Surrender

The sea of chanting, bright-eyed faces was at her eye level for only a moment before she was dragged to her feet. Victoria had an instant to grope for her *vis* before she swung out at the vampires who came at her. She kicked and dodged and punched, had the satisfaction of meeting one of them in the face, and was reaching back to yank a stake from her hair when her arms were grabbed and pulled down to her sides. Dimly aware that it had taken two vampires, one at each arm, to do so, she ducked and tried to twist free.

The grip was too strong; she couldn't break it. She couldn't get to her stakes, her holy water, her crucifix... Hands were on her everywhere, pulling at her dress, her arms, her legs, her breasts. She felt her head being jerked to one side by the hair, felt her coiffure loosen and her neck bare to the sweet-smelling room. The dull, pasty smell of blood on the breath of the vampire nearest her filled her nose, pushing away even the hypnotic scent of the incense.

When his teeth sank into her neck, it was almost a relief.

Praise for The Rest Falls Away

'With its vampire lore and Regency graces,
this book grabs you and holds you tight to
the very last page!'

JR Ward, *New York Times* bestselling author
of *Lover Revealed*

Rises the Night

Rises the Night

The Gardella Vampire Chronicles

COLLEEN GLEASON

Typeset in Adobe Garamond Pro and Cardinal
by Lara Chisp

Printed and bound in Great Britain by
CPI Bookmarque Ltd, Croydon, Surrey

First published in Great Britain in 2008 by
Allison & Busby Limited
13 Charlotte Mews
London, W1T 4EJ
www.allisonandbusby.com

Copyright © 2007 by COLLEEN GLEASON

The moral right of the author has been asserted.

*All characters and events in this publication,
other than those clearly in the public domain,
are fictitious and any resemblance to actual persons,
living or dead, is purely coincidental.*

This book is sold subject to the conditions that it shall not,
by way of trade or otherwise, be lent, resold, hired out or
otherwise circulated without the publisher's prior
written consent in any form of binding or cover other than
that in which it is published and without a similar condition
being imposed upon the subsequent
purchaser.

A CIP catalogue record for this book is available from
the British Library.

First published in the USA by Signet Eclipse,
an imprint of New American Library,
a division of Penguin Group (USA) Inc., 2007.

10 9 8 7 6 5 4 3 2 1

ISBN 978-0-7490-7966-6

BIRMINGHAM CITY COUNCIL. (CBC)	
HJ	23/07/2008
GF	£6.99

WEOLEY CASTLE LIBRARY
TEL: 0121 464 1664

COLLEEN GLEASON has been writing for as long as she can remember, throughout school and college, and on and off during her career in health care and small business start-ups. She is married with three children and two dogs. Rises the Night is the second book in The Gardella Vampire Chronicles.

**Available from
Allison & Busby**

The Gardella Vampire Chronicles

The Rest Falls Away
Rises the Night

Also by Colleen Gleason

The Gardella Vampire Chronicles

The Bleeding Dusk
When Twilight Burns

To Mom, for absolutely everything

Acknowledgements

As always, I'm thankful to be able to work with such a wonderful, talented, and supportive group of people who believe in the Gardella books.

Many thanks to Marcy Posner, for holding my hand and always believing in me and my work, and helping to make my dreams come true.

I'm so grateful, too, to be working with Claire Zion on this and other books – thanks for always 'getting' what I'm trying to do, no matter how clumsy it might be, and helping me make it better. Also, big thanks to Kara Welsh for believing in this series and supporting it, and to Tina Brown for always being so patient. I'm so appreciative of everyone at NAL for everything behind the Gardella books, especially the art department, for creating the most fabulous covers ever, and the marketing and sales staff, who help to get my stories out there.

Once again, I have big hugs for the women of the Wet Noodle Posse, who are always there to celebrate the ups and downs of this business, and to Holli and Tammy for plodding through each chapter and watching me tear my hair out. Thanks also to Jana, Janet, Delle, Mary, Christel, Kelly, Larry Y, Danita and Bam.

And, finally, much love to my family.

Prologue

A Widow Grieves

One month after she lost her husband, Victoria took to the streets of London.

In the darkest part of night, whilst the rest of the city was safely tucked away and the bulk of Society had repaired to the country for hunting season, Victoria Gardella Grantworth de Lacy, Marchioness of Rockley, strode alone through the slum known as Seven Dials.

Dullness permeated her bones. Dispassion and numbness, laced with deep, gnawing grief and rage, caused her limbs to move soldier-like, one foot in front of the other. It was not only in deference to her status of mourning that she wore black from head to toe, but also to allow her to meld with the shadows, in and out, to be seen if she wished to be seen; to become one with the darkness if she did not.

She wore men's clothing for ease of movement and because they smelt like her husband. She also wore them as a silent protest against the strictures of

Society that demanded she sit in her dark-swathed home and do nothing for a twelvemonth. Her lips curled humourlessly at the thought of what the ton's matrons would say if they only knew.

The beaver topper, tall enough to tuck her thick braid up into, had also been Phillip's. She had smelt his rosemary-scented pomade on it when she first placed it on her head. Now the comforting, familiar, painful scent was lost in the stench of horse droppings, human waste and other refuse that littered the streets of one of London's worst neighbourhoods.

These streets were narrow and close, with buildings built barely a man's width apart. Windows were fairly non-existent, and every other structure had hanging shutters or sagging doors, or both. Carriages and even hacks were a rarity, especially in the early hours of the morning, when it was still dark and the ruffians and thugs were on the prowl for an unsuspecting mark.

Victoria knew she would not find vampires to hunt tonight. They had all fled the city with their queen, Lilith, a month ago.

No, Victoria did not expect to find an undead to stake tonight, but she wanted to. Oh, she wanted to. She needed to.

She needed to feel the blood coursing through her body again, the blood that felt as though it had slowed to a crawl and sat, stewing, like a scum-covered pond, in her veins. She needed to move, to exert, to *feel* again. She needed revenge.

She needed absolution.

Victoria turned the corner and immediately ducked into the shadow of the old brick building she skirted. Across what passed for a street in this area of London, she saw two figures.

One, a tall, burly man. The other, a slender young woman; a girl, really, for she barely reached the man's armpit. The half-moon stippled light over the street and illuminated them quite well. Victoria could see that the girl was frightened, pleading, struggling… whilst the man, using the ease of his bulk and height, manhandled her against the wall, holding her by the throat as he groped her breasts, tearing away the bodice of her dress. Her small hands pulled and scratched at his hairy arms, alternately trying to cover herself, pull his hand from her neck, and bat his other hand away.

Victoria glanced around as she let herself into the light, easing from the shadows. There was no one in the vicinity; whether the girl had been brought here by the man, or whether she'd become lost on her own, it appeared as though there was no one to help. She whipped off Phillip's hat and let the long braid fall along her spine. She wanted him to know a woman was going to bring him to his knees.

Ignoring the stake in her deep inside coat pocket, and disdaining the knife she had strapped to her thigh, Victoria walked up behind the man, silent as a cat, and gave a powerful kick to the base of his back.

With a cry of rage he spun, his meaty hand still closed around the girl's neck…until he saw who'd accosted him. He released the girl, who slumped to the ground, and reached for Victoria.

She was ready for him. The blood was moving in her, her hands poised, her knees bent to give her stability, just as Kritanu had taught her. The rage she'd swallowed for weeks bubbled to the surface. Her breathing quickened.

The man spared her a nasty smile, then lunged. Lithe and swift, Victoria waited until the last moment and sidestepped him, grabbing his outstretched arm and using the force of his weight to propel him around, her braid flying. The tiny *vis bulla* she wore gave her the same superior strength and speed as the undead she was used to fighting, and enabled her to slam a man thrice her weight face-first into the brick wall.

He crashed into it with a satisfying 'oomph', but Victoria was not finished with him; she was not ready to contain her exploding emotions. Ignoring the wide-eyed look of the young girl, who'd slunk off to the side and away from the activity, she whipped the would-be rapist back around. Her nerves zinged with energy, her breath came in deep, drawing gasps, her vision edged red as she slammed a fist into his cheek. He stumbled, but righted himself and, with a guttural cry of fury, swung an arm that was thicker than her thigh.

Victoria blocked him with one strong, slim limb, and used her other fist to smash towards his face. His expression blared surprise and shock, but he ducked her blow and bent, spinning, then rose with a blade in his hands.

The world slowed to a crawl and raced ahead at the same time.

Victoria remembered smiling, remembered the feeling of contentment that settled so calmly over her as she reached for her own knife. She recalled the ease with which she withdrew it from the garter on the outside of her trousers, the feel of it in her palm... not so unlike the weight and thickness of a stake. An ash stake.

It was like coming home. It was like being released from some deep, dark confine. She burst free.

She thrust and sliced and slashed. Images burnt in her mind as she flowed in and out of the positions Kritanu had taught her, the ones that had become second nature to her in the last months. The memories – of Phillip, of Lilith, of the myriads of red-eyed vampires she'd fought – all melded, intermingled with this attacker's face, still frozen in shock and then pain...and then emptiness.

Emptiness.

It wasn't until she raised her arm to strike yet again and saw the dull red streak of blood over the tendons of her hand that Victoria came back.

She froze, looking at her hand. There wasn't

supposed to be blood. Vampires didn't bleed when they were staked.

She realised she couldn't catch her breath, that it had escaped and was jolting her body into deep heaves with each inhale. Her shoulders jerked up and down; her lungs burnt. Her arms and legs shook. Her eyes and nose leaked.

Victoria looked down. She was holding a knife, not a stake. A knife dripping with blood. Her hand was not only streaked, but dotted, splattered with blood in a horrific pattern. She was kneeling…kneeling over a massive body that no longer moved.

His eyes were open, dull and glassy, and blood covered his chin and cheeks, even his lips, in the same ghastly pattern that was on her hands. His chest barely rose and fell.

Victoria stared down at him and gingerly pushed to her feet.

She looked at the knife. She would have dropped it, but her fingers would not release the hilt. She shoved it into her pocket, still clutching it, and looked around.

The girl. She dimly remembered the girl.

But there was no one. No one to see what she'd wrought, what the rage and devastation had done when it erupted from her.

Victoria looked down at her hands again. She'd killed before…but she'd never had blood on her hands.

* * *

Eustacia Gardella heard the noise before the man sleeping beside her did. She reached automatically for the stake she kept beside the bed, rolling off the mattress with an agility that belied her eighty-one years. Kritanu, his black hair shining in the moonlight beaming through the window, shifted and woke at her movement.

He saw the stake in her hand and then his dark eyes met hers, silent; then he too slid his wiry body from beneath the sheets. He reached for the knife, and Eustacia felt him behind her as she turned to slip from the room.

The noise had been faint, but her sensitivity as a Venator allowed her to recognise and process danger and warning much more acutely than an average mortal. She had heard something once, and then nothing more.

Despite the fact that she did not sense the presence of an undead, Eustacia gripped the stake like the hand of her lover, and moved down the stairs swiftly and in silence. There was only one other servant, Charley, and he would not have awakened.

She had half descended the stairs when she saw the figure standing in the grand entrance of her home, recognised her, and her breath seized.

'Victoria!' she cried, lifting her night rail, bunching its soft linen with her grip on the stake. 'What has happened?'

Her great-niece stood in the foyer, looking up at

her in the dim light always left burning in the gold lamp beside the stairs. Dark streaks on her face and hands, and the wide, shocked eyes that stared up at her told Eustacia part of the story.

'I didn't want to go home looking like this.' Victoria's voice sounded remarkably calm. 'What would the servants say?'

'*Cara*, what has happened?' Eustacia wrapped her gnarled fingers around Victoria's cold, stained ones and gently tugged her towards the sitting room.

Kritanu, bless him, had whisked a blanket from its trunk and settled it around Victoria's shoulders. 'I shall make some tea,' he said in a voice just as soothing as the Darjeeling he would no doubt bring.

'I nearly killed him,' Victoria said, looking at Eustacia with eyes like olive pits. 'There was a lot of blood. I didn't know what to do.'

The words were simple, calm, logical. She stood straight and relaxed. But the expression in those eyes had Eustacia's brows drawing together. She directed her niece onto the davenport and settled herself next to her. 'Tell me what happened, Victoria.'

'I went out tonight. I didn't expect to find any vampires – I know Lilith took them all with her – but I went out anyway. I needed to.'

'You needed to do something.' She repeated the words purposely, hoping they would help drain the shock from her great-niece's eyes. 'Of course you did. You are a Venator.'

A brief smile flitted over Victoria's face. 'Max said that. The night Phillip…died. He said I was truly a Venator.'

'Did he?' Eustacia's protégé, Max, had left for Italy immediately after the tragedy, and she had not yet heard from him. The tension between him, an experienced Venator, and Victoria had been palpable. She found it interesting that Max had given her niece such a compliment; for he'd been so adamant that she would be more concerned about beaux and balls than vampires and stakes. 'So you went out. Tell me what happened. Whose blood is this?'

'I almost killed a man. I don't remember doing it, Aunt Eustacia. He was going to rape a woman, a girl, and I stopped him. He was very big, much bigger than I. We started to fight, and when he pulled out a knife, I took mine out too…and the next thing I knew he wasn't fighting back. There was blood everywhere. There's never been blood.' Her eyes were vacant again, and Eustacia's heart squeezed as she looked into her niece's beautiful face. Her brave, smart, strong, lost niece.

How many times had she regretted making her a Venator and bringing her into this world? This world of violence and evil?

But she was here, and they needed her. She and Max and the other Venators needed Victoria if they were ever going to destroy Lilith, Queen of the Vampires. The destruction of the evil that stalked their world was worth every sacrifice, great and small. Eustacia had lived this truth for more than sixty years.

Victoria would live it too. Eustacia just wished she had not experienced such a great sacrifice, and so very, very early.

'No, there's never any blood,' she replied, selecting the last comment to respond to.

'It sickened me. He…I left him there. I didn't know what to do.'

'Victoria. Listen to me. The man was attacking a girl, and you saved her. You helped her. And he would have cut you if you hadn't cut him. You had to protect yourself.'

'I did. But I didn't have to slice him to ribbons!' Then, finally, the tears came.

Eustacia held her, feeling the jerks and heaves of her delicate shoulders as if they were her own sobs. This had been a long time in coming, since Phillip's death, and she was relieved Victoria had finally released the grief and anger that had built up inside of her. Losing her husband less than a month after marrying him, and in a horrific way, had caused her to withdraw and cloister herself away. At least tonight she had found a way to confront some of those emotions.

But what a terrible way to do it.

After a very long time, after the heaves turned to small jerks and then to gentle little hiccups, Victoria pulled away. Her eyes were swollen, her cheeks blotchy. Tiny brown ovals splattered her face, and one long streak edged her jaw. Some of her dark curls had come loose from their single braid, curling wildly around her face.

Victoria began fumbling with the shirt tucked into her man's trousers, yanking it free and pulling it up and away from her belly. Eustacia cast a quick glance, but Kritanu hadn't yet returned.

'I can't wear this. I can't let it control me.'

Eustacia knew what she was talking about. Victoria lifted the shirt and there, resting in the hollow of her navel, was the *vis bulla*, the holy strength amulet worn by Venators. Vampire hunters. Crafted of silver from the Holy Lands, the small cross had been soaked in holy water from Rome before its small matching hoop was pierced through the top of Victoria's navel, just as Eustacia's own *vis bulla* had been when she had accepted her duty as part of the Gardella family legacy. She still wore hers, of course. A Venator never removed the *vis*.

She and Victoria were Venators, born, trained, and blessed. A select few were asked, and even fewer accepted. There were only a hundred or so Venators in the world who had actually passed the test and wore the *vis bulla*.

And now Victoria wished to give it back. Eustacia opened her mouth to speak, but her niece interrupted.

'Do not fear, Aunt. I will take it again – when I can be sure I will not abuse it. I terrified myself tonight, but I learnt that I am not yet ready to hunt again. It is one thing to kill an undead, an immortal evil being… but I do not wish to see human blood on my hands again.'

Eustacia grasped her niece's bloodstained hands. It pained her and, at some deep level, it frightened her… but she understood. 'There is no danger in London now. Lilith has taken her followers away, and although she will return, there is no imminent threat.'

Victoria's eyes cleared; her mouth tightened fiercely. 'Never worry. I will have my revenge on Lilith for what she did to Phillip, I swear it. What before was a duty is now my personal accountability.'

Chapter One

In Which Lady Rockley's Weapon Is Alarmingly Ineffective

Victoria tightened her fingers around the ash stake, more out of habit than necessity, and peered around the rough brick corner. It was dark and damp, as London was wont to be shortly after midnight, and the streets just past the safety of Drury Lane were strewn with refuse and scattered with the occasional thief, prostitute, and other such dodgy persons.

Unfortunately, none of said dodgy persons were wreaking any havoc, picking any pockets, or biting any necks.

Now a year had passed since Phillip died, and Victoria was back on the streets hunting for vampires for the first time since the night she'd removed her *vis bulla*. She'd spent the last twelve months practising her fighting skills, learning to control the rage and grief that had driven her to nearly kill the man in St Giles. She wanted to be sure she was ready, and able to temper those emotions before reinserting her strength amulet. The silver cross shivered in the hollow of her navel when she walked, and Victoria felt complete again. She was ready.

Which was why she'd been taking to the streets late at night, stake in one hand, pistol in the other. Looking for something to do. Someone to save.

She would never stop looking for someone to save.

Victoria shook her head abruptly to dislodge the memory and chase away the guilt that still crawled along her nerves. Her temple scraped against the brick, sending crumbles of mortar dusting to the ground and a dull pain over her skin. And she returned her thoughts to the matter at hand.

Barth would be along shortly in his hackney to pick her up and take her back to the echoingly empty Rockley estate known as St Heath's Row, where she would continue to live until the arrival of the new marquess, who was somewhere in America and hadn't yet been located.

No sooner had she had the thought than the hackney in question rumbled around the corner and came to a rather slower stop than usual. It wasn't that Barth's driving had improved; it was that he'd been combing the streets, looking for Victoria.

As she climbed into the carriage, she made the decision she'd been putting off for a week. 'Barth, I'm not ready to go home yet…take me to St Giles. To the Chalice.'

And before he could protest, she closed the door.

There was a bit of a wait, as though he were considering arguing, but then she heard Barth cluck to the horses and she lurched as they started off at a smart pace. Victoria settled back in her seat and tried not to think about the last time she'd been to the Silver Chalice. More than a year ago.

It was well past midnight, and the streets of St Giles were deserted. Only very foolish or very brave people ventured into this area of London during the relative protection of daylight; at night, even fewer would dare to trespass. As they rumbled along St. Martin's Lane and crossed the intersection of the seven roads known as The Dials, Victoria cast her glance down one of them. She had not forgotten Great St. Andrews Street, nor even the block where she'd nearly killed the man. She could find it again in her sleep, for though she did not recall the actual event in all of its terrible detail, the location had imprinted itself on her brain.

Perhaps someday she would return.

Several streets later the hackney jerked to a stop, drawing her from her uncomfortable reverie. Anticipating the jolt, Victoria had already put out a hand to brace herself. Lifting the small lantern from the interior wall, she ducked out of the vehicle and slipped away before Barth could speak or follow her.

Her feet were soundless on the cobbled street as they skirted piles of trash and stepped over small puddles left from an early evening rain. The stench no longer bothered her; nor did the weight of eyes peering from the shadows.

Let them come. She was ready for a fight.

Across the street and down she walked, head held high, hand on her pistol, the legs of her men's breeches swishing faintly against each other, the lantern light slicing through her shadow. A welcome summer breeze lifted the smell of rotting carcasses and animal waste back to her consciousness, then brushed on away. The back of her neck cooled slightly under the beaver topper she wore, but it was from the wind, rather than a sign of approaching danger.

Victoria stood in front of what had been the doorway to the Silver Chalice. She had not visited the place since the night she came looking for Phillip, and found instead the smouldering ruins of what had been an establishment that served vampires and mortals alike.

Did she imagine it, or was the oaky smell of ash still in the air? It couldn't be, all these months later –

The chill had returned to the back of her neck.

She froze, stopping her breath to listen. To feel.

Yes, it was there; it was real, raising the hair on her nape in a warning she hadn't felt for a twelve month: a vampire was near. Below.

Now, the rush of anticipation fuelling her actions, Victoria climbed over the rickety remains of the door frame and started down the steps into the cavernous chamber. She felt along the stones with her left hand whilst her right carried the lantern, shining onto the wood and stone rubble that littered the steps. If she could have approached without the illumination, she would have done so; but seeing in the dark was not one of the gifts bestowed upon Venators. Some of the element of surprise would be diminished, but that was better than trying to make her way through the mess silently, and in the dark.

Miraculously, the ceiling had not completely caved in over the stairs, and she soon found herself at the bottom. Victoria paused, thrusting the lantern behind her to block some of its light, and peered around the corner into the dark, misshapen cellar.

What was left of Sebastian's place.

Although the tingle at the back of her neck still played there, confirming her instinct, she did not feel or hear any sign of movement. She stilled, but for the fingers slipping into the deep pocket of her coat.

The stake felt comfortable in her hand, but she did not withdraw it yet. She let her grip close around the wood, warm from her body, and waited, listening and feeling.

The chill on her neck edged colder, and she breathed the proximity of the vampire and the impending exhilaration of battle. Her heart rate picked up speed; her nostrils flared, as if to smell the presence of an undead.

At last, satisfied that she was alone in the chamber,

Victoria drew the lamp forth. Shining it around, she saw the same scene of destruction that had greeted her months ago; but now her mind was not numbed by fear and apprehension. Now she saw the blackened ceiling beams, the splintered tables and broken glasses…perhaps she even smelt the faint tinge of blood in the air.

. The lantern bobbed as she climbed over a fractured chair, and glass crunched like gravel beneath her feet. She was making her way towards the innermost, darkest part of the wall, hidden under a lowering ceiling. The growing sensation at the back of her neck told her she was moving in the right direction.

Sebastian Vioget had disappeared the night the Silver Chalice burnt. Max had been there too that night, and he told Victoria he didn't know whether or not Sebastian had escaped from the fire; and she knew that he didn't give a whit what had happened either way.

Victoria knew she shouldn't care either…but she had not been able to forget the bronze-haired man who welcomed vampires into his establishment. He'd once told Victoria that it was better to know them and to offer them a place where they might find ease, where their tongues might loosen and information might be gained…

She found the secret door Sebastian had taken her through the very first night she'd met him. Tucked away under a low stone ceiling and set in among the stone walls, it remained fairly unscathed. Marked with black streaks, it was ajar.

And the cold at her nape tingled more sharply.

Victoria pushed through the door, leaving the lantern at the entrance of the passageway. She felt the weight of the pistol in her pocket as it bumped against the edge of stone – the pistol, useless against a vampire, of course, but helpful for other purposes. In the dark, narrow passageway, Victoria couldn't help but remember facing Sebastian, with the damp brick behind her, and him much too close for propriety's sake as he reached to sweep off the hat of her gentleman's disguise.

He hadn't kissed her that time.

Moving down the faintly lit hallway, quickly, as though to leave the thoughts behind her, Victoria made her way to the small room on the left, the one Sebastian had used as an office and sitting room.

He, she, it, or they…were in this room.

Her lips curled in a feral smile, and anticipation kicked up her pulse. She had been ready for this for months.

The door was ajar, giving her the opportunity to peer around into the room. It was lit from within; only a large lantern could illuminate the chamber well enough for her to see the intricate brocade design on the sofa from where she stood. Interesting that a vampire or two would use a lantern.

From what she could see through the open door,

the room had been untouched by the fire, with the exception of a lingering smoke smell that had likely been trapped in the couch and chair upholstery. There was no sign of any disturbance…the books were still lining shelves, the pillows perfectly arranged on the furniture…even the silver tray with the brandy and sherry bottles was in place across the room.

The only things out of place were the two figures bent over Sebastian's desk. At least one vampire.

Slipping the stake from her pocket, Victoria let it hang behind the folds of her jacket and stepped into the room.

'Good evening, gentlemen,' she said as they turned. 'Are you looking for something?'

Her year of grief had made her a bit slow.

One of them was at her before she expected it, his eyes blood red and his incisors flashing. Victoria stepped back, felt the wall behind her, and twisted away. He followed, and she tripped over the leg of a chair, nearly stumbling to the floor. The error made her more determined, and the skills Kritanu had taught her came flooding back to her muscles like the fit of a well-worn glove.

When Victoria gained her balance, the vampire was reaching for her, inadvertently opening his chest to her driving stake. She slammed it in, felt the familiar *pop*, and stepped back as he disintegrated into dust.

Barely breathing, she looked up at the other man, who'd not moved. He watched her with a twitch of a smile, but he'd not changed. Instead, he adjusted his jacket and looked at her with glinting black eyes.

'Came prepared, did you?' he asked, walking easily from around the other side of the desk. Coming closer, but easy. Unthreatening and unthreatened.

'What are you doing here?' Victoria wanted some answers before she staked him too. It could be no coincidence that they'd both chosen this night to visit Sebastian's rooms; and by the amount of dust here, and the neatness of the room, she gathered this was the first visit anyone had made.

'Merely curiosity.' He stood so that the sofa was between them. 'This is what remains of the infamous Silver Chalice; I was interested in seeing the place owned by Sebastian Vioget.'

His fangs had not protruded; his eyes remained unexceptionally dark.

'Do you know him?'

The vampire, who was no taller than most other men in London, had nondescript brown hair brushed back from his face. His nose, a bit too large to make his face attractive, rounded on the end like a garlic bulb. And his brows were straight, narrow strips over his eyes. He shook his head in response to her question. 'I'm afraid I haven't had the pleasure of meeting Monsieur Vioget. From what I have heard,

I'm not altogether certain it is any longer possible to do so.'

'I haven't seen a vampire here in London for months,' Victoria said, watching him. 'Since Lilith took herself and her followers off. Did she send you back to ascertain whether it was safe for her to return?'

He looked at her for a moment; then recognition shifted into his black eyes. Not red, not yet. They were normal. He looked like nothing more than an average English gentleman, except for his ill-fitting clothing. 'You are the woman Venator.'

Victoria bowed her head in acknowledgment.

His eyes narrowed thoughtfully. 'What a coup it would be for me to bring you to Nedas. He would reward me greatly.'

A spike of anticipation jolted through her. 'You could certainly attempt it. I'm certain that whoever Nedas is, he would appreciate your martyrdom.'

'I'm not quite as capricious as my dearly departed companion,' he replied. 'But I am much stronger and faster.'

Then he was there, across the room, next to her, reaching for her throat. Victoria spun back, but he grabbed at her arm, and he was indeed strong.

She tried to wrench away, caught in his suddenly glowing red eyes, and felt the sofa against her legs. She pretended to stumble, dodged, and knocked him off balance. He came after her again, close behind, without giving her a chance to catch her breath, and the next thing she knew, she was whirling back to face him.

Raising her stake at shoulder level, she lifted her face to look at him, ready to slam it home, and faltered. *Phillip.*

It was Phillip.

It was as if her body had turned to ice, and then raging fire. The stake fell from her limp fingers, and the scream was knocked out of her as he shoved her aside, sending her to the floor.

On the rug, dragging dust and lint into her panicked breaths, Victoria looked up at the figure looming over her. How?

But it wasn't Phillip who bent over her. It was the same nondescript man, now with glowing eyes and a determined line for a mouth.

She scrabbled for her stake…surely it hadn't rolled far on the rug. He lunged for her and she twisted away, suddenly trapped against the edge of the sofa. She felt something under her hip, round and hard and long, and rolled sharply to the right, towards his feet, grabbing the stake.

The force of her motion sent him off balance, and Victoria propelled herself to her feet, stick in hand. She turned, using the momentum of her leg to whip around, then shifted her centre of balance as she plunged the stake into the centre of his chest. She pulled it away, stepping back to watch him dust to the floor.

Nothing happened.

And he came at her again, his mouth drawn in a frightening, feral smile.

Victoria recoiled in shock, stumbling backward, and tripped over the flipped-up corner of the thick Persian rug. She tumbled to the floor, slamming her head against the wall as she fell, and stared up at the red-eyed man who advanced towards her.

Calm and steady he moved, and Victoria could barely get her mind around the fact that she'd stabbed him, sunk a stake into his chest, and *nothing had happened*. Neither blood nor dust…he'd just come after her again.

As she gaped up at him sprawled against the tapestried wall, readying the stake for another plunge, his face turned towards her again.

'Phillip?' she cried softly.

'Venator,' he said, sweeping down towards her. 'Come now…relax…I shan't hurt you.'

'No!' she grunted, slamming the stake upward with all of her might.

She stopped him, impaled his body on the wooden pike, but he did not disintegrate. His movements slowed…but he did not die. With a scream of horror and desperation, she used the stake and her hand to shove him away. The stake came free, and she bolted to her feet.

She needed another weapon. The pistol in her pocket…she pulled it out, aimed it at the creature, and squeezed the trigger. The explosion kicked the gun in her hand, and the bullet slammed into the chest of her attacker.

The focused part of her was not surprised when he barely paused…drew himself to his feet, and came at her again.

Victoria launched herself backward over the sofa, frantically looking for something that could be used as a weapon…but what?

He was so fast, so strong…she had no chance.

He was after her, on top of her, and they rolled on the floor, slamming into furniture. The sharp-edged silver tray of brandy and sherry clattered to the rug, spilling the sharp-scented liquors.

Through the fog of panic and shock, Victoria's mind scrambled through a warren of possibilities, of the need to survive, of the anger at being taken by surprise. She felt the heavy tray behind her, and closed her fingers around its sharp edge. Not certain she knew what she was doing, Victoria pulled it up and over her head, slamming it down onto the skull of the man bending towards her.

He staggered, losing his footing, and she shot to her feet, still clutching the tray. Grabbing the sofa, he propelled himself around towards her, his eyes back to burning red, his mouth grim. Victoria said a prayer and swung the tray in a mighty blow, into and through his neck, severing the head in one powerful, ragged stroke.

His eyes rolled back and his head lopped to the floor, and Victoria braced herself, waiting, trembling, panting as though she'd fought ten vampires.

As she watched, the face changed...it shrank and deflated, turning leathery brown with sunken eyes and shrivelled lips, and metamorphosed into ribbony black...then sank into the floor and disappeared.

Chapter Two

In Which Lady Rockley Disdains a Discussion Regarding Fashion and Becomes Overset

'It had to have been some sort of demon,' Victoria said when she finished describing her experience. It was early the morning after she had visited the Silver Chalice, and she had slipped out of St Heath's Row long before most of the ton would have been stirring. 'Even though I've never met one before, and there haven't been any in England for centuries, it couldn't be a vampire. I couldn't kill him with a stake. And he changed appearance.'

Aunt Eustacia, whose glittering eyes had grown worried during the telling of the tale, nodded. 'A stake to the heart will always kill a vampire, *cara*; you are correct. Even Lilith would fall to that, though it might be difficult to drive it into her.'

Her blue-black hair, still without a trace of grey in its coiled coiffure, gleamed and rippled like ink. Even her face, more than eight decades old, bore little sign of her age…but her hands – the ones that held the small metal amulet Victoria had given her – twisted old and gnarled, with arthritic joints that made it difficult for her to grasp a stake.

'I stabbed him two times,' Victoria continued. Her heartbeat still hastened when she remembered those moments of panic. Unlike the time in the alley of The Dials, where it had been all too easy to nearly kill a man, this had been a nightmare in which she couldn't kill a vampire. 'Two times, full in the chest…it slowed him, but when I removed the stake it was as if nothing had happened.'

'You say he was with a vampire? That is peculiar. Demons will never coexist with vampires if they can help it. They are as much enemies as we are.'

'I don't see why they wouldn't, for both races do the bidding of Lucifer.'

Aunt Eustacia nodded. 'One would think. But we are fortunate that they are too jealous of the other to do so. Both races vie so mightily for the partiality of Lucifer that they would never wish to allow the other to attain any great favour from him.'

When one considered it, it made sense, in a warped sort of way, Victoria thought. The demons had been heavenly angels before turning to follow Lucifer, long before human history began.

In comparison, vampires were relatively young. Judas of Iscariot, the infamous betrayer of Jesus Christ, had been the first of these immortal undead. Unable to believe that he would be forgiven after turning his friend over to his enemies, Judas had committed suicide and chosen immortality, aligning himself with Lucifer, who in turn gifted him by making him father of the vampires, a new breed of demons. In a horrible irony, the devil had taken the words of Jesus: 'This is my blood, take and drink of it' – and deemed that Judas and his vampires would be required to do just that in order to survive.

It was no wonder those two races of creatures were rivals for the powers of Hell. One had been with Lucifer for an eternity; the other had been created by him, wooed from the side of Jesus Christ by thirty pieces of silver and the promise of protection from the wrath of God. Apparently these detestable beings were no different from their human counterparts in their zest for power and recognition.

'Victoria?' Aunt Eustacia looked at her as though a new thought had placed itself forefront in her mind. 'I must ask you – and think on it before you answer – after you had killed the vampire, did you sense the presence of another one? Was the back of your neck cool? Do you recall?'

Victoria stilled and took herself back, reviewed the conversation she'd had with him and tried to remember...had her neck been cold? At last she had to shake her head. 'No...it wasn't like I was sensing a vampire, but there was something. I smelt something...odd. Off. Strange, but I cannot say it was as discernible a sensation as when I am near a vampire.'

Aunt Eustacia smiled. 'Well, that is quite interesting. Most Venators cannot sense the presence of a demon like they can a vampire; in fact, most cannot sense the presence at all. If you felt something, anything, that is unusual for a Venator.' Her smile faded. 'I shall contact Wayren and show her this. Perhaps she will have an idea what would bring a vampire and demon together.' Aunt Eustacia looked down at the bronze disc Victoria had found where the creature's body had sunk into the floor. 'Whatever it is, it cannot bode well.'

The disc was perhaps the size of a large man's thumbnail, stamped or engraved with a sinuous doglike animal. Although she couldn't be sure it had come from the creature she'd decapitated, Victoria's instinct told her that it was important. When she'd touched it to pick it up, an uneasy sensation skittered along her arms, flowing over the back of her shoulders so that she'd whipped around as though someone had come up behind her. Or some*thing*.

'Where is Wayren?' Victoria asked, wondering about the serene, yet mysterious woman Eustacia often consulted when research needed to be done. Her attention darted to the small bookcase of aging, fraying manuscripts. They looked like something Wayren would have loaned to Aunt Eustacia – old, important, sacred. Perhaps they were part of Wayren's library, which she managed and studied…somewhere. Victoria had never learnt exactly where Wayren lived.

Her aunt placed the amulet on the mahogany piecrust table next to her favourite chair. 'She was with Max, in Roma, but she will come if I send for her. She was helping him with a problem.'

'Max has a problem?' The sarcastic words slipped out before Victoria could catch them. 'I would never have guessed it. In truth, I'm flabbergasted to hear that all things are not splendid in his world. So how does Max fare, back in your homeland?'

'He has not been in contact for several months.' Her aunt kept her eyes downcast; perhaps she didn't wish Victoria to see the expression therein. 'Victoria, I realise it seemed rather callous that Max returned to Italy so immediately after the events last year with Lilith…and what followed, but he had been called back by the Consilium – the council of Venators – weeks earlier, and had chosen to stay until we could stop the threat of Lilith here in London.'

'Callous? No, that thought never crossed my mind,' Victoria said. 'It was past time for Max to return to Italy, indeed. You and I are well able to handle any vampire threats here in London. Until tonight, I hadn't even seen a vampire since Lilith left.'

Aunt Eustacia reached over and patted Victoria's hand. Her gnarled fingers were warm, and their pads were soft and smooth. 'It's been a difficult year, *cara*,

I know, and the last few months especially, as you've begun to receive some of your family's close friends and think about your return to Society. With all the questions about Phillip, and—'

'The most difficult part has been that I've had nothing to do!' Victoria heard her voice spiralling up into a wail, and she stopped. If Max were here, he'd make some sardonic comment about how good Venators couldn't let their emotions get in their way, citing himself as the perfect example of one who did not.

But…perhaps not. The last time she'd seen him, Max had said something that was high praise coming from him. He'd called her a Venator. As if he'd accepted her as his equal.

'It may be that you haven't had much to do in the last months,' her aunt said, 'but what you did in your first months as a Venator far surpasses what anyone could have expected. And after what happened… Victoria, you needed a rest. You need to let yourself heal.'

'I *need* to stake vampires. Not just one. More. I need to get back to work.' Victoria was on her feet, her heavy ink-coloured skirt swaying. 'You cannot imagine how it is, Aunt! I sit in my black gowns, drab as a scarecrow, and do nothing all the day, unless Mother or her two friends come to visit. And then we speak of inane things. Of gowns, and jewels, of who's marrying whom, and who's fornicating with whose spouse. Apparently now that I am a respectable widow, I can be privy to these conversations.

'But outside of that, and a few other visitors like my friend Gwendolyn Starcasset, I hardly leave the estate. And I do not know when I will be asked to leave Phillip's home. The new marquess is in America, of all places, and has not responded to any of the letters sent by the solicitors. We do not know when, or if, he will be coming to claim the title and estate. I'm fortunate that Phillip had the foresight to settle quite a bit on me, or I would be forced to move back in with my mother.' She had paced over to the streetside window and looked out at the dreary, rainy streets. July was supposed to be green and pretty, not drab and grey.

'That might not be such a travesty, Victoria. At least you would not be alone.'

Victoria let the curtains fall back into place. 'Aunt Eustacia, how could I live with my mother – especially after what happened? Endanger her again? She knows nothing about my life as a Venator. She and the rest of London have no concept that vampires and demons actually exist! Besides, she will try to find me a husband again as soon as I am out of these widow's weeds. And after what happened with Phillip…well, of course I cannot marry again.'

'It seems to me that you could have been in half-mourning grey for months now, Victoria,' her aunt replied gently. 'A lovely pearl grey that will make your complexion look rosy and your dark eyes brighter. You are well past the year's mark of mourning. I think you are still wearing black only to keep your mother at bay.'

'Please, Aunt! You are beginning to sound like my mother. Let us talk about stakes and amulets and… and stopping the evil in this world – instead of gowns and fashions. I do not care if skirts are beginning to grow wider.'

'Victoria…you must have a care for yourself. You still grieve. Ignoring your loss will only make it worse.'

'Aunt Eustacia, I am *not* ignoring my loss. I want to *avenge* it. But there are no vampires here in London… at least, until last night.' She'd been so upset about the vampire who would not die that she'd missed the implication of last evening's events.

Perhaps the undead were returning.

And if the vampires returned, then she could learn where Lilith was…and how to get to her.

Rest? No, Victoria would not take her ease until she plunged her own stake into the fiery-haired vampire queen's heart. Or died trying.

Eustacia drew in a long, deep breath…then expelled it, slow, easy. She opened her eyes to find Kritanu watching her.

He sat on the floor, as she did. One of his ankles was behind his neck, the other leg stretched out in front of him. As she watched, he lifted the foot from his nape and brought it gently to the thin mat on which he sat, raised his wiry, ropy arms, and drew in a deep breath.

Eustacia straightened her own legs, dismayed to hear the soft click of muscle and tendon that hadn't been there only a year ago, and lifted her arms for a deep breath.

They did not speak until they were finished.

'*Yoga* should be relaxing and meditative,' he said, padding over in bare feet to sit next to her. 'Yet the worry did not leave your eyes.' His short, loose pants rose up to expose two muscular calves covered with blue-black hair. Not one white or grey strand stood out over his tea-coloured skin anywhere, despite the fact that he had recently turned seventy-three. He could still position himself in the most difficult of *asanas* when they practised *yoga*…ones that Eustacia had long ago lost the flexibility for.

She still stretched and breathed, as Kritanu had taught her when they'd first begun to train together… oh, well more than fifty-five years ago. But she could no longer put her ankles behind her head, nor could she hold her folded body up on one flat palm, fingers splayed, as he could.

'It did not? And how would you know, if you were meditating as you should have been?'

'I was meditating upon the familiar face of *mere hum-safar*, and I was dismayed by what I saw there.'

She smiled at him, and in the old way, as she had done when they were much younger, Eustacia drew his head into her cross-legged lap so she could look down at his face. Never mind that her knees did not touch the ground as they once had, and that her arthritic ankles throbbed with the weight of his head. It was familiar, and it was a comfort to touch him.

She replied, 'It is true. I have been able to concentrate on little else since Victoria's visit this morning. It cannot bode well that she found a vampire and a demon together, yet I fear I haven't the energy to determine what it means. The demon spoke of someone named Nedas as well: a familiar name, but one that I cannot place. Wayren will know.'

'At least it is not Beauregard who is making mischief.'

'Unfortunately, there is no reason to believe that. Nedas could be one of his followers, or even one of his rivals. If I were not cursed with the mind of a *strega*, I should be able to recall who he is. And then there is the amulet that Victoria found...it fairly reeks of evil when I touch it.'

'I have been thinking on that as well as the worry in your face,' Kritanu said, looking up at her. 'The hound on it makes me think of the *hantu saburos* of the Indus Valley.'

Eustacia smoothed her hands along his wide jaw in an automatic gesture. 'The vampires who lived in caves and fed on animal blood?'

'No, *mere sanam*. The *saburos* in the stories I heard supposedly trained dogs to hunt humans and bring them back for them to feed upon. I do not know if there is any truth to the legend, but…the hound figure on the amulet reminded me of it. I do not know if it is worth mentioning to Wayren in your correspondence…but then, you have already sent it, haven't you?' He drew himself from her lap and smiled into her face. 'Of course you have. With the swiftest of pigeons, haven't you?'

'Wayren should have the letter in four days or less. I will send her another letter with your thoughts, however, as I have learnt never to discount your impressions.'

'At least you have learnt something in more than fifty years.'

They laughed together, a comfortable, close chuckle, their breaths mingling and their noses brushing.

When the humour faded from her face, Kritanu picked up her hand. 'And you are worried about Victoria.'

'*Vero*. She is like my daughter. The pain is still so fresh for her. And there has been all the gossip, all the pity for the new bride of the Marquess of Rockley, so shortly married, so soon a widow.'

'The story told is that he died at sea. A reasonable one.'

'*Si*, although there have been more than a few

comments about why he left for the Continent without his new bride, if they were so much in love… Even the servants do not know what truly happened. And certainly not her mother. And Victoria has held her head up bravely during it all…but she is only just twenty – so young to have this sort of burden and grief. Our life is difficult enough as it is.'

'It is not your fault, Eustacia. What happened was not your fault.'

A sudden sting burnt her eyes. He knew her so well. 'I know that…yet, I cannot relieve myself of the blame. If she had not become a Venator…if I had not pushed her…'

'You did not push her. She was meant to be…just as you were. As I recall, you were none too shy about taking on the task…and not demure in the least when a younger man came to teach you to fight using *kalaripayattu* and to meditate using *yoga*. You wanted nothing to do with me, as I was so much younger than your twenty-four years.' He smoothed his fingers over the ugly, knobbly knuckles of her old woman's hand. 'And see what a difference you have made in the world, *sanam*. Without you…without your gift and your bravery, the mortal world would be very different than it is now. Remember that Christmas Eve in Venice? Eustacia…if you had not stopped those Guardians, the whole city would have been lost.'

'And Lilith would have had the Gold Clasp in her hands.' A tug of a smile caught her mouth. 'We have thwarted her more than once, have we not, *amore mio?*'

'We have. You have.' His eyes, pupil and iris the same black colour, glittered with seriousness. 'You and Max and the others…but you, most of all. And now it is Victoria's turn. She is destined for greatness. You know it, because she carries two generations of Venator skills, from both your brother and her flighty mother. You must let her achieve it.'

'I think in the end it was best that Victoria's mother didn't accept her calling as Venator. I don't believe Melly could have given up her love for Society in favour of hunting vampires.' The last bit of levity and comfort seeped away. 'Kritanu, it's Max I am most worried about.'

'You have no word from him?'

She shook her head slowly. 'Not in more than ten months. I was not completely truthful with Victoria when I told her Wayren was with him. She was in Spain, and then Paris, until a month ago, when she learnt I had not heard from Max since last August, shortly after he arrived in Venezia. Wayren went back to Italia to see if she could find him…but she has not. No one seems to know where he is.' Lifting her eyes, she looked at her *sanam*, her beloved. 'She writes that the Tutela is rising again. I am afraid it is the doing of this vampire called Nedas.'

'They have risen before, and we have stopped them.'

'There is something different this time, Kritanu. And I fear I do not have the energy, nor the clarity of mind, to know what it is…what to do. I am old and slow. And I ache.'

'It is Victoria's turn, *pyar*. You will do what you can, but you cannot do it all. And do not worry for Max. He wears the *vis bulla*, though he was not born to it. He is one of the few who passed the life-and-death test to do so. There is a reason for it.'

'I know that. But I fear for him still.'

Chapter Three

An Encounter with a Most Discreet Gentleman

Victoria had walked the night many times since she had taken on her duty as a Venator. The freedom of wearing trousers and going where she wished to go had been a joyful adventure, despite the danger of stalking the undead. Knowing that no other woman from the ton would desire – or be able – to walk empty, dangerous streets alone fuelled her excitement.

Knowing that even a man would be in more danger, travelling Great St Andrews or Little White Lion of St Giles alone, on foot, made her feel invincible.

But tonight she was uneasy. Her nerves felt like her hair did after her maid, Verbena, brushed it too much – buzzing with static and energy. She waited for the back of her neck to chill or tingle. She gripped her stake, holding it ready in the folds of her man's jacket, when before she would leave it sagging in her pocket until she needed it.

She could have remained at St Heath's Row, safe behind its cross-studded gates and stone walls. She could have given herself another night or two, after her experience at the Silver Chalice. She could even have waited until Aunt Eustacia heard from Wayren about the amulet she'd found. She could have spent the evening poring over the limited selection of manuscripts and scrolls that her aunt kept at her home, looking for some clue as to whether the amulet had been left by the demon she'd beheaded, or whether it was, perhaps, something Sebastian had lost months ago.

But she had not. If the vampires were indeed back, it was her duty to hunt and kill them. She could not hide in her husband's home and wonder how she would kill a demon if she faced one again tonight.

Her duty was to keep the innocent, the unwitting, safe from the immortals who would feed on their very life. If the residents of London – indeed, of all of England – had any concept how easily evil walked along with them, there would be mass hysteria.

So instead of attending dinner parties, or visiting clothiers and millineries, Victoria trained and planned and hunted.

A shadow detaching itself from the corner of an alley caught her attention as she walked by. She felt it step into her wake and pad quietly behind her, silent, oh, so silent.

The back of her neck did not cool. She didn't sense anything else prickling at her nerves, either.

This, then, was a mortal who stalked her tonight, and Victoria waited for him to move on her, releasing the stake into the depths of her pocket. Despite her wariness, she was ready to fight something she knew how to fight.

Rounding a corner, Victoria took two steps before she saw the other figure coming at her from the left. She tipped with a graceful swoop and slid out the knife she wore strapped to her trousered thigh, letting it glint dully in the dim light. Her fingers trembled, but she kept her mind clear. If she needed to use the knife, she would keep her mind clear and steady. She would not go berserk tonight.

'No need fer that, sirrah,' growled a cockney burr just behind her. Something sharp pushed into the back of her coat.

The second figure blocked the walkway, legs spread and strong, something silver in his hand. His face was shadowed, his bulk generous. The bigger they were…

Victoria stopped, calm, her hand holding the knife dangling at her side. She did not turn to see the man behind, but kept her eyes on the one in front while listening, and feeling, what was behind. Her heart zipped along at a steady pace, her muscles tightened in anticipation, and energy swelled inside her.

'Ye ken put that away; ye won't be needin' it, now, sirrah. All we wan' is yer valyables.'

'I have nothing of value, so let me pass,' she told

them, not attempting to hide her woman's voice.

She saw the jolt of recognition in the man straddling the walkway – the moment he realised she was not a foolish dandy stumbling home from the faro tables, but a defenceless woman. Even in the spare light from the dirty street-lamp, she saw his lips stretch in a smile, saw the gap in front where a tooth might once have grown.

'Oh, ye mightn't have nothin' in yer pockets, but ye got somethin' else we want,' the first man said from behind her. He was no longer poking her with what she'd assumed was the tip of a knife. Apparently, despite her weapon, he did not feel the need for one of his own anymore.

All the more fool he was, and that became apparent when he reached for her.

The moment his fingers closed over her upper arm, Victoria reacted. She whipped easily from his grip and spun, knife flashing. Her hat slipped off, and the braid she'd loosely pinned up fell and swirled about her shoulders as she brought the blade down along his sleeve, then made a point of withdrawing it. The man squealed when she sliced, but her next move was hampered by a shove from behind.

The large man from the front sent her reeling, and when she kicked back around, he was ready for her, half-crouched, knife in hand. 'Feisty one, she is.' He laughed. 'And to think we almost let 'er walk on past.' He lunged and Victoria ducked, slamming her head into his gut hard enough to knock the breath from him.

She pulled away, slicing with her knife, readily controlling the berserker that simmered inside her. Whipping the hair from her face, she came back around to grab the first man by the scruff of the neck. With a great heave she sent him tumbling towards his partner and watched as they rolled onto the ground.

The big one sprang to his feet with surprising agility, coming at her now with the taunting grin wiped from his face, replaced by fury. 'Ye little bitch.'

The arc of her knife in the air gave him pause, and she held him off when she positioned it at the corner of his chin, standing there much too close for the ease of her nose, for the man stank to high heaven. 'Be off with you now. I've more important things to do than tussle with the two of you fools.'

The smaller man slunk into the shadows from whence he'd come, but the larger man stood his ground.

An approaching carriage, turning from one dark street onto this one, crunched over the bricks. Victoria's instincts sharpened when the back of her neck cooled, but she did not take her attention from the man who accosted her.

The man shifted, as if readying himself to launch, just as the carriage slowed alongside them. The chill over her nape was sharper now, definitely connected to the arrival of the carriage. Victoria's fingers tightened over the knife when its door opened. Before she could react, a man jumped out, landing with two solid feet onto the uneven ground.

He was dressed in well-tailored clothing, more like one who resided on Hanover Square than here in St Giles. His face was half-shadowed by the tall, brimmed hat, but she could see the impression of a long nose and square chin.

He spun, brandishing a pistol, and pointed it at the other man. 'Oughta blow your brains out,' snarled the newcomer, 'attacking a woman on the streets!'

A vampire? Speaking in a vaguely familiar voice and lecturing a hoodlum?

Surely not.

The chill was definitely raising the hair on her neck, heightening her senses, but this man wasn't an undead. She knew it…yet…her senses were still on alert.

Then Victoria saw the faintest shift of shadow, grey-black moving into ink black, behind the carriage.

Ah.

Stepping back from the altercation in which the newcomer's cloak was whipping and churning about as he advanced on the bandit, she reached into her pocket and grasped her stake, then replaced the knife.

She turned and saw the faint glow of red eyes between two wooden buildings across the road – barely enough room for a man to walk through shoulder-square. Her pulse notched up and she smiled there in the night, slipping in front of the parked carriage and across the street…into the narrow space.

She heard an alarmed shout behind her, as if the newcomer had seen her walk into the dark alley…but she ignored it.

As she moved deeper into the slender opening, Victoria stepped on something that shifted and scuttled beneath her foot, sending her off balance, bumping into the brick wall. At least it was furry and squirming, not eight-legged and crunching. Her next step landed her boot in something soft, squishy, and putrid, and when she took one more step, she realised that the red eyes had vanished, and that the back of her neck was warming.

The vampire had gone.

The sensation at the back of her neck was gone too.

Frowning in the dark, Victoria stopped and listened and felt. Deep breaths, as Kritanu had taught her, deep breaths to heighten her awareness, and to calm the singing of her nerves.

Nothing. She felt and heard nothing.

Unwilling to believe that her chance for a fight had disappeared, Victoria waited still longer, and contemplated. This was the second time in two nights that she'd found vampires, after months of nothing.

Last night she'd had the unsettling experience of being unable to kill one, or kill what she'd thought was a vampire. And tonight the one she stalked had simply slipped away, silent and quick, leaving her with stake in hand and an odd feeling of unfinished business.

She listened and felt again. Still nothing.

As Victoria turned to take the four or five steps that would bring her from the alley, she heard a shout coming from the street.

'Madam! Miss!'

It was the carriage owner, the one who had taken it upon himself to save her from the thugs. Again she thought his voice was familiar. She stepped back into what passed for illumination on this dark night, out of the alley, then darted across the street and around the carriage. 'I am here.'

He spun and faced her, and their recognition was simultaneous.

'Mr Starcasset!'

'Lady Rockley!'

Victoria could not believe her misfortune. Her would-be saviour was her good friend Gwendolyn Starcasset's brother. And he was staring at her with understandable shock and concern, frozen, as if unable to think what to do.

As would any other member of the peerage, if they found a widow just coming out of mourning alone in the most dangerous part of London in the middle of the night, not to mention garbed in men's clothing.

Despite the awkwardness of the situation, Victoria could not help but be amused at how the man must be struggling to find something polite to say, so she stepped in to help him. 'Mr Starcasset, thank you for your assistance,' she told him demurely. She would not offer an explanation for her presence here.

He appeared to accept her lead. 'Madam, may I escort you…home?' His attention moved from her to the street corner and back again, as though expecting to see another vehicle, or some other person or attendant. 'Surely you must be…chilled?'

He'd removed his hat, which, unlike Victoria's, had somehow not become dislodged during his interaction with the thug. Now she could see more of his handsome, though boyish face; one, that, with its strong chin and long narrow nose, reminded her uncomfortably of Phillip.

But George Starcasset, heir to the Viscount Claythorne, had more rounded cheeks, was golden-haired instead of dark-haired, and his eyes, though not a deep blue, were a lighter hue than the heavy-lidded ones belonging to her husband. Although she could not see them well in the low light, Victoria was aware that they were the colour of an angry ocean, for Mr Starcasset had trained them upon her many times since they had met.

'I am not chilled, thank you, sir, and there is my hack as we speak.' She'd heard the creaking and rumbling of Barth's carriage as it careened down the streets several moments before it actually appeared.

'A hack? Madam, I cannot allow you to take a *hack* home in the middle of the night. Please allow me the pleasure to escort you to St Heath's Row.'

Victoria should have been used to being called *madam*, but she was not. It made her eyes water because she bit her tongue instead of saying what she truly felt. The title might have been important to another woman, and certainly she didn't begrudge the comfort and wealth she'd attained by marrying Phillip, but she'd have forgone all of it if she could still have him. And every time someone used the title, it reminded her of her loss.

For before Phillip, she had merely been *miss*.

Unexpectedly, her eyes dampened. Mr Starcasset must have noticed, for he reached for her arm, guiding it firmly around his, and said comfortingly, 'This has been a trying night for you, I'm certain, Lady Rockley. Please allow me to see you home in the comfort of my carriage.'

'Very well, Mr Starcasset. Thank you for your insistence.' Victoria gave a wave to Barth, who had slid bravely from his seat and was not troubling to hide the stake in one hand and the pistol in the other. If nothing else, he was prepared for any eventuality, including protection provided by the large crucifix that dangled from his neck.

She turned to climb into the offered carriage and, in doing so, brushed against Starcasset.

'What is that you are holding?' he asked, reaching for the hand that still held her stake.

Victoria slid it back under her coat before he could grasp it. 'A stick.'

'I am certainly glad that I came upon you when I did, madam, for I fear that stick would not have served you well in your defence against those thugs.' The carriage jolted as he climbed in after her.

'Indeed.' Victoria kept her response to a murmur and, shifting in her seat, slipped the stake into its pocket on the inside of her coat.

The carriage rumbled off, taking Victoria away in a much smoother, more sedate manner than she'd arrived in St Giles. She and Starcasset sat in silence for a turn, Victoria mulling over the presence of another vampire that seemed to have run away from her…or, the thought struck her, perhaps it had wished for her to follow it.

'Lady Rockley, if I may be permitted to ask, how have you been faring these last months? Gwendolyn tells me you are still receiving only a very few visitors. I think of you often.'

'Thank you, Mr Starcasset. Your sentiments are much appreciated. And as to how I have fared…it has been a long year, but I am of the hope and belief that the worst is over. I told your sister only last week that I am preparing to make a full return to Society.'

In the low lantern-light that bobbed in rhythm with the cobbled bricks below, his smile was exceedingly warm. 'May I say that I am very pleased to hear this. And I know that Gwendolyn has missed your presence quite abominably at the functions this Season. But now that it is drawing to a close, I am sure you know we are preparing to repair to Claythorne. And if I may not be considered too forward, I do believe it would be a great delight to my sister should you attend us there.'

'Indeed. How very kind of you, Mr Starcasset.' Victoria found herself wanting to blush under his warm stare, which made it all too clear that he would be the one most delighted with her presence. 'Gwendolyn did speak to me of it.'

'We were just talking Wednesday last in regards to our house party, which we make on an annual basis, as a celebration of the beginning of grouse season. Of course, last year you would have been invited, but... oh, forgive me, madam. It was not the best of times for you.' He brushed off the lapels of his coat in a rather nervous gesture. 'Gwendolyn was musing aloud as to whether you would be able to attend this year. And how felicitous that I should have the opportunity to reiterate the invitation in person!'

Victoria forbore to point out that felicity had played little role in their meeting on the dark, dank streets of St Giles. Danger and happenstance, perhaps...but not felicity. 'I am most honoured and have already decided to accept the invitation,' she replied. It was time that she at last shed the black clothing she'd been wearing. Of course, she would never be able to wholly embrace the dances and the fetes and the fashions and the teas that were part of Society as fully as she had done before…but perhaps she could find some sort of balance betwixt her two lives.

Or perhaps she would be destined for the loneliness of walking the streets at midnight, instead of riding home with a handsome beau after a long night of dancing.

'I will be delighted to join you at Claythorne,' she added with real pleasure.

'Splendid! I shall tell her tomorrow that you have accepted, although' – he coughed genteelly – 'I shall not divulge to her the exact circumstances as to how we have met up.' His lips stretched in a jovial grin.

'Indeed. I would and *do* appreciate your reticence in that matter.' Victoria smiled back at him, realising that his grin was so very pleasant as to make anyone want to join him in his humour. She hoped that he would honour his statement and not share with Gwendolyn or any other person of their Society the fact that he had found her walking alone on the streets at night. Although she supposed if he did, few would believe him.

As she settled back in the carriage, it occurred to her to wonder, then, just exactly what had taken the Viscount Claythorne's heir himself to those same dangerous streets during the same dark night.

Chapter Four

In Which Verbena Has Her Way

''Tis long past time to see ye in a colour other than black.' Verbena clucked as she tied Victoria's stays. 'Ye cudda gone to half-mournin' six months ago and been wearin' that pretty pearl grey. Even when ever'one was mournin' for Princess Charlotte, God rest her soul, they went to greys after six months. But no, no, you woulden and can't say't I blame ye, what with losin' the marquess so horribly, but my lady, yer skin's been missin' the pretty colours like yeller an' that peach. It's right to be liven your cheeks up a bit.'

Victoria knew better than to attempt a word when her maid was in lecture mode. Likely Verbena had been saving it up the last nine or ten months and wouldn't be dissuaded from saying her piece regardless of what her mistress might wish to interject.

'All I can say is, I'm glad I talked ye into leaving all them black and grey gowns back at home. This is a house party, and ye should have fun. Ye deserve it, my lady. Ye deserve it.' Her impossibly hued orange hair was gathered into two springy bunches, one below each ear, and stuck out like fistfuls of stiff netting.

Their eyes met in the mirror, one pair a sparkling, good-humoured blue, the other thick-lashed, almond-shaped and serious. 'But I'm glad t'see,' Verbena added more gently, 'that ye didn't leave off your *vis bulla*. What would we do wit'out ye, and the other Venators?'

Verbena, whose cousin was Barth the hackney driver, had recognised Victoria's vampire-hunting amulet immediately after she'd begun wearing it more than a year ago. How she knew of vampires and Venators when the rest of London was blissfully ignorant, Victoria was uncertain; but it was a relief that her maid, who also inexplicably knew how to treat vampire bites and was not frightened of visiting places like the Silver Chalice, was aware of her secret. Having one's maid in on the most intimate details of one's life, especially when it involved much sneaking around and wearing clothing belonging to the opposite gender, was a great serendipity.

Victoria shook her head, drawing in a breath that was more restricted now that she'd been laced into her stays. 'I feel better when I am wearing the *vis*; that is certain. Though I don't expect to have need of it whilst here at Claythorne. To be sure, I would not have agreed to leave London had Aunt Eustacia not assured me she would send for me were there any threats to be contained. I've seen only one vampire, other than the one I killed, and found no sign of any others since that night I met Mr Starcasset.'

'Yer Aunt Eustacia is one smart lady,' Verbena said, digging carefully through the pile of gowns so as not to muss them. 'Though that butler of hers, Charley… he sure does know how to keep his mouth shut. Can't say I haven't tried to get'm to talk to me about the goin's-on there, but his lips are's tight as a clam's. And that friend o' hers, Mr Maximilian Pesaro. He's a right fascinatin' Jemmy, too, if I do say. Frightenin'ly handsome, in a bold sort of way.' She shivered. 'If I didn't know better, I'd almost think *he* was a vampire; he's got the elegant, dangerous look o'one.'

'You aren't the first to think that of him,' Victoria replied dryly. She stood, pushing away from the bleached-wood dressing table, and turned to what was sure to be the difficult task of refusing to let Verbena dress her in bold carmine or bright jonquil for her first dinner at Claythorne. 'He is a formidable Venator; that one thing is certain. I can't say that I understand why he left so quickly after Phillip died, but my aunt says he was needed in Rome. Though it wasn't as if he were needed here. I think I shall wear the navy gown tonight, Verbena.'

'*Navy*? My lady, that's near's bad as the black! Wouldn't this lovely mulberry colour be more fittin'? See how't brings out that dusky sort o' rose colour in yer cheeks? And next to yer black curls? An' it makes yer lashes look darker'n a boar's-bristle brush.' She thrust the preferred gown in front of her mistress. 'Well, that Mr Pesaro cert'nly helped ye last summer, when ye were tryin' to keep Lilith from gettin' th' special book she wanted. Maybe he'd decided he'd stayed too long here and needed to get home.'

'Perhaps,' Victoria commented, rather wondering what it would be like the first time she saw Max again. She felt that the animosity that had simmered beneath their politeness and forced proximity might have eased quite a bit, after all that had occurred, even though she was still annoyed that he'd left London so suddenly.

After all, she'd seen the impressive Max brought under the control and thrall of Lilith, showing a weakness she never would have attributed to him... and he had seen Victoria learn how to fight like a Venator and grow from an average debutante into a fierce, brave vampire hunter.

The gown of Verbena's choice was fluttering down over Victoria's shoulders before she realised the moment to stop it had passed. 'Not the mulberry!' she exclaimed in vain. "Tis too bright!'

But the gown was on, and swiftly being buttoned up the back as Victoria looked at herself in the mirror. She did look well in the gown. Heavens, it had been more than a year since she'd been dressed so, and Verbena was right: it did bring out the faintest pink in her cheeks. She bit her lips, bottom, then top, and they plumped and reddened as though they'd been kissed.

'Very nice, my lady,' Verbena told her, making a narrow braid from one long curl at the top of her crown. 'Ye have nothing to feel guilty fer, now. You've mourned your husband fully and completely, and whilst ye'll never stop loving him, ye must remember: you're still here, and ye still have a life to live.' She finished the braid and wound it around the rest of Victoria's hair, piled at the back of her head.

'Yes, a life. And a duty.' Her green-brown eyes glittered above her flushed cheeks.

Verbena's blue eyes met her gaze again. 'A duty you are well suited for.' She slipped the last pin into her hair and smiled with satisfaction. 'But it don't mean ye have to be a nun.'

Victoria nodded at her reflection, then rose from the chair. 'Time to go down to dinner, then. Perhaps I'll have a bit of gaiety before duty beckons me back to London.'

'I'm hoping you do, my lady. Ye deserve it.'

Victoria left her room on the second floor and made her way down to the drawing room, where the rest of the guests would gather before going in to dinner. She'd arrived only two hours earlier, and thus had had a short visit with Gwendolyn, and then had repaired to her room to change for dinner.

Now she walked into the large drawing room and found that several of the eleven who would be dining had already gathered. Three gentlemen stood near one side of the room, and appeared to be holding hostage a bottle of some golden liquid. One of them Victoria recognised as Gwendolyn's father, Viscount Claythorne. He was speaking with Baron Frontworthy, Gwendolyn's most ardent suitor.

'Victoria! You look lovely.' Her friend rose and came to her side immediately. She was accompanied by an older, elegant woman. 'May I make my aunt, Mrs Manley, known to you, Lady Rockley.'

Victoria curtsied and complimented the woman on her gown.

'Good evening, Lady Rockley.'

Victoria turned at George Starcasset's voice. He bowed over her proffered hand, and she made a brief curtsy. 'Good evening, Mr Starcasset. I must thank you again for making me one of your party.'

'Gwendolyn and I are so very pleased to have you with us.' He smiled and tucked her hand over his arm. 'May I provide you with a sherry?'

'Indeed, that would be lovely.' Victoria cast a smile over her shoulder at Gwendolyn, who appeared to be not at all surprised at her brother's attentions. In fact, her friend's twinkling eyes told her that she was quite pleased with the situation.

'The others shall be joining us shortly. Mr Berkley and his sister Miss Berkley, you might perhaps know, along with Mr Vandecourt. And our other guest,' Starcasset told her as he presented her with a tulip-shaped glass, 'I am certain you will be quite pleased to meet. He is rather a celebrity.'

'A celebrity?' Victoria sipped the sweet sherry, looking up at Gwendolyn's brother with her head tilted gently to the side. How wonderful it felt to be thinking, not of vampires and stakes, not of losses and grief, but of the handsome gentleman who stood before her.

'Indeed. Dr John Polidori, the author.'

Victoria blinked. No, apparently even here she could not get away from vampires.

Mr Starcasset took her expression for confusion, and explained, 'He wrote the book *The Vampyre*. It was published in *New Monthly* under Lord Byron's name, but just recently it became known that Polidori is the true author. Though it is said that he based the vampire character of Lord Ruthven on Byron himself!'

'Indeed,' Victoria murmured. It would be interesting to converse with Dr Polidori. She wondered if he'd ever met a vampire. Quite unlikely, for he wouldn't be writing romantic novels about it if he had.

'Dr Polidori and Mr Vioget arrived only some minutes ago, and they hastened to change for dinner. We will wait for their arrival before going in to supper. Lady Rockley, is something the matter?'

'Dr Polidori is not travelling alone?' Victoria managed to make her voice casual, but what should have been a small sip of sherry turned into a rather large gulp and set her to suppressing a rough cough.

'He travels with his friend Mr Sebastian Vioget, whom he met, I believe, while lately in Italy with Byron.'

'Italy? I see.' So it was Sebastian, and he was here. With the author of a book about vampires. How very unexpected.

Victoria finished her sherry. The last time she'd seen Sebastian, she'd left him in his carriage after a most intimate interlude – which ended quite abruptly as he delivered her to a group of vampires out for her blood.

He'd had her half-undressed in that carriage, and lazy with desire, as she recalled, her face warming. He'd been delighted to learn that she'd broken her engagement with Phillip, and had attempted to take full advantage of her newly unbetrothed status…until she sensed the presence of vampires.

Since they had been riding in his carriage, under his direction, and Victoria hadn't seen any vampires for weeks until these three suddenly appeared, surrounding their vehicle, she couldn't help but suspect Sebastian's hand in the matter. His way of denying had been to protest that he had saved her life before; why would he endanger her at that moment…? But Victoria hadn't fully believed him.

'He seems a very amiable gentleman, if a bit shy,' commented Starcasset, hovering rather close to Victoria in a gentle waft of balsam.

'Mr Vioget? Shy?'

'I meant, rather, Dr Polidori, although Mr Vioget is also very pleasant. Ah, and here they are now.'

Starcasset moved towards the door, but Victoria impudently remained across the room and with her back to it, pretending to be admiring an arrangement of tall purple lupine. She would find out soon enough if Sebastian was as surprised by her presence as she was by his.

Behind her, the other guests were being introduced to Dr Polidori and Monsieur Vioget, as Sebastian identified himself. At the sound of his familiar voice and its intriguing accent, Victoria felt an uncomfortable prickle.

Then, at last… 'And Dr Polidori, and M. Vioget, may I introduce to you my sister's particular friend, Victoria de Lacy, Marchioness of Rockley.'

Victoria turned to face the three men. 'It is a pleasure to meet a man of such renown, Dr Polidori. Your work has made quite a reputation for you,' she said, offering her hand to the man with messy dark hair. A quick skim of her attention over Sebastian told her that she had the advantage of him. She had never seen such a look of discomposure on his handsome face. It would be comical if she weren't as taken aback as he.

'Madam, I am very well pleased to make your acquaintance. And thank you for your kind words.' Polidori bowed and released her hand, then turned to take a glass of brandy from the viscount as he remarked on his trip from London.

'M. Vioget,' Victoria said, and offered her hand to Sebastian. Obviously recovered, he took it gallantly, closing his fingers over her gloved ones and raising them to his lips.

He'd not changed in the last year: still impeccably clothed in the highest of fashion, with tawny hair curling over the high collar of his shirt and the same superficially charming smile that always seemed to have a hidden message behind it.

'May I express my condolences, Lady Rockley,' he said as he raised his face from her glove. He let her fingers slip through his as she returned her hand to her side, looking at her intently. 'I was terribly sorry to hear of your loss.'

Considering the fact that he'd been quick to take advantage when he'd learnt she broke her engagement with Phillip, Victoria found that highly unlikely. But there was that hint of abashment in his face…perhaps he was feeling contrite over the events that had left the Silver Chalice in flames, and Phillip and Max ultimately in the hands of Lilith. Although whether it was the loss of his business or the cause of Phillip's death that he regretted, she was not certain.

'I was terribly sorry to experience it,' she replied coolly, and turned back to Gwendolyn's brother with a warm smile. 'Who is that lovely woman in the painting over the mantel, Mr Starcasset?'

Happy to oblige her interest, Starcasset removed her from the presence of his guests and strolled with her to the portrait in question.

Victoria took care to keep him in conversation for the next several minutes, whilst they waited for the last members of their party to join them. As she continued to ask questions regarding this painting and that vase and the statue on the table thither, she kept the edge of her attention focused on Sebastian.

He watched her without appearing to do so, covertly scanning her whenever he turned to speak to someone, letting his eyes wander in her direction whenever he lifted his glass to drink. Instead of the chill over the back of her neck that she felt when a vampire was watching, Victoria felt Sebastian's attention as a never-ending prickle between her shoulder blades. It was accompanied by an unfamiliar squirming in her stomach. She and Sebastian had unfinished business to attend to.

When it was time to walk into the dining room, Mr Starcasset remained at her side and led Victoria to a seat between himself and Dr Polidori. Sebastian was placed at the other side of the table, near the opposite end, between Miss Berkley and Gwendolyn.

'I have had the pleasure of reading your work, Dr Polidori,' Victoria offered, removing her gloves and folding them neatly in her lap. She'd read *The Vampyre* even before becoming aware of her Venator calling. 'It is very unique, as most other stories about vampires portray them as mere beastly creatures of low class, while your gracious and charming Lord Ruthven could easily find himself a place in the ton. How did you ever come to this different understanding of these creatures?'

'Indeed, it was rather Byron's fault. I was visiting him along with Shelley and his wife in Switzerland, and she thought up a game for each of us to write a story about a supernatural or monstrous creature. Byron dabbled with the story for a bit, then moved on to something else, and as the idea piqued my interest, I decided to pursue it.' Polidori's reply was glib, as though he'd given it many times. His hair was an explosion of wild black curls that could not, no matter the amount of pomade, be tamed. They framed his round, youthful face and curled in every direction. Yet, despite his easy carriage and words, a wariness limned his eyes, as though something worried at him.

'You wrote so convincingly, Dr Polidori. Do you believe that vampires exist? That they actually can move among us in Society? Could any one of the peers really be a vampire?' Mrs Manley, Gwendolyn's aunt, who sat across from him, appeared quite taken with the idea that a vampire might be sitting at the very table.

Victoria refused to exchange glances with Sebastian, although he tried. She hoped quite heartily that the woman never came face-to-face with a vampire, in Society or no. 'Only members of the peerage who do not show their faces during the day,' Victoria commented with a smile. 'According to Dr Polidori, they do not come out in the sunlight. If they did, would they die a horrible death…or merely be burnt?'

'I believe they would suffer terrible burns, but they would be unlikely to die unless overexposed.'

'And what of flame?' Victoria asked, remembering last summer, when she and Max had been trapped with vampires in a burning building. 'Would that also burn them?'

Polidori brushed crumbs from the corner of his mouth. 'Flames from a fire do not harm a vampire, at least' – he gave a gentle laugh – 'in my imagination.'

And in reality as well. Victoria thought it quite interesting that Polidori seemed to have an accurate knowledge of the bloodthirsty creatures.

'Dr Polidori is lately returned from Italy.' Sebastian's comment was directed to Miss Berkley.

'Italy? I have never been, but I have heard that Rome and Venice are lovely cities. Where in Italy did you travel?' asked Gwendolyn.

'I spent much of my time in Venice with Byron, until several months ago, when we parted ways. He felt he did not need the personal services of a physician any longer,' he added with a self-deprecating smile. 'I travelled throughout the country and then returned to England near the beginning of the year.'

Victoria's attention was drawn from the physician-turned-author to Mr Starcasset, when he leant closer and said, 'I shall promise you, Lady Rockley, that the gentlemen will not leave you ladies long alone in the parlour after dinner. I am hoping you might partner me in a game of whist this evening, as my sister claims you are a devilish good player!'

'Does she indeed?' Victoria replied, trying to recall if she had ever played whist with Gwendolyn. She didn't believe she had; so now she wondered whether Mr Starcasset had her confused with some other lady, or whether he was merely attempting to make an attachment to her. Smothering a smile, she turned back to him with a demure look and said, 'I should be quite pleased to be your partner in whist, if you will agree to sing when Gwendolyn sits at the pianoforte. She has spoken quite often of your pleasing voice!'

He smiled down at her, his teeth wide and white, and his eyes warm. 'I think I must call you on that exaggeration, madam, as Gwendolyn scarcely allows any of her siblings to sing whilst she plays…but I will happily make the attempt, if all for your hand at cards.'

Indeed, Starcasset made quite well on his promise, ushering the men from their cigars and brandy back into the parlour with the ladies less than thirty minutes after they had separated following the end of the meal. A rousing game of whist ensued, with he and Victoria partners, playing across from Miss Berkley and Mr Vandecourt.

Victoria, who was not known for her excellence at cards, despite Starcasset's claims to the contrary, managed to keep from embarrassing herself…even when Sebastian happened to stroll along behind her and peer over her shoulder as though to ascertain whether her mediocre playing was due to lack of good cards or skill.

It was also possible he was using the opportunity to look down the bodice of her gown, as he stood behind her for quite a long enough time, but since he already was acquainted with exactly what it covered, she rather doubted he would need to stare *quite* so long.

Victoria felt her face warm at the memory that this man behind her – who, by all outward appearance, was a stranger to her…had actually had his long-fingered hands on her bare skin. And she had allowed it.

'I believe I am quite finished with whist,' she said calmly, as the last hand of the second game ended and she stood from her seat. 'Perhaps Gwendolyn and her brother will entertain us at the pianoforte.'

The Starcasset siblings obliged her request, and their lovely duets soon ebbed into a more rousing set of country songs. The others joined in with the singing, and imbibed more brandy and sherry, and soon Gwendolyn's fair cheeks were flushed, Miss Berkley was fluttering her eyelashes quite noticeably at Sebastian, and Victoria was feeling cheerier than she had for months.

But when she saw the way Mr Vandecourt hovered near Gwendolyn, solicitously assisting her to rearrange the pillow on which she sat, and the way his expression softened when he looked at her, Victoria felt a wave of loneliness. It had been that way with Phillip. So kind, so thoughtful, so handsome…she had lost him so very quickly.

Even once she moved beyond this grief that would rear up when she least expected it, grabbing her by the throat when she thought she'd kept it at bay, she would not be able to think about finding a husband or having children. She'd never be able to be like Gwendolyn, happy to be in love, planning a family life, looking forward to the next Season.

Thus was the life she'd chosen, and Victoria was not bitter about it. She'd done it for the right reasons, and the freedoms she received, the things she learnt, the ability to rely upon and protect herself were compensation enough.

But there were times, like now, seeing her happy friend, that she realised how deep the sacrifice had been.

'Lady Rockley, is something the matter?' asked George Starcasset, who had stepped away from the pianoforte to move to her side. 'May I offer you a breath of air on the patio? You look a bit warm.'

'No, thank you, sir,' she replied. 'I fear it is simply

that I am fatigued from the ride from London. I believe I will excuse myself and say good night.'

'Of course. Perhaps you will feel better in the morning. Good evening.'

Victoria bade the others goodnight and left the revelry still in progress. The last things she noticed as she left the room were Miss Berkley and Sebastian in a tête-à-tête in the corner by the whist cards, and Mr Starcasset's gentle blue gaze trailing her movements.

Back in her room, Verbena helped her to prepare for bed. She seemed unaware of her mistress's pensive mood, instead filling what would have been silence with giddy observations about the male species of Claythorne's staff. One in particular seemed to have caught her attention, and Verbena waxed poetically about the under-butler during the entire time it took to unpin Victoria's hair, brush it, and braid it into one wrist-sized plait.

'That will be all tonight,' Victoria said, slipping beneath the covers of her bed. 'Now take yourself off and see if you can find the impressive John Golon and bat your eyelashes at him a bit.'

Despite her relatively early departure from the party downstairs, Victoria was certain she wouldn't find sleep easily. But the next thing she knew she was awakened by a sudden dip on the bed next to her.

She came fully awake and felt the movements of the large body on the mattress as hands groped towards her own person.

'Lady Rockley. V'toria.'

Along with the low murmuring of her name came a waft of spirits. It was so strong it had Victoria turning away and holding her breath. A hand brushed over her face, and another along her arm…alarmingly close to her bosom.

'Mr Starcasset? What are you doing here?' Slipping away from his grasp, she slid from the bed and lit a candle. The illumination was enough to show him blundering about in the blankets, then the lifting of his glassy-eyed face.

'V'toria…if I may c-call you that,' he said, the syllables meshing into one another in a strange cadence. 'I knew it…I knew the signs…'

'Mr Starcasset, I can't imagine what you are talking about, but you are completely foxed.' Victoria nearly had to laugh at the bemused, earnest expression on his face. Perhaps she should be affronted by the man's impropriety, but at the moment he appeared so completely harmless and befuddled that she could almost find the humour in it. The very proper George Starcasset would be mortified if he realised his inebriated self had barged into a lady's bedchamber in the middle of the night.

Certainly it was a common occurrence at house parties such as this one. Victoria had no illusions about the purpose of large parties set on an estate in the country – they were often the perfect excuse and opportunity for illicit trysts. But for some reason she did not picture George Starcasset as one who sneaked about, looking for a chance to tryst.

It simply appeared he had imbibed more than enough brandy after she had gone upstairs. Perhaps the overindulgence was to build up his courage… perhaps it was merely that he'd played too many games of whist.

Or perhaps he got lost on the way to his room. Victoria stifled a soft laugh.

There was nothing left for it. She had to get him out of her room and, hopefully, back to his…or at least to a different area of the house.

A quick glance down reminded her that traipsing around a strange household dressed in a frothy nightgown of little more than French lace and silk was not a prudent thing. With a glance at her late-night visitor, who appeared to have found comfort in her pillows, she pulled a pelisse from the wardrobe where Verbena had hung it, slipped her arms in, and buttoned the three buttons tightly over the bodice. She had to tug on the sleeves of her nightgown to adjust them beneath the narrow sleeves of the pelisse so they didn't bunch up. The cut of the long coat would do little to hide the long silk skirts of her nightgown, but at least her bosom would be covered. Snatching a pair of slippers, she tucked her feet into them and turned back to the bed.

'Come along, dear Mr Starcasset. I suppose after

this I can call you George…at least for tonight.' She giggled and tugged him off the bed. Thanks to her exceptional strength, it was no difficult task to pull him to his feet and sling an arm about his waist. He was beginning to lose track of his eyes; they would focus on her, then suddenly roll up into his head… then come back down and look at her again.

It wouldn't be long before he was out, and so she must move quickly to get him out of there. She could only imagine the horror on his face if he awoke the next morning in her room.

Smiling at the thought, Victoria walked him to the door and out into the hallway. She held the candle in one hand and half lifted, half dragged him with her other arm around his waist.

He was a bit taller than she, and his head began to loll alarmingly. Victoria realised she had no idea where his room was, or even which wing of the house it would be in. So she opted for the safest, easiest route: the library immediately belowstairs.

Thump, thump, thump… She directed him down the sixteen steps and by the time they got to the bottom she was dragging him, as he'd lost the battle with his eyes and neck. His head hung, bobbing easily, and when she peered down to look, his eyes were nearly closed, the lids fluttering as though he were dreaming behind them. His pale blond hair fell in a thick swoop over one temple, and his mouth made the slightest gap. Probably not the way he would want her to see him, Victoria thought, and smiled again, thankful that he would likely not remember much of what occurred. Thus if she said nothing, his pride would be salvaged.

Into the library she went, thankful that it was one of the rooms Gwendolyn had pointed out to her that afternoon. She deposited George in a large wing-back chair near a silent fireplace and tugged the collar of her pelisse back into place.

Something glinted on the floor; she nearly missed it, but the cast of her candle had unexpectedly glanced over it. One of George's buttons, perhaps? Victoria bent and, with a sudden intake of breath, snatched it up from the hooked wool rug.

No, not a button.

The disc was round and bronze and bore the image of a sinuous hound on it. It was identical to the one she'd found at the Silver Chalice.

Chapter Five

Of Balconies and Reprimands

Victoria smoothed her thumb over the bronze amulet. It could be no coincidence that she'd found one at Sebastian's place and then here again…where Sebastian just happened to be.

Lips firming in irksome thought, she cast one last assuring look at George, who snored comfortably in his wing-back chair, then hurried out of the library and up the stairs.

Aunt Eustacia had not received a response from Wayren regarding the amulet before Victoria left London, but she'd been assured of an update as soon as she did. Victoria'd assumed the amulet had belonged to the demon, but that appeared not to be the case, since there were no demons or vampires here at Claythorne.

Focused on her thoughts, Victoria didn't see him until it was too late. He stepped out of an alcove just a short distance from her bedchamber, causing her to falter in her hurried pace.

Sloppy. She should have expected it; she should have known.

'Sebastian,' she said, looking up into his handsome face. Light from her candle flowed over his cheeks, settling a golden cast over his curling hair. His lips were positioned in that sensual, amused smile that alternately annoyed and charmed her.

'Why, Lady Rockley,' he said smoothly. 'What a surprise to find you wandering the halls in the middle of the night.'

She was in no mood to be charmed. 'I suppose I have you to thank for my rude awakening.'

The amusement spread to his eyes as he bowed his head slightly. 'Mr Starcasset is madly in love with your fetching person, and, I have found, is quite biddable when plied with enough brandy.'

Victoria realised they were standing in the hall, where, unlikely as it might be in the wee hours of the night, they could easily be seen. With an angry look, she stalked past him and reached her door, Sebastian at her heels.

Once inside her room, she placed the candle on her dressing table and turned to face him, arms crossed over her middle, and suddenly she was quite glad she'd had the wherewithal to don the pelisse. 'You sent that poor man in here!'

'Let us go out on the balcony,' he suggested. 'Despite the fact that you are a widow, and being found with a man in your bedchamber wouldn't be considered overly scandalous, it is a lovely night. Besides,' he added as he strode past her towards the French doors that opened to a small terrace, 'I don't wish to be in the same room as you and a bed…unless you mean to put it to use.' He paused dramatically. 'Do you?'

Ignoring the spike of interest that sent a warm rush over her bosom, Victoria brushed past him, heading out onto the terrace.

'Apparently not.' Closing the doors behind them, Sebastian walked out to stand across the way from her. 'And as for Starcasset…well, in reviewing the situation, I determined it was much more prudent to get you *out* of your room if I wished to speak with you than to attempt to breach it myself. I had a feeling your hospitality might be a bit…chilly.' His smile shone in the moonlight. 'And yet…here I am. Exactly where I planned to be. And it is not so very cold at all.'

'On the contrary. I find the temperature rather brisk.' A very light breeze brushed the tips of his tousled hair and skimmed over Victoria's cheeks. It *was* indeed a lovely night. The roses and lilies that grew in the garden below scented the balcony. She breathed deeply and smelt fresh country and night air, tangy and dark; so different from the mosaic of artificial smells of London and Society.

The silvery moonlight only enhanced Sebastian's appearance, a factor she presumed had prompted his suggestion to withdraw to the balcony, the proximity of a bed notwithstanding. His arms extended, hands propped on the top of the rail, he watched her with an easiness that irked her. The pale illumination from the celestial bodies tipped the edges of his curls silver, and helped to keep his expression partially hidden.

Victoria waited for him to speak, but he did not; so she said, 'Now that you have gone through such great pains to draw me from my bed, surely you will keep me in suspense no longer.'

'So you have left London.' He looked at her as though searching for something. 'How are you, Victoria?'

She looked away. There were bountiful layers of meaning in his simple question; whether he intended every one that she read there, she did not know. 'Why do you ask? Perhaps because your plan to deliver me to Lilith's vampires didn't work? Because you are ashamed that you ran from the Silver Chalice last year and left Max and Phillip to face the vampires on their own?' Though she kept it steady, surely he could not mistake the anger in her voice.

He stood angled so that his eyes were shadowed, and she could not read what was truly there. 'Ah. Then I have the answer to one of my questions. You still think the worst of me — that I would be so despicable as to make love to you in a carriage as I was delivering you to the vampires. Despite the fact that I warned you when your husband came to the Silver Chalice. Despite the fact that without my assistance with the Book of Antwartha, Maximilian would be dead and Lilith would most likely have it in her possession.' Cool and unruffled he spoke, but there was an underlying emotion that Victoria could not identify. She wasn't sure that she wanted to.

'As I recall, you would have stood by and watched Max perish when he tried to take the book. But regardless of that small point, what else was I to think?'

'That perhaps I simply got carried away by your beautiful mouth, and wanted to distract you from the pain that was so obvious in your eyes – and that the arrival of vampires was no more a part of my plan than to get you undressed.'

Now she could see his eyes, and the look there sent a little shiver over her shoulders. 'According to Max, you would always take the opportunity to undress a woman, particularly in a carriage.'

'I have no wish to hear Maximilian's opinions, for that is what they are, merely opinions – and most likely indicative only of his own inclinations, were he not so bound and determined to be a Venator and nothing more. A hunter, a killer…a man of violence with little left for anything – or anyone – else. I, Victoria…I am not a man of violence.'

'A fact supported by your cowardly escape from the Silver Chalice last summer.'

'Grief has made you harsh. I am sorry for it. I

am truly sorry for your husband's death. If it is any consolation to you, I believed he and Maximilian would follow me when I sneaked out the back entrance of the pub.'

'This is all very enlightening, reliving the events of last summer with you in the middle of the night on my balcony, but I am having a difficult time believing you went through the trouble to trick Mr Starcasset into entering my bedchamber merely in order to show off how well you look in the moonlight.'

'You think I look well in the moonlight? What a serendipitous happenstance!'

'I am finished with this conversation, and I am past ready for you to leave.' She turned and started towards the doors, preparing to lock them behind her if he did not follow. Surely if he could escape from a group of vampires, he could find a way off the balcony on his own.

When his hand closed around her arm, she whirled and whipped off his strong grip with a snap of her wrist and a whisk of silken skirts. It felt good to release some of the tension that had been building inside her. Between them. Let him know she was still in control.

'You still wear your *vis bulla*.' He stepped closer to her, his boot-clad feet grinding on the brick-and-mortar terrace.

'Does that surprise you?' She felt the knob of the door behind her, but other than closing her fingers over its cool brass, made no move to turn it. He was very, very close, but she was not unsettled. After all, she'd faced down numerous vampires, and a demon. And even the Queen of the Vampires. A mere man was no danger to her.

'I assumed since you'd left London that you'd also left your Venator days behind you. Or perhaps you wear the *vis bulla* in order to protect yourself from overly amorous suitors like Mr Starcasset.'

'George' – she used his given name deliberately – 'was not overly amorous until you poked your elegant fingers into the mess.'

'You consider my fingers elegant, then?' Sebastian's smile flashed. 'Two compliments in one evening… how completely unexpected.'

'I have not left my Venator days behind me. Why would I do that?'

His shoulders moved in a nonchalant shrug. 'I thought perhaps after what transpired with Rockley, you might have decided to walk away. After all, you'd done your duty, and look at the result. You lost the love of your life.'

'Walk away? The question would not be whether I would, but how could I shirk my duty? After seeing firsthand the evil of vampires, *how could I*?'

She realised he was closer. She could see the brush of long eyelashes and the slender line of the dimple that barely showed when he was not smiling, as now. 'There's always a choice, Victoria.'

'I made mine. I would not walk away. Nothing would make me walk away, now that Phillip is gone.'

'Nothing?' The word hung on the air between them, as though Sebastian saw the truth in her eyes and hoped to discern it. She held his gaze defiantly.

'Nothing.'

His shoulders moved as he heaved in a long breath, then exhaled as though savouring it. 'You are quite an admirable woman, my dear. Perhaps even out of my league.' He reached for her again, slowly and easily, and closed his fingers around her wrist. 'What is it that you have been clutching here this whole time?'

Again she pulled away, but not so harshly. His fingers were surprisingly strong; it was an effort to break his grip. And then she opened her hand so that he could see the amulet shining in her palm. 'I am quite glad you asked. I believe this is yours?'

Taking it, he needed only a glance and then turned his eyes back to her, still standing close enough that she could smell cloves, see the sprinkling of golden-brown hair beyond the cuff of his shirt. 'Do you know what this is?'

She shook her head, and his expression eased a bit.

'Ah. So why do you attribute it to me, if you do not know what it is?'

'I found one at the Silver Chalice, and then one here tonight. You are the only common factor in both places.'

'Thus and so you came to the conclusion that this

was mine. In that case, perhaps I'll choose not to be offended. You found one at the Silver Chalice you say? When? Where?'

She explained, and included the fact that she'd met and beheaded a demon.

'A demon? With a vampire?' He turned away, moving from her side and breaking the intimacy his proximity had given. 'Nedas has taken no chances.'

'Are you going to tell me what it is, or are you going to mumble to yourself about things I don't understand – and thus can't help with?'

'Ever the impatient one, aren't you?' A quick smile brought the dimple into relief; then it disappeared as his expression sobered. 'This amulet belongs to a member of the Tutela. Do you know anything about the Tutela?'

'No.'

'The Tutela is a secret society, an ancient one. Hundreds of years old, as I've heard it told. Started in Rome, probably in the catacombs right next to the Christians, if you can believe the irony.'

Standing across the balcony from her, he shrugged off his coat, letting the dark material crumple into the shadows at his feet. Now his white shirt, buttoned but not cravated, caught the moonlight and fairly glowed in the darkness that was his backdrop. 'Oh, do not fear, I am not preparing to ravage you. This jacket is rather stifling, and it's not as if you haven't seen my shirtsleeves in the past.'

Instead of the grin she expected, he merely gave her a look that sent her stomach to tingling. When she made no response, he continued, 'The Tutela protect vampires.' He unfastened the wrists of his shirt with great nonchalance. 'They have done so for centuries.'

'Protect them? How? Like offering an establishment where the vampires can come and drink with mortals?' Victoria replied archly.

Although his broad shoulders and darker, muscled arms glowed in the moonlight as he rolled up his sleeves, his face was in shadow again. How did he manage to do that – show off his physique while hiding his expression?

Or perhaps it was merely that Victoria could not help but notice the way his shirt clung to his waist and moulded the very same shoulders she had had occasion to hold on to. And perhaps she didn't really want to know what was going on inside his head.

'Now there you go, bordering on insult again, my dear. Surely your aunt has taught you better than that. No, their purpose leans more towards providing mortals for vampires to feed upon. Bringing innocent people to the undead for their pleasure and nourishment. And gadding about during the day and protecting the interests and secrecy of the vampires while they stay safe in the darkness. Doing the evil work that the undead cannot, or will not, do in an effort to stabilise and increase their power. Members of the Tutela are the whores of the undead.'

'But why? Why would anyone do that?'

Sebastian shook his head. 'Such an innocent you are still, even with all that you have experienced and seen. I do not know if I would wish for that to change or not.' He braced his hands back on the rail. 'There are some people who yearn for immortality. Who find pleasure in being fed upon by an undead. Who believe that if they protect the vampires, they in turn will be protected from the evils in this world.'

The flash of a memory stunned her. Bodies, bloody and ravaged, mutilated from the neck to the legs…the blank eyes, the gashes below the jaws, the tears in the chests, the rank, dull smell of blood. The sight she'd faced after the only time she'd been too late to stop a vampire raid last summer, shortly after she and Phillip had been married. It still had the power to send oily nausea into the back of her throat.

When she relived that image, she could not understand – could not fathom – how any man or woman could protect such creatures, let alone fraternise or mingle with them. 'I cannot comprehend it,' she finally said, when the memory eased and the silence had stretched long enough.

'Victoria, I kept the Silver Chalice as a vehicle to allow the undead to congregate so that any important information might be gleaned from them whilst in their social moods. As I said to you before, I prefer to have them where I can see them, and spy on them, rather than have no idea what they plan. I am not,

and never was, a member of the Tutela. Regardless
of any of my other actions, I hope that you believe at
least that of me.'

She couldn't see his face, blast it! How could she
know what to think? 'Move into the light, where I can
see you.'

'My pleasure.' He stepped away from the balcony,
but did not stop at one or two, or even three paces.
He stopped when he had her upper arms in his hands,
his boots touching her slippers. 'Victoria.' The French
of his voice hung on the syllables, and her breath
stilled.

He bent towards her and she closed her eyes,
waited. It had been over a year since a man's hands
had been on her. A year since she'd been touched with
any affection or sensuality. She'd given no thought to
how much of a dearth it made in her life. But now
she knew.

A tiny huff of breath escaped her lips before he
brushed his mouth over hers, back, and then again.
Fitted to her lips just perfectly, just enough that her
fingers wanted to close over his arms.

And then he pulled away, released her, and opened
his eyes. For the first time that night she read the
message there, and it made her want to step away…or
drag him back for more.

He was back to his cool, charming self. 'Don't
believe for one moment that I didn't want more,
Victoria,' he said lightly, as though to deny the fact.

'But there are more pressing matters to discuss.'

'Pressing matters?'

As if shaking off a slumber, he turned and paced back along the balcony, rolling up a sleeve that had fallen back to his wrist. 'Since you found the amulet at the Chalice, that means someone involved with the Tutela was there…likely the demon or vampire you killed, or perhaps both. There are no other vampires in London, are there?'

'When I left this morning, it was after two weeks of patrolling every night. I found the demon and vampire at the ruins of the Chalice, and I saw one other vampire, who got away…and no others. Lilith has not returned.' She looked up at him in question. 'I don't know where you've been for the last year, Sebastian, but you may not be aware that Lilith took her followers and returned to her hideaway in the mountains after she did not succeed in getting the Book of Antwartha.'

'I am aware of that, although I have not been in England. I made my way to the Continent quite rapidly after my visit from the vampires at the pub.' He looked out over the gardens below, then turned back to Victoria. 'They're looking for Polidori. And someone is here. Someone from the Tutela. Someone must have dropped that amulet. But there aren't any vampires here.'

'No, there aren't. Nor demons either, I don't believe.'

'You can sense demons as well, then. Good. Polidori will be relieved to hear that.'

'Are you going to tell me why they are after him? Or shall I guess?'

His charming smile was back. 'I'm certain it won't be difficult for you to figure out.'

'It must be his book. *The Vampyre*. It reveals too much about the truth of vampires. And you are travelling with him for what reason? Surely not to protect him.'

'Now, Victoria…do not besmirch my capabilities; particularly since you aren't acquainted with the vast array of my talents.' What little seriousness was left on his face shifted away, and his eyes locked on hers. 'Though it is not for lack of desire on my part that you remain uneducated. At any rate, yes, I met him in Italy. Byron dismissed him from his service, not because he didn't need a physician any longer, but because he was afraid for his life.' He sighed. 'I will let John tell you the story; he has all of the details. Suffice to say, I do not expect this to be a quiet and safe house party. Someone is here from the Tutela. Whoever it is, they will be after Polidori, and I should not be far from him until we determine who it is.'

'Why doesn't the doctor just leave?'

'That is what he has been doing for the last year – trying to stay ahead of them. Somehow, they must have found out I was involved; hence, they were looking for me at the Silver Chalice.' He pushed away from the railing. 'At least no one knows that there is a Venator in our midst,' he said, his lips twitching crookedly. 'Polidori will be relieved to hear that; and with you in attendance, he won't be in any hurry to leave. He's safer here with you than anywhere else.'

'That is true. Can you arrange for me to speak with him tomorrow?'

'Of course. If you join us on our hunt in the morning, we should be able to take a few moments to speak alone where no one can hear.'

'Very well, then.'

He started to go, moving towards her, and she suddenly felt exceedingly aware of…him, herself, the quiet and intimacy of the night. Victoria could have shifted out of his path, or opened the doors and slipped into the room before him…but she didn't. His approach sent her gaze up into his face as he neared, and her belly pitched unsteadily.

'If you continue to look at me like that, Victoria, I'll be most happy to give you what you want.' The edge in his voice was unfamiliar and brusque. 'After all, you are no longer an innocent.'

She stood her ground and reached up to touch his cheek with light fingertips. She'd never voluntarily touched a man before…except Phillip. She wanted Sebastian's arms around her, not just a brush of mouth over mouth. She wanted to *feel* and to forget. She wanted to be more than a Venator, more than a widow, more than a sedate marchioness sipping tea whilst discussing the weather and who was fornicating with whom.

Sebastian allowed her fingers on his face for a moment; then, with studied casualness, he reached for her wrist and brought her palm gently to his mouth. A kiss on the inside cup of her hand, and one on her wrist, brought back the memory of the night he'd removed her glove and done the same. She'd never got that glove back.

'If I didn't have to go to Polidori, you would be in quite a bit of trouble, my dear.' He released her hand and, without looking back at her, brushed past and through the french doors.

Chapter Six

In Which a Rather Disruptive Evening Ensues

As it turned out, Victoria did not meet up with Sebastian and Polidori as planned the next morning; nor did she find the comfort of her bed for very long.

Lying there, reviewing the conversation with Sebastian, and considering whether he had been completely forthcoming with her, Victoria became aware that the hair on the back of her neck had lifted. It was as if the gentle breeze from the balcony, where she had left the doors open after Sebastian eased out of the room, brushed over it.

However, since she was lying on her back, the pillow tucked into the curve of her nape, Victoria knew that was not the case.

If Sebastian was to be believed, the vampires had found Polidori.

Even if he wasn't to be believed, the fact remained: Claythorne House had attracted some unwelcome guests.

Flinging the blankets away, along with her confused feelings about Sebastian, she rolled from the mattress, planting her feet silently on the floor. Victoria tucked her long braid down into the back of her gown (all the better to keep it from flying into her face during any ensuing fight) and shoved her arms back into her pelisse. The sleeves caused her nightgown arms to bunch up again, but she was in too much of a hurry this time to fix them. In the bottom of her trunk she scrabbled for her stakes, grabbed one, and also a small vial of holy water, which she tucked into a bulked-up sleeve. Slinging a palm-sized silver crucifix around her neck, she rushed out of the bedroom, not pausing to check whether the door closed behind her.

Out in the hall she hurried along, measuring the chill at the back of her neck. Too soon to tell how many there were. Did they know where Polidori was? Was it truly the author that the vampires sought?

Once at the staircase she had to make a decision: up, down, or continue straight along the corridor? Nerves singing and pulse jumping, nevertheless she made herself pause, draw in a deep breath, and wait. Feel. Listen and smell.

Down.

Victoria fairly flew down the wide, sweeping staircase, stake clutched in her hand, leaping the last few steps and landing light-footed on the floor below. She hadn't felt so alert and in control for months… months! This was what she was born to do.

Here again, she had to pause to sense the undead. Perhaps they had not found a way into the house yet. They had to wait for someone to invite them in; a vampire could not enter a home, even if the door was open, unless asked by someone with authority to do so.

Since someone with authority could include personages as random as butlers, footmen or even maids, that requirement did not provide the level of protection one would expect or hope for.

But, there was the amulet to consider. Whoever had lost the amulet was sure to be the one to have invited them in.

Then she heard it. A clink, then a low, soft scratching sound from the library.

The library. Where she had left George Starcasset!

Victoria slipped behind the tall, thick column at the base of the stairs, her heart ramming in her chest. Resting her cheek against the chalky plaster, she peered from the shadow and could see into the open door of the room. Was he still there? Surely he was… he had been deeply asleep when she left him.

Try as she might, she could not see the chair where he'd slept; it was in the shadows and facing the fireplace, away from the rest of the room. In his sleep, George would be helpless against any threat, but perhaps unnoticeable if he was not snoring.

She saw movement at the window and held her breath. She counted them. Four. Four figures slipping through an open window one by one, silently and without hesitation. The back of her neck was cold. They were all vampires; she could see the faint glow of four sets of eyes…yet they'd come into the house on their own. There was no other movement in the room…either George was still asleep, or he was no longer there.

The vampires must have been at Claythorne House before. That was the only way they could have entered as they did. Someone had invited them at an earlier time, when they were in their human form, and now they were back…with or without that person's knowledge.

Victoria waited, watching them as they conferred with hand gestures and the faintest of whispers, praying that they would not see George in the chair nestled in the shadows. Then, as they began to move towards the entrance, away from the armchair, she felt a wave of relief, a zing of excitement.

She could take on four of them with little trouble. Her eyes narrowed in anticipation; she adjusted her grip on the stake.

Then she saw their faces, their burning eyes, as they turned to move out of the library, only a breath away from where she hid. These were not normal vampires with blood-red irises.

Two of them had pinkish eyes, the colour of rubies. Guardians.

Two of them had eyes of a red-purple colour. They

had long hair and carried gleaming metal swords. Imperial vampires.

Victoria swallowed, her dry throat crunching in her ears. Her palm grew damp, and the stake shifted in her uneasy grip. One could always tell where a vampire was in the hierarchy of his race by looking at his eyes. Pink-eyed Guardians, members of Lilith's elite guard, were dangerous enough, with their poisonous bite and capacity to enthral with great ease…but Imperials, with magenta irises, were the most powerful of the undead – with the exception of Lilith, of course. Imperials wielded swords like second hands, and their strength and speed were beyond measure. They could fly when fighting, and could pull the life energy from a person without touching them.

The first and only time she'd encountered an Imperial vampire, Max had been with her. The match had been difficult, frightening for her to watch…but Max had been victorious.

There was no Max tonight – no one but herself.

They could see in the dark – all vampires could – but, thank heaven, they could not sense the presence of a Venator as she could sense theirs. Her presence as a mere human might be scented, but because the house was full of them, the vampires would not necessarily know exactly where the sensation was coming from or be able to sense her particular proximity as long as she was silent and still.

Victoria held her breath as the four undead swept

from the library, doing nothing to muffle the sounds of their footsteps.

The four moved past her hiding place, close enough that she could have reached out and snatched at the boot of the last one as they swung past her and up the stairs. Her best hope was for them to separate, and for her to take them on one by one.

Victoria eased from her hiding place, staying in the shadows, but shifting so that she could see through the stair railing curving above her. The four did not appear to be interested in separating, so she would have to assist them in breaking up their party.

Slinking from the shadows, she moved along the wall in the foyer to a small table near the library door. The bust of a Claythorne ancestor sat upon it, and Victoria shifted it on its pedestal, creating the soft grating of marble against wood. Then she backed down along the hallway, away from the foyer and the staircase, standing in the middle of the corridor just out of sight of the stairs. She kept the stake hidden in the folds of her pelisse and wrapped one hand around the crucifix, obstructing its form from view.

Her trick worked. She heard footsteps coming back down the stairs and hoped only one had peeled away from the group.

Luck was on her side, for it was not only a single vampire who made his way from the bottom of the stairs towards her, but a Guardian and not an Imperial.

She stood in the hallway, backing towards one side, as he advanced towards her. The sharp metal edges of the crucifix edged into her palm. 'I am sorry, sir,' she stammered. 'I did not mean to disturb…Oh!' She kept the puff of her scream low and soft – no need to draw any other members of the household into the trap – and her stake-filled hand behind the fold of her skirt.

The vampire moved towards her, a glint of humour in the glow of his pink-red eyes. 'You did not disturb me,' he replied in a grating voice as he reached for her. 'But I might find it satisfying to disturb you, my dear.' His fangs, long and silvery in the dim light, bared in a satisfied smile. 'I have a task tonight, but it is hard to pass up the fresh blood of a beautiful young lady.'

Pretending to jerk away in fright, Victoria pivoted, stepping aside so that he did not grasp the arm where she held the stake. Instead he laughed and easily caught at her forearm where it angled over her bosom, holding the cross beneath it.

They had moved down the hallway, towards the back of the house where the kitchens were, and far enough away from the stairs that the other vampires wouldn't hear the details of their altercation.

'If you taste good enough, perhaps I will give you the gift of immortality,' he said with a condescending smile. 'Then you shall always be as young and beautiful as you are now, with your long dark hair

and creamy skin. What a lovely white neck you have
– so long and slender and delicate—'

It all happened quickly: he caught her wrist; she
released the cross and allowed him to pull her arm
towards him, baring the crucifix to his sight. His grip
faltered and he jerked back as though stung, making
his chest vulnerable. Victoria struck.

A tiny pop, followed by a *poof*, and the garrulous
vampire disappeared in a satisfying gust of dust.

Victoria couldn't help a grin – she couldn't have
choreographed it any better. But before she went
haring off after the others, she waited for a moment,
listening. If she were lucky, one of the other three
vampires would separate from the group to come back
and check on the Guardian, giving her the chance to
surprise him too.

But after she waited for several breaths and heard
nothing, Victoria knew she had no more time to
waste. Once again hurrying on light feet, she jogged
back down the hallway to the grand foyer and up the
sweeping staircase. She was only halfway up the first
flight when a bloodcurdling scream echoed through
the house…from below.

Blast it!

What now?

The vampires were upstairs, surely Polidori was
upstairs, but something was happening below…

Victoria stumbled to a pause at the top of the
stairs, forcing herself to wait and try to determine

where the danger was. Her neck was cold and her instincts told her to go on upward…but the scream echoed through the house again.

Footsteps sounded, doors slammed, and suddenly people were erupting in the hallway.

'What is it?'

'Who is hurt?'

'Lady Rockley, is that you?' This last was addressed to her by a man in a nightshirt with spindly knees, his grey curls flattened to one side of his head. She couldn't recall his name – he was a guest of Gwendolyn's father – and she did not have the time to respond politely.

'Get back to your rooms!' she shouted, pushing past him and starting up the second flight of stairs. 'Lock the doors!' Locked doors wouldn't protect them forever, but they would at least slow down the vampires. She hoped.

'What is it, Victoria?' Gwendolyn's voice came, high-pitched, from the landing above. 'What are you doing?'

'Get in your rooms! Lock the doors, and get a cross or a Bible!' Victoria pushed past her friend, who tried to clutch at the tail of her pelisse as she ran past. 'Gwendolyn, *now!* Do as I say!'

The iciness at the back of her neck had not ebbed; it was getting stronger. They were close. 'Where is Polidori?' She screeched to a halt and spun to shout back. 'Where is he?'

More yells, more doors slamming, men running,

and loud, angry thuds from one of the rooms along the hall.

'Last door,' Gwendolyn called, staring fearfully after her. 'Victoria, what are you doing? Come back!'

'Lady Rockley!' It was Mr Berkley, who looked befuddled and rumpled.

Victoria pushed past him and dashed down the hallway, wondering how on earth she was going to fight two Imperials and a Guardian without the element of surprise. And keep the others, who had no concept that vampires had invaded the house, from getting in the way.

But she had to. Polidori's life, apparently, depended upon it.

Something grabbed her from a shadow, and she whipped away, stilling a shriek. 'Sebastian!'

'They're in there. Two Imperials and a Guardian.'

'I saw them; I staked a Guardian already. I thought you were going to be with Polidori after you left my room,' Victoria hissed, pulling away and starting towards the door.

'What in the hell are you doing? I said two *Imperials*.' He wrenched at her arm, and, surprised, she stumbled backward. 'Polidori's not there.'

'Let go,' she snarled, flinging off his grip. 'I've got a job to do. Where is he?' Victoria looked at him, struck by the look on his face. She'd seen Sebastian only with his calm and charming persona, not this intense, angry mood. But she was the one in command here. Not him. 'What I'm doing is what I must. Remember? My choice – to stand and fight, rather than to turn tail and run.'

'You against two Imperials and a Guardian…don't be foolish. Besides, he's hiding.' He pointed to a room across the hall from where she'd been ready to burst in. 'Whoever let the vampires in told them where he slept, and they're searching the room for him. There are two others outside, watching the windows.' He spoke quickly, his words like angry raps in her ear. 'We haven't much time before they realise he's gone.'

Then she noticed. 'What is that you're holding – a sword?' Victoria barked a short, nervous laugh. 'What do you expect to do with a sword?'

Annoyance in his eyes, he shoved her away. 'Think what you will. Are you—' Whatever he was going to say was cut off as someone behind them shouted. They turned to look back down the hallway, where a cluster of party guests were still standing in a wide-eyed group. Several of the men had retrieved pistols, and were starting towards Victoria and Sebastian.

'Get back!' Sebastian shouted, turning towards them. 'You don't understand what is happening here. Get back in your rooms and lock the doors! You will only endanger yourselves!'

'Lady Rockley, what is going on? You must come to safety! What is it?' Mr Berkley, still looking rumpled, but a bit more clear-eyed, ignored Sebastian.

Loath to take the time, Victoria nevertheless turned

and faced him and the others. She spoke calmly, strongly. She knew they had to see the honesty and earnestness in her face. 'You cannot help. You must listen to me. Save yourselves and do as I say. Lock the doors to your rooms and do not come out until it is safe. There are vampires in this house, and pistols will do little to protect you.' Victoria yanked the crucifix from over her head. 'This will protect you,' she said, tossing the heavy amulet to Gwendolyn, who hovered behind the men. 'Now lock yourself away.'

'Vampires?' Mr Berkley backed up, his eyes wide. Another man holding a pistol like a shield took a step towards her as though to argue. Before he could speak, a door slammed open and a tall, glowing-eyed vampire strode out.

Screams echoed through the hall as Gwendolyn and some of the more fainthearted of the men turned and scrambled away.

The sight of the Imperial, with his magenta eyes and long silvery hair, was enough to deflate any argument from the bold man with the pistol. He goggled at the evil-eyed undead and backed away, pointing a shaking firearm at him.

Victoria and Sebastian did not move.

'Where is Polidori?' snarled the Imperial, surging towards them as his companions flowed into the narrow corridor behind him. Through the open doorway, Victoria caught a glimpse of an overturned bed, shattered bedposts and a splintered dressing table. Shreds of bedding and other fabric scattered the floor, which glittered by lantern light with tiles of glass.

Victoria stepped forward, keeping her stake hidden in the folds of her night rail and careful to keep her eyes averted. 'He's not here.' She wanted to add, *What a shame that you'll have to report to Lilith how you you've lost your prey*, but she was hoping to keep the fact that she was a Venator a secret for a bit longer. Just long enough to find an opening for the stake that itched in her hand.

'You lie,' the Guardian said, pushing his way between the two Imperials. His breath hissed like a kettle of evil steam. 'I can smell the dog. Tell me where he is or you die.'

Sebastian shifted beside her, but Victoria took a step to the side and gestured behind her at the long hallway stretching back towards the stairs. Distractions. She had to create distractions. And she had to get him close enough so she could stab him. One chance was all she would get.

'What do you want Polidori for? Is there not enough fresh blood right here?' taunted Victoria.

The other two vampires crowded in the hall behind their leader. In some deep part of her mind – the part that was not focused on the large hand from the Guardian that was reaching towards her – Victoria was glad that the corridor was barely wide enough for three men to walk abreast. The Guardian, by virtue of his stocky body, effectively blocked his companions from moving forward to attack.

Now if she could just get them to move down the hall, away from the room where Polidori was, perhaps Sebastian could help him escape. Somehow. While she attempted the divide and conquer strategy that was her only option.

All other thoughts disintegrated as the Guardian's hand closed over the top of her shoulder and squeezed. Just where she wanted him…close enough to strike. *Don't look at him*, she reminded herself. It would be much too easy to be caught by his enthralling gaze.

Sharp nails dug into her tender shoulder, and she focused away from the discomfort as he bent closer and hissed in his low, menacing voice, 'Right here is some fragrant fresh blood. Shall I feast on your lovely neck right now?'

She was tipped off balance by the thrust of his hand as it jolted her shoulder, or the stake might have found its mark when Victoria reared back and propelled it forward.

Instead, the pointed ash stick slammed into his arm as though she were driving it against a brick wall. The shock of the sudden impediment stunned her, numbed her arm, and she felt an ugly click in her wrist. And pain. Shooting, sharp pain in her awkwardly bent wrist. Victoria gasped and stumbled back, dark spots whirling in her vision before she shook them away.

'What have we here?' growled the Guardian, his burning eyes narrowing as he looked down at Victoria, whose head reached only to his shoulders. He still had a strong hold on her shoulder, but she twisted away when he would have drawn her near.

Don't look at him.

'A bold little girl. Perhaps she will be my reward for a job well done.'

Victoria had blinked away the black spots in her vision, but now as she tried to focus again, she was caught in the vampire's gaze as though he'd yanked her back from a dead run.

The effect of the thrall was instant. She felt as though she were falling into a soft pool of pink velvet folds. Her breath shifted, slowed; her limbs felt like feather pillows. The pulse in her neck surged. She could feel the blood vibrate, yearning for the smooth, sharp bite that would release it.

It was warm in her veins, warm, hot, tingling. It leapt and lapped as though the vampire called the liquid of her life to him, ebbed and surged with each breath. Her body became aware…alive, yet dull… tantalised, yet sleepy…as though she were turning to Phillip's body in the night, half-awake, half-aroused.

Faintly, trying to claw to the surface, to break the spell, her consciousness fought. She had to stop the tug. But the pull…it enwrapped her, like the flow of water suddenly undammed and rushing to drown her. She struggled…if she could blink, make her dry, open eyes close, even for a moment… Dimly she felt and heard movement, shouts…but she could not respond. Couldn't identify them.

Her arms clunked against each other as though someone was moving them, the stake fell from loose fingers; something hard bumped into her sore wrist… something curving and hard that was out of place… Her head tipped to one side, the heat of her shoulder warming one side of her neck, the other damp and cool and vulnerable.

Her hands fluttered as though to fight him away, but he was too close…too strong. Burning pink and ruby filled her world. Hot breath came close, fangs, alluring and promising relief, glistened yellow-grey in the dim light.

Victoria felt the hard, slender thing under her sleeve again as her arms were pushed up against her body, helpless, and she suddenly had a burst of clarity. It was the vial of holy water.

Pater noster. She thought it. Then she said it aloud. '*Pater noster, qui es in caelis…*'

It was like a jolt of lightning through her mind, a streak of consciousness. Focus. She'd been given focus.

A low laugh sounded near her ear. 'He to whom you pray cannot help you now.' The vampire was too close; she couldn't get it in time, though his moving towards her seemed to take hours…days. Her fingers fumbled, clumsy; he came closer; she fought to blink, to break the connection; she pulled on the vial.

As their gazes disconnected, as he came that last inch closer, the vial slid free and she fumbled as the gentle prick of his fangs touched her skin. With the last bit of her strength, she buckled one knee and tipped to the side, twisting the cap off the vial. She fell, throwing the water full into his face as he bent after her.

The Guardian screamed and tore away, hands over his eyes, murderous rage coming from behind them. Victoria scrabbled for the stake she'd dropped, but before she could find it, she saw something better.

The glint of a sword lay near her feet: an Imperial's weapon, dropped and forgotten. She swooped for it and rose, holding the heavy blade.

With a quick slice, like the one she'd used to behead the demon at the Silver Chalice, she rose up and swung it just as the vampire started towards her again.

His head lopped off, tumbling into dust before it hit the floor.

Victoria whirled, the last vestiges of his control over her lifted, and was suddenly back in the present. She saw to her amazement that Sebastian had engaged one of the Imperials with his own sword.

Blades flashed, clanging in rhythm as the two parried in the narrow hallway. Sebastian matched the Imperial blow for blow, blades scraping against each other as they fell away. The other Imperial was nowhere to be seen; but the door to the other room was open.

Victoria hesitated for a moment, but Sebastian shouted, 'Go! Polidori!' He was outmatched, and she knew that if she left, he would die. A sword was effective against a vampire only if it was used to behead him. However, a sword against a mortal could wound, maim or kill in any part of the body.

Sebastian did not have the strength or speed to match the vampire for long, she did not know how he'd managed it so far. It was a blessing that the low ceiling prevented the Imperial from floating and swooping like a bird of prey, or the battle would have been over before it was begun.

'Victoria! Go!' he shouted, and she made her decision. She could wonder later why Sebastian was willing to endanger himself. Bending in a graceful move, she scooped up her stake, and, still holding the sword, darted to one side of the Imperial.

She was not to make it past him, though, for he saw her and spun, whirling with one last blow meant to slice into Sebastian, then arc into Victoria. The clang and slide of three blades meeting was a satisfying yet ugly sound.

Seizing the opportunity, Victoria pivoted and brought her blade around as she slipped to the side of the vampire, who raised his own sword to meet Sebastian's. As she swung with all of her might, slicing towards the vampire, he one-handed his own blade, somehow broadsiding Sebastian while reaching for her.

She brought the blade down, cutting through his arm and missing the vulnerable neck, spinning around behind him.

The arm burst off his body, exploded into dust, and in the blink of an eye another one appeared to replace it.

Victoria swung her blade again, noticing Sebastian crumpled against the wall, and brought it up and around as the Imperial whipped back to meet her. Their blades clashed, sliding angrily along each other, and just as they reached their zenith, separated. Victoria's went up, the vampire's went down, and hers bit into his neck as searing pain exploded along her thigh.

With a scream of determination, she kept her momentum in force, and felt the release as the second sliced through his neck.

She collapsed onto the floor as the Imperial poofed into nothingness. Blood streamed down her leg, sopping her silk night rail and pooling onto the polished floor beneath. She had executed her first Imperial, thanks to Sebastian's assistance.

Shakily, she pulled to her feet and stumbled towards Sebastian.

When she pressed a hand to his chest, sliding her fingers into the opening and over his warm skin to feel whether he was breathing, and tipping his head to one side so she could probe for a pulse, he shuddered a deep breath and forced his eyes open. Weary humour glinted in their amber highlights. 'Not now, Victoria... but later, I promise.'

With an unplanned grin, she pulled herself away, still shaky. She staggered to her feet, satisfied that he wasn't about to expire on the spot. 'One must have one's fantasies,' she told him, then gasped at the pain in her leg.

Still holding the sword, heavy in her sore wrist, she used it to help propel herself to the room in which the author was purportedly hiding. The door was open, hanging half from its hinges.

The Imperial vampire, the last one remaining, spun from the bed to meet her. He did not have a sword; it must have been he who dropped the one she had. Looking past him, Victoria got the impression of blood, a vat of blood spilt over the body that lay there, thick and rust-smelling. The scent of evil, of death.

Her leg screaming, her wrist protesting, she lobbed the sword up, but the Imperial lunged towards her and stopped the blade. It smacked into the palm of his hand, and he caught it, flat against his palm, twisted it from her weakened grip, and sent it flying across the room. His face burnt with anger, edged with blood at the corners of his mouth, and his eyes blazed as he came at her again.

Victoria felt herself lifted and tossed across the room. She slammed into something hard, and everything went black.

Chapter Seven

In Which a Disturbing Question Remains Unanswered

The stench of death roused her.

Victoria opened her eyes, gathering herself to leap back into battle with the Imperial, pushing away Sebastian, who had his hand on *her* chest and was looking down at her with flat golden eyes.

'He's gone,' he told her, removing his hand deliberately. 'The vampire.'

'Polidori?' She pushed herself up on her elbows, then her palms, and saw that her twisted white nightgown was stained dark red.

'Dead.'

'No!' She pushed Sebastian away and dragged herself to her feet, allowing him to help her after she'd got her legs straightened. Her right thigh hurt, stung, ached like a stone was crushing it, and she felt a warm trickle rolling down and curling around her ankle. She turned and saw the bed.

There was Polidori, or what remained of him. Victoria had seen carnage like this before, but it did not make it any easier to observe. What had been unruly dark curls were plastered to one side of his face by crusty brown blood, his hips twisted one way and his torso facing the other. What had been a taupe-and-brown-striped nightshirt had been ruined by dark red splashes. His throat gaped like the entrance to a yawning cavern, and three X marks – in memory of the thirty silver pieces Judas received for selling Jesus – had been carved into his chest.

'The Imperial is gone? I don't remember what happened,' Victoria said.

'I'm not certain…but he was gone when I came in. You haven't been unconscious for very long, and when I came to, I heard a loud thud. I presume it was you going against the wall. He had to have gone out the window, because I looked in right after I heard the crash.'

Then Victoria remembered. 'You wanted me to save Polidori – you were fighting the Imperial and you wanted me to leave you. You could have died.'

'Quite a surprising turn of events, my bravery, hmm? Well, perhaps it was merely an accident – after all, I had to step in when the Guardian was about to feast on your lovely neck, because the Imperial was right behind him. If I had not engaged him with the sword, that would have been the end of you…and then where would we have been?'

Mockery glinted in his eyes. 'Presumptive though it might have been, I figured that even I could hold him off for a few moments. And it was certainly accidental that I distracted the Imperial enough for you to slice his head off. But I must say' – he inclined his head coolly – 'it was a relief when you broke the thrall of that Guardian. I was a bit worried there for a moment. You looked as though you were ready to do anything he wanted, with your parted lips and heavy eyes.'

Victoria walked towards the bed and drew a sheet up over the dead man. 'No one should come in here. We must hide what happened tonight.' She looked at Sebastian.

'I'll take care of Polidori. And the room here. We can burn everything.'

'My maid can help. And perhaps I can send to London for my aunt. She has a way of…relieving people of their memories in situations like this.'

'Her golden disc – yes, I've heard about the spinning amulet that helps…er…adjust what people remember. That would be most helpful. If you send for her now, she could be here by tomorrow afternoon. Surely we can keep everyone here until then. It would not be prudent for tales of what occurred tonight to be spread all over London. We'd have mass hysteria—'

'Not to mention a slew of would-be vampire hunters. A very dangerous vocation for one who is not trained.'

He looked at her as though trying to determine

whether her comment was directed at him. 'Anyone can stake a vampire,' he replied coolly.

'If they can get close enough,' Victoria said. She looked back at the carnage on the bed. 'With all he knew about vampires, you'd think he'd have protected himself somehow. Worn a crucifix, carried a stake... something.'

'A crucifix wouldn't have helped him – Polidori was an atheist. So the holy relics, which meant nothing to him, would have provided no protection.'

'How can one believe in immortal evil and damnation without also believing in divine goodness? One cannot exist without the other.'

Sebastian shrugged. 'You and I know better, for we have understood and experienced this aspect of our world for a time. I think Polidori was still coming to accept that there truly is palatable evil in this world: paranormal, immortal, inherent evil.'

'Perhaps. But why were they after him, anyway? You were going to let him tell me...but surely you know something.'

'All I know is that the Tutela is rising up in Italy, and Polidori knew something about it and its leader, Nedas. Something that the vampires needed to silence, possibly some secret vulnerability or weakness. Or some detail of their plans. But he told me nothing more. He didn't trust me. He allowed me with him because he had no choice, but he did not extend his trust far enough to tell me everything.'

Victoria raised her eyebrows. 'But he would have trusted me?'

'A Venator. Eustacia Gardella's great-niece. Yes, I believe he would have. But now…we will never know.'

'Nedas. You mentioned him earlier tonight. You said he was moving quickly; I presume he's a vampire and not a demon. What did you mean?'

'Yes, of course, a vampire. One of Lilith's sons, in fact. And I meant only that he had found Polidori so quickly, and had sent so many of his men after him – including the demon and vampire you encountered at the Chalice.' His lips twitched. 'I cannot believe it took you so long to ask me.'

She lifted her chin. 'I prefer not to be predictable. Besides, I knew you were baiting me, wanting me to ask…I knew you, or Polidori, would tell me in good time. After all, you went through all that trouble to draw me out of my room.'

Her eyes narrowed. 'Speaking of my room, and the drawing out of it…why weren't you with Polidori when the vampires arrived? I thought you were going to stay with him.'

'I was on my way back to him when I found your enamoured viscount stumbling through the house, so I took a moment to direct him to his own chamber and saw him safely snoring on his bed before I even left the room. By the time I accomplished that, the vampires had stormed through the hall and made their way to Polidori's chamber. He had taken my advice and slept in a different place; not that it mattered in the end.'

'I can see why…you are so inventive when it comes to evading danger.'

'The better to keep my delicate hide safe.' His words were light, but there was an edge of temper in his eyes. 'Now, let me see to this mess, and perhaps your maid can tend that wound on your leg…unless you would prefer to keep it a secret and allow me to care for it.'

'My maid is perfectly capable, thank you very much.' Victoria heard the gravel in her voice and decided it would be prudent to step farther away from Sebastian. He had the unfortunate effect of causing her heartbeat to pick up speed and her nerves to tingle. Especially after seeing the way he'd handled the sword in battle with the Imperial. She'd been distracted, but it hadn't missed her notice that his movements were powerful and graceful.

'And there I go…being predictable myself. I just cannot seem to help myself around you, Victoria.'

And the look in his eyes told her that he was none too pleased with that.

'When,' grunted Victoria as she whipped her leg around, slamming it into the heavily padded shield her trainer wore, 'will you teach me *qinggong*?' Her momentum did not lessen as she lunged forward with the follow-up of a chest-high blow of fist.

However, Kritanu was too agile and he ducked, then returned with his own powerful kick. 'You must master this *kalaripayattu* with the sword before I teach you how to glide in the air and leap while fighting,' he replied. 'And that was a very predictable manoeuvre.'

Kritanu was one of the Comitators: experts in martial arts who were sent as protectors and assistants, as well as trainers, for the Venator to which they were assigned. He had been with Eustacia for decades, and had been acting as Victoria's trainer as well.

Victoria, who pivoted to miss the blow, was more than mildly annoyed that he could speak a whole long sentence with ease, whilst she was grunting and breathing heavily. The man was over seventy, and she was twenty. And she was not even wearing a corset, though her breasts were bound.

Not to mention the fact that she did not want to be thought of as predictable…in battle or with mysterious, charming men.

'Then *when* will we begin training with the sword?' she asked, coming at him fast with her fists in rapid staccato on his chest.

She and Eustacia had returned to London from Claythorne the day before, and Victoria had insisted on a much-needed training session with Kritanu the very next day. If she'd been faster, stronger, more prepared, she might not have the four thin scratches on her neck where the Guardian had been ready to sink his fangs…nor would she have the aching wrist or deep slice along her hip and thigh from the Imperial.

It had already begun to heal, of course. In a week, it would be little more than a scar. But facing an Imperial alone – despite the fact that Sebastian was there, she had been, for all intents and purposes, alone – had made her realise how much more she had to learn, and how much a year of not fighting vampires had cost her.

'We shall start with the sword tomorrow,' he replied. She was pleased to note that this time, his words came out a bit more raggedly.

'Good.' She punctuated her satisfaction with a quick swivel on one foot, followed by a low blow to his solar plexus.

Kritanu *oof*ed softly behind the shield, doubling over. But when he looked back up, he was smiling. '*That* was not predictable.' Then he looked towards the doorway and stopped.

Victoria turned and saw her aunt standing there.

'Very nice, *cara*' Eustacia told her, nodding. 'It is difficult to surprise Kritanu as you did. *Vero*, I have been trying for years. Now, Wayren has arrived. Will the two of you join us in the parlour?'

Wayren was a tall, slender woman who reminded Victoria of a medieval lady. She had pale blond hair that she wore unbound, falling in gentle waves over her shoulders and nearly to her waist. The two times that Victoria had met her, she'd worn the same unfashionable gown: long, loosely gathered at the waist with an intricately tied hemp cord, and wrist-length sleeves that fell in points nearly to her knees. The colour of her garment was cream, as though the linen had been woven without adding any dyes or bleach.

She rose when Victoria entered the room and, to her surprise, enfolded Victoria in a gentle, firm hug. 'I am very happy to see you again, my dear. I congratulate you on your work with the Book of Antwartha. I understand from Max that you were the reason everything turned out as it did.' The woman, who was of an indeterminate age, and seemed to be older than Victoria but younger than Eustacia, had such a slender build that Victoria was surprised at the strength of her embrace. 'But most of all, I am so very sorry about Phillip.'

Victoria knew little about her, except that Wayren and Eustacia had known and trusted each other for a long time. She always felt that if she learnt that Wayren lived like a sylph among the forest trees, she would not be surprised.

'This life we share is difficult enough without having to lose someone you love because of it.' Wayren set Victoria back away from her, but kept her hands on the tops of her shoulders, taking a moment to gaze in her eyes, as though trying to read her emotions. Wayren's eyes were light grey-blue, and when she was entrapped by them, Victoria felt calm and soothed – a sense that Wayren truly cared about her.

At last, the woman released her, sending her to a seat on the sofa with a fond smile. Victoria turned shyly away, surprised at how moved she was by the caring greeting from a woman she barely knew.

Eustacia had taken her regular seat next to the piecrust table, with Kritanu in the armchair next to her, and now she spoke as though she were calling a meeting to order. 'I have told Wayren about the events at Claythorne, and that together with Sebastian Vioget, we were able to obstruct the reason and cause of Polidori's death from the other house-guests. Some will say that he died from poison, and some will say that he died from an accident. The conflicting stories, along with the erasure of the memories of those at the house party, will help to keep the tragedy from the rest of the ton. Victoria, will you please explain to Wayren what Sebastian found.' Eustacia lifted a delicate teacup and sipped. 'I have told her about the amulet and how you came upon it at the Silver Chalice.'

'When Sebastian was preparing Polidori's body, he found a small leather packet of papers. They were notes about the Tutela and its leader, Nedas. Sebastian had already told me that the amulet was a new symbol of the revival of the Tutela, which is likely why Aunt Eustacia didn't recognise it.'

Wayren looked at Kritanu. 'As always, your instinct was close on. I received the message from Eustacia that you had connected the hound on the amulet with the *hantu saburos*, although not with the Tutela itself. But, of course, the *hantu saburos* are vampires who trained dogs to bring human prey to them for nourishment…and what is the Tutela but humans acting as bitches trained by Nedas and his followers?' Her pale eyes narrowed in dislike. 'An appropriate symbol, the meaning of which is likely lost on the members who wear it…but certainly recognised now by all of us.'

Kritanu bowed his head in acknowledgment of her compliment, and turned to Victoria as though to bring the conversation back on track and away from him. 'The notes?'

'Apparently this revival of the Tutela is under the leadership of the vampire Nedas, who, according to Sebastian, is Lilith's son.'

'Ach!' Aunt Eustacia's hands rose. 'Of course. Lilith's son Nedas. I knew I had heard the name before.'

'How could she have a son?' asked Victoria. 'Did she…breed?' A warmth suffused her face, but she had to ask. She needed to understand.

'Not in this case, although it is possible, though not common, for a vampire to breed. No, I believe…I believe she turned the boy's father some centuries back, and made him her concubine. He at that time had a wife, whom Lilith did not allow to live, and a babe with her. Lilith had the child raised with her, and when he became an age satisfactory to her, she turned him as well, and now calls him her son. She has endowed him with great powers; of course, similar to her own.'

Her question answered, Victoria continued. 'According to Polidori's notes, Nedas has obtained something called Akvan's Obelisk, which constitutes some threat that frightened Polidori so greatly that he left Italy.' Victoria looked at Wayren apologetically. 'His notes were rather difficult to read and wandered all over the scraps of paper, as though he wrote them down wherever he could find space.'

'The Tutela has had its moments of power and glory, and its times of weakness and near extinction. It has been decades since it was a threat – indeed, the last time was after the events in Austria, when we were able to put a stop to them after that horrifying massacre,' Aunt Eustacia said quietly.

Wayren had been listening intently, pressing the pads of her fingers from one hand against the other, her eyes unblinking. Victoria fancied she could see the slow, thorough spinning of the wheels in her mind as she thought. Then she reached into the large leather satchel she'd placed on the floor next to her chair, rummaged through it, and at last pulled out a small, browning, curling-leafed manuscript.

Its edges were torn and crumbly, and it was simply bound with a leather thong stitched along one side of the papers. The manuscript was no thicker than a finger, and perhaps twice the size of a man's hand.

Victoria could see dark scratches of symbols and writing of some language that did not appear recognisable from her vantage point, and likely wouldn't be even if she were looking directly at the pages. It seemed as though Wayren was blessed with the ability to read every language or glyph that she needed to, whereas Victoria was limited to knowledge of English, Italian and a bit of Latin.

Wayren turned the pages carefully, using one slender finger to skim along them, one at a time, and then it was several moments before she said, 'Ah, yes, I believed it would be here.' She looked up. 'Akvan's Obelisk is a large, spear-like stone made from obsidian that, as legend states, when activated, gives a demon or vampire capabilities to call on and control the souls of the dead. Imagine an army of the dead, not vampires, not needing even to feed on the blood of man, but of warped bodies, puppeteered by the strings of their souls, called back from their afterlife and brought forth upon the earth. It would be devastating to us to have to fight an army of that strength and number.'

She glanced back down at the manuscript, scoring her long finger in gentle circles around an image therein. 'According to this book, Akvan's Obelisk was a gift given by the mountain demon Akvan to his lover Millitka, who was later turned to a vampire. In a fit of rage – for, as you know, demons and vampires are in general immortal enemies – Akvan took the obelisk back from Millitka and, during his tantrum, threw it into the earth. It penetrated so far and so deeply that no one could find it again.' She looked up. 'If Polidori is correct, and Nedas has somehow obtained it, there could be serious consequences for us if he activates it. If the legend is true.'

The others remained silent as Wayren returned her attention to the book, reading further. 'The stone is impossible to destroy. Once activated and in the hands of its master, it is infallible and indestructible. The activation has several stages, but once it is fully engaged, there can be no way to stop it.'

'Akvan's Obelisk is indestructible...but what about Nedas? Could he be killed?' Victoria asked.

Wayren's eyes flickered towards Eustacia, then back to Victoria. 'If he were killed, it would break the connection between himself and the obelisk...but it would not lessen the power of the obelisk. Someone else could activate it just as he did.'

'However, you are right, *cara*. Nedas must be assassinated. The Tutela must be infiltrated, and he must be located and killed before he begins the activation.'

'Nedas is a vampire. A son of Lilith, so he is very powerful. We were able to find out that much. But we weren't aware that he had found Akvan's Obelisk,' said Wayren.

'We?' Victoria asked, even though she knew the answer.

'Max and I. Part of the reason he returned to

Italy so soon after everything happened last year was because of the rising power of the Tutela.'

'So Max is going to kill Nedas.'

Eustacia and Wayren exchanged glances again. This time it was much more subtle, but Victoria was not a Gardella for nothing. She caught it, though she was not meant to. Something was wrong. 'What is it?'

'Shortly after we arrived in Rome, the bites on Max's neck from Lilith began paining him more than usual,' Wayren replied. 'You know those bites have never healed, and she uses that to her advantage – she would like more than anything to have Max in her complete control. He's always been able to fight it, but…it has become more difficult since she bit him again last year, when you were stealing the Book of Antwartha.'

'Where is Lilith now?' asked Victoria, remembering the horror of seeing the powerful Max so helpless under the vampire queen's thrall.

'I am certain she is in her mountain lair, hidden somewhere in the Muntii Făgăraş in Romania. She has been there since you chased her from London last year, and I have no reason to believe she has left.'

'So what is wrong with Max?'

'As I mentioned, his bites were becoming more painful, and suddenly he disappeared for several weeks. I know he returned, for he was seen by another Venator, Zavier; but then I was called away to Paris and I have not been able to contact him for more than eight months.'

Victoria's throat felt dry. 'What do you think happened?'

Wayren looked at Eustacia, then back at Victoria. 'I don't know. But I am certain Lilith is somehow involved. Her reach is far; even if she is not in Italy, her influence is great. I am not even certain Max is alive.'

Chapter Eight

Of Smashed Toes, Chatty Drivers and Inflation

'So you are off to Italy, are you, Lady Rockley?'

'Indeed I am, Mr Starcasset,' Victoria replied. She would, in fact, have been on a ship at that very moment had her exit from St Heath's Row not been delayed by a visit from the Starcasset siblings. 'I hope you forgive me for being unable to take the time to send word round before I left. My travel to Venice is of a rather urgent nature, in relation to my elderly aunt's estate there.'

'Of course. I hope everything is well.' George – she would never again be able to think of him as Mr Starcasset, or, even when he inherited, as Viscount Claythorne, after the episode in her bedchamber – appeared to be heavily dismayed at her precipitous departure.

'Victoria, I do hope that you were not put off by the events at Claythorne,' Gwendolyn put in, stepping forward into the foyer of St Heath's Row. From the grimace that flitted over her brother's face, it was quite likely that she'd stepped not only in, but on his toes. It probably served him right, Victoria thought, for he had been rather overzealous in his attempts to monopolise the conversation with her. 'I cannot begin to apologise for the terrible fright we all had that night, Victoria. To think of such a thing happening at Claythorne!'

'Think nothing of it,' Victoria soothed, pressing a gloved hand over her friend's arm.

Gwendolyn, of course, didn't know the half of what had occurred, thanks to Eustacia's glittering gold medallion, which had been used to alter the memories of all of the guests at Claythorne. 'And now, dear Gwendolyn, and G – Mr Starcasset, I am terribly sorry that I must beg your leave. My carriage is waiting, and the ship on which we are to sail is expecting me to arrive momentarily.' Victoria drew her friend into a farewell embrace, realising with a start that Gwendolyn was her only real friend her age. Yet another reminder that the other half of Victoria's world was so very different from the one that Gwendolyn inhabited.

Just as it had been for Phillip.

Perhaps if she'd used Eustacia's medallion on Phillip, things might have turned out differently.

Victoria was drawn abruptly from her regrettable reverie when George bent over her gloved hand to brush his lips against it.

When he lifted his face, he pulled her hand up

and stepped towards her, so that his words were for her ears only. 'Your departure shall put quite a damper on my intended courtship, Lady Rockley.' He pressed a kiss to the underside of her fingers, then to the tips. 'Godspeed, Victoria, if I may be so bold as to call you that…and if you should have the urge, I would welcome any correspondence from you during your time away.' He could not help that his clean, boyish looks made him appear rather more like an earnest schoolboy than a serious beau. But, she allowed, despite the broad smile and the dismay in his eyes, he was rather charming. And in spite of the circumstances, Victoria felt rather pleased at having the attention of a man again. She had been lonely.

'Thank you, sir,' she replied. 'I am not known as an excellent correspondent, but I shall endeavour not to disappoint you. And when I return, we shall have to discuss this idea you have of courting me.' With a smile that she realised was rather more flirtatious than she'd intended, she withdrew her fingers and nodded for Filbert to open the front door.

'Farewell, Gwendolyn. I shall notify you immediately upon my return.'

Victoria saw that the Starcasset siblings were safely in their ornately sprung carriage before the tall, broad man named Oliver opened the door of her own.

The door closed behind her, she sank down in her seat and realised she was not alone.

'Sebastian? Blast it, how on earth did you get here?

And in your shirtsleeves again!'

There he was, lounging in the corner of the seat across from hers. She hadn't noticed him when she climbed in because she was looking at her seat, and he had been prudent enough to keep his feet off the floor – where she would certainly have spied them as she climbed in.

If nothing else, the man had a talent for appearing unexpectedly – and looking utterly casual about it.

He sat with his legs extended along the length of the seat, his back propped against one wall of the coach. His curly brimmed hat sat in his lap, held in place by two elegant hands. His dark jacket had been removed and was hanging from a hook above his feet. He smiled lazily at her as she arranged her gown primly on her seat, lurching slightly as the carriage started off.

'At least he is not as reckless as Barth is,' Victoria muttered.

'Who? Ah…your new driver. Yes, he is a right accommodating fellow, this Oliver. Oh, yes, I was very pleased to get his name and a good portion of his pedigree while we were at it. It was no difficult task to send him off to speak to the other carriage's driver whilst you were exchanging fond farewells with your paramour, George, who, I am quite certain, is devastated by your leaving England. And as it was, Oliver's earnest discussion with the Starcassets' footman allowed me the opportunity to avail myself of the extra seat in your carriage.' His lips closed, settling in a complacent smile, as the carriage made a gentle turn.

'Surely you too aren't here to bewail the fact that our courtship will be on hiatus for several months whilst I am in Italy?' Victoria replied, trying to keep from looking at those lips. She remembered well enough what they felt like; she didn't need to be reminded of their shape.

With him in it, the carriage seemed much smaller than it really was, and if she had been paying closer attention, rather than reflecting on the unexpected visit of the Starcasset siblings, she would have noticed the sharp smell of cloves that laced the air as soon as she'd stepped foot in the carriage.

She didn't even begin to wonder how he knew she was leaving for Italy at this time. He certainly must have an idea as to why she was going, for he'd found Polidori's notes, but his timing, as always, was disgustingly perfect. It was a boon for him that she had sent Verbena ahead with the bulk of her luggage and some furnishings, in order to get her cabin arranged on the ship; otherwise, he would have had to find a way to get rid of her too. The bloody thing was, he would have succeeded.

'Courtship? That's a rather strong word for what I had in mind.'

He must have chosen his position in the carriage purposely so as to keep his face in as much shadow as possible. Again. She needed to make a point of meeting him sometime in full daylight.

'Whatever it is you had in mind,' she replied coolly, 'will have to be interrupted while I am gone. Unless you planned on finishing it during the ride to the docks?'

Her gentle taunt surprised her as much as it surprised him, if the widening of his eyes and sudden grin were any indication.

'Well, now,' he said, swinging his feet to the floor and sitting upright. 'That wasn't particularly the reason I slipped into your carriage, Victoria…but if you insist, I'm more than happy to oblige.'

'I was merely attempting to understand why you would have invaded my carriage as I was leaving the country. I did not mean to suggest that I would go along with it.'

His eyes were no longer shadowed; now she could see their rich amber, and the interest that glittered there. 'Of course you did not, Victoria. At least, with your words. The rest of you says otherwise…However, I am sorry to inform you that despite my extreme interest in picking up where we left off last summer… in a very similar setting,' he added, gesturing to include the interior of the carriage, 'I did not invade, as you call it, your carriage for that reason. I did not want to call on you for fear of being seen—'

'By whom?'

He shrugged, spreading those well-formed hands

that looked as though they'd never done a day's work. 'By anyone. I don't know who or what is still lurking about, and I thought it would be best if we continued, for all intents and purposes, not to know each other.'

'I think it is merely an excuse for you to find mysterious ways of suddenly appearing.' Victoria glanced out the window. 'We are nearly at the docks. If you have something you wish to say to me, now would be a good time to stop prevaricating and do so, please, Sebastian.'

'I do love to hear you ask so prettily. Perhaps if I declined, you might be consigned to beg? I thought not.' He settled back against the seat. 'I neglected to tell you something else I learnt about Polidori when I took care of things. He wore the brand of the Tutela. He was a member of the Tutela.'

'Brand?'

'A symbol printed on the skin. It is called a tattoo, and it is made with ink and cannot be obliterated. He had the symbol of an ornate T intertwined with a snake on his upper arm, the historical symbol of the Tutela. The hound that is on the amulet is the symbol of the new movement rising in Italy.'

'Now I understand. The vampires and demons were after Polidori because he left the Tutela, and because they were afraid he would tell their secrets. Perhaps he knew more about Akvan's Obelisk than he'd written in his notes.'

'I would think.' He glanced out the window, then

back to her. 'I was not informed that he was a member of the Tutela when I was first asked to assist him in getting back to England. It wasn't until later, when I disposed of the body, that I discovered it.'

'But that means he could very well have been the one who dropped the amulet at Claythorne.'

'I would think so…unless there were other Tutela members there. But if so, they would not have been so frightened of the vampires. And there is one more thing. I suspect, although I am not certain, that Byron might also be one of them.'

'Lord Byron…yes, that might make sense. Byron and Polidori were so close, and then suddenly they are no longer friends, and Polidori leaves Italy.'

'An acquaintance with Byron could be the entrée you need to find the Tutela, for that can be the only reason you are going to Italy. Unless it is to visit with your colleague Maximilian.'

She looked at him. 'Do you know anything about Max?'

'I know quite a lot about the man…what precisely would you like to know?'

'Your obtuseness does not become you,' she snapped. She could smell fish, the approach of the sea, and hear the caw of seagulls. Because of the nature of their journey, Aunt Eustacia had booked them passage on a cargo ship headed directly to Italy, rather than a packet that would take them from Dover to Normandy and require an overland trip across the

Continent. She felt it would give them anonymity from any Tutela members, and make it less likely that they would be followed or otherwise interrupted during their journey.

'My aunt has not heard from Max for months. I don't know how or where you get your information, but if you have heard anything about him, I wish you would tell me.'

'Always wanting something from me, aren't you?' Then the last vestiges of humour vanished from his face. 'I wondered why it wasn't he who was handling the problems with the Tutela. I have heard nothing, but that does not mean there is nothing to hear. You fear he is dead?'

'I don't know. My aunt says he has been silent for more than eight months. Well, we are here,' Victoria said, looking out the window. 'Thank you for giving me this information, Sebastian. I will take your suggestion and start with Byron when I reach Venice. You could have sent it in a note, rather than troubling yourself to visit me personally.'

Again that smile. 'But it is so difficult for me to resist an excuse to see you.'

She sent him a withering glance, then looked away, working hard to ignore the deep, squirming sensations in her belly. 'I'm sure you were pining away all the last year during your convenient disappearance.'

'No… I was allowing you to grieve.'

Those words, simple and stark, made her look back

up at him. He'd moved closer, it seemed; perhaps he was sitting on the edge of his seat, perhaps he was leaning forward…or perhaps the carriage had merely shrunk again.

He did not appear to be waiting for her response, or holding his breath for her to react. He was just looking at her as though to fill his eyes with her countenance. She realised with a start that her fingers were trembling and, glancing down, she clasped them together in her lap. 'I certainly did not expect such sensitivity from you,' she said, keeping her voice even.

Suddenly she didn't want to go. It would be lonely there in Venice, with no one but Verbena and Oliver with her, and Aunt Eustacia, of course; but she would not be living with her aunt. They must pretend not to know each other, for fear the Tutela would identify Victoria as a Venator.

She didn't wholly trust Sebastian, yet at least they had a kinship of sorts. At least he made her feel… something. Alive. Attractive.

And when he looked at her the way he was doing now, he made her feel as if she were something more than a hunter, a warrior.

'I do not wish to disappoint you, my dear,' he said, his voice dry, 'but my benevolence was rather more self-serving than you might think.'

The carriage had long since stopped, and Victoria could feel the jolts and jerks as Oliver removed the last of her luggage from the vehicle. She heard the shouts, the calls, the thuds of cargo being lifted and set none too gently on the docks.

Victoria looked at Sebastian, saw the way his face had closed, and wondered what he was retreating from this time. Perhaps the intensity of real emotions was too much for him. Arching an eyebrow, she followed his lead and replied, 'You? Self-serving? Never say it!'

'Of course. The reason was, of course, that even I could not expect…recompense…for my services and assistance until some worthwhile event presented itself. As it did with Polidori, and now.'

Victoria felt the flush starting to creep up from her bosom to her throat. She stopped it by donning an aura of annoyance. 'You wish compensation for your information regarding Polidori?'

'Have we not always had such an understanding?'

'You have had the understanding, not I. What is it – do you wish to see my *vis bulla* again?'

He smiled such a feral grin that Victoria felt an acute stab in her belly. 'I have seen it, and kissed it, as you well know.' The words, the reminder, seemed to take up all the air in the carriage. Victoria felt her palms go damp and her face warm. His voice matched his smile. 'In fact, my price has gone up.'

'You must be utterly joking.' She had to pull indignation about her in order to cover up the varied, frightening emotions that ran rampant through her. Words, arguments, logic failed her, and all she could think of to say was, 'I am about to get on a ship to Italy!' Her words were barely audible over the screeches of the gulls and the shouts of sailors.

'I will be happy to accept a down payment.' He had hardly blinked during the last moments, holding her there with his eyes. 'I'm certain, based on your past demonstrations, that it will be no great hardship.'

She could have argued, could have mocked him right back, could have become affronted…but she did none of those things. She deliberately chose not to; chose to take matters into her own hands as, in other areas of her life, she'd become used to doing.

Her breathing seemed to swell and fill her as she moved towards him. She leant off the seat, her hands reaching for his shoulders, fingers curving around the fine linen broadcloth that shaped him.

He tasted like the clove that scented his clothes, and felt soft and slick and dangerous. It wasn't an easy kiss, a delicate buss of lip to lip. It wasn't gentle or tentative. It was hot and needy, the undamming of controlled desire.

When Victoria returned to herself, breaking the connection, she found her face close to his, held by her hands on the back of his head. He looked at her with an odd expression, then gently released her from his embrace around her upper arms.

'That will certainly do as a start.' Despite the light words, his voice guttered like a candle flame in a pool of wax. 'I shall be looking forward to collecting the balance.'

She smoothed his tawny hair, made more wild by her reckless fingers. 'You will have to wait a long time for that, Sebastian.' And she slipped from the carriage.

Chapter Nine

In Which Mrs Emmaline Withers Annoys an Italian Contessa

Venice, Victoria learnt, was not at its most pleasant in the late summer months. Although it was late September when she arrived at last, it was still hot and sunny. The city itself, shaped like a large fish with its tail pointing towards the Adriatic Sea, evoked dreaminess and calm with its bright gondolas easing up and down the canals. But the stench of refuse rising from the water was made worse by the heat.

'I fussed 'bout the smell o' London when it's hot,' Verbena complained, checking to make sure Victoria's handbag included a small vial of salted holy water. Ever since her mistress had been bitten by a vampire and had to have the wound treated with salted holy water, Verbena had made it her responsibility to ensure Victoria always carried some. 'This city is worse! Why, with the dead fish floatin' in the streets and the muck o' seaweed and that smelly green stuff that grows on top o' the water, I can't know why anyone would live here in the summer! But that Oliver. He says it ain't so bad, and he thinks the city ain't any smellier than a farm is. Well, that's a country boy for ye. He like as left his nose back on the farm in Cornwall.'

She shook her head and replaced Victoria's reticule on her dressing table. 'I still don' understand why m' cousin Barth didn't leave his hackney wi' someone else and come with us, instead of sendin' his friend Oliver. He might not be the best driver – Oliver takes a bit more care in my opinion – but he's certainly got his head on straight when it comes to them vampires. Wearin' his cross and carryin' holy water and a stake. He'd'a been a better man-about-town for us than this green'un from the farms.'

'Oliver seems a gentle sort, for all his size,' Victoria ventured. 'Has he been giving you any trouble?'

'Trouble? Not him, no, my lady, trouble's the least thing he gives me. He's too accom'datin' is what he is. Always askin' what's to be done, how can he help. I say he's a green boy from the country and never been to the city before, and it shows.' Verbena had moved to stand behind her mistress and began to comb through the long stream of curls. 'I shudder to think what'd happen if he actu'lly saw a vampire…he'd prob'ly ask'm in for tea! Hmmph. Now, for yer debut here t'night, we must take care ye're lookin' yer best, my lady. An' I'm puttin' at least two stakes in your hair, just in th' case of runnin' into a vampire. Who knows if they're out 'n' about tonight.'

'I haven't felt any sensation of their presence since we arrived,' Victoria replied. 'Not one cool breeze to the back of the neck except when it comes in from the sea. I'm beginning to wonder if the Tutela is here in Venice at all. And don't you *always* ensure that I look my best?' Victoria added with a fond smile.

She was in a happy mood tonight, the first time in a long time she felt like enjoying herself at a social event. Their first week in Venice had been slow and frustrating. They'd had to set up the household, announce their presence to any and all English expatriates, and wait for invitations.

In the evenings she'd been forced to sit in the house and practise her *kalaripayattu* in the parlour, for she didn't know the city well enough to patrol it in search of vampires. And there was the added complication that half of the streets were not streets but canals.

But at last Victoria had been asked to attend a gathering at none other than Lord Byron's home. She hadn't expected to have such success so quickly: a tea here, a dinner party there, before she made a connection with Byron. But apparently her mention of Dr Polidori's untimely death had garnered her the entrée into Byron's society she needed.

'Y' know I do m' best, my lady,' Verbena said. 'Not that it's a har'ship to make ye look beaut'ful. Ye've got that lovely skin, like a pret' pale rose, and them big green-brown eyes. An' all this hair! Who could find fault with this hair?'

'There have been times when I've thought of cutting it,' Victoria confessed as her maid sectioned off a piece for her coiffure. 'It gets in the way when I am fighting.'

'Ye *can't!*' Verbena exclaimed, her blue eyes goggling like cornflowers in full bloom. 'I willn't allow it, my lady. I'll find a way to dress't so it cannot fall int' your face. An' asides…if ye cut it, how can I put yer stakes in there? Nothin' to hold 'em up, then, if you cut it all off short! I know as some ladies are doin' it, but I won't let my mistress.'

Verbena's chatter did not ease as she finished coiffing and dressing Victoria. This was lovely for her mistress, as it allowed her to sink into a quiet reverie that was pestered only by an occasional too-hard pull on her hair, or a pin stuck in too tightly, or a direction such as, 'Now stand,' or, 'Raise your arms, my lady.'

Unfortunately, her thoughts wanted to centre on that last interlude with Sebastian in the carriage, and the way he'd looked at her when he'd said, *I was giving you time to grieve.*

Even now, remembering that look made her stomach feel like a ball of dough being kneaded. Not that she'd ever kneaded a ball of dough, but when she was young, she'd seen Landa, the cook at home in Grantworth House, do it with such verve and enthusiasm that she rather thought it must feel like her stomach.

But she would never stop grieving, not completely.

The pain would ease, she would move on with her life – she already had, in a sense – but the grief would never completely go away. It would always mark her, somehow.

If she were different, perhaps she would find someone to love again. Widows did; it wasn't unheard of. She suspected that her mother had developed a *tendre* for Lord Jellington, now, three years after Victoria's father's death.

But Victoria couldn't expect to do so.

Certainly, most people who lost a loved one would feel as if they never wanted to love again. Never wanted to go through that horrific pain of loss. But they *could* love again, when the grief eased. They would be able to.

Victoria couldn't.

Well, she could. It was possible and perhaps even likely that love would find her someday, as she was still young and attractive, and if her response to Sebastian was any indication, she appreciated being considered so by a man.

But she was a Venator. Her life was a patchwork of danger and deceit, night patrols, incessant hunting, violence and matches with evil. A greater evil than most people would ever face.

Loving someone would endanger him – and endanger herself by dividing her concentration. The lies, the subterfuge, the lifestyle would pick away at and erode any chance of happiness she might imagine.

She couldn't *allow* herself to love – or, worse, truly worse, to *be* loved.

Her last words to Max had been to tell him he'd been right. He'd been right that she should not have married Phillip for all of the reasons that she now knew. Victoria would never finish grieving because she would never be able to forgive herself for marrying him anyway.

Yet, she missed the feel of a man's lips under hers, the steadiness of his embrace. The smell of masculinity and the broad height of shoulders, the race of her pulse when an attractive man looked at her like he wished to gobble her up whilst he was speaking of the weather or, as in Sebastian's case, about a secret society of vampire protectors.

She didn't have to marry, or even to love, to find pleasure in such a refuge from her world. She was a widow now, experienced in love and more experienced in life than most women her mother's age.

When she was lonely, she *could* find companionship with a man. Selectively, of course. Discreetly. Without the emotional attachment that could endanger them both.

She might be a Venator, a widow, a peer of Society. But she was still, and always would be, a woman too.

Being introduced at La Villa Foscarini was a most unusual experience for Victoria. Arriving at a small party where she knew no one, without a male escort, completely on her own, was something she could not do amongst the London *haute* ton without turning many heads and causing untold whispers of impropriety.

But Aunt Eustacia had explained that Italian Society was not nearly as rigid as that in England, and that their social mores were much more relaxed than what Victoria was used to. And this little clique of English expatriates that had become Lord Byron's miniature circle of Society were even more forgiving of accepted rules.

Still, it felt exceedingly odd to be announced as Mrs Emmaline Withers and to face a small sea of faces that were unrecognisable to her.

In an effort to keep her identity as a Venator a secret, Victoria had agreed with Wayren's suggestion that she use an assumed name during her movements in Italian Society. Lilith most certainly knew who she was, and although many of the vampires she might encounter would recognise her name, they would not know her by sight. Thus, if Victoria were to penetrate the Tutela, she must take care not to be found out.

The consequences, as Eustacia said, were obvious.

'Mrs Withers! How delighted we are that you could attend our little party.' An energetic man, with dark hair even more curling and wild than John

Polidori's had been, bolted from his seat and moved forward to meet her, keeping his limp as smooth as possible.

So this was Lord Byron, poet and, if all the rumours were true, lover extraordinaire.

He certainly had lovely hair. And a tall forehead. But he was rather short.

And most certainly attached to the ravishing red-headed woman who trailed after him to greet Victoria.

'Lord Byron, I am most appreciative of your kind invitation. I have been here a bit more than a week and was beginning to wonder if I should ever see another party again! How dull it has been, and what a lovely party you have here.' She gave a brief curtsy, offered her hand and smiled at the woman, waiting for Byron to make introductions.

'My love, this is Mrs Emmaline Withers, a friend of John's. Apparently, she was unfortunate enough to be in attendance at the house party at which he died some weeks ago. Mrs Withers, this is Teresa, Countess Guccioli. Now! Let us back to our readings!'

With what could only be described as a flourish, the poet turned back to the cluster of chairs where the other seven or eight people sat.

'He is quite loath to be interrupted when he is reading one of his works,' Teresa told Victoria with a fond smile. Her English was perfect, but the syllables were lined with a lilting accent. 'I am pleased to meet you, Mrs Withers. I understand you have come to visit my fair country while recovering from your husband's death. I am very sorry to hear of it. Although there are moments when one could wish to be rid of one's own spouse. Nevertheless, I am certain you will find Venezia a lovely place to celebrate being left with a handsome sum and no husband along with it. Now, come this way and let us find you a seat next to one of our handsome young men.'

It was fortunate that Eustacia had warned Victoria about the Countess Guccioli, or she might have been utterly offended. Teresa and Byron had been in love and cohabiting for two years, some of the time at the Palazzo Guccioli even while the countess's husband was in attendance. That, said Eustacia, was indicative of one of the great differences between Italian and English views on marriage.

In Italy, one married for one's parents and sought lovers for oneself. One treated one's lover with the respect and fidelity most English reserved for their spouse – at least, on the surface. Thus, Teresa Guccioli was not so very different from many of her countrymen and -women, but she had a brash way of expressing it.

Victoria took a seat on a brocade hassock and proceeded to listen with the others for well over thirty minutes while Byron finished the reading of his latest stanzas. She wasn't much for listening to poetry for long periods of time, any more than she was for listening to music and doing nothing, but she managed to sit and appear to be enjoying herself. It wasn't that the stanzas were awkward or uninteresting; it was just that Victoria had a task to complete, and she certainly couldn't go about trying to learn if Byron was a member of the Tutela whilst he was reading about setting suns and the flowing skirts of goddesses.

At last the reading portion of the party ended, and if the rest of the group was as delighted as she was, they did not show it. Everyone stood and began to cluster off into little groups as drinks and lovely little antipasti were served.

Victoria chatted briefly with Teresa before the woman was called away to look at an amateurish drawing by one of her friends. Victoria saw Lord Byron walking out of the room, a definite hitch in his step, and she eased herself towards the entrance.

Where one exited, one must re-enter.

And so he did, shortly thereafter, and when he did Victoria caught his eyes.

'Mrs Withers, I hope you are having a fine time of it here. A bit less stuffy than the ton, do you say?'

'Indeed, there is much frivolity here. I'm having a lovely time.'

'I hope you do not mind if I ask you how my friend John was when you last saw him. I was devastated to hear of his horrid passing.'

The sparkle in his eyes and the way he gestured with his glass of Chianti belied his sentiment, but Victoria was more than happy to go along. After all, she had a role to play as well. 'Dr Polidori was hale and hearty when I saw him last. We were at a house party at Claythorne, and…well, you heard about the accident. I do not wish to talk about that, for it was quite horrible. But we had a lovely conversation about *vampires*.' She dropped her voice to a near whisper on that last word, leaning closer to him and purposely giving him a view down her low décolletage.

He noticed and, closing his fingers gently around her wrist, stepped backward, his gaze fastened down at her bosom, which, she knew from previous experience, was quite appreciated by the opposite sex. Victoria noticed that behind him was a small curtained alcove. She allowed him to tug her gently behind the curtains as she discreetly whisked away the fichu Verbena had tucked into her neckline. Whatever would help her cause.

She just hoped Countess Guccioli didn't notice. Dealing with vampires was one thing; having a jealous Italian contessa flying at her was another situation altogether.

'It was so fascinating,' Victoria continued, widening her eyes and gently pulling her wrist away. 'Vampires! I do believe,' she whispered again, forcing him to move closer to hear her, 'that Dr Polidori was quite convinced that they really exist. Imagine that!'

'Indeed,' Byron replied. Victoria had never been as grateful for low-cut fashions as she was now. The man was half in his cups and quite distracted by the amount of flesh she was showing since she'd removed the fichu. This, then, was one of the benefits of being a widow as opposed to being an innocent maid.

She was certain she could ask him any question and he would answer.

'It must have been a great annoyance to you when *The Vampyre* was published and everyone thought that you had written it.'

'It was nothing. I soon set it right. Although the story idea was mine, I did not care that John made a hash of it. Patterning Lord Ruthven after *me*!' He chuckled, stumbling towards her – whether it was purposeful or not, she didn't know – and catching a brief handful of breast.

Victoria closed her fingers over his hand and gently removed it, but kept a tight grip on him, flattening his hand against the bare flesh of her shoulder and upper chest. A much safer area, one designed to keep him from getting too distracted yet not a complete rebuff. It felt odd to have a man's hand on her skin, particularly a man whom she did not know.

But she did not think about it. No one would see, and if it helped her to get the information she needed, she would suffer it.

'I should think you would make a lovely vampire,' she told him, giggling in a manner more suited to a new debutante than a vampire-killing widow. 'All dark and dangerous… Surely you are not about to spring fangs and bite me in the neck, are you, my lord?'

He grinned lasciviously at her, a thick mop of unruly black hair flopping onto his forehead, mingling with eyebrows and dancing into his eyes. He looked not the least bit dangerous; rather, a bit silly, with his fair skin and too-feminine lips. 'And if I were, would you scream and run away…or would you let me?'

'I would let you.'

His pupils widened, became black as night, and his fingers convulsed on her bare skin. 'Mrs Withers… you tempt me so.'

'But,' she said, deftly removing his hand and setting him back gently, shaking her head, 'there are no such things as vampires…are there? More's the pity, for I think they are terribly romantic.'

'Romantic?' He looked befuddled, as if he wasn't sure how he'd come from being so close to his prey to being set back with nary a bump or a struggle.

'I should love to meet one. A vampire. Do tell me…have you ever met one? Because I am sure, after speaking with Dr Polidori, that they really exist.'

He looked at her, his eyes a bit clearer now. 'You would be dearly frightened if you met one, Mrs Withers, I am certain.'

'No, indeed, for why should I? They wish only to

survive, and they cannot help that they must live on fresh blood. It is the way they are made.' She curved her lips into a promising smile. 'I think that it should be quite…erotic…to have two fangs sinking into my neck.'

Byron had taken a step back and removed his hands from any proximity to her. He looked as if he expected *her* to sprout fangs at any moment. 'To be honest with you, my dear Mrs Withers, I would not be surprised if they did exist. But I, unfortunately, have never seen one.' He coughed. 'I do believe, however, that you are right. John Polidori believed in them too, and I am almost certain that he did meet them. But, I am afraid, I do not know for certain.'

Blast. She thought she had made progress!

'Thank you for your poetry readings tonight, my lord,' she told him, ready to release him before he reached for her again. 'I think I have taken quite a thirst. May I excuse myself to find some more tea?'

'Of course, Mrs Withers. I would be happy to escort you.'

The Countess Guccioli looked none too happy when they emerged from the curtained alcove, but she did not bear down upon them as Victoria expected her to, ready to snatch her lover from a poaching woman's hands.

Instead, she did something utterly unexpected. She turned all of her charm and beauty and coquettishness onto the two gentlemen sitting next to her, and flicked not an eyelash nor the twitch of a nose at her lover. She ignored him.

Victoria watched her in fascination. She had not had very much experience in the womanly arts of flirtation and, apparently Countess Guccioli was a master at it. Poor Byron. He was fairly miserable by the time Victoria was ready to leave…which was two hours later.

She had called for Oliver and the carriage and was stepping out of the villa's door, ready to draw in a deep breath of night air, when she felt a presence behind her.

'Do you leave us so soon, *signora*?'

'Count Alvisi, is it not a lovely night, with the stars out? And, yes, I am sorry, but I am feeling rather fatigued. I had a gorgeous time this evening.'

He was the same height as she, with the same swarthy Italian colouring that Max had. But his eyes glittered just a bit too much, and his lips curled in a most dismaying manner. And he smelt ridiculously, hideously, of lavender water.

Either he had bathed in it, or he'd got much too close to a woman who'd bathed in it.

At any rate, Victoria was near the end of her patience and was prepared to set him down quickly and thoroughly should he become friendly. And friendly was what he had in mind, if the direction of his gaze was any indication.

'But you did not get what you came for, did you?'

She looked sharply at him. He nodded delicately and smoothed a hand down the front of his shirtwaist. 'What do you mean, sir?'

'I had the pleasure of overhearing a portion of your conversation with our wonderful host.'

'Indeed?'

'How you wished to meet a real vampire.' He stepped closer, bringing lavender and…was that lemon?…with him.

'I should think it would be fascinating. Do you think they truly exist?'

'I know that they do. I have seen them.'

She widened her eyes and brought a girlish squeal from her lips. 'Truly? Where have you seen them? Are they dangerous? Have you been bitten?' She dropped her voice.

'I have. Would you like to see my scars?' He showed her, and true enough, there were four little marks on his neck. Rather recent, in fact.

'How? Where?'

'We have a little…group. We see the vampires and we spend time with them – only a few of them, mind you. Because we understand them, you see. They are the most misunderstood creatures I have ever met.'

'I can only imagine! People for years have thought of them as beasts. But they aren't, are they? Are they as romantic and dangerous as I have dreamt?'

'They are. And if you like, I can arrange for you to join us some evening.'

'I should be most grateful, Count Alvisi.'

He slipped something hard and flat into her hand. 'This will be your token of admittance. I shall notify you of the date and place.'

She looked down, already knowing what she would see. A Tutela amulet.

Most grateful indeed.

Chapter Ten

In Which Lady Rockley Acquires an Acute Dislike of Lavender

True to his word, four nights later Count Alvisi sent a cryptic note to Victoria.

"'I shall call for you in one half hour,'" she read aloud. Sending the note wafting onto her dressing table, she looked up at Verbena. 'It appears that I will be attending a meeting of the Tutela very shortly.' She looked at the small clock on her dressing table. 'At ten o'clock tonight.'

'I'll have Oliver bring word 'round t' your aunt whilst we get you ready,' the maid said, bustling towards the door. 'The man's been frayin' each one o' my nerves for the last day, lookin' for somethin' t' do. After I 'splained they're afraid o' silver, 'e got himself so worked up he locked hisself in his room, says he's gonna make a new weapon for fightin' vampires with.' She snorted, shaking her head as she slipped out of Victoria's room, then poked it back in to add, 'The man's never seen a vampire, so I don' know how he's gonna invent a way to kill one. He'll take one look at those red eyes and he'll be runnin' back to Cornwall wi' wet britches, where 'e belongs.'

The door closed behind her, and Victoria picked up the note again. Over the last several days she'd considered the best way to approach the invitation extended by the count. At one point she'd thought of having him followed so she could learn just where he went, and possibly discover the Tutela's meeting place on her own. She would have preferred going in on her own terms, possibly sneaking in, rather than having to wait to be escorted.

If she were escorted, she would have to play the role of the widowed Mrs Withers and to remain with Alvisi during the entire time. If she could go alone, she might simply be able to watch unobserved.

But in the end she'd decided to wait for his invitation and go with the count. He would certainly be aware of the process, and if there were anything special one must do in order to gain entrance, he would know. Once she learnt the location of the meeting, and how to get in, she could investigate on her own. After all, her goal was to find and assassinate Nedas.

Against her better judgment, she allowed Verbena to coif and dress her as though she were going to a social event. Her maid had protested when Victoria originally opted to dress in her loose split skirt and braid her hair in a simple braid.

'You should look as if you're goin' to a party,' she

told her. 'Ye can't dress as if ye're huntin' vampires. And besides…the count prob'ly wants te show you off to the vampires! I'm sure ye'er prettier than any of the other women in the Tutela!'

'More dangerous too,' Victoria added, and succumbed to her maid's ministrations. She was quite certain that half of the reason Verbena insisted on dressing and coiffing her so particularly even when the event didn't call for it was because her sister was the lady's maid for the daughter of a duchess…and they were always comparing notes about their mistresses' gowns and jewels.

When Victoria came down the stairs a half hour after receiving the note from Alvisi, two stakes in her hair and another one affixed to the garter under her skirt, salted holy water in her reticule and in a small vessel attached to her other garter, along with a sheathed dagger and a large crucifix tucked deep down betwixt her breasts where it would not be seen unless she wished it to, she interrupted a fierce, whispered conversation between Verbena and Oliver in the front parlour.

It was comic: the maid barely reached to his collarbones, but she appeared to be doing the talking, with him nodding silently but energetically down at her. Her carrot-red hair, frizzy and bushy, bobbed with her every movement, his darker, more auburn hair following in a slower rhythm. Her hands slapped together in some sort of emphasis, back hand into her palm with a loud crack; then she shifted into a single pointing finger.

'Has the count arrived?' Victoria asked innocently.

'Not yet, my lady,' Verbena responded, stepping away from her counterpart with one last glare. Perhaps she'd been lecturing him on using a crucifix instead of garlic for the best vampire repellent. 'But Oliver here will, I'm certain, be pleased to look out for you.'

Just then, the Italian servant who acted as a sort of butler for the small house they were renting slipped into the room and announced, 'The Count Alvisi, *signora.*'

It was apparent as soon as the count stepped into the small parlour that he had not brushed too close to a woman who had bathed in lavender the other night, but that he had been the one to douse himself. And as though he were trying to extend the scent in some sort of stylistic pattern, his silk shirtwaist was a lavender colour…and the cravat tied neatly, if blandly, at his throat was lavender. And the gem that glittered in the centre of it was…yes…a clear, pale amethyst.

'You look lovely this evening, Mrs Withers,' the count told her, honest appreciation beaming in his dark eyes. 'In fact, you look lovely enough to eat!' He winked and gave a loud guffaw as he stepped forward to take her hand.

Victoria remembered herself, and that she had to play the role of a bold, crass woman – instead of

a fiercesome Venator or a perfect Society woman –
and managed a hearty enough laugh that would
have mortified her mother. She would remember
that for the evening: if she did something that would
cause her mother's jaw to drop askance or her lips to
purse in annoyance, she would be acting just as she
should – just as she imagined a woman who would
be interested in meeting vampires because she found
them fascinating and attractive would act.

'Shall we go?' asked Victoria.

'Indeed, *signora*. The carriage awaits.' He took her
arm and they swept out of the room, shoulder-to-
shoulder, elbow-to-elbow.

'I cannot believe I shall meet a real vampire
tonight,' Victoria said once they were settled in the
carriage. No sooner had the door closed than she
wished fervently to crack a window in order to allow
some of the lavender to escape.

Alvisi sat across from her, not as Sebastian would
have, relaxing in the corner with an arm extended
along the back of the seat, but on the edge of the
bench, stiffly upright, hands clasped in his lap. He
looked as though he might be ready to bolt at any
moment. 'Er…*si, signora*. We may not see an actual
vampire tonight. I have seen one myself only one
time.'

Victoria sagged back, stifling her disappointment
and budding annoyance. Was this simply a ploy to get
her in a carriage alone?

If it were Sebastian, she would believe it without a doubt. But this man did not send ripples of apprehension through her. He seemed harmless and easily managed – except for the powerful weapon of his cologne. 'Where are we going if not to see a vampire?'

'We are to attend the meeting of a secret society, the Tutela, whose purpose is to protect and care for vampires. But I do not know if we shall be graced with the presence of the immortals.' That glitter she had seen in his eyes at Byron's villa was back, accompanied by a slight sheen on his rounded forehead. 'They do not attend every meeting at this level.'

'Level?' Victoria looked around; the carriage had stopped. 'Have we arrived?'

'No, no. We must cross a canal. Come, *signora*, hurry, or we shall arrive too late and the doors will be barred. It is already after half past ten.'

They climbed out of the carriage and hustled quickly into a waiting gondola that dipped and pitched when he tried to find a comfortable seat. Victoria did not recognise the part of the city in which they had stopped, but she was not all that familiar with Venice as yet. As the gondolier eased them across the canal with his long pole, she glanced back at the shore they were leaving behind. Something in the shadows moved next to the carriage, and then it was gone.

She continued to stare as the grey outline of shore, lit only by random lanterns hung from poles and a smattering of stars in a moonless sky, melded into the darkness that now surrounded them on the wide canal. Someone or something had been there. Following them?

As they poled along the canal, away from either shore, Victoria could hear the excitement growing in Alvisi's breaths. They were coming faster and more shallowly, a bit raspier, often with a little catch, like a tiny gasp, at the end. The single lantern of punctured tin that hung from the back of the gondola gave enough light for her to see his hands clasped onto the sides of the vessel, and a shinier sheen on his forehead. Either he didn't like water and boats, or he was becoming very excited about the meeting of the Tutela.

They went on for a long while, travelling away from the city, silently moving atop the water. There had been a few other gondolas in the vicinity when they started out, but as the distance from town and their carriage increased, the number of other vessels decreased until there were none other about. Even the lights from homes along the canals, and the squares of buildings silhouetted against the shore, eased into darkness and the jaggedness of tumbledown structures and rocky terrain, illuminated only by chance when their gondola lantern swayed in a lucky direction.

Victoria began to feel a bit apprehensive as she realised they'd left Venice behind. This was so very different from London, where she at least had a sense of direction and knew where she was. And where a hackney could be hired to take her home from most any place in the city, even St Giles. She realised she should have paid much better attention to where they were going in the carriage, and watched for landmarks along the canal.

She wasn't frightened, but she should have made better preparations. Having Oliver follow along might have been a prudent choice. Perhaps Kritanu as well.

But she had been so confident of her ability to take care of herself, with her *vis bulla* and other weapons, and so focused on her goal of gaining entrance to the Tutela, that she had planned poorly.

Of course, she could be worrying about nothing. But her uneasiness was beginning to grow as steadily as the moisture on Alvisi's forehead. He spoke little during the voyage, and Victoria, who was trying to watch for landmarks in order to remember their route, didn't attempt conversation.

And then, at last, after what must have been more than an hour of navigating along the dark canal, they arrived.

At least, that was what Victoria assumed when the gondola eased up to a dark shore.

'Come, come,' Alvisi said, his voice strained. He scrambled out of the boat and pulled her after him with none of the gentlemanly aplomb he'd served up earlier at her villa. Once on the rocky shore, Victoria pulled firmly away from his grip – no difficult task, and if he noticed her unusual strength, he made no comment. He was already hurrying along some pathway that she was hardly able to see. Looking back towards the water, she saw that the gondola and its small lantern had shoved away from the shore and it was easing back up along the canal.

She would have paused longer, to take measure of the darkness and its occupants, but Alvisi had come back for her. 'Mrs Withers, come; we must hurry or they will bar the doors!'

This was what she'd come for.

She turned and followed him down the dark path, between bushes and trees that brushed into her and snagged at her light pelisse.

At last they came to a wooden door attached to a tall stone building closely surrounded by trees. It appeared that they'd approached it from the rear; there were no other buildings in sight, nor anything that hinted of civilisation. It was a building alone in the dark woods. Victoria could see the outlines of the grey, black and tan stones that made up the wall, thanks to the small lantern that hung from a short iron stem. It sat only knee-height, and was half-hidden by a bush until one came nearly upon it. Clearly, the Tutela took no chances in having its meeting place found.

Alvisi pulled on the long iron latch of the door and, to his obvious relief it swung open on silent hinges. A red glow from inside coloured the sandy, trampled ground next to the low lantern outside, and tinged the door and stones with a warm hue.

With one quick glance up at the sky, which had cleared to show the moon, Victoria noted that it was approximately midnight already. She followed Alvisi in and, once inside, a tall man dressed as though he were ready to attend the opera closed the door behind her.

'Good evening, madam, and welcome,' he said in Italian. He seemed to be waiting for something, and then Victoria remembered. She opened her hand to show him the Tutela amulet, and he nodded admittance.

She followed Alvisi down the hall, confirming that, according to the back of her neck, there were no vampires in the vicinity.

The half-lit room they entered at the end of the hall contained several dozen people conversing, and was large enough in size to be a ballroom, but not appropriate in decor. Victoria hadn't been able to determine what kind of building they were in, but it did not appear to be a villa or home. The interior walls were the same stone as the exterior. There were no windows – not surprising, as the vampires wouldn't be receptive to having sunlight come flooding in – and as far as she could tell, only one other door. The floor was covered with rugs, and between them she could see the primitive dirt and stone.

There were, however, chairs and benches throughout the room. And at the far end from where she and Alvisi had entered, a small, high dais had been positioned. It was just large enough to hold a long table and five chairs. It reminded her of a theatre, or perhaps a church...although that would be an odd place for vampire protectors to meet.

Curious, Victoria slipped away from her escort and towards the front of the room, for she was too far away to see what was on the table other than two large, shallow bowls that held small fires, one on each end.

The room's red glow came from a roaring fire on one wall near the dais, in a fireplace that could easily hold eight grown men. Candles and sconces flickered throughout the room, and as she passed among the other attendees, Victoria noted that the vast majority were men of all ages and that they were as well dressed as the man who'd asked to see her amulet.

In fact, she saw only three other women, and they did not appear to be ones who would normally be accepted in high society, based on the ludicrously low-cut gowns and pretentious jewels they wore. Perhaps she should speak with them. Since that was the kind of thing that would make her mother's eyes roll up into her head just before she swooned, it would be a fitting action for Mrs Withers to undertake.

The room smelt of smoke and sweat, along with the horrid mingle of Alvisi's lavender, and the rosewaters, minty perfumes and vetiver colognes that clung to other persons. But underlying all of the sweet floral and musky herbal scents, Victoria smelt blood and darkness and evil, and a faint pungent smell she'd sensed only once before: at the Silver Chalice.

It was nothing she recognised, nothing she could name or even compare it to; it was faint, but it was rancid and rank. It made her belly want to seize. She hadn't remembered even smelling it until now, but the memory came back as she inhaled it once again. The only other time she'd experienced it was when she was fighting the demon.

Was this the scent of a demon? Or was it something else entirely?

She looked around and realised that everyone seemed to be selecting a seat. Alvisi was gesturing to her from one of the rows in the back of the room, and Victoria decided it would be in her best interest to remain with him. She had no desire to be singled out until she had a better idea of what was to happen here. In addition, sitting in the back of the room would give her a better view of the entire chamber and perhaps an opportunity to determine whether there was indeed a demon present. So far, there were no vampires.

No sooner had she been seated next to her escort than three men stepped up onto the dais. She recognised one of them as a guest at Byron's villa. Signore Zinnani.

'Good evening,' he said, gesturing widely to the room as the attendees gave him their attention.

'Welcome to the Tutela. You are all here only because you have been invited by one of our members.'

Victoria looked at Alvisi, who gave a small shrug and nodded.

'Let us begin.'

Zinnani opened what appeared to be a square black box that gleamed when it was moved. He reached in with his hand, then sprinkled whatever had been in the box onto each of the small bowls of fire that sat on the table in front of him. Each fire in turn gave a tiny poof, like a huff of breath, and the flames burnt blue, then purple, then back to red again. Almost immediately a faint but enduring sweet scent reached Victoria's sensitive Venator nose.

She didn't like it. The smell made her want to escape from the room even as it rushed through the air, silently and invisibly, like a web.

She didn't like it at all. It was too sweet and too thick, like honey or molasses, and Victoria felt it clogging her nostrils as though a piece of heavy cloth had been tossed over her, pulled tight, and stuffed into her nose. She looked around, next to her, and along the rows in front of her. No one appeared to be bothered by the smell but her. In fact, Alvisi looked as though he wanted to sniff the entire room into his nostrils, the way he lifted his face and closed his eyes and sucked in long, deep breaths.

Victoria was feeling hazy and light-headed. Alvisi swayed next to her, and when she turned to look at him, she saw that his eyes were darker and glassy. Others in the rows in front of her, all the way to the dais, were moving, restless, tipping as though having difficulty keeping their balance as well.

She became aware of a low murmur. She could not understand the words, but they sounded like a chant. It started with the men at the dais and swelled to fill the room, deep and low, as though needing to stay near the ground so that its meaning would not be discerned. Alvisi's mouth was moving and the words were coming out, but they were not recognisable to her.

The sense of muzziness had not left her; Victoria placed her hand on her abdomen, slipping her fingers into a small hole where several stitches had been removed at the seam of her bodice and skirt. This way she could feel under her stays and beneath her chemise to her *vis bulla*, the solid, blessed silver of comfort and strength. When her fingers touched it, she closed her eyes, drew in a deep breath, and let its power flow through her.

The haziness ebbed. It did not disappear completely, but it relaxed its grip.

The chanting stopped, and for a moment the only sound came from the sizzle and pop of the fire in its large stone enclosure.

Then Zinnani spoke again. His voice was low and mellow. 'We have been called, those of us here. We are chosen from among the mortals to protect those who cannot walk in the sun as we do. To protect those who cannot live in ease, those who have been cursed to darkness.'

As he spoke, murmurs punctuated his words, the beneficent list of the tasks and rewards of the Tutela. 'Protect them!'

'Those of us here who can stand the test and who shall prove themselves will be granted safety.'

'Safety!'

'By serving the Immortals, we will remain safe from harm. We will not be hunted or ravaged as the unbelievers will. We will not be their targets when the Immortals rise to rule.'

'Rise, Immortals! Rise!'

'We will be granted pleasure such as we have never known.'

'Pleasure!' This response a soft gasp, nearly a whisper.

'The partaking and giving of life force is the most erotic and pleasurable event ever experienced. This will be ours at will and without cessation! We shall feel as we have never felt before! We shall feel and we shall live for the first time! And we shall be granted the gift of immortal life.'

'Immortal life!'

'Immortal life!'

'*Immortal life!*'

The words filled her ears, slipping into them, spiralling into her consciousness. Immortal life. The prize sought by men for centuries from alchemists to, if legend was to be believed, the Knights of the Round Table who hunted for the Holy Grail.

Was it any wonder that some men would even align with evil in order to attain life everlasting?

Immortal life, the gift of the Tutela. Immortal life until they were staked or beheaded…and then eternal damnation. She shuddered, for she knew it was true.

Victoria turned to Alvisi, wanting to say something to him, to try to penetrate the fog that had hold of him, but even when she tugged at his arm with all of her strength, he merely stumbled into her, righted himself, and then returned his attention to Zinnani.

And then she felt it: the cool wisps across the back of her neck, growing burning cold. Her fingers still pinching her *vis bulla*, Victoria let her gaze scan the room without turning her head, looking for new arrivals. They either needed to enter through the door near the dais, or from the doorway through which she and Alvisi had come. She could not see that door unless she turned around, and she dared not do that for fear of drawing attention to herself.

The cold itch became biting. There must be five or six vampires here.

And then they pushed past her, thrusting themselves through the messy rows of chairs, one by one, six of them, striding towards the dais. Victoria felt cold rush over her entire body. She had never been so close to a vampire that she had not been fighting, that had not been on the attack.

Fingering her *vis* amulet, she thanked God that vampires could not sense the presence of a Venator.

Five of the six vampires had not fed. She saw that from the moment they stepped onto the dais and turned to face the room. Their eyes, pure blood red, had the hunger in them that would drive them to find nourishment at any cost. The sixth vampire, whose eyes were also red, turned to speak with Zinnani.

Zinnani, who had the same unblinking expression on his face as Alvisi, made room for the vampire guests next to him. Even from her position in the back, Victoria could see him vibrating with emotion and pleasure at the proximity of the creatures he so obviously worshiped. His eyes glistened with what must have been tears, and his mouth was stretched in a wide, wet smile that made him look as though he were about to partake of some rich and sinful pastry.

The sixth vampire turned from him and spoke to the room. 'We have come to receive your commitment and promise to the Immortals. Who of the First Trial shall be the first to receive this honour?'

There was a hesitation; then a man stood near the front of the room. 'I shall.'

'Come forward.'

The man, who was little more than a youth touching adulthood, manoeuvred himself between the chairs until he stood at the dais. The vampire leader, the one Victoria had come to think of as the Sixth, effortlessly pulled the young man up onto the stage.

She could see the pulse pounding in a distended vein on the man's forehead, and the way his Adam's apple jerked and jumped. He faced the room, and the Sixth opened his mouth, extending his lethal fangs, and pulled the man's head to the side.

He bent and, as Victoria watched, sank his teeth slowly into the exposed neck. The young man started, his shoulders snapping back, but he did not fight. His eyes closed; his mouth opened; he would have sagged to the floor had the Sixth not held him upright. He moaned, twitching, his fingers convulsing at his sides as though reaching for something, his chest moving rapidly as though he were running. He seemed to welcome the sensation.

Behind them, the other five vampires, the ones who had not fed and were susceptible to the scent of blood, stood and watched avidly. Their noses twitched as though the scent of fresh blood called to them. Victoria could feel their hunger; she could nearly smell their obsession; and she waited with trepidation to see whether they would succumb to the temptation and the need.

But though their eyes burnt like the hottest coals of Hell, they did not, and the Sixth did nothing to alleviate their agony. Instead, after he had fed from the young man for a few moments, he turned to face him, swiping a tiny trickle of blood from his lips. 'You have now entered the Second Trial. When you have completed what is required of you in the next two trials, and have proven your service, you shall be brought into the Centre.'

The man, shaking but glowing with a sort of accomplishment, hurried back to his seat and received the congratulations of the men sitting beside him.

'Who shall be next?'

Another man stood and came forward, and the same process ensued. The Sixth fed from him as he had from the other, ignoring the increasing depravity and impatience of the five other vampires. This time when the man was being fed upon, Victoria, who now knew what to expect, felt herself becoming enraptured along with the man. His cries were not of agony but of ecstasy, his eyes closed in pleasure rather than pain. His hands reached back behind the vampire, who fed from his neck and fondled his shoulder-length coils of hair.

When he moaned, she felt it rumble through her veins. She felt his shivers and the waves of pleasure, felt her own body begin to awaken. What should have been grotesque and frightening became inviting.

She realised then that the sweet, cloying scent had become stronger and noticed Zinnani moving back behind the stage. Reaching beneath her gown, she felt again for her *vis bulla* and closed her eyes.

This went on for a time; Victoria felt as though hours had elapsed since she and Alvisi had arrived: the Sixth feeding for a short time with each of the men who volunteered to come forward. None of the three other women that Victoria had seen stood and asked to complete their First Trial, and she began to wonder if only men were given the opportunity to get to the Centre.

She must find out, for the Centre must be where Nedas was.

To her surprise, Alvisi did not volunteer to go forward, and she remembered through her haze (for she still held her *vis bulla*) that he had said something about a 'level'. Perhaps the trials were the levels of which he'd spoken. That brought her to wonder what level or trial he had attained. He'd shown her his bite marks, so he must have passed at least the First Trial.

When all of the volunteers from the First Trial had come forward, the Sixth stood with his hands on his hips. He'd forgotten to wipe away the last vestiges of blood from his last feed, and a small trickle curled down his chin. His lips were full and moist and red, and his matching eyes glowed a complacent blood colour. 'Now we have finished the First Trial. We have brought sixteen new members into the Tutela, sixteen new men who shall help to protect and serve the Immortals!'

A cheer rose in the room, followed by that

same chanting she had heard at the beginning of the meeting. As before, it started off low and deep, undulating throughout the room, catching her up in its rhythm. She could not fathom the words, but this time the volume swelled and peaked and reached a froth of emotion that sent cold, curling shivers down her back. It was uncontrollable; it was loud, its ebb and flow of syllable and breath rumbling into and around her combined with yet another increase of the sweet, hypnotic scent in the air.

The men about her shouted, punched their fists high. Everywhere about her, she saw eyes lit with fanaticism and fervour.

The chanting continued, rolling into a soft accompaniment to the Sixth's next words. 'The Second Trial! Who shall begin the Second?'

The chanting built, the scent sweetened, the fervour escalated. Someone stood, a man near the front, not one who had been fed upon this night. 'I shall!' he shouted joyously.

And then, instead of stepping forward, as Victoria had expected him to do, he bent to the side and grabbed the arm of the woman who sat next to him. Muscling her to her feet – for by now, she was trying to pull away, obviously apprehensive of what was to happen next – the man shoved her forward.

She stumbled and would have fallen, but the man grabbed her arm again and manhandled her in front of him towards the dais.

'I offer my commitment and promise to the Immortals,' the man said, shouting to be heard above the rising chanting. And he pushed the girl hard.

The Sixth reached down from the dais and easily plucked her up before she fell, sweeping her up onto the platform. Her creamy white gown swept along with her, spilling over the edge of the stage as she tripped again.

'Your commitment is accepted!' shouted the Sixth above the room's frenzy, effortlessly holding the woman's wrists behind her back. He then released her to two of the unfed vampires.

They fell upon her, one at each side, tearing their fangs into her white flesh, one at the side of her neck, one at the juncture where neck met shoulder. The woman screamed, kicked, bucked; but a third vampire came behind her and pulled her arms back, holding her steady while his companions fed.

Victoria watched in abject horror, her mouth drying and her heart pounding. This was so different from the scenes before. The unwilling victim at the mercy of the two vampires who ravaged her neck and shoulders, made crazed by their need to feed, by the smell of blood and by the agony of having watched sixteen others being fed upon.

But what could she do? One woman against a room of men, against six vampires. Her mind was still foggy; her limbs didn't want to move. The instant she was discovered to be a Venator, she would be killed before she could take her next breath.

She looked back up at the stage and saw that the woman's bodice had been torn away and one white breast, streaked with blood, bounced and swayed as she twisted and fought. These vampires did not bite delicately; they were starved, so they gouged and tore and destroyed. The woman's moans were choked, her cries fading. The stench of blood filled the air, just as the chanting continued.

And then Victoria noticed that another woman was on the other end of the stage. Two more vampires were sharing her, but she did not fight with the same vehemence as the other. Her flesh was torn, and blood streamed from her neck and bosom, and she cried, and suddenly Victoria felt a great, hard jerk on her own arm.

She pulled away from Alvisi, whose face had become determined and fanatic, whirling from his grip, but she slammed into another man, who shoved her forward. Victoria sidestepped him, swinging out with her fists, but she faced another one. Everywhere she turned, another man stood, blocking her, shoving her forward towards the stage.

The chanting continued as Victoria was spun around, trying to fight her way through the wall of men, but there were too many. She was pushed and prodded, pulled and tripped. She kicked and fought, her head swam, the sweet smell built back in her nose

again. She could not touch her *vis bulla*; she could not
stand straight; she could not see where she was. She
couldn't breathe.

Suddenly hands, many hands, grabbed her – too
many to fight off. She felt herself being lifted, and
the roaring fire to her left tipped in front of her, then
around to her other side as she kicked and bit and
bucked. Then she felt herself launched through the
air, and landed on her hip and shoulder on something
hard, her cheek smashing onto the floor. The smell of
fresh blood filled her nose.

The sea of chanting, bright-eyed faces was at her
eye level for only a moment before she was dragged
to her feet. Victoria had an instant to grope for her
vis before she swung out at the vampires who came
at her. She kicked and dodged and punched, had
the satisfaction of meeting one of them in the face,
and was reaching back to yank a stake from her hair
when her arms were grabbed and pulled down to her
sides. Dimly aware that it had taken two vampires,
one at each arm, to do so, she ducked and tried to
twist free.

The grip was too strong; she couldn't break it.
She couldn't get to her stakes, her holy water, her
crucifix…

Hands were on her everywhere, pulling at her
dress, her arms, her legs, her breasts. She felt her head
being jerked to one side by the hair, felt her coiffure
loosen and her neck bare to the sweet-smelling room.

The dull, pasty smell of blood on the breath of the vampire nearest her filled her nose, pushing away even the hypnotic scent of the incense.

When his teeth sank into her neck, it was almost a relief.

Chapter Eleven

Two Fortuitous Doors

Teeth sank into her once, twice, three times. Victoria felt the warm ooze of blood seeping along the crease of her neck, trickling into the cleft between her breasts, and the soft lull of relief…the easy haze that tempted her to let go.

She couldn't stop fighting; her body shifted and tilted as they pawed at her, nibbled on her. She felt something heavy shift and slide under her bodice, and then fall free with a gentle weight tugging at the back of her neck.

There were cries of surprise and fear, and the hands clawing her fell away, and she felt herself falling, tumbling and then smacking onto the ground again.

Her crucifix thudded against her chest, and she reached for it automatically, her ears filled with shouts and cries, and held it up like a small shield as her other hand slammed palm-first onto the wooden stage.

Though its sudden appearance had surprised them, the crucifix would not keep them back for long; it would not prevent a mortal from tearing it out of her hands and returning her over to the hungry vampires.

Victoria's fingers scrabbled at the floor, trying to find purchase so she could haul herself upright, and they felt something other than polished wood. Metal. Set into the floor.

The haziness still gripped her mind, but since the vampires had stopped feeding on her, she was more in control, and some of her strength and clarity were coming back. She had the presence of mind to close her fingers around the metal object, and through the dizziness recognised it as hinges. In the floor.

Where there were hinges, there was – *please God* – a door.

Hands were grabbing at her now, pulling her fingers away from the crucifix so they could tear it from her throat and give her back to the vampires. Victoria twisted, bucking away from the puny strength of the mortal man – Zinnani – who had taken the place of the Immortals and bent over her.

She stopped fighting his hands and kept twisting until she was on her face towards the ground, putting what was above and behind her out of her mind as she felt around, trying to find a door handle. Where did the door open? She felt someone – or something – pulling at the chain around her neck, and she kicked out and back, her foot connecting with something quite soft and squishy, and she had enough presence of mind to hope it was some man's private parts. Zinnani's, if she were lucky.

She was on the door; now that the shadows above and behind her shifted away, she could see the faint outline of the door in the floor and that her weight kept it from opening. If it were old and stuck or locked, or was not a door after all, she would have no other chance. Her fingers found what they sought at her waist, and she tensed herself up, ready.

She felt the chain of her crucifix snap, scoring into her throat in that last instant before it fell away, and the roar of delight as the air surged above her with the vampires swooping back down for the kill.

Victoria was ready for them, and she rolled away, off the door, knocking into the feet of the vampires as she splashed the vial of salted holy water at them. They screamed and fell away, and she yanked on the handle in the floor.

It stuck for an instant, then *whumped* up next to where she crouched, and Victoria rolled through the opening.

She felt her gown catch on the rough edge of the door, but it didn't stop her from going through and falling. The rectangle of light above disappeared as the door closed after her, and she hit the ground.

The door above opened again immediately, spilling dull yellow light into the space in which she'd landed. Pulling to her feet, she brushed against a rough wall just as one of the vampires vaulted through the opening and landed next to her.

His red eyes glowed in the dim light, and he lunged for her.

Victoria was ready. The stake solid in her hand, she thrust it into his heart with considerable satisfaction.

Before his ashes filtered to the ground she was dodging into the darkness, hoping it was a passage that led somewhere. Behind her there were the sounds of feet thumping on the ground; but she did not stop to check whether it was a red-eyed vampire or a brave mortal who'd come after her this time.

Victoria found the wall and, moving as silently as she could, felt along it, praying that it wouldn't end in a corner that signalled a dead end.

At least down here she had the advantage of limited space, as she had when fighting the vampires at Claythorne. If they all came after her, she would have a better chance of fighting them off one by one than if they all leapt on her at once.

Whoever was behind was gaining; a quick glance back confirmed the red eyes of a vampire. He had night vision, which gave him a decided advantage when traversing through a pitch-black tunnel.

Victoria picked up her pace, keeping her stake at the ready. If she had a moment to pause, she might be able get the other vial of holy water from her garter; yet if she escaped, she would need it to pour over her bite wounds.

They throbbed and oozed blood; she could feel it

trickling down her throat and arms. It was chilly on her skin, no longer that velvety release she'd experienced when the vampires were feeding.

She put one hand out in front of her and ran as fast as she could, but she was blind and the vampire was not. He was close enough to grab at her clothing, but she jerked free and dodged to the side and back again, trying to keep him off balance.

There were other footsteps behind them; at least one other was coming closer. She could not continue to outrun the vampire; sooner or later she was going to come upon a wall or door or something that ended, and he would have seen that long before she would feel it.

Getting away from the hypnotic incense in the Tutela meeting room had helped to clear her mind a little, and Victoria decided she had to do something drastic. And she also noticed that there was a faint line of light far ahead of her.

Where there was light, there was a door and possibly sunlight. Was it late enough? She'd been here for hours…but was it close enough to dawn?

She put on her last burst of speed, dodged to one side, and dove to the ground, tumbling head over heels. The vampire didn't move in time and he tripped, falling palms-flat onto the ground. Victoria leapt towards him, felt for his nape, and slammed the stake down through the centre of his back. He disintegrated under her.

But a third vampire was there, coming at her, grabbing at her hair to pull her to her feet. Victoria couldn't hold back a soft cry at the unexpected pain. His red eyes burnt furiously as he closed his fingers around her throat, his grasp slipping in blood. They lit the small area with an evil glow, casting enough illumination that she could see part of his face. Enough to recognise him. The Sixth. Not one of the starving, depraved vampires, but their leader.

'Who are you?' he growled, giving her a little shake.

She would have raised her stake, but he caught her hand in midair and shoved her up against the wall. It was cold, and she felt the grit of dirt and stone on her bare shoulders.

'Who are you that you have killed two of mine?' He moved closer, and she smelt the blood on his breath, old blood, and the stench of the damned.

Her other hand was free, and she tried to dig under her skirts to get the vial of holy water, but he was too quick and seized that wrist as well. Imprisoning both hands, pressing them back into the damp stone wall, he moved closer. His grip was vicious, and she dropped her stake. 'A Venator, of course. I have never tasted a Venator.'

His red eyes moved closer, and she waited until he was just about to press his lips to her skin. Then, using his hold on her for balance, she raised both legs and slammed her feet into his calves.

It surprised him enough that she was able to twist free and reach for the second stake in her hair, but it had fallen when he yanked her to her feet. Victoria lunged at the vampire, knocking him off balance, and started off towards the faint light.

He was behind her, not far, but enough that she had a lead. She tried to reach under her skirt to pull her last stake out, but it was too long and she couldn't find the slit while she was running.

Please, a door. Please.

She was close enough now; it was a crack of light. She slammed against the wall, which had to be a door, *had* to be, and felt him coming up behind her. Scrabbling around with her fingers, she felt for a latch again, praying for sunlight. She had no idea how much time had passed since coming to the meeting, but it had been hours…

Sunlight, please.

She slipped her fingers into a crack just as he slammed up behind her. He grabbed her by the shoulder and whipped her to the ground, hoping, obviously, to slow her down. But he'd actually given her an advantage. She flipped back and kicked her feet up into his abdomen, sending him sprawling as she rolled back around and grabbed with her nails under the bottom of the door.

Pull, pull, pull…

And it opened. Dear God, it opened!

And a low beam of light flooded into the tunnel.

The vampire screamed and rolled away and Victoria followed him, slipping the last stake from under her skirt. She drove it into his back, straight through to his heart, then turned to stumble into blessed, blessed dawn from a sun just peeking through the trees at the horizon.

She slammed the door behind her and staggered three or four steps away from the building.

She ran, her eyes smarting from the sudden brightness, blinded again, brushing through trees and bushes until she crashed into someone.

Two someones.

'My lady?'

'Lady Rockley?'

Victoria picked herself up from the grass and, still blinking away sunburst tears, said, 'Verbena? Oliver? What on earth—'

'My God, she is bleeding!' Oliver's horrified voice penetrated, and she was finally able to focus on him.

'Everywhere.' His voice cracked, easing into a horrified hush.

'We have a boat, my lady; come, come.' Verbena was tugging on her, and although Victoria could hear the fear in her voice, she also heard her trademark bossiness.

She allowed her maid to lead her back to the same canal on which she and Alvisi had travelled hours ago.

A half a day ago.

The voyage along the canal took well over an hour, during which Victoria had the overwhelming impression of warm yellow sunlight and of little else. Later, she recalled certain moments: the agony when Verbena liberally doused her wounds with salted holy water. The sudden listing of their gondola when Oliver's pole caught on something. The snatches of hissed conversation between her two companions.

'She looks so white.'

'O' course she does! She's been bit five, six times, ye oaf!' And then the splash of water followed by the excruciating sting of salt. 'Can ye not row any faster?'

'I'm not rowing. Do you see an oar? A paddle? No, it is a stick, and it's not like rowing in the pond back in Cornwall.'

'Watch where ye're—'

And then a great lurch, a muffled curse, and the resulting jolts as the vessel went on its way.

Then, later... 'If you weren't being such a stubborn nanny goat about me going, and delayed me, we wouldn't have been so late getting there.'

'Ye weren't goin' wi'out me.'

'Lot of help you were, yelling and squawkin' like a hen out on the canal.'

Followed by an angry huff and jerk of the boat, as though someone had spun away and folded her arms over her middle. 'Ye were goin' in the wrong direction.'

'So we wouldn't be followed.'

'*We* were doin' the followin'!'

'You can't be too cautious in such matters.'

Then another great jolt of the boat. She must have turned back towards him. 'What d' *you* know about fightin' vampires?'

'More than you do, which, by the look of it, says very little.'

Likely it was fortunate that Victoria drifted off at that point and didn't hear Verbena's response. She wasn't aware of anything else until more jolting and then a sudden lurch told her they'd arrived at the dock.

She could walk, she told Verbena, and proceeded to demonstrate just that. The salted holy water had already begun to do its job, and although she was weak and sore and exhausted, she knew she would feel better by the next day. Venators healed quickly and easily, even from vampire bites.

At the villa, however, Verbena insisted that Victoria repair to her chamber to be washed and changed instead of sending word over to Aunt Eustacia.

'Oliver'll take a message to 'er while we get ye cleaned up.'

Victoria didn't like to admit it, but she was shaken by her experience, and although physically she knew she would feel perfectly fine in a matter of a day or so, the memory of the vampires tearing at her amidst the fog and incense and inexorable chanting made her fingers shake and her stomach ball up in an ugly knot.

She slept after Verbena's ministrations, and woke hours later, judging by the position of the sun outside her window. Victoria rolled out from under the light blanket and went to take a look at the damage.

She counted eight bite marks, and six more that were more like gouges, scoring like jagged ribbons into the skin of her neck and shoulders. The blood had been washed away, but the bruises had already begun to show dark purple and black beneath the marks. Victoria touched one of the bites and realised how close she'd come to dying.

She wondered what happened to the other women. Had they been torn apart or had they been set free after their trauma?

She couldn't have saved them; she'd barely been able to save herself. But the knowledge that they'd faced a horrifying, painful death stabbed at her. She was a Venator. Her task was to save lives by stopping the demons and vampires from taking them. She'd failed last night.

She'd seen it happen and been powerless to stop it.

She'd been too late to save Polidori; but at least she'd tried.

She hadn't tried to save the women.

Pushing away from the mirror, Victoria washed her face with a bit of water, using her damp hands to slick back the wisps of hair that had escaped from her braid while she was sleeping.

At the bottom of the stairs she met the Italian butler, a trusted member of Aunt Eustacia's household, who gave a little bow and said, 'Your aunt and two gentlemen have availed themselves of the parlour, *signora*.'

Two gentlemen?

Victoria hurried to the parlour and opened the door.

It wasn't Max. 'What are you doing here?' She stopped short inside the door.

'Bloody hell, Victoria!' Sebastian stood, starting towards her, then stopped in the middle of the room. 'Your maid said you'd been hurt, but this is much worse than she indicated.'

'What is he doing here?' Victoria asked her aunt, ignoring Sebastian to sit down next to her on a divan. Of course she looked like hell. She'd been mauled by three vampires.

But he didn't need to sound so blasted surprised. Or repulsed. And just because he looked as handsome and well-groomed as he always did, with his artfully tousled gilt curls and perfectly folded neck-cloth…

'It looks as though you had a rather close call,' Aunt Eustacia told her, peering at the bites, even poking at one with her finger. 'These are quite nasty, and even though you are a Venator, these kinds of wounds can have consequences, *cara*. Your maid said she treated you with salted holy water; and I have something else that will help the bruising disappear.' She began to rummage in the small reticule she'd pulled from her wrist.

'We are very glad you didn't suffer any worse injuries,' Kritanu said in his soft voice. He reached over from the chair on which he sat and patted Victoria's hand, ending with an affectionate squeeze. 'And to answer your question, Monsieur Vioget arrived at your aunt's villa late last night.'

Victoria turned to look at Sebastian, who had not stopped watching her since she came in the room, and raised her eyebrow in condescending query.

'I did not know where you were staying here in Venice,' he explained, settling back in his seat in an obvious attempt to appear relaxed. He crossed his arms over his middle, his well-cut jacket straining gently over his broad shoulders. 'But I did know how to reach your aunt and presumed she would put me in touch with you, particularly since I came with information that I believe you will welcome. It is unfortunate that I arrived a day late, or I could likely have prevented your bloody mishap last evening.'

'And how is that?' Victoria asked. She was beginning to become weary of his sudden appearances and mysterious pronouncements. He always seemed to be obscuring something. Or trying to get something.

'I could have told you that Nedas is in Rome, not here in Venice. And if you wish to infiltrate the Tutela in hopes of stopping him, you will not do so here in Venezia. And certainly not on the arm of Count Benedetto Alvisi.'

'And you waited until now to apprise me of this? Why did you not tell me this before I left London? In the carriage?' Her wounds throbbed along with the angry veins in her neck.

He spread his hands. 'I did not know it at the time.'

'Victoria, do tell us what happened last night,' Aunt Eustacia interrupted. She closed arthritic fingers around her great-niece's hand. They were chilly, but strong, and her skin was soft and textured with thick weals of veins. 'And here is some cream for your bites.'

With relief, Victoria turned from Sebastian and gave a detailed description of the Tutela meeting.

'So you went alone, without taking any precautions should something go wrong.'

Victoria skewered Sebastian with her look. 'I'm a Venator and we must take chances, dangerous though they might be.'

Aunt Eustacia drew in her breath as though to speak, but Victoria stepped on her words, not wishing to be reprimanded, particularly in front of Sebastian. 'I will, however, acknowledge that I should have prepared for the possibility that things were not as they had seemed. Without Max, I had to act on my own; there was no one else who could have followed along and been able to assist me had things gone awry. Which, of course, things did go wrong. As it was, I was fortunate enough to make my own escape, and to come upon Verbena and Oliver, who were able to take me home. It is not' – she nodded at Kritanu and her aunt – 'an experience that I would wish to repeat.'

'You did not arrange for your maid to follow you, then,' Aunt Eustacia said in a carefully modulated voice, which told Victoria that she was annoyed or angry.

'I did not. She did that on her own.'

'You did not send a message asking for Kritanu to come with you. He could have followed you as well.'

'I did not have the luxury of time to send for you; for I received the message from Alvisi less than a half hour before he was to pick me up.'

'A conscious decision on his part. He has long been trying to find his way into the inner workings of the Tutela,' Sebastian added.

'You seem to be exceedingly well versed in the Tutela yourself, Monsieur Vioget,' Victoria responded archly.

His smile was bland. 'I am very pleased to be of service to you and all of the other Venators. Now, if you will permit me, I will be more than happy to assist in connecting you with the appropriate people in Roma' – he rolled his R with an authentic Italian purr – 'so that you can continue your quest to find Nedas.'

Victoria looked at Aunt Eustacia. She nodded. '*Si*, we shall all make our way to Roma. By ship. It will be safer than by land, where the Tutela might spot us or follow us.'

Chapter Twelve

In Which Monsieur Vioget Calls a Bluff

'Enjoying the moonlight, or patrolling the ship for nasty vampires in order to save the rest of us mere mortals?'

Victoria was not startled; she'd sensed Sebastian's presence as he came up behind her on the ship's deck. She turned easily to face him, leaving one arm propped on the corner of the ship's railing. 'No worries, Sebastian, darling. There's not a vampire to be found on this vessel.'

'Did you just call me darling, or was I dreaming?' He selected a spot to stand next to her, far enough away that her skirts, lifting and shifting in the breeze of the Adriatic Sea, did not brush his trousers. 'Perhaps I am making progress.'

She just looked at him, ignoring the curls that fluttered like pennants around her temples. When he appeared content to stare out over the glittering sea, coloured black and midnight and grey by the moon and stars, she commented, 'I didn't think it would take long for you to seek me out.' She hated to admit it, but she was glad he had.

'I hope I am not too terribly tardy.'

'Not so very.'

'But late enough that you were getting impatient, true?' He turned his face to look at her, his elbows remaining on the railing. 'Perhaps I don't wish to be predictable either.'

'The only thing predictable about you is that you consistently appear when you suppose I least expect it. Perhaps that will be your undoing; for now I shall expect to see you every time I turn around.'

'You were very foolish to go to the Tutela meeting on your own. You nearly died, Victoria. They nearly tore you to shreds.'

'Do you think I do not know that?' She looked away from his face, which had turned to stare out to sea, and followed his gaze. 'I had no choice.'

'You always have a choice.'

'I don't. I'll see this through until the end, and on the way I'll take as many of them with me as I can. I owe it to Phillip.'

'You speak about violence so matter-of-factly, Victoria. Will that always be your life? Your focus?'

'It can be no other. You don't understand; you cannot know what it's like, Sebastian. I'm a Venator, and that will never change.'

He was silent for a long time. She glanced at him once, saw the shift of his jaw bringing his cheek into shadow and back out of it again. 'When I saw you in Venice, all those bites and scars, I...well, I realised it would be quite a loss if the worst had happened to you.'

'Don't worry, Sebastian. There are other Venators to protect you. Or is it the balance on my debt that you are more concerned about?'

He chuckled, but there was an edge to it. 'I know where the Tutela meets in Rome. You won't have to go alone.'

'So you've said, but I cannot help but wonder why you would endanger yourself so, O man of no violence.'

'Why are you angry with me?'

'With you? Don't flatter yourself, Sebastian. It is anger at this whole life of mine that digs into me right now. I carry this responsibility that, despite your naive assumptions that there is a choice, I cannot choose to shirk. I am lonely and see no end to it. I am widowed and can see no other future for myself. I could have died two nights ago, and yet I willingly go back for more. Sometimes...' Here her voice broke at last. 'Sometimes it becomes too much, and it turns into anger. And other times... other times, it is the only me I can be. The true Victoria.'

'There are very few of us who know what sacrifices you and the other Venators make. How your lives are not your own, though you might wish them to be. But without you and your kind, how different would the world be.'

Victoria was silent again. The anger she'd exposed roiled, then ebbed away, leading into an excruciating awareness of the scent of cloves mingled with salty sea, and a long-fingered hand clasping the railing next to hers. She became conscious of the night, and the fact that they stood at the corner of the ship's stern, shadowed by mast, sail and the poop deck, for all intents and purposes, alone. She heard the soft flap of the sails and the distant shout from one of the sailors.

'How odd.' She didn't realise she'd spoken aloud until she felt Sebastian move next to her; not to look down at her, but to adjust the lapel of his jacket.

'What is that?'

'To stand outside in the night, alone with a man, and not to have to fear for my reputation. I could not help but think of all the times during the Season when I was coming out how careful one had to be not to be found alone with a gentleman, even when I was in no danger of having to protect my virtue. And now that I am a widow, it is no longer such a concern.'

'Indeed.' He sounded bemused. 'I'm wondering if I should be distressed at being considered no danger to your virtue.'

'If you were a danger to me, you would have stopped with the gentlemanly repartee regarding compensations. And I would have cut you off at the knees, just as I did some other gentlemen who thought that suggesting a walk outside on a terrace would give them the opportunity to be free with their hands. Among other things. However, I am sure you would not be so foolish, knowing that I am no ordinary chit.'

'I am not. And don't believe for one moment that I will be led, Victoria. You are much smarter than that, and so am I.'

'I am not interested in leading you anywhere.'

He laughed then. Not as though he'd heard something uproarious, but a low, rolling, knowing laugh that made Victoria more than a bit uncomfortable. 'I could play along, *ma chère*. In fact, I am tempted to do so. Very tempted.'

He moved quickly, smooth as a scarf of silk, and suddenly she was caught between the rail and Sebastian, one of his hands on either side of hers, wrapping around the rail. Long arms settled along her own, keeping her centred between them.

His breath was warm at the back of her neck, where her upswept hair left her skin bare and vulnerable. 'It would be very easy to allow you to provoke me into doing what you are too cowardly to do yourself.' The words prickled there, sending echoes all the way down her back.

'And what, in your warped mind, can you imagine I am too cowardly to do?' She was pleased that her voice remained steady and as easy as the sea breeze when she could feel his height behind her, his proximity, yet, disturbingly, no contact but for the bare touch of his hands alongside hers.

His mouth was at the top of her ear, just brushing the back of it when his lips moved. 'As brave as you might be in facing down vampires and demons, you are too gutless to admit that you fancy finishing what we started in the carriage. You would prefer to provoke me with your arch comments, hoping that I will lose my head and ravage you...whereupon you will be convinced that it wouldn't be so horrible to succumb to your desires.'

She drew in an angry breath, her shoulders shifting back and her breasts lifting, and he moved his hands closer together, tightening his arms around her. 'I—'

But his voice, though lower and more even than her outraged syllable, overrode whatever she would have said. 'And then you would have an excuse for putting aside your suspicions and mistrust of me, your reputation and your fears. The truth is, Victoria, you want me as much as I want you. You just don't want to have to make the decision.'

He moved, and now she felt him behind her, the unmistakable validation of his words pressing into the small of her back. He pushed her hips against the rail, holding her there from behind, as he placed a gentle kiss on the sensitive skin just behind her earlobe. His mouth opened, warm and sighing with breath, and feathered delicately over that same area, light and sensual, sending great, tickling shivers along the back of her shoulders.

'The truth is, Victoria, you don't have to trust me, or to feel any emotional obligation to this alliance in order to assuage your desires. You need not fear that I will be another Rockley and demand what you cannot or will not give.'

She felt his chest rise and fall behind her as he drew in a deep breath and kissed along the tendon that jutted from the side of her neck; she'd tipped her head to the other side as if he were a vampire who'd caught her in his thrall.

Her knees wanted to buckle, but the railing was there to catch them and save her from that indignity. She'd had no idea – *no idea* – how much she'd missed this awakening, this enlivening of her body. Even his mention of Phillip did not allay the growing pleasure.

His hands had moved from the railing to her breasts, and they lifted in his palms when she drew in a deep, quavering breath and reached to touch his head behind her. One finger eased down beneath her bodice to find her nipple and brush over it, and then his arms dropped from her, hands moving back to the railing on either side of her.

Victoria tried to move, to turn to face him, but he kept her in position, looking out at the sea, with his hips and another insistent appendage. 'No, you don't, my dear,' he said in a most uneven voice, deep in her ear. 'I told you I would not be provoked, and I won't. And don't think I will allow you the excuse of my earlier demands for recompense. I have decided that you have quite fulfilled any debt you might have to me.'

She realised she was shaking, and damp everywhere, and quite suddenly alone.

Left alone, standing at the rail with the sea breeze brushing over her like the wisp of his mouth.

Damn him.

'I wonder who shall be the first to give way,' Kritanu murmured into Eustacia's ear. He stood behind her, arms wrapped around her waist, and rumbled a chuckle against her back.

They'd been enjoying the sea evening from a high deck near the stern of the ship when Victoria positioned herself at the railing below. When Sebastian joined her moments later, Kritanu and Eustacia could have moved on, but didn't.

Thus they had been privy not so much to the actual verbal exchange betwixt the two young people, but enough of their activity to discern what was occurring.

'I certainly hope Victoria has enough sense not to make an impulsive decision, or one ruled by desires instead of reason,' Eustacia replied. But she had seen the way her niece sighed and leant into Sebastian, and how she'd drawn deep, shaky breaths after he'd left.

When she thought no one would see.

'I'm certain she wouldn't do something so imprudent. Gardella women are certainly not known for their impulsiveness when it comes to matters of the heart.'

Eustacia could not contain a smile. 'What a shrewish *strega* I've become, *vero*? Age is getting to me and becoming too heavy a burden. I have forgotten what it is like to be young and tempted by a young, handsome man.'

'A young, handsome man nearly eight years your junior.' He was laughing behind her and pressed a kiss to her ear. 'Oh, how you fought your attraction to me. I was too young, much too young, and I was only a Comitator – a mere trainer – not a Venator, so I was beneath your notice.'

'I was furious when Wayren sent you to me! As if you, at seventeen, knew more about fighting vampires than I, a chosen Venator, who had been *vis bulla*ed for nearly four years, since I was twenty. Of course, I had no idea how much I would learn from a Comitator.' She half turned to look at him, and he adjusted to her side, so they leant on the railing, looking at each other. They were exactly the same height: his golden, compact body and her slender one that stooped just slightly with age.

'I know it. And I was stunned by your beauty and put off by your rudeness, your cheeky attitude and your abhorrent fighting skills.'

'I never tire of hearing you reminisce about my stunning beauty.'

'And I never tire of hearing you claim that, thanks to Wayren's insistence that I train you, your life was saved numerous times.'

They smiled at each other, companionable and comfortable in the night and with their memories. Though her joints throbbed more than usual, and despite the fact that she was apprehensive about returning to Rome, Eustacia would not have wished herself back to those younger years.

'Your niece is just as beautiful and talented and stubborn as you were. It is no wonder Vioget looks at her the way he does.'

'I do not know all that has transpired between them; I fear it is more than I would like, and I hope there is no lasting attachment there.'

'You do not wholly trust him.'

'No. I cannot. He can be a valuable ally; he already has proven himself helpful to us. But I cannot take him at face value, for he plays whatever role it suits him to play, whenever he wishes. And he plays it well. He will say and do whatever he must to get what he wants.'

'And what is it that he wants?'

'That is what disturbs me the most, Kritanu. I do not know. I do not know what is truly in his heart.'

'Perhaps you are feeling a bit chary about your

own intuition because of Max's disappearance. You trusted him implicitly.'

'*Trust*. I still do and will until my grave. He is either dead, or… Well, I do not care to think on it. I was able to learn nothing about him or his whereabouts in Venezia; I can only hope we shall find him in Roma.'

'If not, then you fear the prophecy will come to pass.'

She nodded once. 'As our mystic Rosamund wrote: *The golden age of the Venator shall end at the foot of Roma*. If Nedas does indeed loose the full power of Akvan's Obelisk, I fear this battle in Roma will be the end of us all.'

Chapter Thirteen

A Wager Is Made

After her interlude with Sebastian, Victoria stubbornly stayed away from all areas of the ship's deck when the stars and moon were out, confining her strolls to sunlit ones.

It was odd seeing him every day, including during those daytime walks around and between the masts and other objects fixed to the deck. She was used to having him appear unexpectedly – not being seated across from her at a meal. He acted as though he barely knew her, politely bowing and calling her Mrs Withers whenever they came in contact, and spreading his charm evenly among the four other females on the ship. The captain's wife and her sisters were duly charmed.

Victoria preferred him at a distance. It was easier to keep hold of thoughts of Phillip and how much she'd loved him and how recently she'd been widowed when she saw Sebastian only in passing.

But the fact was, she had thought of Sebastian,

and quite often. It was hard to banish the reminder of his muscular body pressing her against the rail, and near impossible to forget the kisses they'd shared – particularly when his sensual mouth was curved in that welcoming smile whenever she walked in the room. His intentions were clear to her, at least; she hoped Aunt Eustacia hadn't read them as well.

And the fact was, Victoria did wonder what would be the harm in giving in to what they both wanted. He'd made it clear that he had no interest in anything other than a mutually beneficial dalliance, which was all she wanted, or could allow herself to engage in, anyway. And there was no possibility of a baby to result from any liaison she might wish to embark upon, as Victoria had been provided a medicinal potion when she was married to Phillip to prevent pregnancy. It was an old tradition of the Gardellas; for no one, least of all Victoria, wished to have a Venator carrying a child.

If she were going to see what it was like to take a lover to whom she was not married or had no other attachment, Sebastian would be a rather logical choice. At least he understood and accepted her life. He was aware of her obligations, and didn't have that overbearing sense of protectiveness that any other man would have. He wouldn't need to be lied to; nor would she need to hide her *vis bulla* from him; nor would he expect anything more from her in the way of marriage.

He was attractive and charming, and he made her feel a bit reckless, even for a Venator. There was, of course, the whole issue as to whether she could completely trust him. But, trustworthy or not, he was a fine kisser, among other things, and she was a Venator and could take care of herself.

It was certainly something to consider.

Other than trying to avoid Sebastian – and thus her confused, tantalising feelings about him – during the course of the voyage, Victoria had little to do.

At first, she tried to keep sharp by practising her *kalaripayattu* in the small chamber she shared with Verbena, but it was much too small. She kept kicking one or other of the beds, and at one point slammed her elbow into the wall when she misjudged a spin.

That sent her searching for another place on the ship that might accommodate a bit more movement. More accurately, it sent Oliver to search for such a space for her. He did manage to locate a storage room that, because the trip was less than a fortnight, was not being completely stuffed with supplies that would have been needed for a longer voyage.

So Victoria practised there, sometimes with Kritanu and other times without, while Oliver sat just outside the door in case anyone tried to come in. It would have been exceedingly embarrassing for one of the shipmates to barge in on Victoria wearing loose pants and a tunic-like shirt, as she was spinning and kicking throughout the room.

One day she had been practising for well over an
hour, using the crates scattered throughout the room
as part of her moves. She spun and kicked, launched
herself up onto one of them, whirled with the
momentum of her movement, and leapt down and
across the room onto another one.

Victoria was perspiring and her hair had begun to
straggle from its braid, plastering to her face and neck.
She whipped around and snatched up a machete she'd
been using in her battles with Kritanu in days past,
and when she turned back around, she saw the door
to the room opening.

It was, of course, Sebastian.

'How did you get in here?' she asked, huffing and
puffing. She stood on one of the crates across from
the door and swiped a hand over her damp forehead.
Her sword dangled from a loose grip. She would not
even think of how she must look, with damp patches
along the sides of her shirt and the loose, unfeminine
trousers. And her feet, wearing only light stockings.

'Your man Oliver, of course. He and I have had
several conversations during your practices – a matter
of gaining his trust, you know. So today I suggested
that it might be acceptable to allow me to watch for
a bit.'

He walked over and picked up Kritanu's matching
machete. 'Learning to fence, are you?'

'The skill is called *ankathari*, and it is much more
lethal than a Frenchman's pretty fencing pirouettes

and parries. Notice the inflexibility and width of the blade. Our weapons are much more serious than those slender, bendable ones you use.'

'Oho! So you wish to challenge me to a duel, do you? I am pleased to accept.' He swung the sword, whistling it through the air, then put it aside as he stripped off his coat and cravat. She tried not to notice as he unsnagged the two buttons of his collar and rolled up his sleeves, showing skin tanned the colour of toffee.

'There is padded gear there, if you wish to wear it.' Victoria nodded her head towards the pile of armour that Kritanu would normally don during their sessions.

Sebastian considered it, then looked at her. 'You do not wear it?'

'No. But I—'

'—am a Venator. Yes, yes, I am aware of that.' He stepped into the centre of the room. 'I'll take my chances.' He looked up at her, where she still stood. 'Do you not wish to duel with me? Or are you finished practising for the day?'

'I'll duel with you.' She jumped down, landing flat-footed on the ground. 'There is little else to do on this ship.'

They faced each other, the length of two machete blades apart. His golden-brown eyes pinned her when she looked at him, and she recognised pleasure and challenge there.

'We must have a prize for the winner of this duel,' he said, grinning slyly. 'You didn't think I would allow such an opportunity to pass, did you?'

Victoria couldn't hold back the huff of a surprised laugh. 'Of course not. And, coincidentally, I'm sure you have something in mind.'

'A boon. The winner chooses a boon that the other must give freely.'

Now she really laughed. 'Sebastian, you are utterly predictable!'

Instead of being offended, he grinned in return and nodded. 'Of course. When opportunity presents itself, I am most delighted to grab it.'

'That means, of course, that you must win in order to collect on your boon.'

'You do not appear concerned.'

'I'm not.' And she lunged at him.

He didn't move except for his sword hand, neatly blocking her machete. 'Nor am I.'

They parried and teased for a bit, their feet remaining in a stationary position for the most part as their blades slid along each other, clanged each hand-guard against the other, then fell away. Victoria held back, wanting to gauge her opponent's skill; for though she wanted to best him, she did not want to injure the arrogant fop who disdained padded armour. Certainly he must be more used to handling an épée or other fencing blade, which was lighter and more flexible, yet he kept pace with her, even as she increased her speed and the power of her lunges and thrusts.

Soon they were dancing about the room in an odd sort of waltz, and Victoria felt herself needing to concentrate to stay with him. He was quick and inventive, and she was by no means outmatching him. In fact, she was beginning to wonder how he kept such pace with her and blocked her so easily. But then she caught his machete at just the right angle and flipped it from his hands, sending it tumbling to the floor.

She barely registered the fact that she had won when he somersaulted, swept up the still-vibrating sword, and came at her, lunging fiercely enough to back her towards one of the crates.

Their blades clashed and clung together as though glued, pausing in mid-battle, their faces so close together Victoria could see one golden copper hair from his eyebrow curling out of place and catching in the bangs that had fallen over his forehead. A line of sweat trickled down one temple. He grinned and her stomach dipped.

Then, as if reading the other's mind, they both moved at the same time, and in a frenzy of blades and a dangerous tangle of sliding metal they caught again, stuck, heaved, and then one machete went flying and the other clattered to the floor at their feet.

Sebastian slammed his foot down on the blade that fell and kicked it aside before she could reach for it.

'Victory is mine, my lovely. I shall claim my prize!'

'No victory for you. The battle ended in a draw.'

'Indeed. Well, as long as I may claim my boon, I do not much care if you wish to call it a draw.'

'But what if my request is that your boon be null and void?'

'But you would not, *ma chère*. You are not a coward.'

Her eyes narrowed but she stepped back, nodding. 'Yes, then. Name your prize.'

'I wish...' – he stepped towards her, capturing her hands before she could react, and tugging her gently in his direction – '...an honest answer to the question I am about to ask you.'

'No kisses? No viewing of my *vis bulla*? No lewd propositions? Sebastian, you are frightening me!'

He reached, closing his fingers gently around her chin and lifting it. 'If you are disappointed, recall that you still have a prize to collect.' He gave a small, affectionate jerk to her chin, then released it, brushing his fingers over her cheek. 'I wish to know why you married Rockley – out of familial duty or out of love?'

The question surprised her, and she hesitated. Then: 'It was no duty. I loved him.' Her voice sounded rusty, and suddenly the room felt stifling. Why would he ask such a question? Why would he care?

He squeezed her hands, then released them and stood waiting. She looked at him in his white shirt, damp in places and veed open to show the sheen of sweat at his throat and bronze-haired chest. She'd mused more than once over the way he reminded her of a golden angel, all tawny haired and golden skinned and tiger eyed. The darkest aspects of his face were slashing brows, of walnut mingled with blond and auburn, and the lashes that framed his eyes. Otherwise, he was all bronze.

But certainly not an angel, particularly when he looked at her as he was now…as though he was expecting her to collapse into a pile of lust at his feet.

'Victoria?' he prompted.

She smiled at him, a smile she'd used only with Phillip…one that she'd learnt after discovering how a man's desire worked, and how a woman could use it to her advantage. And pleasure.

She smiled that smile at him; perhaps there was a name for the type of expression it was, but she didn't know it. She stepped up to him, close. She smelt clove, and man, and perhaps some other scent that might have been on his clothing or in his hair…bay… and put her hands on his shoulders. They were broad, wide and solid, and his skin burnt damp and warm through the fine, thin shirt he wore.

She could see the gold, copper and brown of stubble beginning to show beneath the skin of his jaw, and feel the expectancy in his breathing. His eyes were half-closed, but she felt them watching her, heavy. He wasn't smiling.

Victoria drew herself up on her toes, bringing her mouth to his neck, and whispered, 'I want to know how you know so much about vampires.'

Then she let her heels thump to the floor and stepped back, releasing his shoulders as they sagged with discharged tension. His eyes opened fully.

'How you do tempt a man, Victoria,' he said lightly. But his expression belied amusement. 'The answer to your question is much more involved than I can or will share at this time, but I will tell you this: like you, I lost someone I loved to the vampires.'

'Your wife? A lover?'

'My father.'

Chapter Fourteen

In Which Mrs Withers Has Double the Fun

Victoria's first glimpse of Rome caused an unexpected shiver along the tops of her shoulders. As she looked upon the city of so much history, she felt a sense of foreboding prickle her, as though the sight of the city portended some catalyst of which she was ignorant.

But when the wagon that had brought her and the others from the port of Ostia finally stopped and she alighted, Victoria didn't feel the sensation, nor the trembling of the earth underfoot that she might have expected when stepping into a place that burnt with such a sense of prophecy. She merely felt that her consciousness would be overwhelmed by the sounds, the smells, the sights of the streets…of Roma.

Despite the lure of the city, Victoria didn't have much opportunity to enjoy or experience it. Within a day Aunt Eustacia had her settled in a small town house with Oliver and Verbena and a retinue of Italian staff, approximately fifteen minutes from where the Gardella matriarch herself was staying. As in Venice,

Victoria and Aunt Eustacia had deemed it prudent to keep their connection under wraps.

Victoria didn't know where Sebastian had gone.

They'd seen each other only at meals after their mock sword-battle and tête-à-tête confessions, and he was nowhere to be seen when Victoria and her retinue disembarked from the ship back in Ostia. He had apparently found other means of transportation into the city.

She was content not to see him, for she wasn't sure how to react to his announcement. What did it mean that he'd lost his father to the vampires? That he'd been killed by them? Or, perhaps, turned into a vampire? It was also possible, she supposed, that his father was a member of the Tutela. That could explain why Sebastian knew so much about them.

It made sense. That would account for how he'd got involved with Polidori, and how he claimed to know where they would be meeting here in Rome.

He made no contact with Victoria for three days after they arrived in Rome, leaving her to stew and wonder if they'd come here only to be manipulated by Sebastian; but then on that third day, he sent a message that he would call in the afternoon.

She was waiting for him in the parlour. She would have mistaken the tiny room for a broom cupboard if it hadn't been for the two chairs and small table that made it what the Italians who'd let the town house to her claimed to be a parlour. Whatever it was, it was much too small for her and Sebastian. She felt the room condense as he came in and closed the door behind.

'I presume you've spent the last three days working very hard to establish the clandestine location of the next Tutela meeting, and determining the best way to sneak me in,' was how she greeted him. She sat, despite the fact that he remained standing, making the room feel even smaller.

His eyebrows drew together but his words were drier than chalk. 'Now, whatever would have made you think that? I had other business to attend to, acquaintances to call upon, an opera to see, and the Trevi Fountain to drop a coin in for a wish. But in regards to the Tutela meeting, yes, indeed, you shall be attending. I hope your calendar is free tonight.'

'I had box seats to the opera myself, but I shall forgo them in lieu of going with you to the meeting, of course. Duty before pleasure.'

'Not in my book.'

Before she could fathom what he was about, he came in towards her and closed his hands over her shoulders, pressing her into the high-backed chair and clamping her in place with his fingers curling over the top. He bent to kiss her, covering her mouth – which had opened to protest in surprise – with his as he slid his knee onto the cushion next to her skirt.

Her face tipped up, the high centre of the chair digging into the back of her skull as she welcomed his kiss with lips that parted more to taste him. She felt the bulk of her hair, pinned up behind her head, loosen with every movement of her head as it scrubbed against the wood frame and velvet upholstery, and the sharp poke of two pins as they dug into her scalp.

A warm, languid feeling coursed through her limbs, and she sighed into his mouth. He tasted as golden and warm as he looked. His knee in the chair next to her had her tipping slightly to the side, leaning against its solid weight, her left hand brushing against the hem of his trousers.

He pulled his mouth from hers and pressed sliding kisses along her jaw towards her ear. He was definitely breathing deeply, and his fingers had closed more tightly over her shoulders, but with one last buss at the corner of her jaw, he stopped. Leveraging himself off the chair, he looked down at her and said, 'That is payment in kind for your little display after our sword fight.'

She didn't have to ask what he meant; her heart was beating much too hard in her chest, and she felt warm and damp everywhere.

'I'm fully prepared to go to whatever lengths you wish to go, and when you decide to, Victoria. The only thing holding us back from what we both want is you.'

She nodded. It was true. And she wasn't even sure why she was holding back. Goodness knows, she wasn't innocent, and she had most certainly enjoyed making love with Phillip. But he was gone, and she had little pleasure available to her in this life.

'Now,' Sebastian said, as though the interlude had never happened, 'we must talk about the Tutela meeting. There is a gathering tonight that is more of a social event but will include many of the Tutela members. It is not a meeting or ritual, but Conte Regalado, one of the more prominent Tutelas, is hosting it as a way to recruit more followers.'

'I'd like to go.'

'I was certain you would. They are heavily recruiting, Victoria, and there is almost an edge of hysteria and panic to their need for more. I believe that whatever it is Polidori learnt from his interaction with them has something to do with this need for more members. They are preparing for something – probably the activation of Akvan's Obelisk.

'The event tonight is held under the guise of the unveiling of Regalado's latest portrait – he fancies himself an accomplished artist. There will be Tutela members there, and they will be searching for opportunities to lure interested parties to their cause, so a few words dropped here or there will certainly be to your advantage. I believe he will be welcoming visitors as of eight o'clock.'

'I'm certain if I ask how you obtained all of this information, you won't tell me.'

'You continue to impress me with your intelligence, determination and needless virtue.' He looked at her pointedly for a long moment, causing a warmth to rush over her bosom and up into her neck and cheeks when she read the blatant message in his eyes: *Blast virtue!*

'You will attend with me, then?' she asked when she had to tear her eyes away.

'Actually I will not. It would not be prudent for me to be there tonight – Tut, tut! Don't ask why, my dear. A man must have some secrets.'

'*Some* secrets? Sebastian, there is nothing about you that is *not* secretive.'

He raised his brows. 'Indeed? And here I thought my desire for you was quite flagrant.'

The blush returned with his forthright words. She'd never heard it put aloud, so bluntly and boldly. But she would ignore it. For now. 'So I am to attend alone?'

'No, that would be awkward at best. I happen to be acquainted with two young women who are also friends of Conte Regalado's daughter, Sarafina. They will be attending tonight and were more than happy to include you in their party. As Mrs Withers, of course, the recent widow who seeks solace from the loss of her husband. Along with some distraction, and perhaps a chance at immortality.'

'Two young women?' Victoria looked at him knowingly. 'So that explains where you have been for the last three days.'

'Does it?' His smile was enigmatic, and to her

annoyance, she found herself…well, *annoyed*.

'Perhaps I might learn more about your many secrets whilst I am in their company this evening,' she replied with a teasing smile of her own. 'It will be rather interesting.'

'Hmm…perhaps I spoke too soon.' But he was chuckling, his tiger eyes lit with humour. 'Their names are Portiera and Placidia Tarruscelli, and they have agreed to call for you at eight o'clock. It would not do, apparently, to be on time to such an event.'

'I see that Society in Rome is no different from back home,' Victoria commented. 'Very well, then, I shall be prepared for their arrival at eight. Thank you very much, Sebastian, for the assistance you've given us in this.'

He took her hand and raised it to his lips for a rather tame kiss, as Sebastian kisses went. 'I hope you shall still be grateful when this is all over.'

Portiera and Placidia Tarruscelli were dark-eyed, dark-haired beauties with voluptuous figures, and each with a small mole on the side of their luscious pink mouths: Portiera's was at the left of her lips; Placidia's was on the right. They were twins.

Victoria couldn't help but wonder just how well Sebastian knew them.

Everything about them was in duplicate: their gowns (one in garnet and one in mauve), their reticules (one beaded with pearls, the other with jet beads)…even their compliments on Victoria's spring green gown came in rapid succession, with slight variation – one loved the lace around the bodice, the other *adored* the three layers of ruffles at the hem.

When she sat across from them on the carriage ride to the Regalado villa, Victoria felt as though she were being accosted by two twittering cats – cats didn't twitter, but they did move sinuously and had a certain slumberous look about their eyes. The non-stop commentary and questions, punctuated with giggles and squeals, accounted for the twittering part.

Victoria was fluent in Italian, and the twins in English, so their conversation was easy and multilingual. And exceedingly difficult to keep straight.

While one twin asked a question regarding London, the other was following a train of thought along the lines of fashion, asking different things. And to Victoria's added confusion, they switched back and forth in their prattle, each picking up the other's conversational thread until she was never quite sure to whom she was responding at any given moment.

She was delighted when they finally arrived at the villa.

Inside the spacious home, past the traditional Roman fountains that graced the arching entranceways, Victoria and the Tarruscelli twins were announced and then passed through into the main ballroom.

It was not outfitted for dancing tonight, although a string quartet played unobtrusively in one corner. There were paintings hung on every wall – all, by the looks of them, in the hand of the same mediocre artist. Apparently Sebastian and Victoria shared a similar opinion of Regalado's art.

In the centre of one of the short walls of the rectangular room was a small dais where the orchestra would normally play during a ball, but where tonight's highlight was the latest painting by Regalado.

Victoria nearly laughed aloud when she saw it. A portrait it was indeed, of the Tarruscelli twins and their moles flanking a pretty blonde girl of the same age and proportions. They were painted to represent the three Fates, each in a flowing Grecian gown that exposed a shoulder here and rather quite a lot of a bosom there. Six nipples pointed through their flimsy garments.

'Do you recognise me?' asked someone next to Victoria, speaking in heavily accented English.

She turned. 'You must be Signorina Regalado, the artist's daughter.'

'*Si*, and you must be the *inglese* friend Portiera and Placidia brought tonight. Emmaline Withers? I am so very pleased to meet you, I could not wait for them to introduce us. I came *immediato* to *discorrere* with you.'

Victoria glanced about the room to find escape; the last thing she needed this night was to be commandeered by another young and foolish girl. She had work to do. '*Grazie* for your hospitality, *signorina*—'

'Oh, *favore*, I am Sara to you! I am so pleased to practice my *inglese* with another woman. Men do not know the *importante* words. Such as lace and ruffles and gloves and flounces and—'

'Where is your father? I should like to congratulate him on such a lovely piece of work,' Victoria interrupted before she was treated to an entire list of every fashion term under the sun. 'He has made you look so beautiful.'

'My *amore* has said the same thing.' Sara beamed and slipped her arm through Victoria's. 'I shall introduce you to him later, but first I would like you to meet my father, and also two of your countrymen. They do not wish to speak on fashions with me, so I shall push you in their faces and make them *geloso*.'

When Sara at last located her father, who was standing with a group of three other men at the other side of the room, she nearly towed Victoria over to them. Victoria was not the least bit reluctant to meet the count, of course, for if he were one of the more prominent members of the Tutela, it would behove her to make friends with him.

'Ahh, Sarafina, who is this lovely beauty you have brought?' he asked, turning from his conversation.

'*Padre*, this is my new friend, Mrs Emmaline Withers.'

The man, who was short and stocky with scarcely any of what had been dark hair left on his skull – but compensated for it by growing a full, bushy beard and moustache – bowed and took Victoria's hand. He raised it and kissed it with soft wet lips, and looked at her with exceedingly interested dark eyes. Not a surprise; after all, this was a man who painted the nipples of his daughter and her friends. 'I am most gratified to make your acquaintance. May I introduce you to some of my companions?'

That was when Victoria turned and saw, for the first time, the very confused, very familiar face of George Starcasset.

Chapter Fifteen

Lady Rockley Receives a Set-down

Victoria looked at George and smiled as though it were nothing out of the ordinary to be introduced by a false name.

To his credit, he did nothing but bow and raise her hand for a brief kiss, but moments later, after all the introductions had been completed and Victoria managed to excuse herself before he said something awkward, he made his own excuse to follow her.

'Perhaps you will permit me to escort you to find something to drink,' George said, taking her arm firmly.

When they got out of earshot of the count and his companions, George pulled Victoria off to the side and looked down at her. 'I do not know what serendipitous happening has brought us together so soon after my arrival in Italy, but whatever it was, I am most grateful.'

'You made no mention of travelling to Italy when we bade farewell,' Victoria commented, wondering why he wasn't asking her about her assumed name. Perhaps he was merely being as polite and circumspect as the time he'd found her stalking vampires on the midnight streets of London. Perhaps he was merely an unsuspicious person.

But could there be another reason? While surprised, he did not look as startled as she had been when Regalado had turned to introduce them.

'I had not planned to make my way to Italy at that time, to be sure…but I must confess, I felt it highly regrettable that you had to leave England just as we were becoming better friends.' He squeezed her elbow as though to add an extra layer of meaning to the word. 'And after some thought, I realised it would be a good time to return to Rome to check up on some business interests I had here. I felt sure that since we were both in the same country I would be able to ascertain how to find you and to pay a call. I had no idea that happenstance would bring us to the same social event only two days after my arrival.' His smile was wide and boyish, and with the two deep, curving dimples that framed it, along with the deep cleft in his chin, he looked even more youthful.

'How very fortunate.' Her lie was accompanied by a smile that was just as false. She had to find a way to dislodge George so that she could pump Regalado about the Tutela. And then another uncomfortable thought occurred to her. 'How did you happen to come here tonight?'

Surely it wasn't because he was interested in the Tutela. Surely it was a coincidence.

But there had been vampires and Polidori – a Tutela member – at Claythorne. And she wasn't altogether certain that Sebastian wasn't a Tutela member since it was possible that his father was.

Then another just as black thought opened in her mind. Sebastian had said it would be imprudent for him to attend the party at the Regalado villa. Was that because he knew that Starcasset was going to be here? And he didn't want to be recognised for some reason?

'Polidori mentioned to me when we were at supper that night at Claythorne…that night…that if I ever visited Rome, I should be certain to acquaint myself with his friend Conte Regalado. He seemed to believe that the count and I would find each other exceedingly amiable.' He squeezed her elbow again. 'And I have found it to be true. Regalado and I have much to discuss.'

Victoria decided to chance it. 'Has he spoken to you of the Tutela?'

'The Tutela? Why…not that I recall. What is that?'

'I am not sure,' she replied blandly, casting her glance around the room. 'I just happened to hear the word mentioned and was curious.' And that was when she saw Max.

'Well, I would be most pleased to ask about it if you

don't wish…Lady Rock – Mrs Withers, is something the matter?'

He – Max – was standing across the room from them as though he'd just walked in, greeting a cluster of people. Just as tall, just as dark-haired and arrogant-looking as he'd been a year ago. He was smiling as he shook their hands.

'No, indeed,' she replied to George, only a moment after he'd posed the question and it had sunk in. 'Except perhaps that I am a bit thirsty. Would you…?' She allowed her voice to trail off as she slanted him the convenient look that branded her a helpless female.

'Of course, of course, madam,' he replied, appearing a bit flustered. 'I have delayed you in your quest for a beverage, and I must apologise. I shall fetch a tea for you, or would you prefer a glass of that wine they call Chianti?'

'Tea would be lovely, or lemonade,' Victoria replied, trying to keep her attention from spanning back to where Max stood.

As soon as George started towards the tables where drinks were poured, she pivoted in the opposite direction and began to make her way through the loose clusters of people in the ballroom. She was about halfway across the room when Max saw her.

He had not expected it; that was clear by the poleaxed expression that flashed over his face, gone as quickly as it appeared. He did not hold contact with her eyes, but returned his attention to the cluster of people in which he was gathered. Someone said something amusing, and the group, including Max, responded with laughter.

He looked relaxed and well. Handsome and aristocratic, with his olive skin and high cheekbones, long, straight nose, and square-angled chin. His dark hair had grown long enough to be pulled back, but tonight was not and fell nearly to his shoulders. Certainly he didn't appear as though he'd experienced any travail or other casualty. Nothing, by the looks of him, that would account for his lack of communication for nearly a year.

Victoria knew she couldn't simply barge into the group and accost Max, nor even insinuate herself into the conversation with the four or five men with whom he was speaking. He glanced once more in her direction, and she could see the expression in his eyes from where she stood: dark, cold, flat.

'Mrs Withers! I have been searching all over for you. I was wondering where you had got off to. May I call you Emmaline?'

'I was searching for you as well, Sara, and of course you may call me Emmaline,' Victoria replied. How might she use Sara to accomplish what she needed to?

'*Splendido!* Now, I must introduce you to *amore mio*. He has just arrived.'

Of course. Victoria wasn't surprised at all. Why should she be? Along with vampires, her life had become full of coincidences and unexpected arrivals. Sebastian appeared regularly as if out of thin air. George Starcasset simply happened to attend her first social function in Rome. So why would Max not be the beau of her new acquaintance, the daughter of one of the most powerful men in the Tutela?

'*Caro*, may I introduce you to my new friend, Mrs Emmaline Withers,' Sara said, sliding her arm proprietarily through Max's. 'She has recently arrived from London. Emmaline, may I present *fidanzato mio*, Maximilian Pesaro.'

Her *fiancé*?

He gave the barest of bows; really, it was more insolent than polite, flickered an impersonal glance over Victoria, and said, in Italian, 'London, you say? And whatever would induce you to leave such a charming city?'

'Do not be offended, Emmaline. Max simply hates London,' Sara interjected. 'He had to spend several months there last year and says he couldn't wait to return.'

'Indeed? Well, I am certain there will be no need for him to return ever again if he despises it so much. But did you not go with him? And how did you find London?'

'Alas, I had not yet had the pleasure of making the acquaintance of my fiancée when I was there,' Max said in his deep, smooth voice. Very, very easy. Nonchalant. 'That happened shortly after my return.'

'May I be among those who wish you congratulations on your impending marriage,' Victoria replied. 'When is the happy date?'

'It cannot come soon enough,' Max said, looking down at the beaming Sara, who gazed up at him as if he were a bonnet she just had to have. She did not even reach his shoulder; she was so petite, yet soft and curvy. Her blond hair, unusual in Italy, must have been what attracted him; that, perhaps, and the long-lashed brown eyes in a sweet, heart-shaped face. 'It is unfortunate that you won't be able to attend, Mrs Withers, as I'm certain your travel plans will soon take you from our fair city.'

The message couldn't have been clearer if he'd written it.

Victoria realised her fingers were trembling. 'I see Mr Starcasset has returned with a beverage for me,' she said to Sara. She refused to look at Max, for fear someone else might read the murderous expression that would surely be on her face. 'And I simply must take another look at that painting. Please excuse me.'

'It will be our pleasure.' Max's under-the-breath comment went straight to her ears as she hurried away.

Deep breaths. Victoria took deep breaths and made herself slow down. She would not allow him to see that he'd upset her.

And of course he'd upset her. He'd disappeared nearly a year ago, and now she found him happily ensconced with his fiancée in the bowels of the Tutela! Surely he could not be ignorant of his fiancée's father's involvement; he was, after all, a Venator.

As she reached George, who, luckily, had appeared with a drink for her just as she returned, Victoria recognised there were two explanations for Max's involvement with Sara Regalado and his conduct tonight.

Either he was acting a part, as she was, in trying to infiltrate the Tutela; or he had changed alliances and as a result had cut off all interest and communication with Aunt Eustacia and Wayren. If it were the first, Victoria did not understand why he would not have been in contact with them. There were discreet ways to do it; surely Max would know how. If he had joined the Tutela, the protectors of the vampires, then he must have denounced his position as a Venator.

That she couldn't believe. Not even for an instant.

But there was a third possibility.

Everything could be exactly as it seemed, no more, no less: he'd fallen in love with Sara Regalado and was planning to marry her.

Victoria had to endure George Starcasset's clumsy attempts to kiss her during the carriage ride back to her villa. She wanted to plant him back in his seat with a well-placed shove calculated to give him whiplash, but she refrained from so blatantly using her Venator powers. Instead, she chose to 'accidentally' grind her sharp heel into his toes hard enough to deflate any other amorous ideas he might have. Not only did it cool his ardour, but it would likely keep him from dancing for a week.

What she really wanted to do was hit someone. Preferably Max.

After she'd had a chance to reflect on the situation, Victoria had come to the only conclusion she could: that he was playing a role, and that as soon as they had a moment to talk privately, he would clear it up.

It was the only explanation that made sense. Max was a Venator, the most powerful one after Aunt Eustacia. He would never betray them.

And as for Sarafina Regalado? Victoria would not believe Max had fallen in love with that fairy-headed chit. If he ever deigned to allow himself to be distracted by a woman, it would be someone... different.

Having come to her conclusion, Victoria assumed that Max would be as anxious to make the truth known to her as she was to receive it, so she hovered near one of the ballroom entrances in hopes of catching his eye and hinting for him to leave. But he did not glance her way even once, and he seemed perfectly content to mingle among the guests, with or without Sara clinging to his arm.

When at last she had run out of excuses for Portiera and Placidia as to why she did not move from her spot, she allowed them to manoeuvre her to a cluster of young Italian men – the equivalent of the rakes and rogues that made their way through the ton in London – and present her to them.

For a short time, Victoria allowed herself to be lulled by the pleasure of being nothing more than a young, attractive woman interacting with young, attractive men. She'd forgotten what it was like to be concerned only with providing witty comments or flashing demure smiles.

This was the life she'd given up: a simple one, where the biggest worry was what gown to wear to which event, whether her dance card would be filled, and whether, once wed, she would provide an heir and a spare. It was filled with gossip and parties and little else.

Oh, and blissful ignorance.

Yes, that was definitely part of the life she'd given up.

Portiera and Placidia's handsome friends were complimentary and charming and falling all over themselves in an effort to speak with Victoria, to retrieve a drink for her, a *biscotto*, an *antipasto*, a walk on the terrace to steal some air. As an English widow, she was unusually attractive to them, in particular to one of the elder of the group – though he couldn't have been more than thirty – Barone Silvio Galliani.

'Perhaps I could convince you that some fresh air would be delightful, Mrs Withers,' he suggested, elbowing another, less bold competitor out of the way. 'The gardens at Villa Regalado are particularly beautiful in the moonlight.'

Italy flavoured his English, admiration glinted in his dark eyes, and his smile was compelling enough to send a little twinge into her belly. When she acquiesced and he took her arm, she felt the fine cloth of his jacket and the sinewy muscle underneath it.

'Have you known the Regalado family for long?' Victoria asked him as they strolled along the cobblestone terrace.

'For many years,' he replied. 'I am the *contessa's* cousin. Was I not truthful when I claimed that the gardens are most beautiful by moonlight? Do you see those roses there?'

She looked at the creamy white blooms, made silvery by the moon. 'They are beautiful, but seem to be blooming rather late in the season.'

'Indeed, they are! I dabble a bit in the breeding of flowers, and this one is one of my own creations. I named it Sara in the Moonlight – *Sarà nel chiarore della luna* – but perhaps I was rather hasty in choosing a name.' He cast a meaningful look at her. 'Its delicate colour reminds me of your beautiful English skin, and the silver glaze from the moon is the same as the shine in your dark hair. *Il chiarore della luna di Emmaline* would perhaps be a more fitting name: Emmaline's Moonlight.'

Victoria felt the sway of his charm. After all, she'd never been described as a rose. 'I am most complimented,' she replied, walking on. 'You must be very close to Sara and her family to name a rose after her.'

'*Si*, I have known her since she was young. A bit frivolous at times, but a nice enough girl. Pretty in her own way.'

'It sounds as though the family is quite pleased about her pending nuptials. Have you met her intended?'

'Many times. Pesaro is quite the gentleman and seemed to become rather quickly attached to young Sara. It was only a matter of a month, perhaps half again, and they were announcing their engagement. Of course, when one finds true love, time means nothing.' He was looking at her again with that same intense look. Did he really think she was going to fall for it?

'Does the *conte* approve of such a quick decision for his daughter's marriage?'

'He is very pleased. He and Pesaro have extensive business dealings, which is how I believe he came to meet Sara. Now, my dear Mrs Withers, enough talk about Sara and her beau…let us talk about yours. I noticed quite a bit of interest from that English boy back in there. Tell me true, and do not break my heart…is he of special interest to you, or is there the possibility that another might attract your attention?'

'My attention is not attached to anyone at this time, *barone*.'

'Then I may count myself as a fortunate man.' Barone Galliani's brilliant smile flashed in the moonlight. 'It would make me very happy if you would call me Silvio. Would you care to take a turn along the pathway yonder? I should be happy to show you some of my purple sweet-peas.'

'I would be very happy to see them, but I fear I must find my way back into the ballroom. I do not wish Placidia and Portiera to worry on my absence. They may be preparing to leave.'

He was clearly disappointed, but he acceded to her wishes and escorted her inside. Just as they came back into the ballroom from the terrace, Victoria saw the tall figure of Max striding towards the opposite door.

He was leaving the room, and she was going to follow him. This would be her chance to catch him alone.

She told Silvio that she must excuse herself for a moment, and made her way through the people chatting and drinking without appearing to be in a hurry. She even paused at the drink table to dash down an unladylike gulp of lemonade, then continued on her way. By the time she reached the exit, nearly ten minutes had elapsed.

The doorway through which Max had disappeared was not the one through which she'd originally entered the ballroom; instead of leading to an entry foyer, it led into a spacious, curve-ceilinged hall lined with doors and alcoves, studded with shoulder-high pillars topped with marble busts. In keeping with Regalado's theme, several of them also sported nipples.

Victoria paused at one of the doors, unsure whether Max had gone this way to meet someone else, to obtain some solitude from the demanding social event, or, perhaps, to seek her out.

There was silence in the hall, then, from a distance, the rumble of a low voice followed by a low, delighted feminine squeal. Someone had taken the opportunity for a tryst.

Victoria moved along, wondering if she dared to open one of the doors. Max could be anywhere; he could be in a completely different area of the villa. But if he'd slipped out in order to create an opportunity for them to meet, he should be nearby. Waiting for her. He must have seen her come back in from the terrace and must know she was behind him.

A doorknob turned, and Victoria scooted into the shadow of one of the busts, tucking herself behind it, wishing she were as petite as Sara. With a low *whoosh* the door opened, and the rustle of skirts told her that a woman was coming along the hall.

Victoria held her breath, but the woman rushed along back to the ballroom with nary a glance. It was Sara Regalado.

An ugly feeling stirred in Victoria's belly. She stepped from behind the pillar and waited.

The door opened again, and out strode Max. His thick hair was rumpled and the collar of his shirt was crooked. Other than that, his hawkish features made him appear cool and removed, his elegant cheekbones as though they were carved from ice. He looked down his long, straight nose at her, standing there in the hall, and said, 'You again?'

He would have brushed past her, but she planted herself in the centre of the passage. 'What's going on, Max?' she asked in a low voice.

'Whatever do you mean?' he asked, flicking at what had to be an imaginary speck on his coat sleeve. 'Perhaps you've caught me in an awkward position, but after all, she is my fiancée.'

'Why haven't you been in contact with Aunt Eustacia?'

His look was bland as porridge. 'I've been busy. Wedding plans and such. You know how distracting they can be.'

She felt as though he'd slammed her in the stomach. 'Yes,' she breathed.

He waited a beat, then said, 'Is there anything else?'

'No.'

'Very good, then...er, Mrs Witters, was it? Will you permit me to return to my fiancée? I hope your journey back to London is comfortable – and *imminent*.' As she stepped back, he walked past her, tall and dark, and she could not miss the air of annoyance that accompanied him.

Now, hours later in the carriage across from George,

who'd enthusiastically offered to see her home when the Tarruscelli sisters weren't ready to leave, Victoria still seethed.

She simmered and stewed, but beneath the anger was emptiness, disbelief, fear. Arrogance and rudeness were nothing new where Max was concerned, but it was the blithe put-off when she'd asked him about Aunt Eustacia that really bothered her. He loved her aunt like a mother, a mentor, a teacher, and a liege. For him to dismiss her boded nothing good.

Surely it wasn't what it seemed. Surely it wasn't that he'd fallen in love and denounced the Venator world and duty.

Or that he'd joined the Tutela.

She'd never believe it.

Chapter Sixteen

In Which a Small Italian Parlour Experiences Much Activity

Victoria wasn't surprised to find Sebastian waiting at the villa when she returned. It just seemed to follow with the rest of the way things had been going. When she came in to find him awaiting her in the cushion-sized parlour, she had a brief moment of regret that she hadn't taken George up on his hints to be invited in.

It was only a brief moment, however, and was replaced with the more fervent wish that she'd allowed Silvio to take her home, and to come in with her. The presence of the attentive and handsome Italian baron would have wiped the expectant smile off Sebastian's face.

As it was, Victoria's hand itched to wipe it off. She truly wasn't fit for company, as her mother would say. But that was the risk Sebastian had taken, showing up here uninvited. Sending her off alone tonight. Not telling her everything he knew.

He was asking for it.

'I hope I didn't keep you waiting too long,' she said by way of greeting.

He'd shed his coat and gloves before she arrived, unknotted his cravat, and unbuttoned the two buttons of his collar. For that presumption alone, she ought to be annoyed. 'Not at all, *ma chère*…in fact, I thought it would take you quite a bit longer to extricate yourself from all of those salivating young bucks you were sure to meet. Or was it a worthless evening?'

'I had to fight off George Starcasset's *attempts* to kiss me in the carriage on the way home.'

'Should I be pleased they were only *attempts?* And gratified that my attempts of the same were successful?'

'*And* I survived a stroll in the moonlight with Barone Galliani. Not that that was a hardship.'

'Galliani?' His smile thinned for an instant; then it was back, cool and sensual.

'A friend of yours?'

'Not particularly. Other than deciding to save yourself for me…how was your evening?'

'Oh, did I save myself for you? I had no idea. My evening, such as it was, was full of surprises. I'm just trying to ascertain whether you knew about all of them, or just some of them.'

She was pacing the room, which consisted of ten strides in one direction, turn, and ten in the opposite. If she were careful, she could keep from brushing against the arm of the wider chair.

Sebastian watched her for a moment, then, with an insouciant grin, selected the narrower seat and sank into it in a blatant show of rudeness whilst she remained pacing. 'I can think of other, more pleasant ways to blow off steam,' he commented. 'If you come over here.'

She stopped pacing. 'Unfortunately for you, that is the last thing I'd like to do right now. Did you know that George Starcasset would be there tonight?' She stood to the side of his chair looking down at him. His shirt gaped open in a long, narrow vee, and she could even see the sprinkling of golden and bronze hair peeking through. The intimate view made her stomach tingle in that special way, and she had to think about looking away before she did.

Right into his hot amber eyes.

'Come here, Victoria,' he said, and reached out to tug her into the chair. 'This has gone on long enough; and I can tell you are in no mood for prevaricating, even if you don't realise it.'

She fell – let herself fall, to be truthful – across the hard edge of the chair, sprawling across his lap. One arm curled around the other side of the chair, finding a grip on the edge of the back, and her hip jutted into the side over which she'd tipped. Her other hand found its own place to hold on just behind Sebastian's ear...but she wasn't thinking about the smooth wood under her fingers, nor the shiny but worn brocade upholstery.

No, she was kissing Sebastian with the same fervour she'd seen in his eyes moments before she closed her own.

The twinge in her belly sparked sharply and shot low as he released the arm he'd yanked and slid the cup of his thumb and forefinger up under each breast. She arched into his hands and adjusted herself on his lap so that she sat on one hip, legs bent. She could feel the rhythm of his thumbs over her nipples sending shivers through the thin material of her gown, and the warmth of his chest, textured with hair, under her hands.

Victoria pulled his shirt apart, opening it so she could see those broad, golden shoulders. He liked the feel of her fingers spread over the hair on his chest: she could tell by the way he closed his eyes and let his head sink back against the chair. His skin tasted warm and a little salty, smelt like clove and rosemary and man, and she could even feel the pulse thumping in his neck beneath her lips.

When she would have brought her hands farther down, to pull up the rest of his shirt, he caught at them, opening his eyes with a lazy smile. 'What's the hurry, my dear? We've both waited a long time for this.' Grasping her shoulders, he pulled her forward for a long, slippery kiss, sliding his hands over the tiny sleeves at the uppermost part of her bodice and pulling them down.

With them went the front of her gown, and her breasts tipped out from her low corset, loose and warm and trembling.

A year ago Victoria would have been mortified at the thought of straddling a man in the parlour, her gown being pulled down to her waist as Sebastian worked the buttons at the back. But she was not an innocent, and neither was Sebastian a proper gentleman.

And he'd been right: she was in no mood to feign disinterest. She needed something tonight – *something* after everything that had happened in the last weeks.

When he kissed one of her breasts it was a soft, gentle buss, so delicate that it was barely more than his breath; but it made her tighten up, and little bumps erupted, radiating from where he touched her. He did it again, gently nuzzling, and sent the same sensations coursing through her. Like a lazy wave, lapping gently, insistently, through her, unfurling warmth and liquid down where she straddled him, her gown caught and stretched under her knees.

Her head tipped back, and she steadied herself with hands on solid, square shoulders. They were warm and smooth and solid. He kissed her again, his mouth harder now, his lips wet and hot against her nipple. His breath spread wide over her breast as he breathed deeper and rougher, his fingers clamping her skin more closely now.

Victoria felt herself straining below; the warm burning between her legs where it pressed against him. She rocked a bit, he groaned, and she rocked again.

'And I always thought our first time would be in a carriage,' he murmured, working her gown and shift up from the hems so that they bunched around her waist, and skimming his fingers over the tops of her thighs under the bundle of silk, lace and linen.

Reaching behind her, he fitted his hands under her skirts and around the back of her hips, drawing her forward, closer, so that she fell against him in the chair. Her breasts pushed into his chest and he moved to touch the top of her head, tilting it to the side so he could kiss the long tendon that stretched from jaw to shoulder. Her vampire bites were long healed, but the sensitivity in her neck was still sharp; sharper than before she was bitten, and when he closed his mouth over the smooth skin, she felt everything focus there.

So different from the ugly, evil fangs that drew out her life force, yet frighteningly similar. Everything slowed as Sebastian nibbled and bit and licked, long and smooth, from ear to shoulder and back. Victoria was shaking, wanting to twist away from the intensity, yet wanting to push herself into him, wanting *more*. Her eyes had closed, her hands fallen from their grip on the chair; she was lost in the tailspin of pleasure.

Then he slipped his fingers down and beneath her

skirts again; they found their way through the slit in her drawers, where she was hot and pounding and wet. They brushed over her swollen flesh and she seized up, catching her breath at the opulence. How had she forgotten this? Pleasure surged from one of her centres to the other, from his lips and tongue to his fingers, stroking and sliding. His palm cupped her from the front, pressure built, and yet his rhythm did not waver.

She felt his breath faster against her breasts, heard it rasping in her ear as his mouth fell away from her skin.

Skilful, oh, his fingers were skilful…teasing her to the edge, then drawing aside to let her slip back; then back in, gently probing, slick and sure, until finally he let her go over.

Victoria caught herself before she cried aloud; some part of her remembered they were in the parlour, and she buried her face in his shoulder as the orgasm shuddered through her.

So long. It had been so long.

She was weak and lazy and alive. Her fingers shook along with her breath, and she realised his hands were moving at his own waist and she put her attention to helping him.

When she would have removed his shirt, he stopped her, pushing her hands to the bulge in his trousers, and murmured, 'No, here, if you please,' with a bit of strained, wry humour in his voice. 'Victoria.'

'This is an efficient way to distract me from my question,' she whispered into his ear, working to unfasten his breeches. When she slipped her hands inside, she found him hot and ready, heavy under her fingers.

'About George? You already suspect the answer.' His breathing was definitely off.

'You knew.'

'Let's not let George come between us,' he murmured coaxingly.

'How about Max?' she asked.

'Max too?' His fingers stilled. 'So that is what this is about.'

'What?' It took a moment, but the haziness of desire spiralled away when she saw the serious look on his face.

'Your easy capitulation. Did you talk to him?' He kept his fingers closed around the stays caging her ribs, just below her breasts, but they were still, and his mouth distant and thin.

'He's getting married to Regalado's daughter. Don't tell me you didn't know that.'

'I didn't.' Sebastian looked at her, his expression dark as he slipped his palms up under her breasts again. 'I understand now, and it is fortunate that I have no qualms about seizing an opportunity that falls in my lap. Literally.' His smile had an unfamiliar edge to it.

With a sudden movement he pulled her back to

him for a hot, rough kiss that brought more out of her than he'd taken before. Her breath hitched and she kissed him back, caught up in the emotion, renewed desire pulling down through her belly. His hands were more insistent on her breasts…

And then something changed.

He slowed, caught back his breathing, gentled his kiss, let his warm hands settle at her waist. 'Apparently I am not the opportunist I thought I was,' he said ruefully, shifting and setting her off his lap.

Victoria stood there, suddenly chilled, her gown at her waist, her shift bunched up underneath her skirts, her breasts jiggling with the movement of her breath and his sudden release.

Sebastian rose, then, his billowing shirt brushing against her torso. He looked down at her as he refastened his trousers. 'I can't decide if it's because you expect him to walk in on us at any moment, or because you're angry at him. Or both. Likely both.'

The last vestiges of arousal fell away. 'You are addled!' She yanked up her bodice to cover her breasts.

'Most likely I am,' he replied, tucking his shirt in. 'But I'd rather be addled than be manipulated.'

'Thank you for your assistance with the Tutela,' she said frostily. 'I hope that you'll remember tonight with fondness, for there won't be a repetition of it anytime soon.'

His lips twitched to one side as he grabbed up his

coat, gloves and cravat. 'You are so very predictable, Victoria, donning the spurned-woman facade.'

'Spurned woman?' She laughed in real delight. 'I would say not. You left me with little to regret, and I wager *I'll* sleep better tonight than you.' She raised a brow and looked at him meaningfully.

'If you keep that up, I'll be happy to rectify the situation.' He turned to go, his hand on the parlour door, and slanted her a last look. 'Or I'll call on the Tarruscelli twins.'

Victoria regretted telling Sebastian about Max's appearance at the Regalado villa, not so much because of the way it inexplicably ended their intimacy, but because she still cringed inside when she thought about what it could mean.

She wanted to keep that information to herself so she could turn it over in her mind and somehow make sense of it. She felt as if once she told Aunt Eustacia, or anyone, it would be too late to take it back; it would be real. And it would worry her aunt needlessly, for Victoria just did not believe Max had turned from the Venators.

And she also believed – *knew*, deep inside – that Max would seek her out. If he was playing a role, which was what she *had* to believe, despite all evidence to the contrary, he wouldn't take any chance of their being overheard or seen. They could have been noticed in the hall beyond the ballroom; he was being overly discreet…which was nothing less than what she'd expect of Max.

Even though he infuriated her, Max didn't make mistakes. He was deliberate and careful and very, very dangerous.

As for Sebastian's odd accusations…Victoria put those off to the fact that she could never understand what made Sebastian tick at any time, let alone when he was in the throes of passion. There was no love lost between the two men for reasons she did not know, but which appeared to be part of a long history. Apparently the mere mention of Max's name was a douse of cold water to Sebastian.

So certain was Victoria that Max would call on her or send some kind of message now that he knew she was in Rome, she remained in the villa for the next two days, refusing even to leave to visit Aunt Eustacia at the Gardella villa. She didn't want to miss him if he came.

She did not explain to her great-aunt that she'd seen Max. Not yet. She wanted to make sure…she wanted to wait until they could speak again in private.

But he did not contact her.

She did, however, have to greet George Starcasset when he called on her the day after the party, bearing flowers and a glitter in his eyes. They sat and took tea in the cramped parlour, chatting inanely about London Society and their friends back home. It was thirty minutes before she could get rid of him.

The following day, when he called, she was 'not at home'.

The third morning after the party at the Regalado villa, the Tarruscelli sisters brought Sara Regalado to call on Victoria.

'We were certain you'd fallen ill,' gushed Portiera. 'We'd hoped you'd come to tea yesterday and were so disappointed when you did not attend.'

'We missed you so very much at tea yesterday, we were quite convinced that you'd been stricken with some ache in the head or some other illness,' said Placidia in her sister's wake.

'I was feeling rather under the weather,' Victoria admitted, watching as Oliver and Verbena attempted to arrange the minuscule parlour for three guests plus their mistress. 'I had such a lovely time at your father's party, too, Sara.'

'I hope you are feeling quite the object today,' Max's fiancée said in her imperfect English.

'I am feeling much more the thing, thank you very much.' In truth, she was feeling worse every hour that went by that she hadn't heard from Max.

Unless…perhaps Sara was unwittingly to deliver the message.

Indeed, it seemed possible, when the young woman continued and said, 'We were hoping you would join us in our box at the opera tomorrow evening. We four will be escorted by my father and Maximilian, as well as Barone Galliani, on whom you seem to have made quite an impression.' She smiled without a bit of malice and continued, 'My cousin appeared to be so smitten with you that he has threatened to change the name of the rose he created for me!'

'I'm certain your fiancé was overjoyed,' Victoria could not resist saying.

Sara looked at her quizzically. 'Maximilian? Why, he has not a jealous bone in his body; he could not care if Silvio named twenty flowers after me. And if he should change the name for someone as lovely as you, my new dear friend, well, I should not be *adirato* at all. For I have my Maximilian to name flowers after me himself.'

Victoria had to turn an unladylike snort into a fit of coughing. The vision of Max tending to a rosebush, let alone naming it for a chit of a girl, was ludicrous.

When her coughing subsided, amidst a flurry of 'oohs' and 'ohs!' (from the Tarruscelli twins, their mirror-image moles twitching accordingly) and clapping on the back (from the dainty Sara, who wielded quite a lusty clap), Victoria smiled through watery eyes and accepted the invitation. If nothing else, it would give her another opportunity to see Max and scrutinise what he was up to.

No sooner had her visitors left than Victoria, who had planned to steal away for some training practice, was called back to the parlour.

Aunt Eustacia had arrived.

Victoria kissed her aunt's soft, wrinkled cheek

and settled her on the most comfortable chair in the sitting room. She was looking more fragile, she noticed; as though all of the travelling had taken a toll on her. It was odd, for Victoria had expected that returning to her homeland after so many years away from it would have brought a sparkle to her eyes. Instead, they bore a hint of sadness and worry.

'Have you news?' her aunt asked without preamble.

'Sebastian assisted me to attend an event at one of the Tutela leaders' homes,' she replied, and explained about Regalado. 'I am to attend the opera with him and his daughter and some others tomorrow night. I hope that will give me the opportunity to find out more about the Tutela. I have not been out to hunt for vampires since we arrived in Rome; I was planning to practise my training just now, and go out on a patrol tonight. I know it is important to stay ready and sharp. And I miss it.'

Eustacia was looking at her with steely black eyes, as though she knew Victoria was equivocating. 'You learnt nothing at the villa when you were there?'

Victoria hesitated. 'George Starcasset was there, whom I did not expect.' Her aunt's eyes sharpened with interest. Victoria drew in a deep breath. 'And Max was there.'

'Max? *Grazie a Dio!* Did you speak to him?'

She nodded. 'He is apparently engaged to marry Regalado's daughter. He made no mention of the

Tutela or of anything related to the Venators. I have been expecting him to contact me, but he has not. I…don't know what to think.'

'What did he say to you, exactly?'

Victoria repeated their brief conversations and watched her aunt's expression. It remained neutral, even as she replied, 'I would never believe Max has forsaken us. He must be involved in something.'

'Of course – he's involved with Sara Regalado. He's in love.' Victoria was beginning to wonder if it might actually be true. 'He has no time for us anymore. He's been too busy even to let you know he is alive.'

Aunt Eustacia slanted her a narrow glance. 'I cannot tell you the number of times I had a similar conversation with him last year when you were intent upon marrying Phillip, *cara*. I told him then as I tell you now: we must trust that he will manage all of his obligations. There is no stricture that says a Venator can't marry.'

'But I did not forsake my duty!'

'And you do not know that Max has either, Victoria. For all you know, he's been hunting vampires every night, and finding a way into the Tutela at the same time. Perhaps you will have an opportunity to speak with him tomorrow night at the opera. It is very promising that you have made friends with Regalado's daughter.'

'Indeed. And with or without Max, I intend to do what I can to find out more about Conte Regalado and his Tutela. His wife died many years ago, and he is not married. And,' Victoria added, recalling the nipples in his painting, 'he seems to appreciate women. Perhaps I shall flirt outrageously with him.'

Aunt Eustacia nodded. 'Very good, *cara*. I know you shall take care, and I hope that you will have some news to report shortly.' She sighed. 'I am filled with worry, and Wayren, who has been here in Roma since she left London, shares my concern. Nedas has the obelisk, and it is only a matter of time until he has control of its power. We do not know when or where, although Wayren is studying her books and scrolls to see if she can find any prophecy or description of how or where. At this time, you are the only one we can rely on to find out. The other Venators here in Roma, and even in Italia, are too well-known and would be recognised immediately by the Tutela. Your advantage is that you are a woman, and you are not well-known. When they speak of the woman Venator, they think of me and only me.'

'Unless they realised I was a Venator during the events in Venice,' Victoria reminded her.

'It is possible, but not probable. You killed the only vampire that named you thus, and the rest of them would not have lived to see you fight so well or so strongly. We must use this advantage as long as we can. *Vero*, they know that my niece is a Venator, but they do not know who you are and what you look like, or that you are here in Rome. So it is important that you are not seen with me, and that you are not observed fighting a vampire anywhere. For any reason.' She looked at her fiercely. 'Do you understand?'

'I could not stand by and watch a vampire maul another person,' Victoria replied, thinking of the events in Venice. 'It is not in my nature.'

'You must. You must act like any other female should you come face-to-face with one.'

'Aunt Eustacia—'

'Victoria, you will obey me in this. There are some times when an individual sacrifice must be made to protect the greater good. I know.' Her eyes saddened. 'I know this, Victoria, for I have seen it happen. You must learn to think about the larger event instead of the singular moment in which you breathe.'

Victoria pressed her lips together, but nodded. She didn't know if she could stand by and let the worst happen, but she would try if the circumstances called for it.

'We must find a way to stop Nedas. The more information you can obtain, the better we can plan for such an event. Perhaps we will have to find a way to steal the obelisk, if he has already begun to activate it.'

Aunt Eustacia shook her head. 'I will leave you now to your training. I will contact you the morning after the opera; there is no need for you to send for me. I know better how to move with subterfuge here in Roma. And do not worry about Max. All will be fine.'

But Victoria did not believe her. She had seen the change as they talked, how the lines had deepened in her face, and the way her eyes had become shadowed, and she knew Aunt Eustacia didn't even believe herself.

Chapter Seventeen

In Which Maximilian Considers Gardening

'It has happened before, Eustacia,' Wayren told her. 'Much to my dismay, I will confirm it. We have lost Venators to the lure of the vampire. As there have been in every battle throughout history, there have been traitors to us as well.'

'That may be, but Max? After what he's done? No. There is some other explanation.'

Wayren looked as remote as Eustacia felt numb. 'I wouldn't believe it either…but recall his history. And that he still fights Lilith's thrall; that her bites still burn on him. It is a horrible battle for him that can arise and weaken him unexpectedly.'

'He has learnt to distance himself from it. At times.'

'I know it. He is a fiercely strong man. But I fear that if any Venator could be turned to the Tutela, he would be a likely candidate, if only because of his ties to Lilith, as horrific and unwelcome as they are. Since she bit him the first time years ago, those bites have not healed, and she tries to exert her control over him. Last year when she fed on him again, it just strengthened those ties. So far he has been able to resist, but anything can happen. There are no absolutes.' Despite her grave pronouncements, she looked serene and ethereal, as she always did – as she had from the day Eustacia had met her nearly sixty years ago.

She had no idea how old Wayren was; nor was it important to know. She just knew that somehow, Wayren was always there when she needed her. She was the wisest person she'd ever met, and she never lied. In spite of what she'd just said, *that* was an absolute.

Wayren had seen so much over the years; perhaps nothing was shocking to her.

'It is possible he will seek you out now that he knows Victoria is in Rome. There may be a reason he won't speak with her.' Her pale blond hair, which framed her face with four braids as narrow as a child's finger, fell down over her shoulders and into her lap. The braids were tied with delicate gold chains, and from each one hung a pearl the size of a pea.

Eustacia nodded, feeling old and inelegant. 'That is possible. Have you found anything else that might be of help to us? And do you know where Lilith is?'

Wayren fumbled in her ever-present leather satchel and pulled out a sheaf of curling papers. Placing in their position the square spectacles she always wore when reading, she began to flip through the pages.

Eustacia couldn't help a smile. If she thought age had warped her memory, she had nothing on Wayren, who'd been around much longer and who relied heavily on her notes and journals and memoranda written to herself during research sessions.

'I do not believe Lilith is directly involved in this plot with Nedas; at least, if she is, she is not here in Italy. She is still hidden away deep in the mountains of Romania, with an entire city of vampires. I am certain she must be aware that Nedas has found Akvan's Obelisk and intends to activate it. He is her son, after all. They have ways of communicating, just as we do.' Her rueful smile revealed three little creases near her chin. 'From what I have gleaned since I arrived, Beauregard and his vampires were prepared to overthrow Nedas here in Italy, but once it became known that Lilith's son had the obelisk, Beauregard was forced to back down. I can only imagine he is waiting to see what occurs before declaring his loyalty – or attempting to usurp him.'

'Beauregard is smarter and has more experience, but Nedas is Lilith's son. *Dio mio*, we cannot let *either* of them have it. Wayren, if we do not stop it, it could be another scene like Praga.'

'I pray it is not. Twenty thousand people massacred by the vampires and Tutela…here in Rome. They will surely target the Papal states, as well as our Consilium and as many mortals as possible. It would be devastating.' Wayren looked at her, and Eustacia saw understanding in her eyes. 'You are thinking of Rosamund's prophecy, aren't you? The…hmph.' She bent to dig in her satchel again, drawing out five large books of various sizes, shapes and conditions that could not possibly have fit in the bag but somehow had.

'*The golden age of the Venator shall end at the foot of Roma.*' Eustacia quoted the words she'd never forgotten. A short phrase, one of many she'd read over the years, studied, perused…but none had stayed with her, resonated with her, as this one had.

Colourless blue-grey eyes, framed by square lenses, met sharp black ones. 'It could mean anything, Eustacia.'

'It could. But I fear this could be our last battle. Rosamund was graced with many gifts, the least of which was her mystical writings.' She clasped her hands together in the raven-like gown she favoured for her age. 'Our only hope is to stop Nedas from activating Akvan's Obelisk, or, barring that, to somehow steal it.'

'The only thing we know for certain is that he has not completely harnessed its power yet. He is waiting for something – for the right time, or for some other thing he needs – or else he would have done it by now.'

'I shall have to join Victoria; she cannot do it alone.'

Wayren fixed her with eyes that had changed from pale moonstone to brilliant, stirring sapphire in a blink. 'The moment the connection is made between you and Victoria, any chance we have will be over. The precise second you step into any gathering of the Tutela, or the presence of Nedas, it will be done. You are a legend.'

'You think I am too old to fight?' It stung, hearing it come from Wayren. Even though she knew it was true.

'A Venator is never too old to fight. But there are better uses for you and your experience than to have your presence announce our intentions. Eustacia, I love you. But this is something that Victoria will have to do alone.'

'Alone? How on earth… No, I'll call together the Consilium. And perhaps Vioget can be persuaded to assist. He will have to choose sides at one point or another.'

'Perhaps he will. Perhaps he won't. I do not place much faith in him.'

Neither of them mentioned Max.

The opera house was no different from the theatres Victoria had visited in London: opulent and ornate and crowded with members of high society dressed in their finest, more interested in seeing and being seen than actually watching the opera.

A carriage with the Tarruscelli twins and Barone

Galliani had called for her, and she had been seated next to the *barone*, much to his obvious pleasure. He'd greeted her immediately with apologies for not calling on her before now, and said that he understood she'd been ill.

During the ride, Victoria allowed him to be as attentive as he liked, and more than once caught the speculative glances from Portiera and Placidia. She smiled demurely as he made a great show of taking her arm and the arm of one of the twins – she didn't see which one – and led them through the opera's hall to the Regalado box.

Inside the small, shadowy room, which hung just to the left of the stage at approximately the height of two men, and close enough that Sara would be able to see the detail of every costume's button, Conte Regalado and his daughter were waiting.

'How kind of you to join us,' Conte Regalado said with a smile that reminded Victoria of molasses. He bowed, took each of the twins' gloved hands in turn, and kissed them. Then he turned to her and bowed again, took her hand in the same manner, but did not release it after the kiss. 'Mrs Withers, I am particularly pleased that you accepted my daughter's invitation tonight. We did not have enough of a chance to speak at my art showing, to my dismay.'

'Conte Regalado.' Victoria made a curtsy even as he held her hand as though he were not about to allow her to have it back. 'I cannot tell you how lovely it has been to be so welcomed here in Rome by you and your family and friends. And I did not have the opportunity to tell you how fascinating I found your painting.' Fascinating was definitely one way to describe a man who painted his daughter's nipples.

'I am hoping that I might persuade you to sit for me someday. I believe you would make a lovely Diana.'

The huntress. How appropriate. 'I would be most flattered to oblige at your request,' Victoria replied, wondering if his image of Diana included the same filmy gowns as did his Fates.

'Emmaline!' Sara had greeted the twins and now pushed her way between her father and Victoria in order to greet her. 'You must sit near me so that we can talk. *Padre*, excuse us, please.'

'Good evening…Mrs Twitters, is it?' Max's deep voice startled Victoria. He'd been standing to the side, in the shadows, where he wasn't easily noticed. She was sure he'd done it purposely just for the effect.

'Max, do stop teasing. You are *stupido*. Of course you remember her name. This is Mrs Withers; surely you recall meeting her at Papa's showing?'

'Of course I do.' But he sounded baldly uncertain and Victoria wanted to slap that indolent smile off his face. But then, when she looked up at him and their gazes met, she was so shocked by the animosity in his eyes that she nearly stepped back.

Victoria turned to Sara and asked brightly, 'Did you ask your fiancé about a rose?'

'Oh, no, I had forgotten.' Sara turned to Max, gripping his arm, and looked up at him with an ingenuous smile. 'Silvio, *il malfattore*' – she giggled at this point, taking any sting out of the insult for her cousin – 'has decided to change the name of my rose to call it after Emmaline, and so she suggested that you might be willing to grow one of your own for me. And I told her I was certain that you would concur.' Victoria watched in fascination as she actually batted her eyelashes.

Max raised his eyebrows and looked at Victoria. 'Is that so?'

'Well, actually, that was not exactly how it occurred, but' – she tipped her head to one side as though considering his fitness – 'I do see that being surrounded by flowers and digging in the dirt might suit you very well.'

It was so quick Victoria wasn't certain she'd seen it, but she would have sworn there was a flash of humour or admiration, or *something* that relieved the harshness there, *something* of the old Max…but then it was so brief that she might have been mistaken, for that awful arrogant and cold look was back. 'I see. Well, *adorate mio*, for you, I shall consider it.'

At that moment the box door opened again and in walked Sebastian. 'I am terribly sorry for being late,' he said, his gaze scanning the small room.

He looked delicious – his thick lion's-mane hair combed neatly off his forehead and curling about the nape of his neck and his ears. His jacket was rich topaz and his breeches were dark rust, his cravat a masculine design of carrot, persimmon, and gold; and the entire ensemble, as always, was cut and tailored to perfection. And his smile, the way his upper lip shadowed his lower one and the hint of a quirk at one corner…

Victoria felt the heat rush from her bosom up over her throat and to her cheeks in one great wave. She hadn't seen him, nor heard from him, since their erotic interlude the night of the party. And all she could think of was where his hands had been and what his fingers had done.

And what still remained unfinished between them.

'Mrs Withers, are you feeling quite the thing? You appear to be rather…red.' Somehow Max had come up behind her, and when he spoke in her ear she nearly jumped. Again. 'It is rather disconcerting when people show up where they shouldn't be, and *are not welcome*, is it not?'

Victoria swallowed and turned her head enough to see how close his silky blue-and-grey neck-cloth was. It was nearly brushing her shoulder. 'I have no idea what you mean,' was all she could think of to say.

Just at that moment she turned back and found the man in question in front of her. 'Mrs Withers, how delightful to see you again.' There were so many nuances in Sebastian's tone, Victoria was not sure whether to blush or to slap him.

'It is indeed,' she replied with a curtsy, and allowed him to kiss her gloved hand. But when he released it and pulled his hand away, her glove came with it, dangling like an unstarched cravat.

'Oh, dear,' Sebastian said, looking at it. 'You do have a penchant for losing your gloves, do you not?'

Of course, he was reminding her of the time he'd taken another of her gloves, in nearly the same manner. The one she'd never got back. 'I already have one pair of unmatched gloves,' she replied lightly. 'I do hope you won't cause me to have another.'

'But then you can put your single glove together with this one, and you will have a complete pair. And then…well, perhaps I will find a mate for this one too.' And he stuffed it in his pocket. 'Good evening to you, Maximilian.'

'Sebastian.' Max's nod was cool and sparse, and he drifted away.

Victoria could say nothing else about her glove without drawing attention, so she had to be content with directing a glare at Sebastian and removing her other glove, which, fortunately, wasn't as much of a crime as it would have been in London. Italians were a bit less rigid about such proprieties than the English.

Sebastian looked at her with a mild expression, then turned to speak to the Tarruscelli twins, who had been thrilled, as evidenced by their clapping hands and genteel squeals, with his arrival.

It did occur to her to wonder, just for a moment, if Sebastian had followed through on his threat to call upon Poitiera and Fiacidia after their unsatisfactory tête-à-tête in the parlour.

As Victoria cast a covert look at him, flanked by the two dark-haired beauties and their beside-the-mouth moles, she realised she didn't like that idea at all. In fact, it made her rather queasy.

And annoyed.

In fact, she was annoyed enough to consider the age-old female retaliation of using her nails to scratch their pretty eyes out. Of course, being a Venator, she would probably gouge more than scratch, and it would be a bit messier than normal...

'Mrs Withers, are you quite certain you are feeling all right? Perhaps you ought to return home; you've not recovered from your illness, I see. That sort of discomfort often happens to people when they thrust themselves into a situation they should not.' Max had returned. He was looking down at her with that bland expression, and she realised that the others were preparing to take their seats.

She was saved from the indignity of having no quick retort – things had just been going so upside down that her wit had disappeared – by Conte Regalado's approach. 'Mrs Withers, may I seat you?' he asked, slipping her arm into the fold of his elbow.

'I would be delighted,' she cast over her shoulder as they walked away. Not her best rejoinder, but at least she'd had the last word.

But when Conte Regalado seated her in the front row of the box and took a seat beside her, she felt Max and Sara sit down behind them, and she heard Max's innocent question: 'And when is your friend returning to London, my dear? I am sure it cannot be too soon.'

Galliani took a seat next to Victoria with a little bow, and had one of the Tarruscelli twins on his arm – Portiera, she could tell by the cornflower blue gown. She always wore the darker colours. And behind them sat Sebastian with Placidia, in sky blue.

Thus Victoria was, in effect, surrounded by an array of men: an insufferably rude one, a father who painted his daughter's breasts in detail and who cultivated the company of vampires, a *barone* who grew roses, and a man who'd made her shiver and tremble with passion only days before and now sat flirting with another woman.

Conte Regalado claimed her attention, reminding her of her plan to flirt with him in hopes of learning more about the Tutela. 'The opera is ready to start,' he said. He smelt like wine and lavender. 'I hope you enjoy it.'

The opera was long. The box became warm. And Victoria became squirmy. She wondered why she had decided to come after all. It had mainly been so that she would see Max again, and hope to have an opportunity to speak with him, but that was obviously not going to come to pass.

At the end of the first act she heard movement behind her, and glanced back to see Sebastian leading Placidia from the box, his head bent solicitously to her face as they left the stifling room. Unfortunately it wasn't a formal intermission, or Victoria would have been able to go with them. As it was, it would seem odd for her to insist on joining them.

If she'd known Sebastian would be there, she might have stayed home, just to avoid the awkwardness.

No, on the other hand, she would have come regardless, for she hadn't stopped thinking about him and his sensual mouth and talented fingers, and the fact that it really was a shame that he'd gone all cold and proper on her. And had chosen to sit beside one of the twins. And escort her out.

Then, suddenly, her mind sharpened, pinpointed, and she realised that the back of her neck was cool. The hairs were rising as though a chill breeze was brushing over them. Vampires. Somewhere nearby. One, perhaps two.

Victoria held her breath, keeping her attention focused on the stage. Thinking. She had to do something.

Despite the fact that Aunt Eustacia had impressed upon her the importance of not giving away the fact that she was a Venator, Victoria had not been allowed – by Verbena – to leave the villa without one stake, slipped into a garter under her gown.

It was the beginning of the second act; the curtain had just risen. The single intermission wouldn't be until the end of this act, which could be an hour away. She couldn't wait that long.

The sensation grew stronger.

Max would feel it too.

She shifted in her seat, trying to figure out a way to make eye contact with him where he sat directly behind her, and bumped Galliani's arm.

'Are you uncomfortable?' he murmured, leaning towards her. 'Would you like to get some air?'

Thank you. She nodded and replied, 'That would be wonderful.' She could somehow slip away from Galliani once out of the box and see what was happening.

Victoria started to rise and could not. Something was holding her gown in place. From behind. Low on the seat.

Conte Regalado was looking at her now. 'Is something the matter, Mrs Withers?' he asked, placing a heavy hand on her arm.

'I just…felt the need for some air. It is so stifling in here. Lord Galliani has been so good as to agree to escort me.' She tried to rise again and found that she could not.

Galliani was waiting, looking at her expectantly.

Her neck was colder; the prickles had begun to rise

along the back of her shoulders, telling her that the vampire was drawing nearer.

The diva onstage below sang on, her voice clear and true, her pudgy hands glittering with rings and bracelets.

Victoria had to resist the very strong urge to turn to Max and command him to release her gown. She wanted to, but something held her back – besides his grip.

He was stopping her for a reason.

Aunt Eustacia had warned her she could not reveal that she was a Venator, even if danger approached. She would have to let the threat pass by, let it play itself out.

But how could she?

Galliani nudged her gently. 'Mrs Withers? Have you changed your mind?'

'I am feeling better now,' she replied reluctantly, making the decision to follow Aunt Eustacia's direction. Her stomach felt odd, as though some thick and heavy liquid sloshed inside it.

What if the vampires attacked and killed some of the patrons, and she did nothing? Could she sit here and let it happen? Did she have that kind of resolve?

The chill deepened and Victoria fisted her fingers into her skirts, crinkling the light silk and staring straight down at the stage, seeing nothing, hearing nothing, aware of nothing but the growing cold at the back of her neck.

And then the door of the box opened.

Two men came in.

Their eyes were not red, their fangs were not extended, but Victoria knew they were vampires.

Chapter Eighteen

A Most Welcome Interruption

The vampires looked like any other gentlemen, dressed for the opera in dark coats with tan or fawn-coloured breeches, adequately knotted cravats, and gloves. 'Our apologies for being tardy,' one of them said with a bow to Conte Regalado, who had risen to greet the men.

Not men, vampires.

Victoria remained in her seat, turned away from the opera, watching and waiting. Her nerves tingled, and the nape of her neck prickled. Her fingers itched to pull the stake out from under her gown.

There was a sense of expectation in the air, and she did not know where to look. Max studiously refused to turn in her direction as he stood and greeted the newcomers; Regalado and Galliani seemed pleased to welcome the new arrivals.

What did this all mean? Did Regalado know they were vampires? Surely a powerful member of the Tutela would.

'Mrs Withers, may I present an acquaintance of mine to you…Signore Partredi.'

The vampire bowed, took her hand with his surprisingly warm one, and raised it to his lips. 'A pleasure to meet you, I'm certain.' Being familiar with vampires, as she was, she read an entirely different message in his eyes. And it wasn't pleasant at all.

To her dismay, he took the seat next to her that had been vacated by Galliani. Regalado sat back down in his seat, and there she was, sandwiched between a vampire and a Tutela leader. When the second vampire chose the seat behind her, where Max had been sitting, she felt even more boxed in. Surrounded on all sides by danger. And she could do nothing.

Victoria was uncertain where Max was, and of course Sebastian was still gone with Placidia. She dared not turn around to look about the room. She must appear as though nothing were out of the norm.

As the opera dragged on, with one aria after another, she reflected on that terrible night at the Tutela meeting; remembered the horror of being controlled, of being attacked from every side, of the warm surge of her blood under the teeth of the vampires. Her head felt lighter, easier…her pulse slowed; she had to blink to focus. The small box became stifling and warm.

Victoria closed her fists, digging nails into her palms, using pain to send away the gentle lull she'd begun to feel. Sitting next to a vampire, feeling the sleeve of his jacket brush against her bare arm, allowing his presence to sink into her consciousness... it was a different way of becoming enthralled. Not a common one, for most often when she was faced with a vampire, the moment was all action, movement, battle.

This was a different sort of battle. One of wills.

Thus far, truly, it had been easy. The vampires had made no threats, no move to hurt anyone. She could sit and focus her energy on fighting off the subtle attempts to capture her consciousness, pretend to watch the opera, and perhaps, just perhaps, that would be the end of it.

But it was during a rare, brief moment of silence from the stage that Victoria's hopes deflated. A soft gasp and sigh caught her ears, and she felt the hair along her arms lift, sending a surge of sharp prickles over her abdomen.

She turned in her chair. Behind her, the vampire who'd taken Max's seat had also taken his place at Sara's side. When Victoria looked, the truth of what was happening struck all of her senses at one moment: the smell of fresh blood, the faint, very faint whistle of suction, the dull glow of Sara's white neck and half-exposed bosom with her blood trickling down it, and the renewed rush of sensation over Victoria's own body.

She looked away, her eyes skittering from the scene that appeared more sensual than horrific, and clashed with Max's gaze. He stood near the door at the back of the box in a pose that struck her as being imminently dispassionate. When their gazes met, she looked for something there, some signal or sign…but he merely raised his brows in that sardonic manner of his and casually shifted his glance.

Apparently it was of no concern to him that his fiancée was being attacked by a vampire.

On the other side of the vampire Partredi, Portiera was watching the performance, seemingly unaware of what was going on behind her.

Victoria shifted in her seat and returned her attention to the opera. Her heart was pounding. She made herself think through everything that was happening, even though every instinct in her body urged her to grab for the stake and plant it in the chest of the being that stole from Sara.

But Sara wasn't fighting. She was not restrained. She made no sounds, other than soft sighs and gasps that sounded as though she were responding to a lover rather than an attacker. She did not need Victoria's help. She was not being mauled or torn apart. A vampire could feed without permanently injuring a person, as Victoria well knew.

She could leave it alone. In good conscience, she still did not have to act.

Licking her lips, she tried to watch the opera, tried not to listen to the sounds behind her. Tried not to feel the pull, the incessant pull, of the one next to her.

She knew the moment the vampire behind her finished feeding and braced herself for what might happen next.

Partredi placed his hand on her wrist, holding it on the seat's arm. Victoria's breath caught. She was strong; she could pull away…but should she?

Then on the other side of her, Regalado closed his fingers over her other wrist. 'Now, just relax, my dear,' he murmured into her ear. 'You might find it as enjoyable as my daughter has.'

Her heart rammed in her chest. Victoria felt her breath catch as something happened in front of her to obliterate the stage below…someone was pulling the box curtains closed.

Max.

She stiffened in her seat, unable to move, her pulse increasing and her breath shortening. The vampire next to her moved, showing her his red eyes, and she found herself weakening as she was caught in them.

Deep breaths. Close your eyes.

She tried to, but found it impossible to break the connection there. She tried to pry her wrist away from the vampire, from Regalado, but somehow they held them down. Her strength was weakening, but she was still a Venator. She could fight.

But she had to let this happen. She had to listen to Aunt Eustacia. If she fought, her powerful strength and fighting skills would surely give her away. She'd been bitten before; it would heal quickly.

Max was here. Surely…surely he wouldn't let them really hurt her.

Something grasped her head from behind, fingers plunging into the twisted coiffure near the top of her head, pulling it back, jerking her head to one side. The other vampire's blood-scented breath wafted over her tilted face.

Her neck was bare, and she felt Partredi move towards her, shifting in the seat next to hers, his knee bumping her leg. He leant against her imprisoned arm and brought his gleaming fangs towards her vulnerable throat.

Her pulse thumped harder; she tried to twist away, somehow remaining silent – purposely or not, she did not know.

Now her eyes sank closed. The smooth teeth whispered against her skin. She couldn't control the urge to fight any longer; she strained up, trying to pull free, and found that she could not. The sounds of the orchestra, the rustles in the room, all faded away, until she could hear only the breathing of the vampire as it matched her own. His pulse as it beat with hers.

Her head was held rigid, her arms, her legs, all held fast by unrelenting fingers.

His breath was cold on her skin, icing her throat along with the back of her neck. He sighed and pricked her with his fangs.

'Stop.' Somehow the single syllable penetrated her fog.

There was a pause, a hitch in the vampire's movement…then suddenly she was released; the thrall was broken. The weight came off her. She could breathe. Focus.

'This one is mine,' the voice continued.

She recognised the voice, the face, as it came into her view. Sebastian had returned.

The vampires had released her on his command?

He appeared calm and utterly in control, but the vampires looked abashed as they moved away from her. 'Vioget! We did not know,' said Partredi.

Regalado had stood up. 'What? What is going on?'

'She is not for your use,' Sebastian told him coldly. 'They will not touch her. She is mine.'

Regalado's dark eyes were furious. 'You have no authority here!'

Sebastian lifted one brow. 'If that is the case, then why do they back away on my command? You do not wish to anger me, Regalado. The Tutela does not wish to displease Beauregard. Or do they?'

'*Beauregard?*' Regalado stepped back. 'How do you—'

'Begone,' Sebastian told the vampires, ignoring Regalado's stammered question as though it were that of a two-year-old.

The vampires bowed to him as they left and, absurdly, Victoria noticed that someone – Max? – had reopened the curtains in the box. The orchestra continued to play; the chorus continued to sing.

She did not know what to think. Where to look. Whom to look at.

How to feel about being called *mine* by Sebastian.

Of course, that was probably just for effect. But it still echoed in her mind, along with the fact that she'd been bitten yet again. Fortunately, it was a shallow bite; hardly worth noticing. A short trickle of blood curved along her neck.

Victoria surreptitiously opened the small vial of holy water in her reticule and dampened her handkerchief with it. Then she took stock of the other occupants of the room as she pressed it to her wound, hardly feeling the salted holy water.

Sara sat in her seat, eyes glazed, holding a white scarf to her neck. She didn't seem to notice Victoria, or if she did, she didn't care.

Galliani and Max stood near the back of the box, half-shadowed. Regalado stared at Sebastian, but made no further comment. He sat in his seat, looking less like a vampire protector than a sulking child whose game had been cut short. Placidia stood behind Sebastian, as though they had just come into the room and he'd stepped in front of her. Portiera was next to her twin.

Victoria looked at Sebastian, who gave her a look that told her he couldn't wait for her to ask him the questions he knew were going through her mind, because he wasn't going to answer them.

She could only imagine what kind of compensation he would attempt to extract from her.

What else could she do? She sat back down in her seat to watch the rest of the opera, relieved that she'd come out of the situation with no one the wiser of her Venator status.

But as she sat in her seat, she realised belatedly that the chill at the back of her neck had not eased. Its persistence told her that the vampires were still nearby.

And, as if to confirm this, only moments later someone screamed. It was a horrible, terrified scream.

Victoria bolted to her feet. Fortunately she wasn't the only person in the box to respond in that manner, and Sebastian was right next to her, slipping his hand through her arm as though to steady her. Or hold her back.

There was another scream, perhaps a bit closer, from the passageway behind their box. A few shouts. The diva continued to sing. The orchestra continued to play. The cold at the back of Victoria's neck had not subsided.

'Who is it?' cried Portiera, clutching at Galliani. 'Someone's hurting her!'

'Someone is being hurt!' echoed Placidia, tugging at Sebastian's other arm.

With Portiera in tow, Galliani had opened the door of the box and was peering out. 'I see nothing!'

There was another scream, louder now that the door was open. Victoria tugged away from Sebastian, all thoughts of listening to Aunt Eustacia's warning suddenly evaporated. She moved around the seats, heading for the door, and was caught by Max's dark eyes. When she saw the grim expression on his face, she stopped.

As she grabbed at the back of the velvet-covered seat next to her, trying to decide what to do, she glanced at Conte Regalado. He was leaning against a side wall of the box, near the seats. Unconcerned. Watching her.

Victoria took a deep breath and closed her fingers tighter into the velvet cushion, anchoring herself there.

But she wavered. She needed to get out of this room. The vampires had been sent off by Sebastian – only to wreak havoc elsewhere.

The sounds of cries and running feet had grown; yet the opera continued. Perhaps they could not hear, so far away and over the sounds of the orchestra. But it was an odd sensation – from one side of the box was beautiful music; from the other were the sounds of terror and panic.

'Someone must do something!' Placidia cried. 'And I do not wish to stay here… What if it is a fire? Or bandits! I do not wish to be trapped!' Her voice rose in a spiral of nerves as she looked up at Sebastian. Apparently vampires were not a concern to her.

Victoria seized upon the opportunity and lifted the back of her hand to her forehead as she'd seen her mother do when complaining of vapours. 'I am feeling quite warm,' she said, adopting a whiny voice. 'Mr Vioget, I do think I will need your escort out of this small room. You will protect me, won't you?'

And before he could respond, she slid her arm around his other elbow and began to gently direct him towards the door. She heard the other women speaking, but Victoria and Sebastian, along with Placidia, were already out of the box and into the narrow passageway that led behind the lower theatre seats. Other doors were opening, people were coming out and looking around in fear and concern, and the hall was filling.

In the distance, Victoria heard the sounds of chaos – running feet, screams and yells, and loud noises that could be doors slamming or large items falling to the floor. As soon as they were out of sight of the opera box door, and the others behind them, Victoria pulled loose from Sebastian and started off down the hallway, slipping betwixt the other opera-goers.

She heard the shout behind her, but she didn't listen to him… She listened to the cold on her neck, the barometer that would tell her where the vampires were.

Down the hall, past the doors to the other boxes, towards the staircase that led down to the main entrance…or up to the higher box levels.

Victoria didn't remove her stake as she pushed

through the people. There were more than two vampires here, she realised, and she wondered what they were doing – if they were snatching people as they could, feeding on them and then releasing them, or if they were dragging them off as prisoners to feed on later.

Then she heard the shout: 'Fire!'

A wave of screams rolled through the narrow hall, and the people began to push and shove to get through.

'Fire!' echoed in her ears, up and down and throughout the theatre. The orchestra had stopped playing, and the only sound was that of cries and shouts.

People were leaving the building in droves, which was good. Outside they had a better chance of escaping a vampire attack simply due to the fact that they would scatter. But her neck was still cold, so the vampires were still about.

She hurried down one of the flights of stairs, listening to her instincts, hoping to find them somewhere. A faint smell of smoke told her that there really was a fire burning somewhere in the opera house, but Victoria was not ready to leave yet.

She didn't know how long she pushed her way through the throngs of people, or exactly where she was going as she made her way down hallways and up and down varying flights of steps. But as time passed, the smoke grew thicker, and she could hear the crashes of parts of the building falling, and the muted roar of flames.

At last she burst out of a door and found herself in a balcony on the opposite side of the stage from where the Regalados' box had been. She knew there was a vampire nearby; she looked up and over and saw him, three boxes away and down.

He looked up from the man on whom he'd been feeding and saw her.

The flash of recognition was instant. It was the one Imperial vampire who'd escaped after murdering Polidori.

'You!' he cried, blood streaming messily from his mouth. 'I thought you were dead!' He dropped his victim and leapt from the small balcony to the one next to it, clambering along its edge so he could position himself to launch up to her level.

Victoria saw the flames snake up the curtains an arm's length away, saw that it would take the vampire two more inhuman leaps to get to her own box, and made the decision: she had to face him.

He recognised her; if he got away, he would expose her to the Tutela. She had to fight him.

Dipping to pull the stake from under her skirts, she did not feel the movement behind her until she was snatched back from the balcony. A hand clamped over her mouth and strong arms pulled her back, into the darkness of the box.

'Don't,' Max snarled in her ear, 'fight.'

She heard the vampire coming closer, struggled to tell him, but he was strong and relentless, and pulled her swiftly and smoothly out of the box.

The smoke was thicker in the hallway, but Max charged along the hall, pulling her behind him. It stung her eyes and made her cough, but it was not at a dangerous level yet. She could still breathe, still see. The flames were far away.

Max shoved her down a flight of stairs and into a small room, following her in and closing the door silently behind them. He pushed her up against the wall, face-first, sliding a hand over her mouth and holding it there much too tightly. She struggled to force him away, but he did not move except for the rhythm of his laboured breathing against her back.

'Go *home*. Back to London. You cannot do anything here. Nedas is too strong. He is going to win.' His lips brushed her ear as he spoke.

She struggled anew, tried her favourite move of slamming her head back into his face, which he easily evaded.

'Do you understand? Nod.'

She nodded, then shook her head as much as she could under his hand. His other fingers were clasped around both of her wrists, holding them at the base of her back.

'Of course you aren't going to listen to me, are you? You're too damned naive. And headstrong. Be quiet or I will hurt you,' he said fiercely in her ear, then released her. Victoria spun around and faced him.

There was a small window in the room that allowed enough moonlight in to illuminate his face. She saw nothing there that gave her comfort. It was harsh and angry and determined; his eyes, barely discernible, were flat.

'Perhaps this will convince you that I mean what I say.' He was pulling at his unbuttoned shirt, yanking it back from his muscular shoulder and turning away from her so that she could see the mark there.

It was dark and heavy, there on the back of his shoulder, just above his scapula, and she recognised it. A T entwined with serpents.

'You see. I'm a member of the Tutela, and I adhere to their strictures. Does that convince you?' He was breathing harshly now, and turned back around to face her. 'I'm bound to assassinate Venators. I am one of theirs.'

'I don't believe you.' But something inside her was turning. They were alone. No one could hear. Why would he lie? 'If it's true, you must tell me why.'

He drew in a deep breath and took her by the shoulders. His fingers were strong but not painful, and he positioned her so that his unbuttoned shirt brushed against her bosom as he looked down at her. 'I made a bargain with Lilith. She promised to release me from her thrall if I joined the Tutela.' His fingers dug into her skin and she twisted away. To her surprise, he allowed it.

'Is Lilith here, in Rome, then? Is that where you've been – with her?'

'No.' His voice was strangled, as though he could barely force the word out. 'She has been in her mountain hideaway far from here. I've seen her only once, when she offered to release me from her influence if I came back to the Tutela.'

'So why do you not kill me now if you are bound to assassinate Venators?'

'I am giving you the chance to get away. This is your last chance. If I see you again, I will betray you to Regalado and the others. If I do not, then they will have no reason to trust me any longer.'

Victoria laughed, short and bitter. 'You've done nothing to protect me, then. That vampire I saw in the theatre, the one you took me from when I would have fought him, recognised me. He knows I am a Venator and he will expose me. So the decision has been taken from you.'

'So it would seem.' He looked at her, stepped away. 'All the more reason for you to go back to London. You will be needed after this is all over.'

'After what?'

'Go back home, Victoria.'

Then he reached over and smashed the window next to her. Before she could react, he picked her up and shoved her out, and she found herself tumbling to the ground below. It was not a long fall, and she landed on a small bush.

Struggling to her feet, she looked up, but Max did not follow.

Max made his way out of the opera house, leaving behind a smoke-filled cave and who knew how many victims of fire and vampire.

He had one thing left to do this evening, and it would not take long.

Indeed, he found Bertrand strolling along towards the place the Tutela and the vampires were all to meet. It was just up one more block and down a narrow alley – Fettuch's Locanda, a place not so very different from the Silver Chalice Vioget had owned.

Max greeted him. 'Pleasurable evening, was it?' he asked the vampire.

'In some ways,' Bertrand replied. 'I did not finish what I set out to do, but I have some glad tidings to bring to Nedas this evening. The woman Venator I thought I'd killed in England is here.'

'Indeed? He will be greatly pleased.' He made a show of pausing to look into a long, narrow shadow. It was the last alley before the one they must turn down. 'What, say? What is this?'

When Bertrand followed him into the darkness, Max spun around, slamming the stake into the vampire's heart before he drew another breath.

Pocketing the stake, Max brushed off the last bit of vampire dust and continued on his way.

Chapter Nineteen

Santo Quirinus's Secret

The morning after her experience at the opera, Victoria received a message from her aunt, requesting her attendance at a small church located across the Tiber River from the most populous area of Rome. The message came by way of a peddler delivering milk at the back entrance of the villa, and was brought to Victoria as she ate breakfast.

Thus it was shortly thereafter that she entered the small church, Santo Quirinus, and found her aunt, swathed in black veils and holding prayer beads, kneeling in a pew near the altar. Unlike many of Rome's other churches, Santo Quirinus was not overwhelming in its splendour. Its windows were few and plain. No marble floors or painted murals. It smelt of age and holiness, and wisps of long-used incense hung in the air.

The decor was stark and simple: brick swaddled with mortar in thick bands down the walls, leaving wide, naked brick stripes separated by the

cream-coloured mortar. Fourteen tarnished silver
crosses, numbered in the Roman style, hung on
the walls, seven on each side of the small nave, on
the mortared sections. The pews were stained dark
and uncushioned. The altar itself was little more
than a stone table on a dais one step up from the
congregation. The ceiling of the little church rose
into a small round dome with three circular windows
that allowed matching beams of afternoon light to
shine down through their wrought-iron filigree.
There were no stained-glass windows in sight.

As she walked through the church, which was
empty with the exception of one other man sitting
in the shadows, also kneeling to pray, Victoria felt
her *vis bulla* sway against her navel, something she
had not noticed it doing since she had become
accustomed to wearing it.

But today she felt particularly aware of it, and
the strength that it gave her sizzled through her
belly and out into her limbs. She felt warm and
confident, almost like a renewal of the intent
she'd had when she had first accepted the strength
amulet.

Not wishing to interrupt Aunt Eustacia, Victoria
knelt next to her to pray, and waited until she
finished her rosary. At that time, without speaking,
her aunt stood and beckoned for her to follow.

Instead of leaving the church, Aunt Eustacia
walked towards the altar, past the iron railing that

separated the priest from the congregation, and up two steps on the left side.

When Aunt Eustacia opened the small door of a confessional at the edge of the altar, Victoria hung back in confusion. But her aunt gestured her to follow, so Victoria joined her in the small room, the door closing after her.

She watched in wonder as Aunt Eustacia reached behind the small screen that would separate the penitent from the priest – if there were one in attendance – and flip a latch. A well-hidden door popped ajar, and the older woman led the way into the opening.

'Have a care, and do not tread on the middle stair,' Aunt Eustacia told Victoria, gesturing to the three steps that led from the hidden door into a narrow hallway stretching approximately fifty paces before it ended in a stone wall. The passage was lit by sconces, and icons painted on wood hung all the way to the end, where a life-size statue of Saint Quirinus stood holding a sword.

Victoria closed the door behind her and, taking care not to step on the middle stair, followed her aunt as she paced down the hall. At the end, Aunt Eustacia shifted aside a small icon of Jesus with the two Archangels, Gabriel and Michael, to expose the brick wall behind it. 'Step here,' her aunt commanded, gesturing for Victoria to move next to her.

As Victoria watched, her aunt pushed on the intricate brickwork that had been hidden by the painting, and suddenly, the floor on which she'd been standing only moments before slid away to reveal a set of spiral stairs that led down into darkness.

'The Consilium is below,' Aunt Eustacia told her, haltingly leading the way down, one of the lanterns bobbing in her hand.

The Consilium? A jolt of excitement ran through her at the realisation that she was to be introduced to it. Victoria knew very little about the Consilium, other than that it was the formal entity that oversaw the Venators.

When Aunt Eustacia had mentioned it once, more than a year ago, Victoria had been surprised that there even was such a group. But her aunt had explained that someone needed to report to the Pope, and that there had to be a way to manage and pass on the knowledge of the Venators over the ages. There had to be some way for them to share what they learnt, and to band together if necessary.

Now, as she descended in her aunt's wake, Victoria felt that same renewal of energy she'd felt upon entering the church, and she thought she understood why. This was the centre of the Venator world, the place where decisions were made, where the *vis bullae* were forged and blessed, where the leaders met and prayed and discussed.

'Anyone could come in here,' Victoria whispered

to her aunt, somehow feeling as though a normal-toned voice would be blasphemous. 'The door wasn't locked.'

Aunt Eustacia stepped from the last stair onto the stone floor and turned to look back at her. Her eyes were dark and lively in the glow from the lantern. 'Indeed not. Did you not see the others in the church? They are our trainers, our Comitators, every one of them.'

'I saw only a man praying.'

'*Si*, and two beyond him near the door through which you entered. And another in the apse across from the statue at the top of these stairs. You did not see them, for they were meant not to be seen, but they were there.' She smiled, her elegant face creasing in slender lines next to her mouth. 'Wayren and Santo Quirinus have ensured that we are well protected here. Even if the vampires or Tutela learnt that this tiny, simple church led to our Consilium, they would not be able to cross the threshold. The doors are lined with silver and covered with crucifixes; holy water is sprinkled throughout several times a day. And our Comitators, though not Venators, are well equipped to deal with any intruders.'

Victoria nodded in understanding and anticipation. Her palms tingled as her aunt drew off the dark veil she'd huddled under. She smoothed her sleek black hair, which was caught into an intricate, curling coiffure studded with pearls and emeralds, giving her a queen-like look. When she slipped off the heavy black cloak, she showed a magnificent green gown under a tight-sleeved, long pelisse of brocaded forest green so dark it was nearly black.

In a matter of moments Aunt Eustacia had gone from the image of a hunched, prayerful crone to an elegant, powerful lady.

It made Victoria glance at her own attire in rueful dismay. Certainly her hair was done, the thick, dark curls pinned up in their own pretty mass; but not studded with jewels or pearls. Not even a ribbon, come to think of it. Although Verbena had slipped in one slender stake, just in case. Nor was Victoria's gown anything more than a simple afternoon calling dress, made of pale yellow silk with a basic cream lace overlay.

She felt like a little girl still in pinafores.

Aunt Eustacia bundled up her veil and cloak and rested them on a small table near the door at the bottom of the stairs. Tall and regal, she opened the door and walked through.

Victoria followed.

She found herself in a vast chamber that brought to mind how a cathedral would look if it were circular. The walls and floor were marble; heavy, shining, black- and grey-threaded marble. Around the entire room were columns of the same marble, and between them pointed arches that gave way to smaller alcoves or doorways. It was through one of these arches that

Victoria and her aunt entered the room.

The chamber was large, and the centre of it was broken up by a large round pool, with water cascading down a fountain in the centre of it. The space was so cavernous, Victoria could not see what was on the other side. There were chairs and tables, benches and desks scattered throughout the room, which, though it was underground, was exceedingly well lit by torches and lamps. The tables held books and papers, inkwells and pens, even some stakes and other weaponry. Except for the fountain and the churchlike arches, it felt rather like the gentleman's club in which she'd had to stop a vampire raid last year.

And there were Venators. Or, at least, men who looked as though they belonged there, and Victoria presumed they were either Venators or Comitators. As they became aware of the presence of the two women – for there were no other females that Victoria could see – the occupants of the room put aside what they were doing – reading, writing, talking, fondling stakes – and rose if they were sitting, and turned if they were not, and looked at them.

There were perhaps a dozen in all, and, Victoria noted, none of them any older than forty, perhaps fifty at the outside. The youngest was likely about her age. Some of the men had the swarthy skin of Italians; others had even darker skin, perhaps from India or Egypt; whilst there were others who were fair enough to be Celtic or English.

Wondering if they were all from the far-reaching branches of the Gardella family, or if they were Venators who chose their profession, as Max had, Victoria watched as her aunt greeted each of them by name and in various languages. They were deferent to her, kissing her hand, making little bows, as though she were some kind of royalty.

Victoria had always known that since her aunt was the most direct living descendant of the first Gardella, she was special in the world of Venators; but this display of affection and respect towards her elderly aunt made her heart swell.

'Signora Gardella!' A voice carried from around the other side of the pool, over the rushing noise of the fountain, and drew Victoria's attention, thankfully, from the others who stood watching.

'Ilias,' Aunt Eustacia said, a warm smile stretching her lips, even as she clasped the hand of a man who had approached her in welcome. 'How wonderful to see you again!'

The man was nearer her age than any others there, but she still had him beat by a generation. He was perhaps sixty to her eighty, and he looked distinguished enough to be someone of importance.

Victoria watched as he came to her and they embraced. 'And this is your niece? The new Gardella?' he said, turning from Aunt Eustacia to face Victoria. 'The one who sent Lilith back to the scourge of her mountains?'

'The very one. Victoria, may I present to you Ilias de Gusto. He is the keeper of the Consilium, and has been for many years. Ilias, please meet Victoria Gardella Grantworth de Lacy.'

Victoria made a curtsy, and found herself looking into twinkling grey-blue eyes. His brows, bushy grey-and-brown spiders, lifted and arched as he looked upon her with pleasure. 'We are honoured to have you here today, Signorina Gardella.' He smiled wider as she began to correct him. 'No, no, to us you will always be a Gardella, *signorina*. And someday, you will be *Illa* Gardella.'

The Gardella. The most direct connection to the original Venator. A leader, a decision-maker, a figurehead for all the other Venators, regardless of where they fell in the worldwide family tree. The one around whom they rallied when great threats descended.

There was a blur of introductions as Victoria met the others; and she'd been correct – most of them were Venators, visiting the Consilium for training or other reasons. Three others were studying and training to be Comitators. Kritanu was a Comitator, of course, and his nephew, Briyani, was Max's. Or, at least, had been. Victoria had been working with Kritanu, but eventually she would be assigned her own trainer.

Victoria had rather expected to be met with suspicion or condescension by the others, as she had been upon first meeting Max last year. He'd believed she would be more interested in dance cards and gowns and beaux than hunting and killing vampires – and he'd been wrong. At last, he'd finally come to accept the fact that she was a real Venator.

She wasn't even going to contemplate what had happened, what had changed Max in the last year since he'd come back to Italy...especially after last night. There would be time for that later. In fact, she suspected that was part of the reason she and Aunt Eustacia were here today. If indeed Max had defected, the other Venators would have to be told.

But Victoria did not want to be the one to do that.

Despite Max's initial begrudging acceptance of her calling, the other Venators appeared to have no such hesitation. In fact, Victoria felt as if she were making her debut at a ball as gentlemen of all ages and looks crowded forward to meet her.

'Would ye like to see the Consilium chambers, Signorina Gardella?' asked one of them with a faint Scots burr. He was not much taller than she, but he was as large and muscular as an ox. His hair was the colour of polished copper, much too long to be fashionable, in London, anyway, and tied back loosely with a leather cord. Unfortunately, she couldn't recall his name, which she'd just learnt. 'I would be pleased to show you around whilst your aunt speaks with Ilias and Wayren.'

'Wayren is here?'

He smiled, taking her arm and slipping it through his as though to stake his claim. His muscles were so large, her fingers felt as though they would be squashed in the cleft of his elbow. 'Aye, of course she is. She is nearly always here, ye ken. Or, at least, it seems that way.'

He swept her away, and as they walked off one of the others called, 'Do not dare to monopolise the *signorina*, Zavier!'

Ah. Zavier. That was his name.

'How kind of you, Zavier. I am very interested in learning all about the place.' It felt odd to be calling a man she'd just met by his familiar name, but apparently Venators didn't stand on ceremony – except with her and Aunt Eustacia – as he had not been introduced with a surname.

Zavier took her first to the fountain and bade her put her hand in it. 'It is the most holy of water,' he told her when she'd dipped her fingers. 'Do ye feel your *vis bulla* now?'

Victoria wanted to blush at the mention of the silver cross because of where it dangled; he was a gentleman, after all, and a stranger. But he seemed so casual about it that she didn't allow herself to feel uncomfortable. Much, anyway. And, yes, he was correct. 'I do feel it. It's as if it knows we are here.'

'Aye. Ye might wish to have it blessed again before you leave today. I would be happy to assist if you like.' His eyes twinkled as they swept over her, and Victoria could not hold the blush back any longer. She might be used to Sebastian's overt comments, but she was still not comfortable with such teasing from other men.

'I think that I should be able to manage it all on my own,' she told him reproachfully.

He laughed and tugged her closer to his side, so that she bumped into his tree-trunk arm. She could only imagine how horrendously strong he was! 'I kenned ye would say that, but I could not resist making the offer. It is so very rare that we are honoured with the presence of a female Venator that one often forgets oneself.'

Although she was sure it was not the case of him 'forgetting' himself, Victoria forbore to comment. Instead, she said, 'How many other female Venators have you met?'

'Well, as ye and your aunt are the only living female Venators – only two thus far,' he replied with a smile. 'Of course, only a woman directly of the Gardella line can be a Venator. The rest of us…well, we are diluted Gardellas, from the very furthest branches of the family, spread or sent all over the world. And some of us – of course you know Maximilian Pesaro – are not of the Gardella blood at all, but have been called in a different way, and have met the deadly trials and tribulations that allow them to wear the *vis*.'

'Indeed.'

'I have not seen Max in some time. The last news I

had of him was that he had travelled to England. That is where you have come from, aye?'

'Yes, of course. I had the pleasure of working with Max to retrieve the Book of Antwartha before Lilith obtained it.' Calling it a pleasure to work with him was a bit of a stretch, but Victoria was attempting to be polite.

'Ah, aye, we have all heard the story of your adventure, and your sacrifice.' The teasing had gone from his face now, as they walked away from the fountain, and was replaced with a soberness that made him look more like a warrior than the flirtatious humour had. 'I am quite in awe.' And he was so serious that she believed he was not merely flattering her.

'Thank you,' was all she said.

'Since ye asked about women Venators, perhaps ye would like to see the gallery?' Zavier asked, leading her towards one of the arches that contained a heavy mahogany door.

He opened it and gestured for her to precede him in. This chamber was long and low, more of a hallway or passage than a chamber. Portraits and sconces alternated on the walls. Occasionally there was a hip-high pedestal with a statue or bust on it, or a glass cabinet, or shelves.

'Every Venator since the first stake was given to Gardella has a portrait here. And we have some other artefacts and mementos as well. It is a bit morbid, perhaps – more like a museum than anything – but it is important that we do not forget those who have given of themselves before us.'

Victoria walked slowly along the line of portraits. They all seemed to be done in the same hand, by the same artist, though some of them were obviously centuries, perhaps a millennium old.

She stopped in front of the painting of a striking woman. 'Catherine Gardella,' she read aloud. Catherine's hair was bright, shining like polished copper, looped and curled and coiled at the sides of her head with ribbons and jewels. She was dressed in court clothing from perhaps three or four centuries ago, with a ruff fringing her neck and split velvet sleeves, puffed, with red satin behind them. She looked more like a queen than a Venator. In her lap, amid reams of skirts, she held a stake. A large emerald glinted on her other hand, painted so realistically that Victoria almost expected the hand to move and the facets to shine in a different direction.

'Our Cat,' Zavier said with a smile in his voice. 'She was well named. A spitfire if there ever was one, from tales I've heard. Her temperament matched her hair.'

'Lilith's hair is the same hue,' Victoria commented, remembering the glowing beacon of the vampire queen's hair, unholy in the way it lit the room.

'You are not the first to have commented on that, and you have seen Lilith, and are here to tell of it. I had forgotten that.' Zavier's voice hushed. 'Ye and

Max Pesaro, and your aunt, of course. Some of the few, the very few of this era, who have walked away from her. I dinna ken how Max has remained so strong all of these years.'

Victoria remembered what Max had said last night, about making a bargain with Lilith to be released from her thrall if he joined the Tutela. She'd wondered what he'd meant; surely he'd never shown himself to be under any kind of control by the vampire queen. His skill at stalking and hunting vampires was legendary; how could he be controlled by Lilith and still be so fearsome? There had not, of course, been time to ask him – and, of course, she knew better than to expect him to answer her. He had been intent on getting her out of the opera house, out of Rome, out of Italy.

'What hold does Lilith have over him?' she asked. 'I have worked with Max, but he is not terribly forthcoming about…certain things.'

'Of course. Ye ken that is Max's way.' Zavier looked over at her; he did not have to look down, as they were of a height. 'Her bites dinna heal, even for a Venator. Even with the balm we use, or the salted holy water. They are always there, and cause him pain when she wishes, for she chooses to remind him of her influence over him.'

'Why?'

Now he looked at her in an odd way. 'She wants him as her concubine, is my understanding. I am certain he would do anything to be released from that position. To be a Venator yet tied to the vampire queen is a burden heavier than I could ken.'

He offered his arm and she slid her fingers around the bulge of muscle that seemed to be flexed at all times, even when at rest. 'Here is another of our lady Venators. Lady Rosamund, meant to take holy vows, but instead she left the abbey when she learnt of her calling, and went on crusade to the Holy Lands.'

Victoria stood before the picture of the young woman. Dressed simply, in a sapphire-coloured gown similar to Wayren's long, loose garments, with pointed sleeves that brushed the ground, Lady Rosamund looked serene and calm – very different from the mischievous Catherine Gardella. Long honey-coloured hair fell from a simple headdress of pearls. She held a stake in one hand and a rope of prayer beads in another.

'She was a mystic, and during her time in the abbey, before she knew she was called, she wrote many manuscripts about the revelations she received during her meditation and prayer. Many of her works have become known as our prophecies, and Wayren studies them a great deal. Aye, she is the one to whom was revealed the whole story of how Judas, beloved of Jesus, came to betray him and turn to Lucifer, and was thus turned into the first vampire.'

'There are some who say Jesus asked him to turn him over to the Jews in order to set all of the following events in motion,' Victoria commented, looking at the portrait of the serene woman whose calm grey eyes reminded her of Wayren's.

Zavier laughed, a low, rolling laugh that fit his bear-like physique. 'Och, that is what Lucifer would like us to believe. If ye study Rosamund's writings, as I have, ye will learn that for whatever reason, Judas indeed sold Jesus for thirty pieces of silver, and even today the presence of that particular metal is cause for a vampire to shrink back. Perhaps Judas knew what would happen because of his betrayal; perhaps he did not. But the truth is, after Jesus was crucified, Judas d'nae believe he would be forgiven for his role in the betrayal, and Lucifer was easily able to convince him to turn to him for protection.'

'You are quite a historian. Do you remember such detail for all of the Venators?'

He grinned back at her. 'Ye ken, it is the female Venators' stories I am the most fond of, because men are *expected* to be warriors and hunters. When a woman is called to do so, she has more hurdles to leap than the men ever do. It is hard enough for a man to be chosen and called as a Venator. I have the greatest respect for a woman who answers the call.'

Victoria thought of Melly, her own mother, who had been chosen to be a Venator, but who had ultimately decided not to take on the responsibility because she had just met the man who was to be Victoria's father. Because of that, Melly's mind had been wiped clean of any memory related to vampires and Venators, and any innate skill that she would have had had been passed to her daughter. In that way, and because Melly's father – who was Aunt Eustacia's brother – had also chosen not to accept the Venator call, Victoria had inherited the skills and sense of two previous generations of Venators.

Zavier was clearly pleased to be in the presence of a female Venator, and had no hesitation in showing it. Victoria decided to be flattered and to enjoy his acceptance. 'And where is Aunt Eustacia's portrait?' she asked.

'There is no portrait yet. The paintings are not made until the Venator's work is done. The biggest question regarding your aunt will be how to portray her – as the young, fierce Venator of legend, or the older, elegant matriarch.'

Before Victoria was able to ask about the next portrait, they were interrupted.

'Pardon me, Zavier, Signorina Victoria, but the Consilium is drawing to order.' The man gestured towards the door with a great flourish, torchlight glinting off his round spectacles.

'*Grazie*, Miro,' Zavier replied, and led Victoria out of the room. 'He is one of our weapon masters,' he explained to her. 'A Comitator who has a finesse for creating new ways to fight vampires and protect ourselves. We will have to see if he can create a special, more ladylike stake for ye. Perhaps one that will fit in your reticule, or down a stocking. Or some form-fitting leather armour?' He winked.

The Consilium, which was both the name of the governing body and also the name of the chambers through which they walked, met in a different room. This one had a circle of chairs arranged in a half-moon shape about a semicircular dais.

Most of the twenty seats were taken; Victoria selected one near the back and noticed that her aunt and Wayren had been seated on the dais behind a table.

They did not waste any time. Wayren spoke, referring to the sheaf of notes in front of her.

'Nedas has Akvan's Obelisk, and it is clear he intends to activate it; in fact, he has already begun the necessary steps to do so. My research indicates that the Day of the Dead, All Souls' Day, is the optimal time for such an event. This is the day on which the souls of the departed are released from their bodies, making it a perfect time for Nedas and the immortals to attempt to capture them and use them for their purposes. It is, of course, November the second, which is two days from now.'

She shuffled the curling papers into a pile and looked at Aunt Eustacia, who continued: 'As many of you know, I was present the last time the Tutela gained vast power and unleashed it upon the mortals. It was the Battle of Praga, where twenty thousand people were massacred by vampires and the members of the

Tutela, in the name of the immortals. Although we were ultimately able to stop them, it was only after great devastation. With the power of Akvan's Obelisk controlling the souls of our departed, Nedas will be impossible to beat back and we expect the damage to be even greater, should he succeed.' She paused and looked around the room. 'I believe it will be the end of our battle with them, for their power will overmatch ours.'

'So how do we stop it?' asked Zavier. His face was expressionless. 'How do we destroy the obelisk? And where does he keep it?'

'Last night there was a fire at the Blendimo Opera Theatre,' Wayren said, with a glance at Victoria. 'It has not been completely destroyed, by some odd happenstance, but it has been closed to the public and will not reopen for months, if at all. And there were some reported vampire attacks at that location as well. I do not believe it is a coincidence, for several reasons. First, my research indicates that Nedas will need a very large space in which to complete his activation of the obelisk, and the theatre is one of the largest and tallest chambers in the city – other than cathedrals, of course, which would not be a welcoming place for a group of vampires bent on calling an evil power to life. Second, the theatre, as you well know, is perched on a small hill near the city's largest cemetery. This makes sense, for it will be much easier for him to draw the dead souls from the nearby cemetery; although I do not believe he would be restricted to only those that are close to him. I am certain that this is where Nedas plans to activate the obelisk. However, there is no known way to destroy the object, so we must consider other alternatives.'

'Then we must assassinate Nedas. If he is dead, he cannot activate the obelisk,' offered another Venator, one of the older ones. Perhaps he was nearing fifty.

'That would have been our hope,' Wayren agreed. 'But once the…mm' – she squinted down at her papers, plugged a word with her finger, and looked back up – 'shadow has been broken and has wrapped around the being who broke it, even assassinating the holder of the obelisk will not solve the problem. Its power can be transferred quite easily to another. And another. We certainly do not want any other demon or vampire to obtain it and its powers.'

'Beauregard would be waiting to snatch it up with both hands if Nedas were taken from the picture,' agreed Zavier.

That caught Victoria's attention. 'Beauregard?'

'A rival vampire to Nedas. He's older and very powerful; but Nedas is Lilith's son, and has been given more favour as a result. If only we could turn their attention to the other, and engage them in their own internal battles, we could let them destroy each other.'

Aunt Eustacia was nodding. 'Indeed. In fact, that is how we were able to stop the horror in Praga thirty years ago. But I do not think it will work now, for from what we have been able to learn, the obelisk's shadow has already been broken. Nedas has already begun the steps to activate the obelisk, and Beauregard, powerful as he might be, is no match for Nedas with his obelisk. There is no chance of distracting them in that manner.'

'What can we do, if the obelisk cannot be destroyed and Nedas is already bound to it?'

'Two things. We must prepare for the worst, and expect that Nedas will succeed. We shall commence with that discussion shortly and put our preparations into place immediately, for we have less than two days. The only other possibility is for someone to get close enough to assassinate Nedas and steal Akvan's Obelisk before its power can be transferred to another.'

'I will do it,' volunteered the same Venator who'd first suggested assassination.

'You will not get close enough to do so,' Eustacia told him. 'The moment the Tutela recognised you as a Venator, you would be slain. As would any of you.' Her eyes lingered on Victoria. 'Except perhaps one.'

'I have already agreed to do it,' Victoria said, rising. 'In London I agreed. There is no question that it must be me.' She had not told Aunt Eustacia what had occurred at the opera house last night – that she had been seen by the Imperial who would recognise her as a Venator. Or of her conversation with Max.

She opened her mouth to speak, then decided

better of it. There was no one else who could do it. The others here would more certainly be recognised as Venators than she would.

There was a chance – slim, yes, but a chance – that the Imperial vampire had not betrayed her to the Tutela, or that he did not know for certain that she was a Venator.

And then she remembered what Max had told her: *Nedas is going to win. He is too strong. You will be needed after this is all over.*

However and for whatever reason Max had become involved with the Tutela and with Nedas was no longer important. The worst was going to happen, and he accepted it. He would allow it to happen. Somehow he knew that Nedas would succeed.

At that moment her last vestige of deep-seated hope poofed like a staked vampire. There would be no help from Max. From anyone.

She really was on her own.

Chapter Twenty

Lady Rockley Dines Out

When Victoria arrived home from her visit to the Consilium, a carriage waited in front of the villa.

It was past teatime, nearing supper – late for a casual social caller.

Her steps were quick as she hurried up the stairs to the entrance.

'You have a visitor, *signora*' the butler told her; but she was already flinging the parlour door open.

Sebastian looked up from the newspaper he was perusing. 'I don't know who you were expecting, my dear, but I'm sure you must be disappointed. Such enthusiasm could not have been meant for me, much to my regret.' His attention wandered over her figure in a way that reminded her of the last time they were in this room.

And then of his threat to call on the Tarruscelli twins when he became inexplicably angry with her.

And then back to last night, when he'd called her *mine*. And casually invoked the name of a powerful vampire.

'It's a bit late for tea, Sebastian,' she said coolly, trying to keep her breathing easy and her stomach from fluttering. The way he was looking at her…it made her want to cover her cheeks to hold back the blush, to touch his thick, golden brown hair, to back out of the room before he put his hands on her, as it was clear he intended to.

Apparently something had changed since he'd chased the vampires away from her neck.

'We must talk,' he said, but there was a wholly different message in his eyes. Now she couldn't stop it – the unfortunate warmth billowed up from her bosom over her neck and to her cheeks. 'Will you permit me to take you for a drive?'

'It is unfashionably late for a drive in the park,' she countered.

'Other than my attire, I thrive on being unfashionable. Will you come with me?'

Victoria knew that if she accepted his invitation, it would be tantamount to accepting whatever was to develop between them. Most likely to continue what they'd started in this very room only a few days ago, but what had been simmering betwixt them for more than a year.

And then there was the minor fact that he had questions to answer, and having him closed up in a carriage with her would be conducive to getting those answers…among other things. She gave him a thoughtful look, then said casually, 'I'll freshen up, and then I will be delighted to accompany you.'

'*Merci, ma chère.*'

Victoria hurried up to her bedchamber, calling for Verbena. It didn't take long for her to have her hair re-pinned, to change into a more flattering gown of rose pink and to pull on a matching pelisse to keep the cooling autumn air away. It had long sleeves that buttoned tightly from elbow to wrist, and would keep her arms warm even if she had occasion to remove her gloves. Which would come in handy with Sebastian around, since he seemed to have a penchant for relieving her of her handwear.

'You look much refreshed,' he told her in the foyer when she returned back down the stairs. 'I took it upon myself to ask for a dinner basket to be prepared for us; it will be some time until we arrive at our destination, and I would not wish you to become famished.'

'I did not realise we would be gone for so long.'

Sebastian paused in the act of placing the tall, curly brimmed hat on his head. 'Do you have another engagement this afternoon? This evening? I did not realise.'

'No,' she replied, eyeing him suspiciously.

'There were other callers today, my lady,' Verbena interrupted as she and Oliver walked in carrying a large basket. 'Their cards are on the table.'

Annoyed that Sebastian's presence had distracted her from that simple task of looking at the front table, Victoria turned and thumbed through the small stack of cards. The Tarruscelli twins and Sara Regalado. Silvio Galliani. Obviously they'd all made it home from the opera unscathed. She was thankful she hadn't been home when they called, for how on earth could she have conversed casually with them after watching Sara succumb so wantonly to a vampire bite? Even her mother would have been hard-pressed to accomplish such a feat.

No one else had called.

Victoria would not even acknowledge that she'd hoped for anyone else; she knew Max had told her all he was going to tell her.

It just confirmed her realisation earlier today at the Consilium. She was on her own.

'Shall we?' Sebastian asked, donning his gloves and then offering her his arm.

There was much more room for her fingers inside the crook of his elbow than there had been in Zavier's. And he was taller. And much handsomer.

And less trustworthy.

Yet, she did trust him after a fashion. He had, at least, saved her from being mauled by the vampire last evening. That must count for something.

Inside the carriage, they sat across from each other as it lurched off, reminding Victoria of Barth's erratic driving back in London. She smiled, and Sebastian noticed.

'Fond memories, my dear? Or are you merely thinking how brilliantly I handled getting us alone in a carriage yet again?'

'Your technique was brilliantly transparent.' Victoria watched him warily.

He noticed and laughed. 'Are you afraid I will leap across the carriage and tear your clothes off? It is not that it hasn't occurred to me, but I would hope you would grant me more finesse than that.'

'I am never quite sure of what you will do, Sebastian. In fact, I was more than surprised by your actions last night.'

His eyebrows rose, as they tended to do when he played the innocent. 'Do you mean my extended attentions towards Portiera? I do hope it didn't bruise your pride, *ma chère Victoire*. You must know that it is you who has truly captured my regard.' His voice was light and merry, as if to cut the meaning of the words, but the sentiment caused a sudden sharp tingle in her middle.

'I was not referring to your gross flirtations with the Tarruscelli twins,' she replied. 'And you know it. I was expecting your visit, as I was certain you would wish to claim some sort of acknowledgment from me – not *compensation*, Sebastian; I know you have decried that motive in the recent past – some *acknowledgment* that you saved me from a very unpleasant experience last night. I was, and am, very grateful.'

'Ah, but you are a Venator,' he reminded her, still with that light tone, 'you did not truly need my assistance. I merely stepped in because I could not bear to see that lovely neck marred again.' His voice slipped into a low tenor, and all humour evaporated from his countenance. 'And you are dying to know who Beauregard is and how I know him.'

'Of course I am. And I know that you will tell me only if you wish it, and so there is no point in asking. I don't wish to play this game of cat and mouse with you, Sebastian.' Her words were steady, unlike her fingers, which, if she hadn't been clasping them in her filmy silk skirt, would have been trembling.

'Then we shan't play.' In a trice he was sitting next to her on the bench. He swept off his hat and tossed it indolently across the carriage, ignoring the fact that it rolled and landed on the floor near the door. 'Will you kiss me this time, Victoria, or will you make me do the dirty work?'

'I kissed you at the docks in London.'

'Of course you did, because you knew it was safe. You were getting on a ship to come here. But now…' After shrugging out of his jacket, he settled back in the corner and looked at her, his arms crossed over his waistcoat. His leg pushed against hers in the centre of the bench, his chest rose and fell, and his shoulders jolted off rhythm with the movement of the carriage. 'Are you brave enough, my lovely Venator?'

She leant forward, and he pulled up from his relaxed pose to meet her halfway. Their mouths met in a tangle of lips and tongue and her delicious, deep sigh of pleasure.

Before she knew it her hair was falling around her, the pins scattering from Sebastian's fingers to her shoulders, the cushioned bench and the floor below. He pushed his hands through her curls and the coils Verbena had made, combing from her neck along her upper arms, then moving to unfasten the pelisse that buttoned tightly over her bosom.

Pulling the tight jacket off her shoulders, pushing it down over her arms, he continued to kiss her on the mouth, the jaw, the neck, until she struggled beneath him. 'The sleeves…need to be unbuttoned,' she told him, trying to shrug out of the tight jacket.

'I know,' he said in her ear, and pushed the sleeves farther down her arms so that the coat slipped over her hands, leaving her wrists trapped inside the arms, pulling the pelisse taut behind her hips.

'Sebastian,' she said, a warning note and a tinge of panic in her voice. 'I don't like this.'

'Shhh,' he murmured against her neck, brushing his eyelashes over her cheek. 'Just relax. Enjoy.' He sucked on her earlobe, his mouth warm and slick.

Victoria took a deep, shaky breath and realised that the hint of panic was subsiding as he spread his hands over her shoulders, pulling the bodice away, then slipping behind to unfasten the buttons and unlace the top of her stays – mainly because of what his mouth and hands were doing to distract her.

He was quick and smooth, her breasts free and bare, jouncing in the darkening carriage before she realised it. He covered them, lifted and thumbed them, gentle and then firm in his touch. Victoria closed her eyes and sighed when his lips closed over one nipple and drew it sharply into his hot mouth, flicking over it with the tip of his tongue. The pulsing sensation matched the throb between her legs, and she shifted her hips beneath his weight.

With one last tug from his lips, Sebastian chuckled against her breast. 'Patience, my dear,' he said, but lifted himself away to attend to his breeches. She saw them fall, baring muscular thighs, and then his drawers; and then he bent forward as his hands smoothed up beneath her skirts, sliding along her thighs, baring her legs and piling her gown into a mass of silk and lace in her lap.

His fingers slipped and played where she ached and burnt, making her sigh and shift and leaving her wanting the rest. She felt the brush of his hair over her cheek as he kissed her neck, his breath rough in her ears.

Victoria wanted to reach for him, but her arms were still trapped behind her. 'Sebastian…' she began to say, but the rest was lost when he covered her mouth with his, closing off everything but her soft moan as his hands moved up and under her gown to touch her *vis bulla*. She felt them brush over it, tug gently on the silver cross. Then his hands spread over her belly, under her shift and stays, and lifted her hips so that her piled-up skirts rode higher.

Sebastian moved away, releasing her mouth with a low, delicious pop that made it clear he would have kissed her all night. With one last look up at her, as if to confirm this next move, he gave a gentle sigh and fitted himself into her with one smooth slide.

Oh. Victoria closed her eyes as her heart thrummed and the lovely feeling of being joined with a man settled over her. A pleasure tear trickled down into her hair, and she drew in a deep breath and just *felt*.

She realised he wasn't moving; they were joined there in the rumbling carriage, his hands positioned next to her shoulders, one knee bent next to her thigh on the bench. When she opened her eyes, it was to see him looking down at her with a grin.

'I always knew our first time would be in a carriage,' he told her. And drew a deep, shaky breath. Then exhaled. Closed his eyes.

And still he didn't move.

She shifted under him because her hands were trapped. 'Sebastian.'

'What's the hurry, *ma chère*?' He bent to kiss her again, fondling her lips with his, tasting them as they rocked gently against each other with the carriage rhythm. It was enough of a movement, that incessant jolting, that Victoria felt every bit of her attention focused there where he'd slid in, and where her nipples brushed against the shirt he hadn't bothered to remove. Her gown bunched between them, spilling over the bench, and his legs were warm against hers.

He moved forward and she tasted the skin of his neck, faintly salty, and felt the hard pumping of the pulse in his throat. The throb between them ached and burnt, and she felt the way they slid together ever so slightly, and the long-lost familiar coil that would begin to unwind deep inside her. That great need dug at her, incessant, until all she could think of, focus on, was him inside her and not moving.

Sebastian rested his cheek on her forehead and at last shifted. Slowly, drawing each stroke in and out with deliberation, he pressed down and in and up, his hands moving in the cushioned seat next to her shoulders, tangling in her hair, fingers crushing into her skin. Their breathing matched, rushed and urgent, capped with sighs and soft groans.

Victoria moved too, felt the tension that had sat dormant as it built inside her, and it wasn't long before she shuddered beneath him, more tears sliding from her closed eyes, then felt him bow into her one last time, and the pause as he came inside her.

'Ah, Victoria,' he murmured next to her ear, his voice low and barely audible over the carriage rumble, 'I am so glad you changed your mind.'

'About what?' She could barely form the words.

'About making me wait a very long time for this.'

'You gave me little choice,' she said, her lips brushing against the beginning of stubble on his jaw. 'You were quite convincing. And Sebastian…my wrists are hurting.'

'Of course.' He pulled out, sat back, and tucked himself back into his breeches, leaving her without the pleasure of seeing his chest or any other part of his body. Then he helped her extricate herself from the pelisse and tuck her breasts back into the dress.

'Are you hungry?' he asked, lounging back in his seat.

'How long until we arrive to wherever we are going? Or was it truly a ploy to get me into this carriage?'

He smiled with great insouciance. 'It was indeed a ploy. I wanted desperately to get you into this carriage. But we can still eat, can we not?'

The basket had been tucked under one of the bench seats, and Victoria helped him to pull it out, her long hair sliding down to get in the way as she bent forward.

'What a pleasure to see your hair unbound like that,' he commented as they hefted the basket next to him on the seat. 'I've been wanting to see it that way since the first night we met at the Silver Chalice.'

'It gets in the way,' Victoria told him. 'I have considered cutting it, but I cannot bear to.'

'Thank heaven for vanity!' he said, opening a bottle of wine. 'Will you look to see if there is any cheese in there?'

While she rummaged in the basket, he poured a glass for her, and when she handed him the cheese and bread, he gave her the wine and they settled back to eat.

Her body still thrummed, and there were still a lot of questions to be asked and mysteries to be solved. Such as what he looked like underneath all those clothes.

And who Beauregard was.

As she sipped her wine and nibbled on a piece of bread, Victoria felt lazy and sleepy and content. It wasn't until her cup was half-empty that she realised it was an unnatural lazy, sleepy, content feeling.

She bolted upright and the carriage pitched. She grabbed at the wall next to her.

'May I take that, *ma chère*, before you spill it?' Sebastian was quick to relieve her of the wineglass.

'*Salvi*' she accused. Her tongue was thick; but she forced herself to say it again. 'You put *salvi* in…this. You…lie…' The words were hard to get out; her eyes were drooping.

'I did not lie when I said it was a ploy to get you in here,' he told her. 'I am sorry it had to be done this way…but you would not have come otherwise. You are, after all, a Venator, and used to doing things your way.' She thought… Was there a bit of mockery in his voice?

'Sebastian…' She put as much accusation in her voice as she could muster.

'You will be more comfortable if you come here.' He helped her settle next to him, her head propped in the corner opposite him, her knees drawn up on the bench, her feet pushing into his leg.

'Why?'

'Unfortunately, you were becoming a problem for the Tutela's plans, and I was asked to remove you.'

'You…liar… You…bastard.'

'Such language! But it is only temporary, my dear. I promise no harm will come to you. You will be safer outside of Rome until after the second.'

'Who is Beau…re…gard…?' Her eyes were closed. Sleep dragged her away.

He said something; perhaps he answered her question. She thought she heard it, but then she remembered no more.

Chapter Twenty-One

In Which Monsieur Vioget Makes an Unflattering Comparison to Our Heroine

When Victoria came back to herself, the first thing she noticed was that the nape of her neck was cold.

Then, that she couldn't move her arms. Or her legs.

She slitted her eyes open in an effort to pretend she was still unconscious, but it obviously didn't work.

'Ah…our lovely Venator has returned to us.' Sebastian's voice was very near, and so Victoria opened her eyes all the way and managed a sleepy glare.

He was sitting in a chair next to where she was lying on a narrow bed or sofa; she wasn't quite certain. She was certain that her wrists and ankles were bound, however, and that she was going to kill Sebastian.

A quick dart of eyes around the small room told her they were in some kind of residence: curtains covered the windows, rugs protected the floor, a table with a wax candle on it sat next to Sebastian's elbow. Nice and homey.

Somewhere there were vampires, though. Not in the room, that she could tell; but somewhere nearby.

'I'm going to kill you,' she said behind her teeth.

'Why do you think I took the precaution of confining you?'

'Did you say Beauregard is your grandfather?'

'Well, more precisely, he is my great-great-great-great…some vast number of generations back… grandfather.' Sebastian smiled benevolently, as though he'd just announced his relationship to the king. He'd left his jacket off and sat in his shirtsleeves and breeches with a glass of wine next to him on the table.

'He's a vampire.'

Sebastian bowed his head in acknowledgment.

'A vampire whose name obviously carries a great amount of weight and influence.'

'So you heard me through the fog of their thrall? I wasn't certain what you remembered.'

'I heard it all, including the part where you claimed that I belonged to you, like some piece of horseflesh. I had no idea you meant to spirit me off like a primitive and take advantage of me.'

He looked at her then with tiger eyes that gleamed warning. 'Might I remind you, Victoria, that I did not take anything you did not freely give.'

She forced away the blush of fury and mortification and turned the conversation. 'Who ordered you to take me away?'

'I was not *ordered* to do anything. I was asked quite reluctantly, and I readily agreed, knowing that it was to my benefit as well as your own, since it would keep your pretty skin from being caught in the crossfire and myself from being forced to take sides. And, might I clarify, I did so without requiring any compensation. Do you not think that heroic of me?'

'Heroic? Or self-serving? After all, it appears you took great advantage of the situation and got your compensation after all.'

'Now, Victoria, you must admit that our lovely intimacies were a long time coming, and in truth, were merely an unexpected benefit of my task. Truly, my only intent was to see you safely out of the way while things progressed the way they will.'

'What do you think I am, a helpless female? I am a Venator! I didn't need to be spirited away, you bloody fool! I needed to *be* there!' She pulled at the ropes around her wrists, causing whatever she was tied to to creak softly. When she saw the interested gleam in his eyes at the reminder of her helplessness, she quickly started up her inquiries again. 'Who asked you to take me away? Beauregard?'

He appeared to be enjoying the situation quite immensely, which made Victoria all the more determined to wipe that sardonic grin from his beautiful mouth. 'You mean you haven't figured it out yet?' He laughed. 'You really don't know? It was Max, of course. Max, who would never have asked such a thing of me if he'd had any other choice – which, of course, he did not. Poor sot.'

Victoria stopped. Yes. It made sense. Max had told her to leave Rome, had known she would not listen – which, of course, she wouldn't have – and had taken matters into his own hands.

'Why is there such enmity between you and Max?' she asked.

Sebastian shook his head. 'That is not something I wish to discuss with you at this time. But feel free to ask any other questions you might have. Perhaps you will hit upon another topic of interest. We do have some time to kill. Unless you would like to indulge in some other pleasant activities.'

'You truly are addled if you think I will ever let you touch me again.'

'Now you are beginning to sound like those heroines in Mrs Radcliffe's novels, not Venatorial at all. Is this what happens when the best has been got of you? It's a wonder you made it as far as you have if you fall into those clichéd protestations.'

'Why don't you untie me and we'll see how much of a Gothic heroine I am.'

'And allow the Venator her full strength?' he replied in mock horror. 'I think not. Although…' He moved and was suddenly sitting next to her, his hip touching the side of her waist. 'I don't know why I shouldn't take further advantage of the situation; for, as you've pointed out, once you've been set free, I'm not liable to get within a few yards of your lovely person. Which I would find to be quite distressing.'

He curled his fingers firmly around her jaw to hold her head in position and bent forward. She expected a rough, controlling kiss, but was surprised when it turned out to be soft and gentle: the antithesis of the forcible way he confined her. She told herself she kissed him back just to lull him into complacency. When, after a moment, she tried to bite his lip, he pulled back, laughing, and released her face. 'There's my fighter.'

He trailed a finger along her chin, over her neck, and down through the little dip at the base of her throat to the swell of her breasts, leaving a trail of gooseflesh in his wake. 'Very tempting, you are, my dear; so much so that I've risked more than I should have since we met. But, then, I am not the first Vioget to allow a woman to influence my better judgment. The men in my family do have their weaknesses.'

Sebastian had not moved from his place next to her side, and the warmth of his legs next to her body was becoming unbearable. He'd shifted and was leaning over her, propped up on a palm on the other side of her arm, his cravatless shirt brushing her gown.

She didn't give him the satisfaction of asking the obvious question; just glared and tried not to think about how near he was. She refused to notice the way the pulse beat calmly in his throat, and the way the shallow opening of his shirt exposed just a bit of the golden hair that grew on his chest. And how one of his fingers played gently with the curls near her ear, sending uncomfortable prickles along her neck.

Instead, she focused her attention on the fact that he'd tricked her again. Certainly he claimed it was to keep her safe…but he was the grandson of a powerful vampire. She couldn't trust him, even if he was a delicious lover. Their lovemaking had merely been a way for him to catch her off guard and abscond with her somewhere to keep her safe.

Her! A Venator!

'My great-great-grandfather was deceived into his current predicament by a lovely, conniving female vampire centuries ago. And my father was mauled and killed by a lascivious one. She happened to be the first of the only two vampires I ever killed.'

'You claim you are no member of the Tutela.'

'I am not a member of the Tutela, Victoria, although there may seem to be similarities between us. The Tutela is interested in protecting vampires as well as attaining their immortality. They wish to see the vampire rise in power and are fascinated by their lives. I have no desire to become an immortal, nor to see mortals destroyed. The price is too high, and I find little to recommend their lifestyle. If one can call it that.'

'But if the vampires have taken two members of your family from you…I don't understand how you can ally yourself with them in any fashion.'

'My grandfather wasn't taken from me. To me, he is who he is and has always been, and I love him. If he were killed by someone like you, he would be damned for all eternity.' He sat upright, looking down at her with an unfamiliar expression. '*Damned* for *eternity*, Victoria, with no chance of reconciliation. Do you understand what that means?' She'd never seen him so flat and humourless. 'Every vampire was once a person, someone's beloved mother, daughter, father or son, Victoria. As you have cause to know. Sending one to his death is tantamount to passing judgment.'

'The vampire is damned only if he has chosen to feed on a mortal; if he has not done so then he can be saved from that eternal hell. And Venators are called to pass such judgment as part of their calling,' Victoria told him fiercely, trying not to think about the man she could have killed back in the streets of St Giles, when she had passed judgment she'd not been called to do. 'We are given that gift and meant to use it to eradicate the evil in this world.' She had tried and condemned a mortal being, and she hated that she'd done so.

'And I would refuse that burden of passing judgment. All vampires are not wholly evil, Victoria, as I well know. If they were the arbitrarily bloodthirsty cretins you believe them to be, I would not be here right now. My grandfather would have turned me or mauled me long ago.'

'But once a mortal is turned to a vampire, he

ceases to be the person we once knew. He becomes a monster, a demon, driven only by his need. I have never met a vampire who hasn't been set on taking from another. I've seen the carnage they leave, the way they mangle and tear and destroy men and women. They are damned for a reason, Sebastian, damned because they take promiscuously, and without need, because they must drain the life of others in order to exist. Knowing that I could prevent it from happening, that I am called to protect mortals, I could never abstain from doing so. I cannot see how you can forgive that evil, even in your own grandfather.'

'And that,' he said lightly, standing, moving away from her both physically and emotionally, 'is what attracts me so about you, to my great regret. Your conviction, your bravery, your sacrifice. Your strength. How, even when presented with an argument, you are not easily swayed. Let me ask you something, Victoria. If my grandfather, Beauregard, walked in this room, and I gave you a stake, would you kill him here in front of me?'

She looked at him, her heart thumping along harshly, audible in the sudden silence. Sebastian was not an evil person; she knew that. He might be an opportunist, he might walk a tightrope and play two sides, but she could not believe he wished evil on anyone. Even her.

Especially her.

'Knowing that with one plunge of the stake, you

would send him – or any being – to an eternity of Hell?' Sebastian stood over her.

Knowing what she knew, would she? Would she pass that judgment on the man – no, the immortal, the vampire – whom Sebastian knew and loved?

How could he love a vampire?

'I don't know.' Her voice was a whisper; it was the best she could do. 'If he… I don't know, Sebastian.'

His mouth caught at one side. 'It appears you might be able to see at least some shade of grey, unlike your dear friend Max, who sees only black and white.' He turned and walked across the room, twitched the curtains to look out.

The movement allowed a bit of light into the room; it was lighter than it had been when she last remembered being in the carriage. She must have been here overnight.

That meant that tonight at midnight would begin the Day of the Dead. If she were going to have any chance of stopping Nedas, of attempting to kill him, she had to get away from Sebastian and the vampires that lurked somewhere nearby. Her neck was still chilled.

Victoria pulled on her arms, fixed above her head, elbows bent. 'How long are you going to keep me like this?' she asked.

He turned, half-shadowed by the sunlight streaming in from the window, reminding her that no one was completely shadowed or lit; no one was wholly good or wholly evil. Even, if he were to be believed, vampires. 'Since I rather relish seeing you in such a helpless position, I'm not motivated to make any changes to the current arrangement.' His smile was back, but it showed the signs of strain.

She tugged at her wrists again. 'My arms are hurting.'

'I'm certain I can find a way to take your mind off the pain.'

'You might find it more enjoyable if I were able to participate.'

One of his brows lifted. 'Your idea of participating would probably not be what I had in mind. I think I'll leave you just the way you are.'

'Where are the vampires? I know they are here. Friends of your grandfather's, I presume?'

'Just as a bit of added insurance,' he said. 'Outside the door there. You should be flattered that I felt the need to have additional assistance.'

He walked towards her and stood, looking down. 'When this is all over – tomorrow, perhaps – I'll release you and then you can start to pick up the pieces. For now, though, I bid you *au revoir*.'

He bent, gave her a gentle kiss next to the corner of her lips, where he was far from her angry teeth, and left the room.

As soon as he was gone, Victoria started to look about for an opportunity to escape; but no sooner had the door closed behind Sebastian than it opened again and another man came in. A vampire.

His eyes glowed red and his fangs were out, and for one horrible moment she thought he meant to attack her. Surely Sebastian wouldn't allow it. But Sebastian was gone.

As the vampire walked over and stood next to her, her vision swirled and her stomach fluttered.

'Quite a shame that we must leave you untouched. I've never had a Venator before.' The implication was clear, and she felt her panic begin to subside.

But then the vampire traced a cold finger over her neck, using his sharp nail, and she felt the prick of its point, surely deep enough to draw blood. He bent towards her and she stiffened, pulling at the ropes beyond her head, feeling them jolt something above her, but he did not bite. Instead he dragged his wide, cold tongue over the place he'd cut. Victoria turned her head away, her stomach pitching, her back arching, hoping that whatever protections Sebastian had put in place for her would be enough once the vampire had smelt and tasted her blood.

Her veins surged, her blood pulsing through them as though shooting to the place on her neck where he'd scratched her. Victoria's breathing became trapped, slow, sluggish. The world funnelled into a whirl of sensation: the cold moisture of his tongue, long and slow on her flesh; the scrape of his teeth; the sharp-nailed fingers that now dug into her scalp, beneath her heavy hair; the beat of her heart racing, pounding through her limbs as she struggled to free them.

When he pulled back he smiled, and his eyes were glowing deep blood red. Hunger glistened there, and she smelt blood on his breath. 'That was lovely,' he murmured, tracing a long nail gently down her neck and to her breast. 'I am so very tempted.' His nail paused, pressing into the tender skin that swelled over her bodice.

The mad thumping of her heart pounded so harshly that her breast jolted in rhythm as she scarcely dared to breathe.

The vampire's eyes glowed red, then redder, then softer again as he seemed to contemplate his options.

But at last he pulled away. 'It is fortunate for you, Venator, that I value my own existence more than what delights you offer,' he said, looking down at her. 'Perhaps later, when Vioget tires of you…but for now…I must regretfully decline.' He said this last over his shoulder as he walked away; and she relaxed, watching as he went back out the door.

If it hadn't been for Sebastian – and possibly his grandfather's influence – she would have been in trouble. The vampire's actions put quite a damper on Sebastian's arguments: the vampire was clearly ready to take from a helpless woman, and only fear for his own safety stopped him.

But now…now she must attend to finding a way out.

When she'd pulled hard on the bonds of her wrists, she'd felt something move above her. Giving her attention more closely to her environment, she recognised that she was bound to a bed and that the headboard had become loosened by her struggles. Perhaps she could break it free.

She didn't know if the noise would bring the vampire guards in, but she had to attempt it. Trying to keep the banging to a minimum, she pulled on her wrists, felt the ropes scrape over her skin, and jerked around, trying to see if she could get the top of the bed loose. She wasn't even certain what it was made of; it sounded like metal of some sort.

Victoria struggled, then began to tug on her feet in the same way, causing low, deep creaking sounds to emanate from below – hopefully low enough that it wouldn't alarm the vampires. If she could loosen those ropes, she could bring herself closer to the headboard and perhaps be able to use her hands instead of just pulling on her bounds.

The end of the bed gave way first, and when she finally flipped her feet up, the whole iron footboard came too, and crashed onto her legs. Groaning with pain, she scooted up closer to the headboard and was able to feel around with her fingers, trying to get a grip on the metal.

But then she found something better. The wrought iron was rough and ornate, and the back of her hand scraped against part of it that was rather sharp. If she could position herself and move her wrists to saw the ropes against the edge…

It took a long time. Her arms were already sore from being held in such a position and from pulling; but she wasn't a Venator for nothing. At last the ropes loosened enough that she was able to pull them apart.

Her arms free, Victoria sat up, shook them out, and began to work on her ankles. Soon she was on the floor, hurrying to the window, carrying the rope that had been around her legs. It was still daylight – past noon, if she were to judge by the position of the sun. She had less than twelve hours to get from wherever she was back to the opera theatre to try to kill Nedas.

She could go out the door and fight the vampires; there would be a certain satisfaction in plunging a stake into the one who'd sampled her blood. But that would take time and there was the chance that she'd get captured again. Not a good chance, but one nevertheless.

The window was four storeys above the ground, however, which was why she was going to put Sebastian's rope to good use. And once she was outside the window, climbing down, the vampires would be helpless to follow her in the full sunshine.

And then she saw it: the silhouette of San Pietro's Basilica. She was still in Rome! That, at least, was in her favour.

When she looked down, she swore and stepped back from the window. But it was too late – Sebastian, who'd just alighted from a carriage, had seen her looking down from the window. He gave her a mocking salute as if to say, *Nice try,* and hurried up the steps below.

So he didn't think she'd go out the window, did he? She thought he knew her better than that!

Her filmy skirt swirling about, Victoria grabbed the metal footboard that still lay on the bed and smashed it through the window, which had been painted shut. She could hear the pounding of feet on the steps below, and knew she had little time. Swiftly she tied the rope to the stone railing, just outside the narrow window ledge at the edge of a balcony the size of a mere pillow.

The door to the room flew open and the vampires rushed in, but she was already out in the pool of sunlight, climbing over the rail, rope in hand. Victoria could hear Sebastian's curses when he came into the room, but she was halfway past the third floor, her skirt gusting in the slight breeze and obscuring her view below. The plaster wall in front of her was scrubbed with a dark orange colour that flaked off when she tried to brush her foot against it for a toehold.

Fortunately, the building backed into a small rust-walled courtyard instead of a street, so there was less chance of an alarm being raised about a woman lowering herself down from a window. Nettle bushes grew along in the insides, thrusting up and obstructing the steps and half of the windows. She would have to take care not to land on one of them.

The rope ended just below the third-floor window, and Victoria glanced up, Sebastian was no longer looking down at her; he must have gone back in and was coming down the stairs to stop her below. She had a decision to make: climb in through that window and try to sneak out another way, or drop down and hope she landed on the second-floor window's tiny balcony. Going back into the building would put her in danger of running into the vampires again, but dropping down was also dangerous – and might not give her time to escape before Sebastian got to the bottom.

She had to make the choice.

Looking down past her skirt, which partially blocked her view, she focused on the window ledge below. It was no more than a man's height away in distance. The pointed arch at the top of the window was just out of reach; but by shifting lower on the rope and reaching out with one hand, she was able to grasp it and hold it to steady herself. Clamping her fingers over it, Victoria shifted her weight towards the building, half leaning on the arch, and let go of the rope.

She fell, using her grip on the slender arch to direct her fall, and she landed on the small edge of the window, barely wide enough for her feet. With nary a moment's thought, she vaulted over the same stone railing as on the fourth-floor window ledge, her skirts tangling and billowing, and dangled from the ledge for a moment before dropping, fortunately, next to a nettle bush on the ground.

She dashed towards the narrow entrance of the courtyard, frightening two cats that had been sunning themselves, and she heard the door slam open behind her and Sebastian calling for her. Rounding the corner, she found herself on a narrow street lined with the same kind of buildings she'd just escaped from. He was right behind her; she could hear his footfalls coming closer.

Victoria was not about to be caught now, when she'd come so far. She dashed across the street, down another alley, and ran and ran, around corners and up streets, past chair-weavers and tailors and bakers, until the sound of footfalls were lost amid the noise of midday Rome.

The Quirinale clock tower bonged in the distance: two o'clock.

She had ten hours.

Chapter Twenty-Two

In Which Mr Starcasset Fills in a Number of Details

The ruins of the opera theatre were still smoking when Victoria arrived at nearly half past three on November first, the day before the Day of the Dead, or All Souls' Day, as it was commonly called. The curious stood nearby and gawked. The busy strode past as if nothing had happened.

The fire had destroyed only about one-third of the front of the building, but it was obviously unusable as it was. Victoria wondered how many people had died – either from the fire and smoke, or the fangs of the vampires.

Despite her conversation with Sebastian, she could not accept the idea that vampires were not all evil. It went against everything she'd been taught for the last year and a half, and her own interactions with the creatures.

Victoria pulled her cloak closely about her shoulders in an attempt to cover her unusual garb.

She'd dressed to fight, to hide, to run and climb, in loose black trousers and a matching tunic. Her shoes were soled with leather, thick enough for protection and supple enough to allow the same ease of movement as slippers. Her long hair had been braided in one long plait and stuffed down the back of her shirt so that the tail brushed the base of her back, under her garments. She had holy water, stakes and a knife secreted in various locations under her clothing. Miro, the weapons master from the Consilium, had given her another weapon that would be of use in this particular situation: a small bow that would allow her to fire a specially carved wooden arrow – a stake – from a distance.

She already knew she would never get close enough to Nedas to stab him; so the bow and wooden arrow-stakes would be her only chance to succeed. She wasn't an expert archer, but she could hit her target. She had three stakes, and her plan was to kill him and then, in what she hoped would be ensuing chaos, steal Akvan's Obelisk. At the very least, assassinating Nedas would put a stop – albeit a temporary one – to the activation of the obelisk, giving the Venators more time if Victoria did not succeed.

Verbena had been more curious than worried when Victoria appeared at the villa; she'd known her mistress had gone off with Sebastian and had not been overly concerned when she did not return that evening. 'After all, I seen the way ye two looked at each other – like ye coulden wait to get b'neath each other's clothes. Ye're young and ye've been mourn'n the marquess for more'n a year, so 'twas time to get ye'self a little slap an' tickle, if ye ask me.'

What could Victoria say to that? Her maid's assessment had, as usual, been accurate; how would she have known that Sebastian had other plans besides seducing her?

It had not taken long for Verbena to dress her mistress and prepare her to go. Oliver had brought a message over to Aunt Eustacia's villa, to inform her that Victoria was back – of course, she didn't even know her niece had gone missing, since Verbena had not thought anything of it – and of her plans to go to the theatre and try to stop Nedas.

Oliver had returned, but with the news that Aunt Eustacia had not been at home. He had left the message, of course, but Victoria could wait no longer; time was slipping away.

Now, at the theatre, her biggest difficulty was to gain entrance to the destroyed building without being noticed by a bystander, or, worse, a member of the Tutela. Once she was inside, her plan was to find her way in and attack Nedas by stealth and from a distance.

Victoria waited until she rounded the rear of the theatre, where there were fewer witnesses, and moved nonchalantly towards the building. She spied a small entrance, half-hidden by a hillock, likely for use by servants and merchants. As she came closer to the building, a faint coolness at the nape of her neck began to build.

She'd stepped three paces off the walkway towards the door, past a trio of trees, when she felt someone behind her. Before she could turn to see who'd stepped out from the shade of the oaks, something poked her in the side of her hip: round and hard. And small.

'So it is you, Victoria. I'd begun to wonder. No, don't stop, just keep moving nice and easily towards the door. I'd expected Pesaro to bring you himself, but this will work just as well.' George Starcasset was prodding her along with a pistol to her kidney, low enough that it wouldn't be noticed by any passers-by and would instead appear to be a solicitous arm about her waist.

'I'm afraid I don't know what you are talking about,' Victoria replied calmly, despite the fact that she'd been caught unawares. At least they were going in the direction she wanted to go.

'We weren't certain about you; we had our suspicions, of course, which was why I invited you to come to Claythorne and made certain Vioget and Polidori were there to draw the vampires. You see, at the time, I did not know what good friends' – he poked her hard in the back – 'you were. But since I didn't actually see you in action, or observe what occurred, I couldn't be certain. Come along this way, then.' A quick glance over her shoulder confirmed that he'd lost the smiling, boyish look he usually had, and it had been replaced by a more fanatical, disturbing expression, albeit in a youthful face.

'What is it that you weren't certain about, George?' she asked as they reached the door. She could hardly believe this was her close friend's brother! A member of the Tutela, from the sound of it. He jabbed her with the gun, and she took that to mean she should open the door. She complied, hoping there was no one else about. If she was going to escape from him, she needed as few witnesses as possible. Preferably none.

'That you are a Venator, of course. Don't try to deny it, my lovely,' he said, pulling the door closed behind them, allowing the pistol to drop away as he did. 'We'd had suspicions for a while, but since Lilith left London and took all of her people with her, how could we be certain?'

It was lucky for her that he had been three sheets to the wind that night of the vampire attack at Claythorne; he'd slept through the whole flurry of events. She wondered if he'd been mortified that he'd had to report to the Tutela that he was unable to determine whether she was a Venator because he'd been too foxed to observe her. The thought made a smile tickle her lips. It would have served him right.

'Lilith? Of course she would have known. How amusing that you had to track me all the way to Italy in order to find out.' She turned slightly so that she was half facing him in the small passageway, and noticed that he was carrying a satchel over his shoulder.

'Perhaps she did, but there is no love lost between her and her son Nedas, so why would she tell him something that could protect him? They would as soon see the other sent to Hell than to help each other. This way, my dear.' He pointed the gun and directed her off to the right. 'They will be pleased you have arrived already.'

Victoria strained to listen; the longer they were alone, the better. The back of her neck had turned cold and prickly. There were many vampires nearby. Somewhere.

Her fingers itched for her stakes because they were the most familiar weapon to her, but of course they would do no good against George. And besides…she could kill a vampire without qualm, but there was still that pesky detail of what to do with a mortal being who stood in her way. Especially one who was her best friend's brother, regardless of his own potential violent tendencies. She would have to find a bloodless way to stop him.

It was fortunate that she was still wearing her cloak, with the small bow slung over her shoulder under it, or he might have relieved her of that. As it was, it was apparent George Starcasset was not the most experienced person when it came to holding one at gunpoint and forcing him or her to do his will. The gun slipped and dropped haphazardly, and he tended to use the hand holding it to gesture when he talked.

'In here,' he said, gesturing to a small door. 'We have some time before we must be down below.' The smile he gave her would have sent shivers down her spine if someone more threatening had offered it to her.

Inside the small room, he pushed her away so that she was standing a few paces from him, keeping the gun trained on her as he locked the door. 'Now, I don't want you to scream, or I'll be forced to use this. And I would hate to do that, for that would bring the vampires running as soon as they smell the blood. Take off your cloak.'

Victoria slipped the bow off when she removed the cloak, and tucked it inside the bundle when she dropped it on the floor. There was only a chair in the room; whatever he had in mind – and she rather thought she knew – would not be comfortable in more than one way.

'Were you really that foxed when you came into my room at Claythorne?' she asked.

To her surprise, he appeared to flush slightly. The gun waved as he brushed off the experience. 'I did not realise what he was up to until Vioget had induced me to drink nearly a bottle of brandy…but he suggested that you would welcome a visit from me, and I was not averse to following the suggestion once he led me up to your room and urged me on.'

Victoria felt a spurt of annoyance. So Sebastian

had actually brought George to her room? He'd led her to believe it was George's own idea, with a bit of encouragement from himself!

'Well, he was not so far off with that suggestion,' she told George, wondering if he were as gullible when he wasn't pickled, but was carrying a weapon that gave him a sense of control. She waited to see his reaction to her statement.

The gun drooped a bit lower, and his mouth relaxed. 'I thought I had read the signs, but one can't be too sure when dealing with demure Society ladies. That was the other reason I invited you to Claythorne, you know. I had noticed the way you looked at me whenever we were at the same party or dinner. Even when you were married.'

Victoria had to hold back the bark of a laugh that statement provoked. When she and Phillip were married – the brief time they were – she had had eyes only for him. And certainly not for this young, flimsy man before her. 'When you invited me to Claythorne I was newly out of mourning, so I did not feel it appropriate to be…obvious.' She gave him that smile…the one she'd learnt from being married, and had used successfully on Sebastian little more than a week ago. 'But the fact is, you would not have needed to get foxed to sneak into my room.'

His expression turned hungry, and he stepped towards her. She held firm, even when he bumped the metal-scented gun barrel into the soft underside of her chin, pressing it there as he lowered his face for a kiss.

She expected it to be as inexperienced and uncouth as he appeared to be in other things, but the kiss wasn't. If she hadn't been thoroughly disgusted by him, and distracted by the other things she had to tend to, she might have possibly enjoyed it. Possibly, but by no means certainly.

And therein lay the difference between him and Sebastian. Even when she was angry with Sebastian, she still enjoyed his kiss. *Damn him.*

As it was, she kissed George back with some enthusiasm in hopes of disarming him. When his free hand began to get a bit friendly, she pulled away from his mouth and asked, 'Are you part of the Tutela, then?'

'I am, of course! I have attained the Third Level,' he replied, sliding his hand over the front of her tunic and tracing her breast through the cloth. Any lower and he'd find her stakes... She didn't want anything to throw him off his stride and remind him that she wasn't an average Society woman.

'I would love to see your mark,' she asked coyly, making it clear that that wasn't the only thing she wished to see.

'Would you now? And I would be most happy to show it to you. But first...' He reached into the satchel he was carrying and pulled out a coil of rope. 'I hate to do this to you, my lovely, but I mustn't take any chances.'

That was her opportunity. Victoria moved, quick as a flash, bending then rising up with a great twisting force to slam her head into his chin and her elbow into his abdomen.

The great, loud snap of his teeth coming together, followed by the whoosh of air from his lungs, were the only noises before he tumbled to the ground like a bag of stones: heathen hips.

Victoria pocketed the pistol he'd dropped, then set about tying him up. She bound him tightly; then, instead of leaving him on the floor in the room, where he might make noise and draw attention to himself, thus alerting the vampires to her presence, she slung his inert body over her shoulder and quickly made her way back down the narrow passageway and out the door. She dumped him unceremoniously in the bushes next to the small door by the hillock, hidden from view on all sides, and safely outside of the theatre.

He would not gain consciousness in the near future; and if someone found him ahead of time, they would make no connection to her being in the opera theatre.

George safely incapacitated, she hurried back inside to the room where she'd left her cloak and bow, knowing that it was past four o'clock and the time was drawing near. The sun would set in two hours.

The only clue she had to where she must go had been George's statement regarding going 'down below'. But which direction and where and how... she had no better idea than she had when she first arrived.

The creak of the door through which she'd just come from the outside, snagged her attention, and Victoria peered out from behind the cracked door into the passageway.

A tall, golden-haired man walked casually down the hall towards her. Sebastian.

At last...the opportunity to take a page from his book and appear when he didn't expect it. Victoria stepped out of the room in front of him. 'Why, Sebastian, I thought you'd still be searching the streets of Rome for me.'

'I regret to inform you, my dear, that if you anticipated sending my heart into fast paces by jumping out in front of me, you sadly mistake my skill. I saw you moments ago, when you brought your... parcel...outside the theatre and left it in the bushes. Incidentally, I sent the erstwhile Mr Starcasset off with my coachman in an effort to keep his interference to a minimum. After that, it was rather convenient to find you so easily.'

Blast! Would she never get one up on him?

'I hope you aren't here to stop me. You know how it ended last time you attempted it.'

He looked at her steadily, and she was surprised

to see acceptance in his gaze. 'It is against my better judgment, but I will not attempt to stop you. I will, however, accompany you, if you are certain you wish to do this. Perhaps you are meant to be present for it all.'

'Nedas is going to activate Akvan's Obelisk, and I am going to do my best to stop him. What do you expect to happen?'

'I'm not precisely certain, but I fear it is nothing I would choose to witness. Anything Nedas is involved with can only be repulsive.'

'Do you know where to go, or would that be too much of an advantage to me?'

He smiled at her; but there was a lack of his old spirit. 'I know of something better. A place where you can watch unnoticed.'

Victoria thought of her bow and the wooden arrows. Unnoticed meant she might truly have the opportunity she needed. 'Then let's be off.'

As they started, she added, 'Thank you, Sebastian.'

He shook his head. 'Save your gratitude, for you may well regret it later.'

Victoria could hear voices as she crouched and followed Sebastian through a low, narrow opening. When she emerged, she found herself looking through a tiny aperture high in the shadows above a stage.

It was not the stage on which the opera she'd watched two nights ago had been performed; there were no box seats nor velvet-covered chairs arranged in rows in a half-circle around it. The decor was not gilt and marble, but raw, rough wood and cracked plaster. A small square window studded one wall, near the ceiling just above her head, which, Victoria noticed, was made of open beams and covered with cobwebs.

'Where are we?' she breathed into Sebastian's ear.

'Second rehearsal stage, below the theatre,' he replied just as softly.

She looked back down to watch the people – mostly men, and many of them vampires – move about. They seemed to be congregating in a central area near the stage. The cold on the back of her neck had not relented; her skin there was so frigid it burnt.

Victoria leant towards Sebastian again and was just about to speak when he closed his fingers over her arm and pointed down. As he did, something changed in the air; it felt thick and expectant, and metallic with evil.

A man was approaching the stage, and the others, Tutela and vampires alike, parted ways for him to pass through. She couldn't get a perfect look at him, but she absorbed the image of shiny black hair, worn short and close to the scalp, and his dark olive skin, much darker than an Italian's, and thick brows. It was hard to tell, but she thought he might be perhaps a few years older than she, in his middle twenties. His lips were thin and pinched, and the whites of his eyes were so white they nearly gleamed.

He looked nothing like his mother, whose skin was nearly translucent it was so pale, and her hair like coils of polished copper and ruby, it was so bright red.

She knew he must be Nedas, the son of Lilith, for no other creature would command such immediate and complete attention from the others. And Victoria felt the evil so strongly, she wanted to brush it off, wipe it away.

She'd been so intent on examining Nedas that at first she completely missed him. But then, as three other men joined Nedas on the stage and stood there in the blush of light coming from a myriad of candled sconces, she recognised Max.

It didn't surprise her. No, surprise was not what she felt when she saw him, his confident, easy figure towering over Nedas and the others next to him. She must have moved or caught her breath, for Sebastian touched her arm as if to comfort her.

Comfort. The last thing she needed – or wanted – was comfort.

She ignored Sebastian and watched Max's harsh, handsome face as it softened into a laugh at something Nedas said, tipping up towards the ceiling, exposing his throat as he basked in hilarity for a moment.

Victoria couldn't imagine for an instant what the

evil creature could have said that was so funny.

Focus.

She had to push away the maelstrom of feelings and urges clashing through her and focus on her opportunity. Bless Sebastian; he'd provided her with the perfect location from which to launch her assassination attempt. They were so high up and tucked into the shadows that even Max's sharp eyes wouldn't spot them unless he knew exactly where to look.

The thought crossed her mind, briefly but severely, that it was possible he might. That he and Sebastian had planned this together, knowing that she would do what she wanted to do, and so faked a kidnapping so that she could think they didn't want her there… when in fact, it was all an elaborate ruse to get her here, at this place, at this time. Max was certainly smart enough to do such a thing, and he knew her well.

Wasn't that why George hadn't been surprised at all to see her? He'd thought Max would bring her himself, but it was just as well that she'd arrived alone.

Victoria tensed. Her stomach churned with doubt in spite of herself. No. If Max had wanted harm to come to her, he would not have helped her to escape the theatre only two nights ago.

That train of thought gave rise to another, and she began to search the small crowd of vampires for the Imperial she'd met at Claythorne. She didn't see him, but she did recognise Regalado, and to her surprise noticed that his eyes were glowing red. He had been turned.

Victoria noticed his daughter, Sara, who remained unobtrusively in a corner with a hood half-drawn over her head and her eyes hidden, along with another hooded companion next to her. The only reason Victoria recognised Sara was that she'd tipped her face up for a moment to speak to Max, who stood on the stage.

At that point, Victoria realised the meeting, or whatever one would call it, had been called to order and that Nedas was talking. She also noticed that there was nothing in the vicinity that could be construed as being Akvan's Obelisk. She didn't really know what it looked like, but Wayren had given her the impression that it was a large obsidian object, certainly nothing that could easily be secreted in a pocket or under a cloak.

If they were here to activate Akvan's Obelisk, where was it? Was it possible they'd been wrong about everything? Had he already done so?

'Tonight we welcome one of our own back to the fold. A Venator, who has proven his desire to return to us despite my suspicions to the contrary,' Nedas was saying. His voice, for all his power, was not so loud… yet it seemed to permeate every corner and cranny of the chamber, insidious as the evil that hung in its tones. Victoria found that she did not have to strain to hear any of his words. 'He has but one more task to prove his loyalty, and then he will take his place at my side. The addition of this Venator into my most secret ranks will be instrumental to our success, particularly with the power I will obtain tonight from Akvan's Obelisk.'

He turned to Max, who now stood alone with him on the stage, and continued. 'Despite the fact that you were once a Tutela member long ago, you turned away from our society and became our enemy, striking at us without regard, making a legend of yourself. When you came to me many months ago and indicated your desire to rejoin our ranks, I would have killed you on the spot.' His thin lips stretched in a malicious smile. 'But when I saw that you bore the mark of my dear mother, and that she had claimed you for her own, and learnt that she had sent you to us, I realised what an opportunity we had.

'A Tutela turned Venator turned Tutela. At last you have come home.'

Max stepped forward, gave a brief bow to Nedas, and said in an oily voice that Victoria barely recognised as his, 'Great One, I am gratified that you have taken me in and allowed me to prove my loyalty. The tasks you have set forth have not been simple or easy; in fact, I am aware that no one else in your ranks has been called to do what I have done. I realise it is penance for my disloyalty to the Tutela in joining the Venators all those years, and that it is only because of the wishes of your esteemed mother, Her Majesty, Queen Lilith, that I have been given the opportunity to rejoin your society. It is my hope that tonight this last task will remove any doubt from your mind that I am wholly and completely Tutela.'

Victoria watched, her emotions moving from horror to disbelief to hope. Surely, surely, this was all play-acting – at least on Max's part. He didn't even sound like himself, even as he had been only days ago when they spoke.

But could Lilith really have sent him?

Her fingers were tight; all thoughts of the bow and wooden arrows had fled. A horrified fascination gripped her as she watched the tableau below. Her heart jolted rhythmically in her chest, and her throat was so dry that when she tried to swallow, it creaked.

Max, what are you doing?

A laugh came from below, from Nedas and Max, from some jest shared only between the two of them. And then Nedas, stepping away from the taller man, announced, 'It is time! Where is that female Venator of whom you are so fond?'

Victoria's body turned to ice, and her heart stopped beating for a full breath. Her stomach dropped and pitched nauseatingly, and though she knew she shouldn't move, shouldn't attract attention to her location, she turned to look at Sebastian, fury jetting through her. He was staring down at the scene below just as she had been. Fingers closing around the wooden arrow, she looked at him, ready to drive the wood into his human heart in reparation for this last trick of his.

But then she didn't, for there was activity below. It was not directed up where she was hiding; they were not storming the room and dashing about in search of her.

No. For instead a small, slight figure in black had been shoved forward; she'd been standing next to Sara, there in the back of the room, both of them in matching black cloaks with hoods. Now that she came forward into the light, Victoria recognised her immediately.

Aunt Eustacia.

The female Venator they were expecting wasn't Victoria, but her aunt.

She swallowed the gasp of surprise and stared down. Her aunt shook off the hands that had been manhandling her towards the stage, and walked proudly towards it. She moved through the small cluster of vampires and Tutela. Up three steps, onto the stage.

Victoria could hardly breathe; she dared not blink.

Her aunt stood proudly, and as tall as her stature would allow. Her dark hair was pulled into its simple bun at the back of her head, not the ornate dressing she'd worn to the Consilium. The cloak fell away, revealing a black gown, and Victoria saw that her aunt's hands seemed to be bound behind her.

'Nedas. At last we meet,' said Aunt Eustacia in a calm voice that carried to every corner of the room.

'At last. Unfortunately, the moment will be altogether too brief.' His smile was completely humourless.

'Any moment in your presence is too long for my taste. I pray daily for your demise, and that of your race.'

'How unfortunate for you that my desires will be answered long before yours will.'

Victoria watched, waiting, her breathing finally coming in short, shallow puffs. What should she do? Could she interfere in whatever was about to occur?

She looked at Max. His face was blank and more unreadable than ever. He stood square, tall and foreboding, facing Aunt Eustacia and Nedas.

Max had a plan. Of course he did, and Aunt Eustacia was part of it. If Victoria did anything to interfere, she might ruin it. Still… She eased back from the opening through which she looked and slid the bow from her shoulder, holding it in her lap. Her fingers were cramped and would hardly move; her palms hurt where her nails had dug in.

'Now, Maximilian Pesaro, you have been charged to prove your ultimate loyalty to the Tutela by bringing us one of your own. You will seal your fate and become one with the Tutela by completing this one last task.' Nedas produced a long, gleaming blade.

Even from where she sat, Victoria could see how heavy and sharp it must be. Her heart was pounding faster now, and something nasty bubbled up in the back of her throat.

Max took the sword, gave it a practice swing that whistled through the air, and nodded to Nedas as he tested the blade over his thumb. Victoria saw the thin red stripe of blood appear after the quick slice in his flesh.

As the next events unfolded, Victoria watched, frozen, waiting. Readying herself to assist Max and her aunt when they needed it.

Nedas stepped away, his dark eyes hooded and focused on Max and Aunt Eustacia. 'Execute the woman.'

Max turned to his mentor. She stood tall, barely reaching his shoulders as she faced him, arms locked behind her back, calm. Victoria could see the steady rise and fall of her chest. Tension hung in the air.

Max gripped the sword, adjusted it in his palm, holding it with two hands as though he were about to go into a berserker battle. His face was still unmoving, emotionless as a stone wall, his mouth a straight line. His dark hair was pulled back into a short queue, leaving that stark face free of any shadow.

Victoria saw him swallow, saw his throat move. She watched as he drew in his breath; she saw his shoulders and chest rise. He swung back with both arms, elbows bending sharply, forearm blocking his face for the merest of seconds, and then, with all the power gathered up there, struck out with the blade.

It glistened silver in the light, sweeping through the air in a great arc as Victoria watched, her breath caught in the back of her throat, waiting for Aunt Eustacia to pull her arms free and swing into action in tandem with Max.

A great twist of pain darkened Max's face; he gave a low, guttural moan, and his eyes closed as the blade sliced where it was intended, where it had aimed. There was no sound from Aunt Eustacia as her body crumpled to the ground, her head thumping next to it. Severed. Separate. Blood spraying the floor and Max's legs.

Victoria stared for a moment, not believing her eyes, her breath choking, waiting for something to happen that would prove her vision false.

And when nothing did, and she realised her aunt was really dead in a great, sudden pool of blood, the arrow dropped from her nerveless fingers and landed right on the stage below.

Chapter Twenty-Three

The Ordeal

Victoria was numb to her very core; the back of her neck was cold, but the rest of her body was devoid of feeling. She couldn't see anything but red rage darkening the edge of her vision and Max.

Max holding the sword, wet with her aunt's blood.

Max looking up at her, his own blood-spattered, shocked, betrayed expression blanking as soon as he recognised her.

It could not have been more than a second, perhaps two, that this burst of emotions rushed over her; not more than a breath before the vampires and the Tutela were gawking up at her in anger and amazement and starting after her, slipping in the puddle of Aunt Eustacia's blood. Some of them were climbing the wall, leveraging one another up towards her vantage place, using the rough brick and wood moulding for toeholds. She heard racing footsteps coming up from behind, and the shouts, and knew it was only moments before they would reach her.

She fitted the second wooden stake to her bow and realised dimly that Sebastian was no longer next to her; but that was of no importance at that moment. She would kill Nedas, whom she'd come for, and then she'd kill Max.

There would be no question of judgment, no hesitation in taking up lethal force against a mortal. It would be done.

Cold determination blossomed over her, pushing away the shock as she lifted the bow, the knowledge that her aunt lay dead there on the stage demanding to be put aside for a moment while she focused on her duty.

The impact of her aunt's death would soon set in. First she had to avenge it.

The arrow fitted into the string of the bow, Victoria drew it back to fire into the midst of chaos on the stage, where Nedas still stood, looking up in her direction with a challenging smirk on his face.

Focusing on his heart, she released the wooden bolt. The string of the bow pinged into place, spewing the arrow into a graceful arc as Victoria felt hands seizing her from behind. A face appeared in front, snatching at her, trying to pull her down from the small platform on which she crouched, and once the vampires behind her realised this, they pushed.

She tumbled through the hole towards the

stage below, dropping the bow and her arrows; a multitude of hands – so many, so very many – grabbing at her in a morbid reminder of the Tutela meeting where she'd nearly been mauled.

Perhaps tonight they would finish it. Pain arced through her; somehow she landed below, slamming into the stage. She kicked and fought with all of her might, smelt blood and felt her vision darken into smoke…then ebb into total darkness. The only thing that stayed with her was the fact that she lay in her aunt's blood, and that she hated Max.

Max's betrayal.

She opened her eyes when she felt the hands pull away, the chaos slip into silence. She was looking up into the face of Nedas.

Up close he was more terrifying, more intensely repugnant than he'd seemed from a distance. She smelt something raw and dusty about him that brought to mind burning bones and butchered meat, and her stomach wanted to heave.

But she would not let it. Her aunt had been brave; so brave and strong as she walked to what she had to have known was her death. Victoria's body was shaking with exhaustion and shock, and she had a multitude of hurts that pounded along with her slamming heartbeat.

Drawing in a shaky breath, Victoria pulled her energy about her, refused to think of what had happened, and what her life would be like without her mentor, without *Illa* Gardella, and called on her strength and her wit.

And most of all, she drew upon her rage and loathing of the man she'd once fought beside and trusted with her life, and channelled it into potency.

'The other female Venator, I must presume,' Nedas said, toeing her with his leather boot. His fangs were out now, and obviously her wooden bolt had missed its mark and let him live. 'This one is much prettier and livelier than the last.'

Victoria looked away from the compelling eyes that had begun to glow with bright red rings around the same blue irises of his mother – which indicated the power she'd invested in him. She found Max.

For the brief moment when their eyes met, she saw his stone exterior slip; saw something agonised waver there; but then it was gone and he straightened his posture, giving her that cool, mocking look she'd become used to. 'She is no real threat,' he said. 'Why do you think I chose the other?'

'Damn you to Hell,' Victoria said to Max, as if they were the only two people in the room – softly, as a lover might murmur a soul-deep secret.

He met her gaze without flinching, without distancing himself from the rage she knew was there; even Nedas's presence faded away from the periphery of her awareness. For Victoria, it was just the two Venators.

Then she was whipped to her feet by a strong, dark hand, and she found herself chest-to-chest with, and less than an arm's length away from, Lilith's son.

'No real threat,' Nedas commented, perusing her face as if he were reading the pages of the *Times* and it was devoid of any articles of interest. 'No, not the woman who fought and killed two of my Guardians, and an Imperial whom I sent to bring Polidori back. No. No threat.

'And most certainly, not the woman who escaped from five vampires, even as they fought over feeding on her, during a Tutela meeting. No.' He looked over at Max. 'This one is no real threat.'

Max arched a brow. 'She must have made much improvement in the last year.'

Nedas looked at her, and she remembered to keep her vision from getting trapped by his gaze. She focused her eyes on his eyelashes, noticing how thick and black they were, how they brushed his thick, wiry brows when his eyes were fully open.

She and Nedas were nearly of a height, and he barely had to tilt his face towards her. One hand held her arm; she made no move to shake it loose. It would be a superficial, short-lived victory. Better that he think she was frozen in fright. Or held in his thrall.

'I could kill her now – or have you do it, Max, as your first duty in my inner circle…but perhaps I will, instead, take a page from the book of my dear mother. Claiming a Venator of my own, most particularly such an attractive one, would not be such a hardship. And after tonight…well, she will have little to do, won't she? The rise of Akvan's Obelisk will make the Venators inconsequential.' He smiled at her again. 'And won't you be pleased to be one of the protected, like your colleague here?'

Victoria did not grace him with a reply. It was useless, and she had more to think about than to exchange repartee with the vampire prince.

That thought reminded her that Sebastian had disappeared sometime during the altercation. But before she could make sense of it, Nedas, apparently annoyed that she would not engage with him in a war of words, commanded, 'Disarm her.'

Thank God Max wasn't part of it – part of the pairs of hands that held her immobile as others felt around and removed the stakes and holy water, and the knife she wore in various locations on her body. She bucked and kicked and twisted futilely, but she could not remain still with those ugly, repulsive fingers on her. They even found the vial of holy water tied to the underside of her thick braid, along with the stake looped beneath it as well.

Her tunic shirt was lifted before she knew what was happening, and then the sudden, rending pain at her navel as one of them – surely a Tutela – tore the *vis bulla* from her skin.

She cried out, a low moan as she felt the instant evaporation of her energy and strength, and the surge of weakness overwhelmed her. The pain was great enough that this time she did succumb to the black void where there was no pain and no grief.

Chapter Twenty-Four

In Which Lady Rockley Attempts to Draw Blood

When she awoke, Victoria found herself alone in the dark.

She drew in a deep breath, surprised at how much she hurt everywhere; she was not used to such intense, debilitating pain. Her arms were too weak to prop herself up, so she remained prone for a long moment, measuring her breaths, trying to discern shadows in the darkness.

The memory waited before it came upon her; then it flashed in, overwhelming her mind with all its blood and death. The whistling arc of the blade. The hands groping and pulling and punching at her. The red-rimmed blue eyes of inhumanity. The tearing pain at her navel.

It was no surprise she was weak and hurting. Without her *vis bulla*, she was as helpless as a woman.

It had been a bit more than a year, and already she'd forgotten how much she relied on the strength amulet, how much it ruled her life and what freedom it gave her. Yes, she had removed it herself, but that had been voluntary, and temporary, and she'd been sequestered and safe.

This was terrifying.

She breathed and tried again to move her arms, and was surprised to find that she could. She was not restrained. Her legs, too, were free to shift and allow her feet to move around enough that she determined she had been deposited on the floor in some kind of room.

But why would they restrain her? She was no threat to them now.

No threat.

According to Max, she hadn't been even before they took her *vis bulla*.

The renewal of her rage set her breathing off balance and her stomach feeling like a cannonball rested on it. Victoria had to stop and make herself consciously push away the venom.

She would deal with Max in time.

The first thing she must do was find a way out of here.

What time was it? Were they even now with Akvan's Obelisk, releasing the full impact of its evil? The event that would, as Nedas had said, make Venators inconsequential?

Gingerly getting to her feet, using the wall for balance, Victoria tried to stand, but her knees and head would not cooperate. She sagged back to the floor, scraping her hand down the rough wall. It was as dark as it could get, and once she felt the stone wall and the cement beneath, she presumed she was in a cellar beneath the opera theatre.

She crawled around the perimeter, bumping into something that she recognised belatedly as a camp bed or large chair, and determined that two of the walls were stone and the other two wood, one of them with a door.

No sooner had she reached up to blindly locate the door handle and jiggle it in vain, than she heard what sounded like descending footsteps over her head, and she realised she was in a cubby under a staircase.

She didn't have time to wonder whether the steps portended someone coming for her, for moments after they reached the bottom of the stairs, a cast of light glowed from underneath the door; then something jolted it, making a soft thump. And then the door opened.

Max slipped in and shut it behind him.

'You!' Weak though she was, Victoria launched herself at his feet, pulling up using his body and the wall for balance, the fury she'd held in check at his audacity in seeking her out bursting forth, giving her a wave of strength.

He held the lantern well away from himself, as though expecting her attack, and he let her land a few ineffective blows to his chest and face before snatching one of her arms in mid-air. 'That's enough, and for God's sake, keep quiet,' he said, and bent to put the lantern down. 'You're wasting time and energy.' He grabbed her other wrist when she would have flailed it at him, knocking one of her kicking feet out from under her so that she lost her balance and remained upright only because he had her wrists in hand.

'How long have you been Tutela?' she hissed. 'You are a traitor and a murderer.'

His face was expressionless. 'You heard Nedas. I was Tutela before I was a Venator.'

'Will you murder me now?' she asked, ignoring the black spots that danced before her eyes and the way her body throbbed in pain. Weakness and fear shivered through her, but she would not allow him to see it. Her muscles trembled and she had to work to form the words. 'What reward will Nedas give you for killing another Venator?'

He gave her a little shake that bobbled her head; then as if to collect himself, thrust her from him and stood away, looking down at her as she stumbled back onto the bed. 'I have exactly ten minutes to get you the hell out of here, or you will find yourself in a much less appetising situation than your aunt. For Christ's sake, you can't even stand, can you?'

This last comment was provoked by her attempt to do just that, pulling herself off the thin bed and using her hand to hold herself upright. He reached for her, and she twisted away, tipping back onto the floor in an ignominious heap. 'Don't touch me.'

He ignored her and unceremoniously yanked her to her feet, pushing her towards the bed. 'Victoria, you have to get out of here. There is no time to play the woman scorned.'

'After I kill you, and Nedas too, I'll be happy to leave this place.'

'Despite the fact that you can't even stand, let alone kill anyone, you can't slay Nedas. Not now,' he told her sharply. 'There will be another time, but not now.' Long fingers were unbuttoning his white shirt, and Victoria gawked, trying to focus around the black dots that obscured her vision.

'What are you doing?'

'He's already begun to activate the obelisk; he cannot be stopped. You will be needed afterwards, Victoria. Think about that and not your need for vengeance, for it will soon be moot.' He moved towards her, and she shrank back from his tall, looming figure. She'd never been afraid of Max, but something in his expression, the determined, settled line of his mouth and the angry black eyes, made her want to scoot away.

But she was a Venator. Damn it, even without her *vis bulla*, she was a *Venator*.

She didn't know what she'd expected when he sat next to her on the bed, but it wasn't for him to take her wrist and force her hand towards him. He moved her reluctant fingers under his unbuttoned shirt, palm open, sliding over warm skin, soft hair, and then brushing against his nipple, and something hard. Metal. He pushed her hand flush against it.

An instant before she realised it was his *vis bulla*, hanging from the areola on his muscular chest, Victoria felt a wave of strength course through her. Light filled her vision, chasing away the black spots. The pain melted into puddles of annoyance. Even the injury at her navel, where her own strength amulet had been torn away, ceased to throb. Her head felt clearer.

And as her pain and confusion disappeared, Victoria became aware of the fact that her hand was splayed over Max's bare skin. She felt the brush of his linen shirt over the back of her wrist with the rhythm of his breathing, felt the steady, strong pounding of his heart under her palm and the strength of his fingers around her hand. He was warm and solid, and a brief peek at the opening of his shirt told her there was a lot of black hair on his chest.

Another glance at his face told her he was unmoved: his eyes were closed, his mouth still settled and firm. She wondered if the flow of energy she felt weakened him at all. She looked up again and his jaw shifted, once, twice, and as if he knew she was watching, he opened his eyes. She looked away, suddenly conscious of their positions on the campbed, him half-turned towards her, his knee brushing hers, his strong fingers wrapped around her wrist. Her hand on his flesh suddenly felt as if it were burning. Her throat was dry.

'Feel better?' he asked, not solicitously, not as if he cared, but as if he couldn't wait to be away from her.

'Strong enough to fight you now.' She pulled her hand away and immediately felt the loss of the energy.

He raised an eyebrow, looking at her as he fastened his shirt. 'Stand up.'

She stood; she managed that. Even without the power from his *vis bulla*, she still felt much better. The room didn't spin, and her vision was clear. Her injuries began to hurt again, but not so bad as before.

'When you leave this room, go to the right. Three doors down the long passage you will find stairs leading back to the main floor of what's left of the theatre.' He produced a stake and a gun and tossed them on the bed. 'Take these and get out of here. I have to get back before I'm missed, and I trust, God knows why, that you will go now that I've given you the chance. Again.'

'I hate you, Max. You must know that.' Victoria picked up the gun, cocked it, and pointed it at his chest. She'd become much more familiar with firearms since she'd been forced to use one in her escape from Lilith last year. 'I would do nothing to benefit you.' The gun was heavy, but she didn't allow it to shake in her grip. Moments ago she would have fired without hesitation.

'It no longer matters what you think of me,' he replied. Weariness and impatience laced his voice. 'Go, now, Victoria. Killing me now will benefit no one. And if you pull that trigger, they'll all be down here faster than you would imagine.' A mocking grin flashed. 'Why do you think I gave you a gun and not a knife?'

'Why did you do it?' To her horror, her eyes began to sting.

'It was either her, or you.' Max turned and strode out of the room, closing the door behind him with a soft thunk.

Brushing away the surprised tears, she snatched up the stake and started after him, hearing his footsteps above her once more, but the door wouldn't open. She pulled again, and it came loose, opening into a dark hallway. Max had left the lantern, so Victoria grabbed it up from the floor and started out.

She didn't go right, as he'd directed. She went up the stairs in his wake, shadowing the lantern as much as she could, listening for his footsteps to follow them. She would remain out of sight, safe…but she had to see what was happening. She had to find out if what Max said was true. And…there might be something she could do.

She couldn't leave.

A soft creak in the distance sent her along a passage at the top of the stairs. She didn't need the lantern any longer; it was not the pitch-black of the room she'd left, but shadowy, and her eyes were becoming accustomed to the shapes and shades of grey, so she blew out the lantern and left it. She passed a door that hung ajar, and a quick peek as she went by showed racks of clothing, probably costumes, hanging inside. The scent of smoke permeated the area as she rushed along on silent feet, trying to catch up to Max.

After a time, she realised she'd lost him. Everything was silent and still.

Frustrated and feeling weak again, Victoria retraced her steps, taking more time to explore the area. She was definitely in the lower level of the theatre, obviously used for storage. Costumes, props, chairs, instruments, music...the rooms were neatly ordered with all of these items.

Victoria found another staircase, a wider one, that seemed designed for heavier traffic, and took the steps up slowly, listening. The back of her neck had never ceased being chilled, but now it was becoming colder, and so she took greater care with her explorations. She gripped the stake in one hand and had tucked the gun in the waist of her trousers. It was heavy and dragged on them as she walked, but she wanted to keep her other hand free.

At the top of the stairs she found herself in a hallway, and beyond it she could see behind the stage. This was not the stage on which Aunt Eustacia had been executed hours before; this was the larger, taller performance stage, where she'd watched the opera only two nights ago. Scorched backdrops hung, one in front of the other, and tables sat in the wings, holding smoke-laden props and costumes. And she heard voices.

Someone was on the stage. She hoped it was Nedas.

Victoria crept forward, straining her ears, and nearly bumped into a wooden ladder. She looked up, her skin prickling with an idea. It seemed to lead up into infinite darkness, to the same place where the ropes that held the backdrops and curtains went.

She climbed up the ladder, taking care that the gun didn't slip from her waistband and tumble to the floor below. She resorted to sticking her stake in the other side of her trousers in order to free both of her hands, and wished she still had her bow and wooden bolts.

Thirty feet above the stage the steps continued on, but she found a catwalk that led into the shadows beyond the wings, where she was, and presumably over the stage. The smell of smoke was stronger up here, and she saw patches of black at the tops of the backdrops, and even on the catwalk and the ropes that acted as railings. It was amazing that the theatre hadn't burnt to the ground. There was illumination coming from the stage, and it helped her find her way more easily.

As she crept silently along the narrow wooden bridge that had a tendency to shimmy, the voices grew louder and more distinct. The back of her neck became colder, and she felt that same repulsive, oozing feeling she'd had earlier when Nedas had come into view.

At last she moved beyond the black curtains that blocked the backstage wings from the audience, and found herself above the main part of the stage.

The first thing she saw was Akvan's Obelisk.

It sat on a waist-high round table in the centre of the stage and looked exactly as she'd pictured it: an obsidian object, glinting blue and black in the light of five lanterns that were arranged in a circle around it. Narrow, with a pointed top, it was approximately the thickness of a man's arm, and perhaps as tall as his leg. It speared up at a slight angle, long and shiny and evil.

The stage itself was a bit worse for wear from the fire. One side near the audience was charred and burnt and had fallen away, leaving a jagged black pit below. A swathe of burnt-out chairs cut through the same side of the theatre, and the boxes above them – the one in which Victoria had seen the Imperial – were scorched. Yet, the other two-thirds of the arena were merely covered with ash and smoke stains and showed no other damage. Half of those seats were filled with vampires and members of the Tutela.

At five stations around the stage, with the obelisk and its table in the centre, sat some kind of bowl-like containers. Smoke wafted up from the small fires in them, bringing the sweet smell that reminded Victoria unpleasantly of the Tutela meeting. The theatre was so large that the incense would not engulf the room as it had then; but she could still smell the essence; and along with it came the memory of being nearly helpless under the hands and fangs of the vampires.

Victoria closed her eyes and shook her head, clearing away the reminder that she was even more helpless now, tonight. Bringing her attention back to the stage, she examined the people there.

Standing next to the table with the obelisk were five men. Nedas she recognised because of his lesser height and darker skin, and because of the way her entire body felt ill when she focused her attention on him. Max was the tallest, with his too-long hair clubbed back, and his white shirt standing out among the sea of black clothing and dark hair. Regalado's bald head shone like a flesh-coloured skull, and his thick beard bushed out so far that Victoria could see it even when he stood directly below her. The other two men, whom she thought were vampires, she did not recognise.

It appeared that Max had indeed become one of the trusted inner circle of Nedas, so that he was directly involved in what was about to occur. Victoria's stomach pitched at the thought of what price had been paid for him to align himself with Nedas. Aunt Eustacia.

And why was he so determined she not be there? Why did he even care?

It was either her, or you.

But why either of them? Why would he forsake the Venators?

Tutela to Venator to Tutela.

Had his years of being a Venator been a ploy for only one thing, to this one end? To gain her aunt's trust and bring her to her death?

But why?

Had they had possession of Akvan's Obelisk that long ago?

The thoughts swirled in Victoria's head; she was feeling weak again, and it seemed as though the incense from the pots was going straight to her nose, weaving through her senses and making them as murky as London fog. Perhaps without her *vis bulla* she was more susceptible to the essence. Or perhaps it was because her injuries simply made her weaker and more easily confused.

She became aware of some sort of chanting below. It came from the vampires who sat in the audience, far enough away that they could see what was to happen, but could not be involved or interfere.

A thought came to mind, and Victoria spent a few long moments scanning the viewers in the seats, looking for Sebastian. She should be as angry with him as she was with Max, but she wasn't.

Yes, he had kidnapped her and taken the opportunity to make love to her. It was fortunate that she hadn't expected more from him, for she was bound to be disappointed if she had.

Yes, he had disappeared at a most fortuitous moment – for him. And yes, he had left her to battle the vampires on her own. But at least he had been truthful with her. He was not a man of violence, and would not strike and kill. Not even a vampire. And he certainly didn't have the powers of a Venator to protect himself.

Of course, that meant it was necessary for him to make himself scarce at such dangerous moments; but if he had not, he likely would have been captured too.

But they wouldn't have hurt him, if all he'd told her about Beauregard was true. Would they?

Or perhaps they would have, if Beauregard and Nedas were rivals.

Victoria's head was swimming and her body was pounding with pain again. She couldn't stop the thoughts swirling around her mind, clogging it, softening it from any clear judgment.

The chanting had grown louder and deeper, and the incense did not disperse, but seemed to continue to swirl straight up.

Its smoke was coloured, she noticed vaguely. Black and blue curls and coils, braiding together as they wove up into the catwalk, insinuating themselves into her nostrils and into her lungs. Stifling a cough, she held the sleeve of her tunic over her nose and mouth and tried to breathe the filtered air; perhaps she had waited too long to do so, but it might help to keep the scent at bay.

How was she going to stop them?

He cannot be stopped.

There had to be a way. She had to clear her mind.

Victoria took a deep breath and spewed it out, long and slow and silent, from between pursed lips, trying to send the smoke away from her, to send it dissipating far from where she breathed.

The backdrops hung from heavy wooden poles. She could loosen one, cause it to crash down on them. At least that would stop them momentarily. She might be able to take them by surprise and jump down to stake a vampire or two. Nedas would be her first target.

But...there would be little to no chance that she could get the obelisk away, even if Nedas was dead. She didn't know how long it would take, or what would have to occur in order for the obelisk's powers to transfer to another being.

And...she no longer wore the *vis*. She couldn't jump down without injuring herself; she would be fortunate to have enough strength in her battered body to drive the stake into a normal, red-eyed vampire, not the son of Lilith.

There were ropes looped over the poles from which the canvas backdrops hung.

Blocking out the sound of the incessant chanting, Victoria considered the heavy canvas scenery and, a plan half-forming in her mind, moved carefully towards one that hung exactly opposite where Nedas seemed to stand. Perhaps she could swing down on the rope, using the element of surprise. If she aimed correctly, she could land on Nedas and stab him before he knew what happened.

Of course, after that she would be at the mercy of the rest of the vampires and the Tutela members, and, weakened as she was, she would be unable to fight them. And the obelisk would still be available for someone else to use.

The craving to drive the stake through Nedas's heart, to make him poof into ash, was so strong she considered taking the chance. And what about Max? He was the one who'd wielded the sword! The one who'd actually done the deed.

He deserved to die too.

She could have shot him, vampires be damned.

Her mouth twitched as she realised the irony of that thought. Then it straightened, for this was not a time for humour. Not with her aunt dead.

She could shoot Max from here. The realisation swept over her, and she pulled the gun from her waistband. She could shoot him and be running through the catwalks before they realised what had happened or where she was.

At least then a part of her vengeance would be satisfied.

The firearm was heavy, so heavy. She sighted Max,

trying to line up his tall frame with one eye squinted and the other focused on him. Never still, he moved with the power and confidence that had been so valuable to the Venators.

The best of them.

How could he have fooled them all?

Suddenly flames burst from below, diverting her attention from her target. They were tall black and blue flames, replacing the smoke tendrils from the five small bowls. They shot straight up, high into the air, narrow and hot, one column of eerie flame blazing only feet below where Victoria was perched. This was why Nedas had needed the large theatre chamber.

The chanting had continued, melding into the background, as Nedas stood inside the circle made from the bowls of flame and began to speak, gesturing with his arms as though to bring the air towards the obelisk. He pulled his fingers through the air gracefully, drawing little buffets of movement towards the small table and its burden as though urging the heat towards it.

Victoria could not understand his words, but she did not need to know what he was saying. She knew what he was doing.

The sweet smell had ebbed, to be replaced by the heat of the flames and the deafening sound of their crackling. Max, Regalado and the other two vampires stood outside of the circle, watching.

As Victoria looked down, she saw the flames begin to lean towards the centre, above Akvan's Obelisk. Nedas continued to chant, surrounded by the black and blue flames that reflected the same colour of the evil object, and the columns of flames drew closer and closer together.

At last they knit together as one, at the tip of the obelisk: five ropes of flame merging into one tall blaze that threatened to reach the highest part of the ceiling arching over the stage.

The flames roared and Victoria could see, directly in front of her, the black and blue twining and writhing like rabid snakes, and feel the heat blazing on her face from yards away.

Akvan's Obelisk began to glow and sweat. Green and blue sparks radiated from it in a random pattern on all sides. Nedas reached out to touch one, and laughed when the spark snapped his finger. On and on he chanted; on the fire blazed; greener and bluer glowed the obelisk. Little beads glistened on the obsidian, trickling down and plopping on the floor.

The entire theatre was lit by the weird blue and black flames, casting odd-coloured shadows and plays of light everywhere. The vampires in the seats had ceased their chanting and stared at the flames as though desiring to pull their power into themselves.

Now the flames were changing, and large black drops swam down them faster than rain during a downpour. The drops swarmed down the long blazing tower and melted into Akvan's Obelisk, on and on and on.

Victoria noticed a sudden movement below; something odd. She looked over, down, away from the blaze that had captured her attention, and watched in amazement as Max burst through the flames, something long gleaming in his hand.

He tumbled into the circle, rolled upright, and slashed the blade through the obsidian tower in the same wide arc he'd used earlier.

The obelisk sizzled, then exploded, the flames extinguished, and the scream of fury from Nedas reverberated in the suddenly silent theatre.

Chapter Twenty-Five

In Which All Becomes Clear

When Max felt the sword connect with Akvan's Obelisk, a rush of pure relief blasted through him.

It was done.

The powerful arc of the sword set him off balance enough that by the time he'd regained his footing, the vampires were rushing towards him.

Max caught a glimpse of a shocked, feral-mouthed Nedas and fury ripped through him; anger at what he'd done, for what he'd been forced to do by that creature. He whipped around with the sword, which was made of pure silver, and beheaded one of the vampires who'd leapt towards him.

Another one came at him, and he met him with the same, and then another, and another. They were climbing onto the stage from the audience at Nedas's frantic command. There were too many to fight, and he knew it wouldn't be long before they overpowered him, but until then he would use the acrimony of regret and madness to fuel as much revenge as he could.

He'd do what he'd been unable to for nearly a year.

A year – an eternity – of watching these evil creatures – these vampire-loving members of the Tutela – of living with them, jesting with them, pretending to scheme with them, professing love for one of them. He'd had to submerge his loathing and disgust, and some days it was all he could do not to explode.

He had succeeded in his deception. He would die with a clear conscience, and leave Beauregard and Nedas to fight between themselves.

And Victoria to lead the Venators in defeating them both.

The sword sang in his hand, but even with the weapon forged specially to conquer evil, blessed and containing a vial of holy water in its handle, he could not fight them all back. He was too exhausted, both in mind and body, to use his *qinggong* skills and slip and glide through the air as an Imperial vampire would do.

But his body was conditioned to fight; despite the fact that he knew he would not leave here alive, that he had sealed his death sentence when he first swung the silver sword after the great black sweat began to pour down the obelisk, he kicked and swiped and spun and sliced as though there were hope.

At last he fell, tumbling to the stage floor, and used his legs to thrust at the undead as they lunged down towards him, and then, lying there on his back, struggling to get up, he saw something that made everything else fall away.

Above the stage.

Victoria.

Something slammed into him, bringing him back, and the world tipped, went black, then came back with a vengeance of tearing hands and pummelling fists. And the reality that Victoria was still here.

The sword was gone; he'd dropped it, and he was at the mercy of the undead.

She hadn't listened. After what he'd done, what had been sacrificed, she hadn't done the one thing she needed to do.

Hands were clawing at him, fangs gleaming, red eyes burning. They dragged him to his feet, brought him to stand in front of Nedas in the centre of the stage.

At any moment the vampire prince would order him beheaded, or allow the undead to tear into him. They'd never touched him before, even when they weren't sure whether to trust him, because of Lilith's marks. That dubious protection wouldn't save him this time.

And once he was gone, there would be no one to help Victoria.

He looked squarely at Nedas's nose, taking care to

stay away from those enthralling eyes.

'How did you know?' Nedas's voice was deceptively smooth and soft. The auditorium had grown silent, watchful. The only sound was Max's rough breathing. 'I am the only one who knows how Akvan's Obelisk might be destroyed.'

Max dared not look up, though he burnt to know where she was, what she was doing. If she had gained her sense and left. He wanted to shout at her to run, to escape. He wanted to shake her until her long white neck snapped.

Instead, he had to focus on Nedas, distract him for as long as he could.

'But it has been destroyed, and not by you.' Max's voice sounded hollow even to his own ears. He drew in a deep, fortifying breath and added, 'You have obviously miscalculated.'

Nedas's hand shot out and closed over Max's throat. Long nails bit into the tender skin on the sides of his neck, and Max felt them puncture his flesh. 'Who told you?'

'Was not my presence back with the Tutela a gift to you?' The grasp around his neck made his voice raspy. 'Perhaps you ought to look towards the one who offered it.'

It took a moment; then Nedas understood.

'*Lilith?*' The vampire was so shocked he released Max with a shove, and his head whipped back painfully. 'My mother sent a spy to destroy Akvan's Obelisk?'

'Why else would she gift a son such as you?' Max mustered a mocking smile. 'She bears as much love for you as you for her. Apparently she has not forgiven you for the incident in Athens.'

'How *dare* she! With the obelisk, I would have ruled the world. And what did she promise you in return? Everlasting life? Well, I shall put an end to *that* possibility right now.'

Max had anticipated his attack. He'd bunched the muscles in his deceptively sagging legs and, using his vampire captors as leverage, kicked out with every bit of his great strength and sent Nedas spinning into the air and off the stage.

And then, as if it had been rehearsed, something came hurtling from above and thudded onto the cluster of vampires behind Max. It took him only an instant to recognise that it was one of the heavy canvas backdrops, and its solid wooden beam had landed directly on four vampires, knocking them to the ground.

Victoria, of course.

Max pulled loose from his startled captors and reached for his stake – but it was gone. He'd given it to her earlier. He kicked at a vampire, blocked another from lunging at him, spinning around and looking for an opening of escape, so he could find Victoria.

'Max!' He heard her shout, and looked up in time to see her half-swinging, half-sliding down on a rope.

She was above him, heading towards the side of the stage.

As she came near, she dropped something, and he caught the stake as if they'd practised the move, and spun in time to slam it into the heart of a vampire grabbing his arm.

Running towards the wings, where Victoria had landed in an awkward heap, Max saw Nedas climbing up over the edge of the stage. He was tempted, only for the breath of a moment; but kept on towards Victoria. It was more important to get her out safely than to play to his need for vengeance.

But to send that creature to Hell… His fingers tightened around the stake.

He glanced back. Nedas was coming towards him, his red-ringed blue eyes burning with hatred. He fairly flew across the stage, and the other vampires scuttled out of his path. Max saw a flash of silver out of the corner of his eye and looked back to see that Victoria held a sword – *the* sword. Her face was set, her dark eyes shadowed with the same grief and anger that fuelled him. Even without her *vis bulla*, she looked like a warrior.

'I want him!' she shouted, running forward with none of her usual grace and strength.

Max hesitated; he understood her need, but she could barely lift the sword. Out of the corner of his eye he saw movement, and turned to meet two vampires who had circled around and were coming from behind.

He had no choice but to fight them off, and noticed that his movements were slowing and his breathing becoming more laboured. He actually missed the heart of one vampire the first time, and had to waste precious seconds and energy to bring his arm back up and stake the undead properly.

There was a loud cry behind him, and Max whirled in time to see Victoria rush towards Nedas, clumsy and awkward, with her sword. The blade was pure silver, and the vampire halted in front of her, but did not back away.

As she reached him, just as his hand whipped out to grab her, Victoria's awkwardness caused her to trip. Max watched in horror as she seemed to lose her hold on the sword, and it jolted dangerously in her hand, the tip striking the floor…then in abject disbelief as she used her stumble to duck under Nedas's arm and pivot around behind him with surprising dexterity, and he realised with surprised admiration that the chit had faked her stumble.

With obvious effort and great relish, she rose up from the back of the vampire prince before he could turn, and swung the heavy sword in the same, but slower, lethal movement Max had used only hours before.

The blade severed Nedas's neck before he realised she'd come up behind him, and in an amazing, frozen moment, he exploded into foul-smelling ash.

Max had been running towards Victoria to interfere; now he was intent on sweeping her up and getting them both to safety before Nedas's followers comprehended what had happened.

He wrapped an arm around her waist and lifted her, sword and all, and dashed between two vampires, who stood as though turned to stone, and off into the wings of the stage. A loud bellow sounded behind them; it sounded as if Regalado was calling the undead to action, and Max did not slow.

They ran through the backstage, Max practically carrying Victoria, for she couldn't keep up, and he was certain that by this time the effects of touching his *vis bulla* would have worn off.

It was fortunate that he knew his way around the theatre, for the passageways turned and ended and branched and cut into each other; but he always knew where they were. The sound of approaching vampires echoed in the empty halls behind them, far distant, but always in their wake.

When they finally reached the back door, the one the vampires used because bushes and trees and the small hillock into which the theatre was built obstructed it, Max released Victoria.

She stepped away from him, still holding the sword, and they looked at each other, breathing hard, the relative safety of exit a hand's breadth away. Everything was silent – even the sounds of pursuit had faded.

One glance told him what he'd already known: she might have saved his life, but in her mind, it was on principle only.

She wasn't about to forgive him any more than he would forgive himself.

Chapter Twenty-Six

A Case of Mistaken Identity

Victoria turned away from Max's steady look to place her hand on the door, lifting the latch. The sword still hung from her numb fingers.

She was out of breath, weak and unsteady, but under it all there was a wave of satisfaction. She'd killed the vampire prince without her *vis bulla*, using only her meagre woman strength, her agile mind – and what Kritanu would have to consider the most unpredictable fighting move she'd ever executed.

Satisfaction, yes, it simmered through her.

But when she looked at Max it fizzled away into a mass of uncertain emotion: nausea, grief and shock.

And she knew he saw the anger that still burnt in her eyes. Knew that she didn't know how to look at him, how to feel towards him. How could she? He'd spent a year living with the Tutela, pretending to be one of them so skilfully that even she'd questioned his loyalty…yet in the end he'd destroyed the obelisk and saved them all.

Except Aunt Eustacia. Could she ever forgive him for that?

'What the bloody hell did you think you were doing?'

His words – not the humble ones she'd expected – startled her, but when she looked back at him, the rage in his dark eyes was enough to make her take a step away.

He was angry with *her*?

'I was saving your miserable life!' she shot back, her trembling hand tightening on the latch. 'You destroyed the obelisk and I wanted—'

'You wanted? Yes, it was all about you, wasn't it?' he snarled. 'You gave no thought to anything but what you *wanted*. Revenge – on me, on Nedas, on whoever got in your way. Never mind the fact that you're helpless as a child now, that I risked my bloody neck to get you out of here, nearly lost the one chance I had to stop Nedas. If you don't survive, everything we've accomplished tonight will be in jeopardy.'

He stood tall and threatening over her, his dark hair falling over his face, bloodshot eyes flashing anger, and fingers planted on the wall next to her as though to keep himself from throttling her. 'You are The Gardella now, Victoria. You have an obligation to the Consilium and the rest of the Venators. You can no longer think only of yourself, of your needs and desires, but of the far-reaching consequences of your actions. Or inactions.' He pulled away, straightening, as the sounds of shouts and dashing feet sounded again in the distance. 'It's time you learnt to sacrifice.'

'As my aunt sacrificed?' Victoria spat, anger, grief, shock, all barrelling through her, making her weak and disoriented. Her animosity grew, burning along her nerves. 'You made that choice for her, Max. I made the choice to save your life when you would have died back there.'

'And by doing so, you forced me to live with what I've done. You've done me no favour, and done nothing for the Consilium.'

'Why didn't you tell me that you planned to destroy the obelisk?'

'Hmm. Could it have been because you either would have demanded to know how, and every single detail, and insisted on assisting, or that you would not have believed me? I told you in every way possible that you needed to leave, and apparently even blatant rudeness didn't work.'

'So you had Sebastian kidnap me. But why didn't you tell me when you came to release me? You could have told me then.'

'Yes, and you would have left, wouldn't you? You would have trotted out the door with the stake and pistol like a good chit and that would have been that.'

'I didn't anyway, did I? You could have told me more when you came.'

'Victoria, they were waiting for anything – any

hint or breath or anything from me that would give them reason not to trust me. I couldn't take the chance that they thought something else was going on other than…other than the fact that I didn't want you killed. For whatever reason,' he added sharply. 'I let them think it, for it was better than the alternative. I suspected they even gave me the opportunity to free you in hopes of hearing me tell you something to confirm their suspicions. I didn't dare. I couldn't risk it.'

The vampires were almost upon them. There was no time to linger any longer. It would either be sunrise or starlight, certain freedom or more running. Victoria whipped the latch open.

The door flew open into a dark night. The stars spread across the sky in a wide diamond scarf that, normally, Victoria would have found beautiful, but tonight found disappointing. She had been hoping for pinks and oranges.

Her body gave a sudden lurch as Max shoved her through, and she tumbled out onto the dirt-worn area outside the door. She heard the door close behind her, and she twisted around on the ground.

But no, he was there, standing at the door, looking past her. Still.

Victoria swivelled back around, there on her knees, sword grasped in her hand, panting. A pair of boots stepped out of the shadows and stopped in front of her.

She looked up and saw the shadow of an elegant chin, with silver-tipped hair curling in a moonlit halo around it.

'Sebastian.' The accusation in her voice was unmistakable. 'Once again, your timing is impeccable.'

The boots stepped closer, and his shadow fell across her hand grasping the sword. 'I see you are quite familiar with my grandson's penchant for disappearing at the most inopportune – or, in his case, fortuitous – moments.'

Victoria stretched her neck to look all the way up at him, and noticed several other pairs of booted feet moving out of the shadows. Her neck was frigid again, but she still held a blessed weapon. She pulled to her feet, as slowly and smoothly as she could. Her trousers still clung to her knees where the cold, damp earth had pressed into them. 'Beauregard, I presume. I'd begun to wonder if you were merely a figment of your grandson's imagination.' She glanced over her shoulder and saw that Max was still standing there, the door to the theatre closed behind him.

The elder vampire laughed, reminding her uncomfortably of Sebastian. 'I'm rather surprised he would have even told you about me. Now. Since you are here, am I to assume you were unsuccessful in your task this evening? Has Nedas activated Akvan's Obelisk?'

Now that he'd moved, and the stars and moon

illuminated him, she could see that it was obvious he wasn't Sebastian. There was a resemblance – their hair the same unruly mass of curls, although Beauregard's was lighter blond in comparison to his grandson's honey-coloured ones. He was older, too, but not elderly. Perhaps he had been in his late forties when he'd been turned by the female vampire who'd tricked him. His face bore the same trace of patrician elegance that Sebastian wore, but his nose was wider and his lips not quite as inviting as his grandson's. His eyes were completely different; even though they weren't glowing red, it was obvious they were darker than Sebastian's, and set deeply into his skull, giving him a closed-lidded look that reminded her of Phillip. Still, indeed, he was a fetching enough man for being a centuries-old vampire, and a grandfather to boot.

He was looking at Max, who stood with his back to the door. Perhaps he was leaning against it; Victoria wasn't certain. He still held a stake in his hand, dangling at his side.

'Akvan's Obelisk is destroyed,' Max told him.

Beauregard lifted his chin. 'You succeeded, then. I didn't wish for Nedas to have that immense power any more than Lilith does. And you are still alive? How convenient for me.'

'Not by any fault of his own,' Victoria replied. She moved, and the sword glinted in the moonlight.

This drew Beauregard's attention, and he jerked

his head in command. 'You will no longer need that. And where is Nedas?'

Sebastian stepped out from behind the cluster of vampires, his gaze steady on Victoria as he walked towards her.

'No,' she said, stepping back towards Max, holding the sword in front of her.

'Nedas is dead,' Max replied to Beauregard.

'I'll take it. Now, Victoria,' Sebastian commanded. She couldn't see his face well, but the steel in his voice was very uncharacteristic of his charming personality.

Max moved behind her. He reached around and closed his fingers around her wrist, holding her back with his other arm around her waist, while Sebastian plucked the sword from her weak grasp.

'What are you doing?' Victoria struggled in his arms, kicking back at Max and forward at Sebastian, until Max released her suddenly and she tumbled to the ground.

'Easy, Victoria.' Sebastian stood next to his grandfather, looking down at her. 'You were not wanted, nor expected, to be here.' He didn't offer her his hand to assist her to her feet.

'We have your incompetence to thank for our current situation, Vioget,' Max sneered, still leaning against the door.

Sebastian raised one eyebrow. 'I see that you have managed to keep her under control as well.'

'I had a few other tasks to accomplish.'

Victoria struggled to her feet, trying not to think about how many times she'd had to do that in the last day. And how much more difficult it was becoming. 'Did she really send you?' she demanded of Max.

'Yes, Lilith sent me. Ostensibly as a gift to her son – a Venator pet, as she said. One that would bring the secrets of the Venators to the Tutela and the vampires, and support them when Akvan's Obelisk was empowered. I was the perfect candidate, as I was once Tutela. A long time ago.'

'When—'

'Silence.' Beauregard stepped towards her, eyes suddenly gleaming like pink rubies, his fangs long and lethal. Until now she hadn't known he was a Guardian vampire. 'You are not in control here. Now, both of you, back inside.' He turned to Sebastian, looking in disgust at the sword. 'Get that out of my sight.'

Victoria didn't move, so Beauregard snapped an order at two of the vampires who flanked him. They grasped her by the elbows and easily hustled her towards the door, which Max had opened.

Three vampires spilt out, fangs extended, eyes red, ready for battle. There were more, crowded in the doorway behind them.

When they saw Beauregard, however, they froze.

Victoria looked back to see Beauregard smiling at the new arrivals. It wasn't a pleasant smile; it gave her, one who'd seen altogether too many vampire expressions, an uneasy feeling in her middle.

'We have detained the ones who attacked you and killed Nedas this night,' he announced, stepping forward with a commanding air. 'As your new leader, I shall impose retribution. Immediately.'

It was a familiar scene in some ways, when Sebastian brought Victoria out onto the opera stage where only a short time ago the greatest of evil sources had burnt and sizzled. Ironic how it had metamorphosed from the scene of a bright, loud performance only days earlier, complete with the swell of music and the clear vibration of song, to a blackened shell, with half of the floor destroyed, and the seats filled not with patrons, but with immortal undead, waiting and watching for their own performance.

She had given up deciding whether she should be angry with Sebastian, or resigned to his actions and thus angry with herself. Hadn't she always known he wasn't to be trusted, even when she made love with him? And now here they were, with no longer any question about where he stood and what was important to him.

Squarely opposite her.

And Max…where did Max stand in all of this? He'd destroyed the obelisk, but had forced her to give the sword up to Beauregard – and Sebastian. Of course, they were outnumbered and would never have been able to fight their way through the group of vampires. But it still made her uneasy.

Beauregard was seated in the centre of the stage in a large chair that Victoria recognised as having come from the props area. He looked regal and powerful, with his eyes glowing and upper fangs pressing gently into the flesh below his lower lip.

'What does he want me for?' Victoria asked in a low voice, looking at Beauregard from where she stood in the wings with Sebastian.

'I'm surprised you haven't figured it out, Victoria,' he replied with his customary drawl. 'Beauregard and Nedas have long been rivals for leadership over the vampires. My grandfather couldn't be more pleased that not only has Akvan's Obelisk been destroyed, but that you've rid him of Nedas.'

'Then he should be shouting for joy and releasing us instead of planning "retribution".'

'Of course. And the moment he chose not to execute two Venators, who are the mortal enemies of his followers, how long do you think he would be in control of the Tutela and the vampires? Regardless of the favours done him today, he is not about to relinquish the power he's been seeking simply by sparing the lives of two Venators. Now, come with me and be quiet. Just stand there and look pretty; fortunately, my grandfather has a penchant for beautiful women.'

'It appears you have made quite an indelible impression on my grandson,' Beauregard told her as Sebastian brought her forth to his side. 'You made an excellent choice,' he added to his grandson. 'I can see now wherefore comes your attraction to the woman. She is quite comely.'

'I ask that you spare her life for the sole reason that she pleases me,' Sebastian said with a short bow. 'She has been disarmed and no longer wears the symbol of the Venators. She is little threat.'

Victoria had to fight to keep her face blank. She might be little threat now, but as soon as she returned to the Consilium she would be wearing a new *vis bulla*, and would be back on the streets.

Assuming Sebastian could charm his grandfather as effectively as he'd charmed her.

'I can see that. It would be simple to preserve that beauty for all eternity, Sebastian. She could be your concubine forever, just as she is today.' Beauregard's eyes glinted with a hint of the same flirtation that his grandson often used, but in this case it made Victoria's stomach lurch. 'And it would be my great pleasure to do so.'

'No, thank you, Grandfather. But I do ask that you spare her.'

'I will spare her, only because you have asked, Sebastian. But on this occasion only. If there so be a chance that we meet again, under different circumstances, I cannot make the same promise.' He cast his ruby gaze over Victoria, and she felt the full force of his power, the tug of his thrall, and the faint, brief curiosity of what it would be like to allow his fangs to sink into her neck.

He smiled wider when he recognised her response, then turned to Sebastian. 'Are you quite certain? Well, then, I shall turn my attention to the other. Bring him forth.'

Victoria swallowed, her throat dry and tight.

Max.

She had an awful, spiralling feeling about what was in store for him. Particularly since Sebastian had made his feelings towards Max absolutely clear.

Which was more than she could say for herself.

She stopped, pulling on Sebastian's arm. 'What about Max?'

'I cannot – will not – save him too,' he told her, pulling her after him.

'Your grandfather will kill him. But why? After he made me give up the sword to you, I thought—'

'No, Maximilian shares no love for Beauregard any more than he does for me. He was merely protecting you when he made you give me the sword. Even together you couldn't have won a fight with Beauregard, and now that he knows that I have ensured your safety, he'll accept his own sentence. Now hurry, before my grandfather changes his mind.'

Sebastian was directing her quickly off the stage when suddenly something whooshed past them, hurtling from above and landing with a loud, heavy thud on the stage, just between them and Beauregard.

Victoria jumped back and looked up to see glowing red eyes on the very same catwalk she'd been on hours earlier; someone had done exactly as she had – released another of the heavy backdrops and sent it hurtling to the floor.

Everything disintegrated into mayhem. Vampires swarmed everywhere, new arrivals – or perhaps older ones, who had been lurking in the shadows of the auditorium – attacking Beauregard's men.

'Victoria, come!' Sebastian was clearly shocked and alarmed, and for the second time tonight she found herself being pulled away from the stage, which had suddenly turned into a battleground.

She saw Max as Sebastian tugged her away.

He was standing at one end of the stage, weaponless, defending himself from a single vampire as others fought around him. It would be moments before he was subdued or outnumbered.

Victoria stopped, automatically looking around for something to use as a weapon, and Max looked over at her. Their eyes met across the melee and she read the message there: the same one he'd been giving her since she'd seen him at Regalado's.

Go.

'Victoria!' Sebastian was tugging on her, but she had gripped the hem of the velvet curtain hanging at the edge of the stage and used it to keep herself in place and half-hidden.

She swallowed, watched as Max tried to whirl and

spin away from the vampire who leapt at him…saw him falter, then pull to his feet.

He looked at her again, his face a mask of anger and determination.

She had to leave.

But she couldn't make her feet move.

Despite what he'd done…she couldn't leave him. He was a Venator. She couldn't leave him to die.

She couldn't make that sacrifice!

She needed him.

With Aunt Eustacia gone, she needed Max. Someone she could trust.

Victoria jerked from Sebastian's grip, staggering a step forward at the sudden release, then losing her balance and tumbling to the stage floor. On her knees for a brief moment, she noticed something glinting under the curtain. Reaching to retrieve it, she pulled it from under the heavy velvet and realised what she was holding.

It was a shard from Akvan's Obelisk. Its diameter was no more than the width of two fingers, and its length less than that of her forearm: the size of a stake. She smelt the evil, felt it sizzle when she picked it up and kept it as she backed out from under the table. Energy zinged along her arm.

She used the curtain to pull herself to her feet, and looked back over the stage. Max was still there, but he was weakening, and distracted by looking at her to make sure she was leaving.

She had to go.

She had to put aside her own feelings and sacrifice.

'Victoria!' Sebastian was grabbing at the wrist of the hand that held the shard, and this time, with one last glance back at Max, she let him drag her off.

'What are you doing with that?' he said over his shoulder as they dashed off.

'I'll take it to Wayren,' Victoria replied, pulling her hand away from his grip.

They ran through the theatre, now without the vampires behind them. The sounds of violence still raged and echoed in the half-burnt building.

Sebastian stopped at the door that led outside. 'I must go back.'

'What? What is going on?'

'It's Regalado. He's fighting to win the leadership of the vampires. I cannot leave my grandfather to face him alone. You are safe; you see the sun has risen, and you must go.'

Before she could protest further, he pushed her up against the wall, his fingers clamping her shoulders through the thin fabric of her tunic. His mouth descended to hers, hungry and warm, apology and desire and farewell all mixed in with sensual lips and a strong, slick tongue.

She kissed him back for a moment, her breath rushing between them; then she tugged her mouth away. 'But you don't kill vampires.'

'I know. But even I have some honour.' He kissed her again, fitting his mouth back to hers, then closed his eyes and tipped his forehead to hers. Drew in a deep breath. 'Be safe. Now go.'

He shoved her out the door, slamming it closed behind her.

The sky was pink and orange, just the way she'd hoped it would have been hours before. She blinked in the bright light and turned to look back.

She wanted to go in. God, she wanted to go back in there.

But she'd done the right thing.

For all she knew…Max was dead by now.

And she hoped Sebastian would not soon follow.

Yet, she could not leave. She couldn't just walk away, find a hack and go back to the villa.

She stood on the dew-damp grass, frozen like stone.

Chapter Twenty-Seven

In Which Maximilian Takes on an Unwelcome Debt

Max was ready.

He was bloody damn tired, could hardly see straight.

He'd watched Victoria leave with Vioget, and knew that for all his shortcomings, he wasn't about to let anything happen to her. He'd get her out safely.

And she'd carry on. She'd be as formidable a leader as Eustacia.

The vampire reared over him, where Max had finally collapsed on the floor, the broken chair leg he'd been using as a stake spinning out of his grip. The undead's fingers were curled with menace, tipped with lethal claws, and his gleaming fangs curved like yellow sabres.

Lilith would have no one to torment, now that Max would be gone. The thought made his mouth twitch with wry humour, and he closed his eyes, ready.

But the pain never came.

He opened his eyes to find Vioget standing over him, stake in hand. He reached down to pull him to his feet as the vampires battled onstage behind him. Max shook off his grip. 'Victoria?'

'She's safe. Outside.'

A warning shout drew their attention as two vampires, fighting tooth and nail, rolled towards them. 'Go,' Sebastian said; but Max was already moving towards the wings, towards escape. He turned back.

'I bear you no gratitude for this, Vioget.'

'Which is precisely why I did it. I told Victoria it mattered not to me whether you live or die.'

Max stopped, looking at him from around the edge of a scorched curtain. 'Then why not let me out of my misery? Why play the hero? It so goes against your grain.'

'I didn't do it for you. I did it for her.' And Sebastian turned back to the battle behind him.

When the door to the theatre opened and Max came out, squinting in the bright light, Victoria could only stare.

He stopped when he saw her. 'You're still here.'

Victoria took one step towards him. They stood there in the long shadows cast by the trees and sun just rising above the horizon.

She didn't know what to say. He'd killed her aunt, yet they'd fought side by side. He'd destroyed

Akvan's Obelisk, and helped her to escape. She'd walked away, leaving him to die.

'How—'

'It's not important.' He stood with his hands on his hips, battered and clearly exhausted. 'I told you your vengeance would be moot – I never expected to walk away from the stage once I'd swung that sword.'

'But you did. I saved you.'

'And so I have yet another reason to be grateful to you, is that it? You could not be more wrong.'

'Surely there was another way.'

He lifted his eyes. 'In order to be there to destroy the obelisk at the precise moment it could be destroyed, I had to prove I was trustworthy, down to doing the most abhorrent thing imaginable. There was no other way, Victoria.'

Silence stretched, long and ugly. The gentle lift of a breeze brushed her cheek, and Victoria saw that the shadows had already begun to shorten.

'You said Lilith would release you from her thrall if you joined the Tutela.'

His laugh was short, his words bitter. 'You don't think I believed that, did you? She said it, certainly, but I didn't really believe her. I suppose there is a hope…' He laughed again. 'No, of course not. And it was moot, as I didn't expect to live whether I succeeded in destroying the obelisk or not.'

They stared at each other, and Max came towards her, reaching out to grip her shoulders. Her messy braid caught under his fingers, pulling tight as she looked up at him. 'You will never forgive me for what I did to your aunt, and I will never forgive you for forcing me to live. Do you think I can ever forget what I did?'

She pulled away, and he stepped back as though he'd been burnt. Then he reached under his shredded shirt for a moment. When his hands came back out, he offered her something. His *vis bulla*.

'No, Max.'

'Yes. It's done. I'm done.'

'You can't.'

He was angry now. 'Do you think I can ever face the Consilium again after this? I cannot even think of living with myself. I killed my mentor, my teacher, my friend. Your aunt.' His eyes glistened and he looked away.

'Max.'

'You'll have Wayren, Kritanu and the others. Perhaps even Sebastian, if he makes it out of there alive. You don't need someone whose loyalty will be forever questioned. For God's sake, think of the Consilium and its future, not your emotions. Goodbye, Victoria. *Andare con Dio*.'

For the second time she let him go. Watched him walk away into the dawn, tall, dark and alone.

Chapter Twenty-Eight

A Bittersweet Gift

The next morning, a day after she'd emerged from the opera theatre and watched Max walk away, a small package arrived for Victoria. Inside was a folded piece of silk and a note.

I found this after the battle was over and thought you would want to have it. Perhaps it will replace the one taken from you, for though I searched, I couldn't find it. Have a care, for I do not know when we will meet again. S.

Inside the silk was her aunt's *vis bulla*.

Epilogue

In Which Wayren Mollifies Illa Gardella

'From the moment she stepped foot in Rome, your aunt knew she would not leave it again.'

Victoria and Wayren were sitting in the tiny parlour at her villa. Victoria had moved beyond her initial shock in the day since she'd emerged from the opera theatre.

So many things had happened, and she'd managed to control the grief and anger and the overwhelming sense of being lost. Adrift and aimless.

She'd accepted the challenge of the vast, ominous responsibility ahead and was ready for it. Yes, she grieved. It seemed like only yesterday that she'd had that same hollow feeling as with the death of Phillip…but she'd managed it, just as she would manage this.

She had to. She was a Venator.

She was *Illa* Gardella.

'It was a prophecy from long ago, from Lady Rosamund. Eustacia knew it well, but she did not know exactly what it meant until it happened. *The golden age of the Venator will find rest at the foot of Rome* is the accurate translation. It makes sense now, for your aunt was truly the golden Venator, Victoria, and you will follow in her footsteps.'

'I still cannot accept Max's choice. There had to have been another way!'

Wayren looked at her with easy blue-grey eyes. Her face bore an expression of compassion. 'He didn't want to do it, Victoria. He did not want to. He would have done anything but that. Eustacia ordered him to do it.'

Her eyes dampened. 'What? How could she?'

'She did what had to be done, Victoria. If Nedas had succeeded in bringing Akvan's Obelisk to full power, there would have been destruction and death even worse than we saw in Praga. She sacrificed herself willingly to give Max the chance – the only chance – to stop Nedas. One life in exchange for many others. She trusted that he would succeed. And he did. Against all odds he did, for he had to strike the obelisk at precisely the right moment, or the opportunity would be lost.'

Victoria took the handkerchief Wayren offered her. It smelt like lily of the valley and peppermint, and somehow the combination soothed her. 'Max didn't expect to survive.'

'I'm certain he didn't. You saved his life even when you were at your weakest, a testament to your strength and ingenuity. You are the Gardella now.'

Wayren touched her with a slender, cool hand, and Victoria felt a wave of comfort. 'Who do you think had the more difficult task – your aunt, going to her execution? Or Max, who had to face someone he has loved and admired and respected, and to cut her down? Is it any surprise that he would not want to live with that memory, that knowledge, day after day? It was over for your aunt in an instant; I am certain Max ensured it was fast and painless. But he…'

'He will live with his choice every day, and wonder if there was something different that could have been done.' Victoria remembered that horrible time a year ago when she'd made a choice, and could have killed the man in the alley of St Giles. Remembering her own choice. She knew how much worse it was to have to kill someone you loved.

'Indeed.'

'He gave me his *vis bulla*.' She showed it to Wayren.

'Did you not remove your own *vis bulla* when you feared you could no longer wear it, Victoria?'

She nodded, remembering.

'We must give him time, Victoria. And hope he will return.'

Have you read *The Rest Falls Away*?

Turn the page to find out more...

Also by Colleen Gleason

The Rest Falls Away

Beneath the glitter of dazzling 19th-century London Society lurks a bloodthirsty evil...

Vampires have always lived among them, quietly attacking unsuspecting debutantes and dandified lords as well as hackney drivers and Bond Street milliners. If not for the vampire slayers of the Gardella family, these immortal creatures would have long taken over the world.

In every generation, a Gardella is called to accept the family legacy, and this time, Victoria Gardella Grantworth is chosen, on the eve of her debut, to carry the stake.

But as she moves between the crush of ballrooms and dangerous, moonlit streets, Victoria's heart is torn between London's most eligible bachelor, the Marquess of Rockley, and her enigmatic ally, Sebastian Vioget.

And when she comes face to face with the most powerful vampire in history, Victoria must ultimately make the choice between duty and love.

'A paranormal for smart girls who like historicals. Buffy in a bonnet takes on the forces of darkness in Regency-era London'
Janet Mullany, award-winning author of *Dedication*

'Lush, dark and powerful – deliciously sexy, utterly compelling'
Jackie Kessler, author of *Hell's Belles*

Available in The Gardella Chronicles
from Allison & Busby

The Rest Falls Away

978-0-7490-7956-7 • £6.99 • Paperback

All Allison & Busby titles can be ordered
from our website,
www.allisonandbusby.com,
or from your local bookshop and are also available by
post from:

Bookpost, PO Box 29, Douglas, Isle of Man, IM99 1BQ
Credit cards accepted. For details:
Telephone: +44(0)1624 677237
Fax: +44(0)1624 670923
Email: bookshop@enterprise.net
www.bookpost.co.uk

Free postage and packing in the United Kingdom

Prices shown above were correct at the time of going to press.
Allison & Busby reserve the right to show new retail prices on
covers which may differ from those previously advertised in the
text or elsewhere.

a&b